Thomas Carlyle

Oliver Cromwell`s letters and speeches

Thomas Carlyle

Oliver Cromwell`s letters and speeches

ISBN/EAN: 9783742874986

Manufactured in Europe, USA, Canada, Australia, Japa

Cover: Foto ©Andreas Hilbeck / pixelio.de

Manufactured and distributed by brebook publishing software
(www.brebook.com)

Thomas Carlyle

Oliver Cromwell`s letters and speeches

COLLECTION
OF
BRITISH AUTHORS

VOL. 560.

OLIVER CROMWELL'S LETTERS AND SPEECHES
BY
THOMAS CARLYLE.

IN FOUR VOLUMES. — VOL. 1.

COLLECTION

OF

BRITISH AUTHORS.

VOL. 560.

OLIVER CROMWELL'S LETTERS AND SPEECHES
BY
THOMAS CARLYLE.

IN FOUR VOLUMES.

VOL. I.

OLIVER CROMWELL'S

LETTERS AND SPEECHES:

WITH ELUCIDATIONS.

BY
THOMAS CARLYLE.

IN FOUR VOLUMES.

VOL. I.

LEIPZIG

BERNHARD TAUCHNITZ

1861.

PREFACE

TO THE SECOND (LONDON) EDITION.

THE First Edition of this Work* having, contrary to expectation, spread itself abroad with some degree of impetus, has, as in that case was partly natural, brought me into correspondence with various possessors and collectors of Cromwell Letters; has brought obliging contributions, and indications true and fallacious, from far sources and from near; and, on the whole, has disinterred from their widespread slumber a variety of Letters not before known to me, or not before remembered by me. With which new Letters it became a rather complex question what was now to be done.

They were not, in general, of much, or almost of any, intrinsic importance; might here and there have saved some ugly labour and research, had they been known in time; but did not now, as it turned out, tend to modify, in any essential particular, what had already been set down, and sent forth to the world as a kind of continuous connected Book. It is true, all clearly authentic Letters of Cromwell, never so unimportant, do claim to be preserved; and in this Book, by the title of it, are naturally to be looked for. But, on the

* December 1845.

other hand, how introduce them now? To unhoop your cask again, and try to insert new staves, when the old staves, better or worse, do already hang together, is what no cooper will recommend! Not to say, that your Set of Cromwell Letters can never, in this Second or in any other Edition, be considered as *complete:* an uncounted handful of needles to be picked from an unmeasured continent of hay, — how can you ever assure yourself that you have them all?

After deliberation, the law of the case seemed to be somewhat as follows: *First*, that whatever Letters would easily fit themselves into the Book as it stood, — easily, or even with labour if that were all, — should be duly admitted. *Secondly*, that for such Letters as tended to bring into better relief any feature of the Man or his Work, — much more, had they tended to correct or alter in any respect any feature I had assigned to him or to it: that for these an effort should be made, if needful; even a considerable effort; effort, in fact, to be limited only by this consideration, Not to damage by it to a still greater degree the already extant, and so by one's effort accomplish only loss. *Thirdly*, that for such Cromwell Letters as did not fall under either of these descriptions, but were nevertheless clearly of his composition, there should be an *Appendix* provided. In which, without pretension to commentary, and not needing to be read along with the Text, but only apart from it if at all, they might at least stand correctly printed: — they, and certain other Pieces of more doubtful claim; for most part Letters too, but of half, or in some cases of wholly, official character; — if by chance they were elucidative, brief, and not easily attainable elsewhere. Into which Appendix also, as into a loose back-room or lumber-room, not bound to be organic or habitable, bound only to be maintained in a reasonably swept condition, any still *new* Letters of Cromwell might without ceremony be disposed.

Upon these principles this Second Edition has been produced.   New Letters intercalated into the Text, and Letters lying in loose rank in the Appendix, all that I had or could hear of or get any trace of hitherto, are here given.   For purchasers of the First Edition, the new matter has been detached, printed as a Supplement, which the Bookseller undertakes to sell at prime cost. — And now, having twice escaped alive from these detestable Dust-Abysses, let me beg to be allowed to consider this my small act of Homage to the Memory of a Hero as finished; — this Second Edition of *Oliver's Letters and Speeches* as the final one.   New Letters, should such still turn up, I will not, except they contradict some statement, or fibre of a statement, in the Text, undertake to introduce there; but deposit them without ceremony in the loose lumber-room, in a more or less swept condition.

T. CARLYLE.

London, 11th May 1846.

PREFACE

TO THE THIRD (LONDON) EDITION.

THE small leakage of new Cromwell matter that has oozed
in upon me from the whole world, since the date of that Second
Edition, has been disposed of according to the principles
there laid down. Some small half-dozen of Authentic new
Letters, pleasantly enough testifying (once they were cleared
into legibility) how every new fact fits into perfect preestab-
lished correspondence with all old facts, but not otherwise
either pleasant or important, have come to me; one or two of
these, claiming more favour, or offering more facility, have
been inserted into the Text; the rest, as was my bargain in
regard to all of them, have been sent to the Appendix. In
Text or Appendix there they stand, duly in their places; they,
and what other smallest of authentic glimmerings of additional
light (few in number, infinitesimally small in moment) came
to me from any quarter: all new acquisitions have been punctually inserted; — generally indicated as new, where they
occur; too insignificant for enumerating here, or indeed almost for indicating at all.

On the whole, I have to say that the new Contributions to
this Third Edition are altogether slight and insignificant, pro-

perly of no real moment whatever. Nay on looking back, it may be said that the new Contributions to any Edition have been slight; that, for learning intelligibly what the Life of Cromwell was, the First Edition is still perhaps as recommendable a Book as either of its followers. Exposed, since that, to the influx of new Cromwell matter from all the world, one finds it worth observing how little of the smallest real importance has come in; what of effort has had to expend itself, not in improving the Book as a practical Representation of Cromwell's Existence in this world, but in hindering it from being injured as such, — from being swollen out of shape by superfluous details, defaced with dilettante antiquarianisms, nugatory tagrags; and in short, turned away from its real uses, instead of furthered towards them. An ungrateful kind of effort, and growing ever more so, the longer it lasts; — but one to which the Biographer of Cromwell by this method has to submit, as to a clear law of nature, with what cheerfulness he can.

Certain Dictionary *Lists*, not immediately connected with Oliver, but useful for students of this Historical Period, a *List of the Long Parliament*, and *Lists of the Association Committees*; farther a certain Contribution called *The Squire Papers*, which is for the present, and must for a long time remain, of doubtful authenticity to the world: these I have subjoined to the Second * Volume, which offered space for such a purpose; but have been careful, in Text, Appendix, Index, to make no reference to them, to maintain a perfect separation between all parts of the Book and them, and to signify that these are

* The *Lists* and the *Squire Papers* will be given at the end of the present Edition.

not even an Appendix, or thing hooked-on, but rather a mere Adjacency, or thing in some kind of contact, — kind of contact which can at any moment be completely dissolved, by the very Bookbinder if he so please.

And in general, for the reader's sake, let me again say plainly that all these Appendixes and Adjuncts are insignificant; that the Life of Cromwell lies in the Text; and that a serious reader, if he take advice of mine, will not readily stir from that on any call of the Appendixes &c., which can only be a call towards things unessential, intrinsically superfluous, if extrinsically necessary here, and worthy only of a later and more cursory attention, if of any whatever, from him.

T. C.

London, 16th October 1849.

CONTENTS OF VOLUME I.

INTRODUCTION.

PART I

TO THE BEGINNING OF THE CIVIL WAR. 1636-42.

PART II.

TO THE END OF THE FIRST CIVIL WAR. 1642-46

PART III.

BETWEEN THE TWO CIVIL WARS. 1646-48.

OLIVER CROMWELL'S
LETTERS AND SPEECHES.

INTRODUCTION.

CHAPTER I.

Anti-Dryasdust.

What and how great are the interests which connect themselves with the hope that England may yet attain to some practical belief and understanding of its History during the Seventeenth Century, need not be insisted on at present; such hope being still very distant, very uncertain. We have wandered far away from the ideas which guided us in that Century, and indeed which had guided us in all preceding Centuries, but of which that Century was the ultimate manifestation: we have wandered very far; and must endeavour to return, and connect ourselves therewith again! It is with other feelings than those of poor peddling Dilettantism, other aims than the writing of successful or unsuccessful Publications, that an earnest man occupies himself in those dreary provinces of the dead and buried. The last glimpse of the Godlike vanishing from this England; conviction and veracity giving place to hollow cant and formulism, — antique "Reign of God," which all true men in their several dialects and modes have always striven for, giving place to modern Reign of the No-God, whom men name Devil: this, in its multitudinous meanings and results, is a sight to create reflections in the earnest man! One wishes there were a History of English Puritanism, the last of all our Heroisms; but sees small prospect of such a thing at present.

"Few nobler Heroisms," says a well-known Writer long occupied on this subject, "at bottom perhaps no nobler "Heroism ever transacted itself on this Earth; and it lies as "good as lost to us; overwhelmed under such an avalanche of "Human Stupidities as no Heroism before ever did. Intrinsi-"cally and extrinsically it may be considered inaccessible to "these generations. Intrinsically, the spiritual purport of it "has become inconceivable, incredible to the modern mind. "Extrinsically, the documents and records of it, scattered "waste as a shoreless chaos, are not legible. They lie there, "printed, written, to the extent of tons and square miles, as "shot-rubbish; unedited, unsorted, not so much as indexed; "full of every conceivable confusion; — yielding light to very "few; yielding darkness, in several sorts, to very many. Dull "Pedantry, conceited idle Dilettantism, — prurient Stupidity "in what shape soever, — is darkness and not light! There are "from Thirty to Fifty Thousand unread Pamphlets of the "Civil War in the British Museum alone: huge piles of "mouldering wreck, wherein, at the rate of perhaps one "pennyweight per ton, lie things memorable. They lie pre-"served there, waiting happier days; under present conditions "they cannot, except for idle purposes, for dilettante excerpts "and such like, be got examined. The Rushworths, Whit-"lockes, Nalsons, Thurloes; enormous folios, these and many "others have been printed, and some of them again printed, "but never yet edited, — edited as you edit wagonloads of "broken bricks and dry mortar, simply by tumbling up the "wagon! Not one of those monstrous old volumes has so much "as an available Index. It is the general rule of editing on this "matter. If your editor correct the press, it is an honourable "distinction to him.

"Those dreary old records, they were compiled at first by "Human Insight, in part; and in great part, by Human Stupi-"dity withal; — but then it was by Stupidity in a laudable "diligent state, and doing its best; which was something: —

"and, alas, they have been successively elaborated by Human
"Stupidity in the *idle* state, falling idler and idler, and only
"pretending to be diligent; whereby now, for us, in these late
"days, they have grown very dim indeed! To Dryasdust
"Printing-Societies, and such like, they afford a sorrowful
"kind of pabulum; but for all serious purposes, they are as
"if non-extant; might as well, if matters are to rest as they
"are, not have been written or printed at all. The sound of
"them is not a *voice*, conveying knowledge or memorial of any
"earthly or heavenly thing; it is a wide-spread inarticulate
"slumberous mumblement, issuing as if from the lake of
"Eternal Sleep. *Craving* for oblivion, for abolition and honest
"silence, as a blessing in comparison! —

"This then," continues our impatient friend, "is the Ely-
"sium we English have provided for our Heroes! The Rush-
"worthian Elysium. Dreariest continent of shot-rubbish the
"eye ever saw. Confusion piled on confusion to your utmost
"horizon's edge: obscure, in lurid twilight as of the shadow of
"Death; trackless, without index, without finger-post, or
"mark of any human foregoer; — where your human footstep,
"if you are still human, echoes bodeful through the gaunt
"solitude, peopled only by somnambulant Pedants, Dilet-
"tants, and doleful creatures, by Phantasms, errors, inconcei-
"vabilities, by Nightmares, pasteboard Norroys, griffins,
"wiverns, and chimeras dire! There, all vanquished, over-
"whelmed under such waste lumber-mountains, the wreck
"and dead ashes of some six unbelieving generations, does
"the Age of Cromwell and his Puritans lie hidden from us.
"This is what we, for our share, have been able to accomplish
"towards keeping our Heroic Ones in memory. By way of
"sacred poet they have found voluminous Dryasdust, and his
"Collections and Philosophical Histories.

"To Dryasdust, who wishes merely to compile torpedo
"Histories of the philosophical or other sorts, and gain im-
"mortal laurels for himself by writing about it and about it,
"all this is sport; but to us who struggle piously, passionately,
"to behold, if but in glimpses, the faces of our vanished

"Fathers, it is death! — O Dryasdust, my voluminous friend,
"had Human Stupidity continued in the diligent state, think
"you it had ever come to this? Surely at least you might have
"made an Index for these huge books! Even your genius, had
"you been faithful, was adequate to that. Those thirty
"thousand or fifty thousand old Newspapers and Pamphlets of
"the King's Library, it is you, my voluminous friend, that
"should have sifted them, many long years ago. Instead of dro-
"ning out these melancholy scepticisms, constitutional philoso-
"phies, torpedo narratives, you should have sifted those old
"stacks of pamphlet matter for us, and have had the metal grains
"lying here accessible, and the dross-heaps lying there avoid-
"able; you had done the human memory a service thereby;
"some human remembrance of this matter had been more
"possible!"

Certainly this description does not want for emphasis: but
all ingenuous inquirers into the Past will say there is too
much truth in it. Nay, in addition to the sad state of our
Historical Books, and what indeed is fundamentally the cause
and origin of that, our common spiritual notions, if any notion
of ours may still deserve to be called spiritual, are fatal to a
right understanding of that Seventeenth Century. The
Christian Doctrines which then dwelt alive in every heart,
have now in a manner died out of all hearts, — very mournful
to behold; and are not the guidance of this world any more.
Nay worse still, the Cant of them does yet dwell alive with us,
little doubting that it is Cant; — in which fatal intermediate
state the Eternal Sacredness of this Universe itself, of this
Human Life itself, has fallen dark to the most of us, and we
think that too a Cant and a Creed. Thus the old names suggest
new things to us, — not august and divine, but hypocritical,
pitiable, detestable. The old names and similitudes of belief
still circulate from tongue to tongue, though now in such a
ghastly condition: not as commandments of the Living God,
which we must do, or perish eternally; alas, no, as something
very different from that! Here properly lies the grand unintelligibility of the Seventeenth Century for us. From this source

has proceeded our maltreatment of it, our miseditings, mis-writings, and all the other "avalanche of Human Stupidity," wherewith, as our impatient friend complains, we have allowed it to be overwhelmed. We have allowed some other things to be overwhelmed! Would to Heaven that were the worst fruit we had gathered from our Unbelief and our Cant of Belief! — Our impatient friend continues:

"I have known Nations altogether destitute of printer's-"types and learned appliances, with nothing better than old "songs, monumental stoneheaps and Quipothrums to keep "record by, who had truer memory of their memorable things "than this! Truer memory, I say: for at least the voice of "their Past Heroisms, if indistinct, and all awry as to dates "and statistics, was still melodious to those Nations. The "body of it might be dead enough; but the soul of it, partly "harmonised, put in real accordance with the 'Eternal "Melodies,' was alive to all hearts, and could not die. "The memory of their ancient Brave Ones did not rise "like a hideous huge leaden vapour, an amorphous ema-"nation of Chaos, like a petrifying Medusa Spectre on "those poor Nations: no, but like a Heaven's Apparition, "which it *was*, it still stood radiant beneficent before all "hearts, calling all hearts to emulate it, and the recognition "of it was a Psalm and Song. These things will require to be "practically meditated by and by. Is human Writing, then, "the art of burying Heroisms, and highest Facts, in Chaos; so "that no man shall henceforth contemplate them without "horror and aversion, and danger of locked-jaw? What does "Dryasdust consider that he was born for; that paper and ink "were made for?

"It is very notable, and leads to endless reflections, how "the Greeks had their living *Iliad*, where we have such a "deadly indescribable *Cromwelliad*. The old *Pantheon*, home "of all the gods, has become a *Peerage-Book*, — with black "and white surplice-controversies superadded, not unsuitably. "The Greeks had their Homers, Hesiods, where we have our "Rymers, Rushworths, our Norroys, Garter Kings, and Bish-

"ops Cobweb. Very notable, I say. By the genius, wants
"and instincts and opportunities of the one People, striving to
"keep themselves in mind of what was memorable, there had
"fashioned itself, in the effort of successive centuries, a *Ho-*
"*mer's Iliad*: by those of the other People, in successive cen-
"turies, a *Collins's Peerage* improved by Sir Egerton Brydges.
"By their Pantheons ye shall know them! Have not we Eng-
"lish a talent for Silence? Our very Speech and Printed-
"Speech, such a force of torpor dwelling in it, is properly a
"higher power of Silence. There is no Silence like the Speech
"you cannot listen to without danger of locked-jaw! Given a
"divine Heroism, to smother it well in human Dulness, to
"touch it with the mace of Death, so that no human soul shall
"henceforth recognise it for a Heroism, but all souls shall fly
"from it as from a chaotic Torpor, an Insanity and Horror, —
"I will back our English genius against the world in such a
"problem!

"Truly we have done great things in that sort; down from
"Norman William all the way, and earlier: and to the Eng-
"lish mind at this hour, the past History of England is little
"other than a dull dismal labyrinth, in which the English
"mind, if candid, will confess that it has found of knowable
"(meaning even *conceivable*), of loveable, or memorable, —
"next to nothing. As if we had done no brave thing at all in
"this Earth; — as if not Men but Nightmares had written of
"our History! The English, one can discern withal, have
"been perhaps as brave a People as their neighbours; perhaps,
"for Valour of Action and true hard labour in this Earth, since
"brave Peoples were first made in it, there has been none
"braver anywhere or anywhen: — but, also, it must be owned,
"in Stupidity of Speech they have no fellow! What can poor
"English Heroisms do in such case, but fall torpid into the do-
"main of the Nightmares? For of a truth, Stupidity is strong,
"most strong. As the Poet Schiller sings: 'Against Stupidity
"the very gods fight unvictorious.' There is in *it* an opulence
"of murky stagnancy, an inexhaustibility, a calm infinitude,
"which will baffle even the gods, — which will say calmly,

" 'Yes, try all your lightnings here; see whether my dark
" belly cannot hold them!'

'Mit der Dummheit kämpfen Götter selbst vergebens.' "

Has our impatient friend forgotten that it is Destiny withal
as well as "Stupidity;" that such is the case more or less with
Human History always! By very nature it is a labyrinth and
chaos, this that we call Human History; an *abatis* of trees and
brushwood, a world-wide jungle, at once growing and dying.
Under the green foliage and blossoming fruit-trees of Today,
there lie, rotting slower or faster, the forests of all other Years
and Days. Some have rotted fast, plants of annual growth,
and are long since quite gone to inorganic mould; others are
like the aloe, growths that last a thousand or three thousand
years. You will find them in all stages of decay and preservation; down deep to the beginnings of the History of Man.
Think where our Alphabetic Letters came from, where our
Speech itself came from; the Cookeries we live by, the Ma-
sonries we lodge under! You will find fibrous roots of this
day's Occurrences among the dust of Cadmus and Trisme-
gistus, of Tubalcain and Triptolemus; the tap-roots of them
are with Father Adam himself and the cinders of Eve's first
fire! At bottom, there is no perfect History; there is none
such conceivable.

All past Centuries have rotted down, and gone confusedly
dumb and quiet, even as that Seventeenth is now threatening
to do. Histories are *as* perfect as the Historian is wise, and
is gifted with an eye and a soul! For the leafy blossoming
Present Time springs from the whole Past, remembered and
unrememberable, so confusedly as we say: — and truly the Art
of History, the grand difference between a Dryasdust and a
sacred Poet, is very much even this: To distinguish well what
does still reach to the surface, and is alive and frondent for us;
and what reaches no longer to the surface, but moulders safe
underground, never to send forth leaves or fruit for mankind
any more: of the former we shall rejoice to hear; to hear of the
latter will be an affliction to us; of the latter only Pedants and

Dullards, and disastrous *malefactors* to the world, will find
good to speak. By wise memory and by wise oblivion: it lies
all there! Without oblivion, there is no remembrance possible. When both oblivion and memory are wise, when the
general soul of man is clear, melodious, true, there may come
a modern *Iliad* as memorial of the Past: when both are foolish,
and the general soul is overclouded with confusions, with unveracities and discords, there is a "Rushworthian chaos."
Let Dryasdust be blamed, beaten with stripes if you will; but
let it be with pity, with blame to Fate chiefly. Alas, when
sacred Priests are arguing about "black and white surplices;"
and sacred Poets have long *professedly* deserted Truth, and
gone a woolgathering after "Ideals" and such like, what can
you expect of poor secular Pedants? The labyrinth of History
must grow ever darker, more intricate and dismal; vacant
cargoes of "Ideals" will arrive yearly, to be cast into the
oven; and noble Heroisms of Fact, given up to Dryasdust,
will be buried in a very disastrous manner! —

But the thing we had to say and repeat was this, That
Puritanism is not of the Nineteenth Century, but of the Seventeenth; that the grand unintelligibility for us lies *there*. The
Fast-day Sermons of St. Margaret's Church Westminster, in
spite of printers, are all grown dumb! In long rows of little
dumpy quartos, gathered from the bookstalls, they indeed
stand here bodily before us: by human volition they can be
read, but not by any human memory remembered. We forget
them as soon as read; they have become a weariness to the
soul of man. They are dead and gone, they and what they
shadowed; the human soul, got into other latitudes, cannot
now give harbour to them. Alas, and did not the honourable
Houses of Parliament listen to them with rapt earnestness, as
to an indisputable message from Heaven itself? Learned and
painful Dr. Owen, learned and painful Dr. Burgess; Stephen
Marshall, Mr. Spurstow, Adoniram Byfield, Hugh Peters,
Philip Nye: the Printer has done for them what he could, and
Mr. Speaker gave them the thanks of the House: — and no
most astonishing Review-Article, or tenth-edition Pamphlet,

of our day can have half such "brilliancy," such "spirit," "eloquence," — such *virtue to produce belief*, which is the highest and in reality the only literary success, — as these poor little dumpy quartos once had. And behold, they are become inarticulate quartos; spectral; and instead of speaking, do but screech and gibber! All Puritanism has grown inarticulate; its fervent preachings, prayings, pamphleteerings are sunk into one indiscriminate moaning hum, mournful as the voice of subterranean winds. So much falls silent: human Speech, unless by rare chance it touch on the "Eternal Melodies," and harmonise with them; human Action, Interest, if divorced from the Eternal Melodies, sinks all silent. The fashion of this world passeth away.

The Age of the Puritans is not extinct only and gone away from us, but it is as if fallen beyond the capabilities of Memory herself; it is grown unintelligible, what we may call incredible. Its earnest Purport awakens now no resonance in our frivolous hearts. We understand not even in imagination, one of a thousand of us, what it ever could have meant. It seems delirious, delusive; the sound of it has become tedious as a tale of past stupidities. Not the body of heroic Puritanism only, which was bound to die, but the soul of it also, which was and should have been, and yet shall be immortal, has for the present passed away. As Harrison said of his Banner, and Lion of the Tribe of Judah: "Who shall rouse him up?" —

"For indisputably," exclaims the above-cited Author in his vehement way, "this too was a Heroism; and the soul of it "remains part of the eternal soul of things! Here, of our own "land and lineage, in practical English shape, were Heroes "on the Earth once more. Who knew in every fibre, and "with heroic daring laid to heart, That an Almighty Justice "does verily rule this world; that it is good to fight on God's "side, and bad to fight on the Devil's side! The essence of "all Heroisms and Veracities that have been, or that will be. "— Perhaps it was among the nobler and noblest Human "Heroisms, this Puritanism of ours: but English Dryasdust

"could not discern it for a Heroism at all; — as the Heaven's
"lightning, born of its black tempest, and destructive to
"pestilential Mud-giants, is mere horror and terror to the
"Pedant species everywhere; which, like the owl in any sud-
"den brightness, has to shut its eyes, — or hastily procure
"smoked-spectacles on an improved principle. Heaven's
"brightness would be intolerable otherwise. Only your eagle
"dares look direct into the fire-radiance; only your Schiller
"climbs aloft 'to discover whence the lightning is coming.'
"'Godlike men love lightning,' says one. Our old Norse
"fathers called it a God; the sunny blue-eyed Thor, with his
"all-conquering thunder-hammer, — who again, in calmer
"season, is beneficent Summer-heat. Godless men love it
"not; shriek murder when they see it; shutting their eyes,
"and hastily procuring smoked-spectacles. O Dryasdust,
"thou art great and thrice great!" — —

 "But alas," exclaims he elsewhere, getting his eye on the
real nodus of the matter, "what is it, all this Rushworthian in-
"articulate rubbish-continent, in its ghastly dim twilight, with
"its haggard wrecks and pale shadows; what is it, but the
"common Kingdom of Death? This *is* what we call Death,
"this mouldering dumb wilderness of things once alive. Be-
"hold here the final evanescence of Formed human things;
"they had form, but they are changing into sheer formless-
"ness; — ancient human speech itself has sunk into unintel-
"ligible maundering. This is the collapse, — the etiolation
"of human features into mouldy blank; *dis*solution; progress
"towards utter silence and disappearance; disastrous ever-
"deepening Dusk of Gods and Men! — — Why has the living
"ventured thither, down from the cheerful light, across the
"Lethe-swamps and Tartarean Phlegethons, onwards to
"these baleful halls of Dis and the three-headed Dog? Some
"Destiny drives him. It is his sins, I suppose: — perhaps it
"is his love, strong as that of Orpheus for the lost Eurydice,
"and likely to have no better issue!" —

Well, it would seem the resuscitation of a Heroism from

the Past Time is no easy enterprise. Our impatient friend seems really getting sad! We can well believe him, there needs pious love in any "Orpheus" that will risk descending to the Gloomy Halls; — descending, it may be, and fronting Cerberus and Dis, to no purpose! For it oftenest proves so; nay, as the Mythologists would teach us, always. Here is another Mythus. Balder the white Sungod, say our Norse Skalds, Balder, beautiful as the summer-dawn, loved of Gods and men, was dead. His Brother Hermoder, urged by his Mother's tears and the tears of the Universe, went forth to seek him.   He rode through gloomy winding valleys, of a dismal leaden colour, full of howling winds and subterranean torrents; nine days; ever deeper, down towards Hela's Death-realm: at Lonesome Bridge, which, with its gold gate, spans the River of Moaning, he found the Portress, an ancient woman, called Modgudr, "the Vexer of Minds," keeping watch as usual: Modgudr answered him, "Yes, Balder passed this way; but he is not here; he is down yonder, — far, still far to the North, within Hela's Gates yonder." Hermoder rode on, still dauntless, on his horse, named "Swiftness" or "Mane of Gold;" reached Hela's Gates; leapt sheer over them, mounted as he was; *saw* Balder, the very Balder, with his eyes: — but could not bring him back! The Nornas were inexorable; Balder was never to come back. Balder beckoned him mournfully a still adieu; Nanna, Balder's Wife, sent "a thimble" to her mother as a memorial: Balder never could return! — — Is not this an emblem? Old Portress Modgudr, I take it, is Dryasdust in Norse petticoat and hood; a most unlovely beldame, the "Vexer of Minds!"

We will here take final leave of our impatient friend, occupied in this almost desperate enterprise of his; we will wish him, which it is very easy to do, more *patience*, and better success than he seems to hope. And now to our own small enterprise, and solid despatch of business in plain prose!

CHAPTER II.

Of the Biographies of Oliver.

Ours is a very small enterprise, but seemingly a useful one; preparatory perhaps to greater and more useful, on this same matter: The collecting of the *Letters and Speeches of Oliver Cromwell*, and presenting them in natural sequence, with the still possible elucidation, to ingenuous readers. This is a thing that can be done; and after some reflection, it has appeared worth doing. No great thing: one other dull Book added to the thousand, dull every one of them, which have been issued on this subject! But situated as we are, new Dulness is unhappily inevitable; readers do not reascend out of deep confusions without some trouble as they climb.

These authentic utterances of the man Oliver himself — I have gathered them from far and near; fished them up from the foul Lethean quagmires where they lay buried; I have washed, or endeavoured to wash them clean from foreign stupidities (such a job of buckwashing as I do not long to repeat); and the world shall now see them in their own shape. Working for long years in those unspeakable Historic Provinces, of which the reader has already had account, it becomes more and more apparent to one, That this man Oliver Cromwell was, as the popular fancy represents him, the soul of the Puritan Revolt, without whom it had never been a revolt transcendently memorable, and an Epoch in the World's History; that in fact he, more than is common in such cases, does deserve to give his name to the Period in question, and have the Puritan Revolt considered as a *Cromwelliad*, which issue is already very visible for it. And then farther, altogether contrary to the popular fancy, it becomes apparent that this Oliver was not a man of falsehoods, but a man of truths; whose words do carry a meaning with them, and above all others of that time are worth considering. His words, — and still more his *silences*, and unconscious instincts, when you have spelt and lovingly deciphered these also out of his words, — will in several ways reward the study of an earnest man. An earnest man, I apprehend, may gather from these words of Oliver's, were there even no other evidence, that the character of Oliver, and of the Affairs he worked in, is much the reverse of that mad jumble of "hypocrisies," &c. &c., which at present passes current as such.

But certainly, on any hypothesis as to that, such a set of Documents may hope to be elucidative in various respects. Oliver's Character, and that of Oliver's Performance in this world: here best of all may we expect to read it, whatsoever it was. Even if false, these words, authentically spoken and written by the chief actor in the business, must be of prime moment for understanding of it. These are the words this man found suitablest to represent the Things themselves, around him, and in him, of which we seek a History. The newborn Things and Events, as they bodied themselves forth to Oliver Cromwell from the Whirlwind of the passing Time, — this is the name and definition he saw good to give of them. To get at these direct utterances of his, is to get at the very heart of the business; were there once light for us in these, the business had begun again at the heart of it to be luminous! — On the whole, we will start with this small service, the *Letters and Speeches of Oliver Cromwell* washed into something of legibility again, as the preliminary of all. May it prosper with a few serious readers. The *heart* of that Grand Puritan Business once again becoming visible, even in faint twilight, to mankind, what masses of brutish darkness will gradually vanish from all fibres of it, from the whole body and environment of it, and trouble no man any more! Masses of foul darkness, sordid confusions not a few, as I calculate, which now bury this matter very deep, may vanish: the heart of this matter and the heart of serious men once again brought into approximation, to write some "History" of it may be a little easier, — for my impatient friend or another.

To dwell on or criticise the particular *Biographies* of Cromwell, after what was so emphatically said above on the general subject, would profit us but little. Criticism of these poor

Books cannot express itself except in language that is painful. They far surpass in "stupidity" all the celebrations any Hero ever had in this world before. They are in fact worthy of oblivion, — of charitable Christian *burial.*

Mark Noble reckons up some half dozen "Original Biographies of Cromwell;"* all of which and some more I have examined; but cannot advise any other man to examine. There are several laudatory, worth nothing; which ceased to be read when Charles II. came back, and the tables were turned. The vituperative are many: but the origin of them all, the chief fountain indeed of all the foolish lies that have circulated about Oliver since, is the mournful brown little Book called *Flagellum, or the Life and Death of O. Cromwell, the late Usurper*, by James Heath; which was got ready so soon as possible on the back of the *Annus Mirabilis* or Glorious Restoration,** and is written in such spirit as we may fancy. When restored potentates and high dignitaries had dug up "above a hundred "buried corpses, and flung them in a heap in St. Margaret's "Churchyard," the corpse of Admiral Blake among them, and Oliver's old Mother's corpse; and were hanging on Tyburn gallows, as some small satisfaction to themselves, the dead clay of Oliver, of Ireton, and Bradshaw; — when high dignitaries and potentates were in such a humour, what could be expected of poor pamphleteers and garreteers? Heath's poor little brown lying *Flagellum* is described by one of the moderns as a "*Flagitium;*" and Heath himself is called "*Carrion*Heath," — as being "an unfortunate blasphemous dullard, "and scandal to Humanity; — blasphemous, I say; who when "the image of God is shining through a man, reckons it in his "sordid soul to be the image of the Devil, and acts accord- "ingly; who in fact has no soul, except what saves him the "expense of salt; who intrinsically is Carrion and not Huma- "nity:" which seems hard measure to poor James Heath. "He was the son of the King's Cutler," says Wood, "and

* Noble's *Cromwell*, i. 294-300. His list is very inaccurate and incomplete, but not worth completing or rectifying.
** The First Edition seems to be of 1663.

"wrote pamphlets," the best he was able, poor man. He has become a dreadfully dull individual, in addition to all! — Another wretched old Book of his, called *Cronicle of the Civil Wars*, bears a high price in the Dilettante Sale-catalogues; and has, as that *Flagellum* too has, here and there a credible trait not met with elsewhere: but in fact, to the ingenuous inquirer, this too is little other than a tenebrific Book; cannot be read except with sorrow, with torpor and disgust, — and in fine, if you be of healthy memory, with *oblivion*. The latter end of Heath has been worse than the beginning was! From him, and his *Flagellums* and scandalous Human Platitudes, let no rational soul seek knowledge.

Among modern Biographies, the great original is that of Mark Noble cited;* such "original" as there is: a Book, if we must call it a Book, abounding in facts and pretended-facts more than any other on this subject. Poor Noble has gone into much research of old leases, marriage-contracts, deeds of sale and such like: he is learned in parish-registers and genealogies, has consulted pedigrees "measuring eight feet by two feet four;" goes much upon heraldry; — in fact, has amassed a large heap of evidences and assertions, worthless and of worth, respecting Cromwell and his Connexions; from which the reader, by his own judgment, is to extract what he can. For Noble himself is a man of extreme imbecility; his judgment, for most part, seeming to lie dead asleep; and indeed it is worth little when broadest awake. He falls into manifold mistakes, commits and omits in all ways; plods along contented, in an element of perennial dimness, purblindness; has occasionally a helpless broad innocence of platitude which is almost interesting. A man indeed of extreme imbecility; to whom nevertheless let due gratitude be borne.

His Book, in fact, is not properly a Book, but rather an Aggregate of bewildered jottings; a kind of Cromwellian Biographical Dictionary, *wanting* the alphabetical, or any other,

* Memoirs of the Protectoral House of Cromwell. By the Rev. Mark Noble. 2 vols. London, 1787.

arrangement or index: which latter want, much more reme-
diable than the want of judgment, is itself a great sorrow to
the reader. Such as it is, this same Dictionary without judgment and without arrangement, "bad Dictionary gone to pie,"
as we may call it, is the storehouse from which subsequent
Biographies have all furnished themselves. The reader, with
continual vigilance of suspicion, once knowing what man he
has to do with, digs through it, and again through it; covers
the margins of it with notes and contradictions, with refer-
ences, deductions, rectifications, execrations, — in a sorrowful, but not entirely unprofitable manner. Another Book
of Noble's, called *Lives of the Regicides*, written some years
afterwards, during the French Jacobin time, is of much more
stupid character; nearly meaningless indeed; mere water be-
witched; which no man need buy or read. And it is said he
has a third Book, on some other subject, stupider still; which
latter point, however, may be considered questionable.

For the rest, this poor Noble is of very impartial mind
respecting Cromwell; open to receive good of him, and to
receive evil, even inconsistent evil: the helpless, incoherent,
but placid and favourable notion he has of Cromwell in 1787
contrasts notably with that which Carrion Heath had gathered
of him in 1663. For, in spite of the stupor of Histories, it is
beautiful, once more, to see how the Memory of Cromwell,
in its huge inarticulate significance, not able to *speak* a wise
word for itself to any one, has nevertheless been steadily
growing clearer and clearer in the popular English mind;
how from the day when high dignitaries and pamphleteers
of the Carrion species did their ever-memorable feat at Tyburn, onwards to this day, the progress does not stop.

In 1698,* one of the earliest words expressly in favour of
Cromwell was written by a Critic of *Ludlow's Memoirs*. The
anonymous Critic explains to solid Ludlow that he, in that
solid but somewhat wooden head of his, had not perhaps seen

* So dated in *Somers Tracts* (London, 1811), vi. 416, — but liable to
correction if needful. Poor Noble (i. 297) gives the same date, and then
placidly, in the next line, subjoins a fact inconsistent with it. As his
manner is!

entirely into the centre of the Universe, and workshop of the
Destinies; that, in fact, Oliver was a questionable uncom-
mon man, and he Ludlow a common handfast, honest, dull
and indeed partly wooden man, — in whom it might be wise
to form no theory at all of Cromwell. By and by, a certain
"Mr. Banks," a kind of Lawyer and Playwright, if I mistake
not, produced a still more favourable view of Cromwell, but
in a work otherwise of no moment; the exact date, and indeed the whole substance of which is hardly worth remembering. *

The *Letter* of "John Maidston to Governor Winthrop," —
Winthrop Governor of Connecticut, a Suffolk man, of much
American celebrity, — is dated 1659; but did not come into
print till 1742, along with Thurloe's other Papers.** Maidston had been an Officer in Oliver's Household, a Member of
his Parliaments, and knew him well. An Essex man he;
probably an old acquaintance of Winthrop's; visibly a man of
honest affections, of piety, decorum, and good sense. Whose
loyalty to Oliver is of a genuine and altogether manful nature,
— mostly silent, as we can discern. His *Letter* gives some
really lucid traits of those dark things and times; especially
a short portraiture of the Protector himself, which, the more
you know him, you ascertain the more to be a likeness. Another Officer of Oliver's Household, not to be confounded
with this Maidston, but a man of similar position and similar
moral character to Maidston's; a "Groom of the Bedchamber;"
whose name one at length dimly discovers to be Harvey,***
not quite unknown otherwise; is also well worth listening to
on this matter. He, in 1659, a few months before Maidston
wrote, had published a credible and still interesting little
Pamphlet, *Passages concerning his late Highness's last Sickness*;
to which, if space permit, we shall elsewhere refer. In these

* Short Critical Review of the Life of Oliver Cromwell. By a Gentleman of the Middle Temple. London, 1739.

** Thurloe, i. 763-8; — and correct Noble, 1. 94.

*** The "Cofferer," elsewhere called Steward of the Household, is
"Mr. Maidston:" "Gentlemen of the Bedchamber, Mr. Charles Harvey,
Mr. Underwood." — Prestwick's *Funeral of the Protector* (reprinted in
Forster's British Statesmen, v. 436, &c.).

two little off-hand bits of writing, by two persons qualified to
write and witness, there is a clear credibility for the reader;
and more insight obtainable as to Oliver and his ways than in
any of the express Biographies.

That anonymous *Life of Cromwell*, which Noble very
ignorantly ascribes to Bishop Gibson, which is written in a
neutral spirit, as an impartial statement of facts, but not
without a secret decided leaning to Cromwell, came out in
1724. It is the *Life of Cromwell* found commonly in Libraries:*
it went through several editions in a pure state; and I have
seen a "fifth edition" with foreign intermixtures, "printed at
Birmingham in 1778," on gray paper, seemingly as a Book
for Hawkers. The Author of it was by no means "Bishop
Gibson," but one Kimber, a Dissenting Minister of London,
known otherwise as a compiler of books. He has diligently
gathered from old Newspapers and other such sources; nar-
rates in a dull, steady, concise, but altogether unintelligent
manner; can be read without offence, but hardly with any
real instruction. Image of Cromwell's self there is none, express or implied, in this Book; for the man himself had none,
and did not feel the want of any: nay in regard to external
facts also, there are inaccuracies enough, — here too, what
is the general rule in these books, you can find as many inaccuracies as you like: dig where you please, water will
come! As a crown to all the modern Biographies of Cromwell, let us note Mr. Forster's late one:** full of interesting
original excerpts, and indications of what is notablest in the
old Books; gathered and set forth with real merit, with *energy*
in abundance and superabundance; amounting in result, we
may say, to a vigorous decisive tearing up of all the old hypotheses on the subject, and an opening of the general mind for
new.

Of Cromwell's actual biography, from these and from all

* The Life of Oliver Cromwell, Lord Protector of the Commonwealth.
Impartially collected, &c. London, 1724. Distinguished also by a not
intolerable Portrait.

** Statesmen of the Commonwealth. By John Forster (London, 1840).
Vols. iv. and v.

Books and sources, there is extremely little to be known. It is from his own words, as I have ventured to believe, from his own Letters and Speeches well read, that the world may first obtain some dim glimpse of the actual Cromwell, and see him darkly face to face. What little is otherwise ascertainable, cleared from the circumambient inanity and insanity, may be stated in brief compass. So much as precedes the earliest still extant Letters, I subjoin here in the form most convenient.

CHAPTER III.

Of the Cromwell Kindred.

OLIVER CROMWELL, afterwards Protector of the Commonwealth of England, was born at Huntingdon, in St. John's Parish there, on the 25th of April 1599. Christened on the 29th of the same month; as the old Parish-registers of that Church still legibly testify.*

His Father was Robert Cromwell, younger son of Sir Henry Cromwell, and younger brother of Sir Oliver Cromwell, Knights both; who dwelt successively, in rather sumptuous fashion, at the Mansion of Hinchinbrook hard by. His Mother was Elizabeth Steward, daughter of William Steward, Esquire, in Ely; an opulent man, a kind of hereditary Farmer of the Cathedral Tithes and Church lands round that city; in which capacity his son, Sir Thomas Steward, Knight, in due time succeeded him, resident also at Ely. Elizabeth was a young widow when Robert Cromwell married her: the first marriage, to one "William Lynne, Esquire, of Bassingbourne in Cambridgeshire," had lasted but a year: husband and only child are buried in Ely Cathedral, where their monument still stands; the date of their deaths, which followed near on one another, is 1589.** The exact date of the young widow's marriage to Robert Cromwell is nowhere given; but seems to have been in 1591.*** Our Oliver was their

* Noble, i. 92.　　** Ibid. ii. 198, and ms. *penes me.*
*** Noble, i. 88.

fifth child; their second boy; but the first soon died.   They had ten children in all; of whom seven came to maturity, and Oliver was their only son.   I may as well print the little Note, smelted long ago out of huge dross-heaps in Noble's Book, that the reader too may have his small benefit of it. *

This Elizabeth Steward, who had now become Mrs. Robert Cromwell, was, say the genealogists, "indubitably descended from the Royal Stuart Family of Scotland;" and could still count kindred with them. "From one Walter Steward, who had accompanied Prince James of Scotland," when our in-hospitable politic Henry IV. detained the poor Prince, driven in by stress of weather to him here. Walter did not return with the Prince to Scotland; having "fought tournaments,"— having made an advantageous marriage-settlement here. One of his descendants, Robert Steward, happened to be Prior of Ely when Henry VIII. dissolved the Monasteries; and proving pliant on that occasion, Robert Steward, last Popish Prior, became the first Protestant Dean of Ely, and — "was remarkably attentive to his family," says Noble. The pro-fitable Farming of the Tithes at Ely, above mentioned; this,

---

* OLIVER CROMWELL'S BROTHERS AND SISTERS.

Oliver's Mother had been a widow (Mrs. *Lynne* of Bassingbourne) before marrying Robert Cromwell; neither her age nor his is discoverable here.

1. *First* child (seemingly), *Joan*, baptised 24th September 1592; she died in 1600 (Noble, i. 88).

2. Elizabeth, 14th October 1593; died unmarried, thinks Noble, in 1672, at Ely. — See Appendix, No. 20, a Letter in regard to her, which has turned up. (*Note of* 1857).

3. *Henry*, 31st August 1595; died young, "before 1617."

4. Catherine, 7th February 1596-7; married to Whitstone, a Parlia-mentary Officer; then to Colonel Jones.

5. OLIVER, born 25th April 1599.

6. Margaret, 22d February 1600-1; she became Mrs. Wauton, or Walton, Huntingdonshire; her son was killed at Marston Moor, — as we shall see.

7. Anna, 2d January 1602-3; Mrs. Sewster, Huntingdonshire; died 1st November 1646: — her Brother Oliver had just ended the "first Civil War" then.

8. Jane, 19th January 1605-6; Mrs. Desborow, Cambridgeshire; died, *seemingly*, in 1656.

9. *Robert*, 18th January 1608-9; died same April.

10. Robina, so named for the above Robert: uncertain date; became Mrs. Dr. French; then wife of Bishop Wilkins: her daughter by French, her one child, was married to Archbishop Tillotson.

and other settlements, and good dotations of Church lands among his Nephews, were the fruits of Robert Steward's pliancy on that occasion. The genealogists say, there is no doubt of this pedigree; — and explain in intricate tables, how Elizabeth Steward, Mother of Oliver Cromwell, was indubitably either the ninth, or the tenth, or some other fractional part of half a cousin to Charles Stuart King of England.

Howsoever related to Charles Stuart or to other parties, Robert Cromwell, younger son of the Knight of Hinchinbrook, brought her home, we see, as his Wife, to Huntingdon, about 1591; and settled with her there, on such portion, with such prospects as a cadet of the House of Hinchinbrook might have. Portion consisting of certain lands and messuages round and in that Town of Huntingdon, — where, in the current name "Cromwell's Acre," if not in other names applied to lands and messuages there, some feeble echo of him and his possessions still survives, or seems to survive. These lands he himself farmed: the income in all is guessed or computed to have been about 300*l.* a year; a tolerable fortune in those times; perhaps somewhat like 1000*l.* now. Robert Cromwell's Father, as we said, and then his elder Brother, dwelt successively in good style at Hinchinbrook near by. It was the Father Sir Henry Cromwell, who from his sumptuosity was called the "Golden Knight," that built, or that enlarged, remodelled and as good as built, the Mansion of Hinchinbrook; which had been a Nunnery while Nunneries still were: it was the son, Sir Oliver, likewise an expensive man, that sold it to the Montagues, since Earls of Sandwich, whose seat it still is. A stately pleasant House, among its shady lawns and expanses, on the left bank of the Ouse river, a short half mile west of Huntingdon; — still stands pretty much as Oliver Cromwell's Grandfather left it; rather kept good and defended from the inroads of Time and Accident, than substantially altered. Several Portraits of the Cromwells, and other interesting portraits and memorials of the seventeenth and subsequent centuries, are still there. The Cromwell blazonry "on the great bay window," which Noble makes so much of, is now gone, destroyed

by fire; has given place to Montague blazonry; and no dull
man can bore us with that any more.

Huntingdon itself lies pleasantly along the left bank of the
Ouse; sloping pleasantly upwards from Ouse Bridge, which
connects it with the old village of Godmanchester; the Town
itself consisting mainly of one fair street, which towards the
north end of it opens into a kind of irregular market-place,
and then contracting again soon terminates. The two churches
of All-Saints and St. John's, as you walk up northward from
the Bridge, appear successively on your left; the churchyards
flanked with shops or other houses. The Ouse, which is of
very circular course in this quarter, "winding as if reluctant
to enter the Fen-country," says one Topographer, has still a
respectable drab-colour, gathered from the clays of Bedfordshire; has not yet the Stygian black which in a few miles
farther it assumes for good. Huntingdon, as it were, looks
over into the Fens; Godmanchester, just across the river, already stands on black bog. The country to the East is all
Fen (mostly unreclaimed in Oliver's time, and still of a very
dropsical character); to the West it is hard green ground,
agreeably broken into little heights, duly fringed with wood,
and bearing marks of comfortable long-continued cultivation.
Here, on the edge of the firm green land, and looking over
into the black marshes with their alder-trees and willow-trees,
did Oliver Cromwell pass his young years. Drunken Barnabee,
who travelled, and drank, and made Latin rhymes, in that
country about 1635, through whose glistening satyr-eyes one
can still discern this and the other feature of the Past, represents to us on the height behind Godmanchester, as you approach the scene from Cambridge and the south, a big Oak-
tree, — which has now disappeared, leaving no notable suc-
cessor.

> *Veni Godmanchester, ubi*
> *Ut Ixion captus nube,*
> *Sic, &c.*

And he adds in a Note,

> *Quercus anilis erat, tamen eminus oppida spectat;*
> *Stirpe viam monstrat, plumen fronde tegit; —*

Or in his own English version,

An aged Oak takes of this Town survey,
Finds birds their nests, tells passengers their way. *

If Oliver Cromwell climbed that Oak-tree, in quest of bird-nests or boy-adventures, the Tree, or this poor ghost of it, may still have a kind of claim to memory.

The House where Robert Cromwell dwelt, where his son Oliver and all his family were born, is still familiar to every inhabitant of Huntingdon: but it has been twice rebuilt since that date, and now bears no memorial whatever which even Tradition can connect with him. It stands at the upper or northern extremity of the Town, — beyond the Market-place we spoke of; on the left or river-ward side of the street. It is at present a solid yellow brick house, with a walled court-yard; occupied by some townsman of the wealthier sort. The little Brook of Hinchin, making its way to the Ouse which is not far off, still flows through the court-yard of the place, — offering a convenience for malting or brewing, among other things. Some vague but confident tradition as to Brewing attaches itself to this locality; and traces of evidence, I understand, exist that *before* Robert Cromwell's time, it had been employed as a Brewery: but of this or even of Robert Cromwell's own brewing, there is, at such a distance, in such an element of distracted calumny, exaggeration and confusion, little or no certainty to be had. Tradition, "the Rev. Dr. Lort's Manuscripts," Carrion Heath, and such testimonies, are extremely insecure as guides! Thomas Harrison, for example, is always called "the son of a Butcher;" which means only that his Father, as farmer or owner, had grazing-lands, down in Staffordshire, wherefrom naturally enough proceeded cattle, fat cattle as the case might be, — well fatted, I hope. Thomas Cromwell, Earl of Essex in Henry Eighth's time, is in like manner called always "the son of a Blacksmith at Putney;" — and whoever figures to himself a man in black apron with hammer in hand, and tries to rhyme this with the rest of Thomas Cromwell's history, will find that

* Barnabæ Itinerarium (London, 1818), p. 96.

here too he has got into an insolubility. "The splenetic cre-
"dulity and incredulity, the calumnious opacity, the exag-
"gerative ill-nature, and general flunkeyism and stupidity of
"mankind," says my Author, "are ever to be largely allowed
"for in such circumstances." We will leave Robert Cromwell's brewing in a very unilluminated state. Uncontradicted
Tradition, and old printed Royalist Lampoons, do call him a
Brewer: the Brook of Hinchin, running through his premises,
offered clear convenience for malting or brewing; — in regard
to which, and also to his Wife's assiduous management of the
same, one is very willing to believe Tradition. The essential
trade of Robert Cromwell was that of managing those lands
of his in the vicinity of Huntingdon: the grain of them would
have to be duly harvested, thrashed, brought to market;
whether it was as corn or as malt that it came to market, can
remain indifferent to us.

For the rest, as documents still testify, this Robert Cromwell did Burgh and Quarter-Session duties; was not slack but
moderately active as a country-gentleman; sat once in Parliament in his younger years;* is found with his elder or other
Brothers on various Public Commissions for Draining the
Fens of that region, or more properly for inquiring into the
possibility of such an operation; a thing much noised of then;
which Robert Cromwell, among others, reported to be very
feasible, very promising, but did not live to see accomplished,
or even attempted. His social rank is sufficiently indicated;
— and much flunkeyism, falsity and other carrion ought to be
buried! Better than all social rank, he is understood to have
been a wise, devout, stedfast and worthy man, and to have
lived a modest and manful life in his station there.

Besides the Knight of Hinchinbrook, he had other Brothers
settled prosperously in the Fen regions, where this Cromwell
Family had extensive possessions. One Brother Henry was
"seated at Upwood," a fenny district near Ramsey Mere; one
of his daughters came to be the wife, second wife, of Oliver
St. John, the Ship-money Lawyer, the political "dark-lantern,"

* "35to Eliz.:" Feb.—April 1593 (Noble, i. 83; from Willis).

as men used to name him; of whom we shall hear farther. Another Brother "was seated" at Biggin House between Ramsey and Upwood; a moated mansion, with ditch and painted paling round it. A third Brother was seated at — my informant knows not where! In fact I had better, as before, subjoin the little *smelted* Note which has already done its duty, and let the reader make of that what he can.* Of our Oliver's

* OLIVER'S UNCLES.

1. Sir Oliver of Hinchinbrook: his eldest son John, born in 1589 (ten years older than our Oliver), went into the army, "Colonel of an English regiment in the Dutch service:" this is the Colonel Cromwell who is said, or fabled, to have sought a midnight interview with Oliver, in the end of 1648, for the purpose of buying off Charles I.; to have "laid his hand on his sword," &c. &c. The story is in Noble, i. 51; with no authority but that of Carrion Heath. Other sons of his were soldiers, Royalists these: there are various Cousin Cromwells that confusedly turn up on both sides of the quarrel. — Robert Cromwell, our Oliver's Father, was the next Brother of the Hinchinbrook Knight. The third Brother, second uncle, was

2. Henry Cromwell, of Upwood near Ramsey Mere: adventurer in the Virginia Company: sat in Parliament 1603-1611; one of his daughters Mrs. St. John. Died 1630 (Noble, i. 28).

3. Richard: "buys in 1607" a bit of ground in Huntingdon; died "at Ramsey," 1628; was Member for Huntingdon in Queen Elizabeth's time: — *Lived* in Ramsey? Is buried at Upwood.

4. Sir Philip: Biggin House; knighted at Whitehall, 1604 (Noble, i. 31). His second son, Philip, was in Colonel Ingoldsby's regiment; — wounded at the storm of Bristol, in 1645. Third son, Thomas, was in Ireland with Strafford (signs Montnorris's death-warrant there, in 1630); lived afterwards in London; became Major, and then Colonel, in the *King's* Army. Fourth son, Oliver, was in the Parliamentary Army; had watched the King in the Isle of Wight, — went with his cousin, our Oliver, to Ireland in 1649, and died or was killed there. Fifth son, Robert, "poisoned his Master, an Attorney, and was *hanged at London*." — if there be truth in "Heath's Flagellum" (Noble, i. 35) "and some Pedigrees;" — year not given; say about 1635, when the lad, "born 1617," was in his 18th year? I have found no hint of this affair in any other quarter, not in the wildest Royalist-Birkenhead or Walker's-Independency lampoon; and consider it very possible that *a* Robert Cromwell having suffered "for poisoning an Attorney," he may have been *called* the cousin of Cromwell by "Heath and some Pedigrees." But of course anybody *can* "poison an Attorney," and be hanged for it!

Oliver's Aunt Elizabeth was married to William Hampden of Great Hampden, Bucks (year not given, Noble, i. 36, nor at p. 68 of vol. ii.; nor in Lord Nugent's *Memorials of Hampden*): he died in 1597; she survived him 67 years, continuing a widow (Noble, ii. 69). Buried in Great Hampden Church, 1664, aged 90. She had two sons, John and Richard: John, born 1594, — Richard, an Oliverian too, died in 1659 (Noble, ii. 70).

Aunt Joan (elder than Elizabeth) was "Lady Barrington;" Aunt

Aunts one was Mrs. Hampden of Great Hampden, Bucks: an opulent, zealous person, not without ambitious; already a widow and mother of two Boys, one of whom proved very celebrated as JOHN HAMPDEN; — she was Robert Cromwell's Sister.   Another Cromwell Aunt of Oliver's was married to "Whalley, heir of the Whalley family in Notts;" another to the "heir of the Dunches of Pusey, in Berkshire;" another to — In short the stories of Oliver's "poverty," if they were otherwise of any amount, are all false; and should be mentioned here, if still here, for the *last* time.   The family was of the rank of substantial gentry, and duly connected with such in the counties round, for three generations back.   Of the numerous and now mostly forgettable cousinry we specify farther only the Mashams of Otes in Essex, as like to be of some cursory interest to us by and by.

There is no doubt at all but Oliver the Protector's family *was* related to that of Thomas Cromwell, Earl of Essex, the Putney "Blacksmith's" or Iron-master's son, transiently mentioned above; the *Malleus Monachorum*, or, as old Fuller renders it, "Mauler of Monasteries," in Henry Eighth's time. The same old Fuller, a perfectly veracious and most intelligent person, does indeed report as of "his own knowledge," that Oliver Protector, once upon a time when Bishop Goodman came dedicating to him some unreadable semi-popish jargon about the "mystery of the Holy Trinity," and some adulation about "his Lordship's relationship to the former great Purifier of the Church," and Mauler of Monasteries, — answered impatiently, "My family has no relation to his!"

Frances (younger) was Mrs. Whalley. Richard Whalley of Kerton, Notts; a man of mark; sheriff, &c.; three wives, children only by his second, this "Aunt Fanny."   Three children; — Thomas Whalley (no years given, Noble, ii. 141) died in his father's lifetime; left a son who was a kind of Royalist, but yet had a certain acceptance with Oliver too. Edward Whalley, the famed "Colonel," and Henry Whalley, "the Judge-Advocate:" wretched *biographies* of these two are in Noble, pp. 141, 143-56. Colonel Whalley and Colonel Goff, after the Restoration, fled to New England; lived in "caves" there, and had a sore time of it: New England, in a vague manner, still remembers them.
    Enough of the Cousinry! —

This old Fuller reports, as of his own knowledge. I have consulted the unreadable semi-popish jargon, for the sake of that Dedication; I find that Oliver's relationship to Thomas Cromwell is in any case stated *wrong* there, not right: I reflect farther that Bishop Goodman, oftener called "Bishop Badman" in those times, went over to Popery; had become a miserable impoverished old piece of confusion, and at this time could appear only in the character of begging *bore*, — when, at any rate, for it was in the year 1653, Oliver himself, having just turned out the Long Parliament, * was busy enough! I infer therefore that Oliver said to him impatiently, without untruth, "You are quite wrong as to all that: good morning!" — and that old Fuller, likewise without untruth, reports it as above.

But, at any rate, there is other very simple evidence entirely conclusive. Richard or Sir Richard Cromwell, great-grandfather of Oliver Protector, was a man well known in his day; had been very active in the work of suppressing monasteries; a righthand man to Thomas the Mauler: and indeed it was on Monastic Property, chiefly or wholly, that he had made for himself a sumptuous estate in those Fen regions. Now of this Richard Cromwell there are two Letters to Thomas Cromwell, "Vicar-General," Earl of Essex, which remain yet visible among the Manuscripts of the British Museum; in both of which he signs himself with his own hand,

* The date of Goodman's Book is 25th June 1653; here is the correct title of it (King's Pamphlets, small 4to, no. 73, § 1): "The two great Mysteries of Christian Religion; the Ineffable Trinity and Wonderful Incarnation: by G. G. G." (meaning Godfrey Goodman, Glocestrensis). Unfortunate persons who have read Laud's writings are acquainted with this Bishop Goodman, or Badman; he died a declared Papist. Poor man, his speculations, now become jargon to us, were once very serious and eloquent to him! Such is the fate that soon overtakes all men who, quitting the "Eternal Melodies," take up their abode in the outer Temporary Discords, and seek their subsistence there! This is the part of the Dedication that concerns us:

"To his Excellency my Lord Oliver Cromwell, Lord General. My Lord, — "Fifty years since, the name of Socinus," &c. — "Knowing that the Lord Cromwell (your Lordship's great uncle) was then in great favour," &c. — "GODFREE GOODMAN."

"your most bounden Nephew," — an evidence sufficient to set the point at rest.   Copies of the Letters are in my possession; but I grudge to inflict them on the reader. One of them, the longer of the two, stands printed, with all or more than all its original misspelling and confused obscurity, in Noble:* it is dated "Stamford," without day or year; but the context farther dates it as contemporary with the Lincolnshire Rebellion, or Anti-Reformation riot, which was directly followed by the more formidable "Pilgrimage of Grace" in Yorkshire to the like effect, in the autumn of 1536. **   Richard, in company with other higher official persons, represents himself as straining every nerve to beat down and extinguish this traitorous fanatic flame, kindled against the King's Majesty and his Reform of the Church; has an eye in particular to a certain Sir John Thymbleby in Lincolnshire, whom he would fain capture as a ringleader; suggests that the use of arms should be prohibited to these treasonous populations, except under conditions; — and seems hastening on, with almost furious speed; towards Yorkshire and the Pilgrimage of Grace, we may conjecture. The second Letter, also without date except "Tuesday," shadows to us an official man, again on business of hot haste; journeying from Monastery to Monastery; finding this Superior disposed to comply with the King's Majesty, and that other not disposed, but capable of being made so; intimates farther that he will be at his own House (presumably Hinchinbrook), and then straightway "home," and will report progress to my Lord in person.   On the whole, as this is the earliest articulate utterance of the Oliver Family; and casts a faint glimmer of light, as from a single flint-spark, into the dead darkness of the foregone century; and touches withal on an acquaintance of ours, the "Prior of Ely," — Robert Steward, last Popish Prior, first Protestant Dean of Ely, and brother of Mrs. Robert Cromwell's ancestor, which is curious to think of, — we will give the Letter, more especially as it is very short:

* I. 242.   ** Herbert (in Kennet, ii. 204-5).

"To my Lord Cromwell.

"I have me most humbly commended unto your Lordship.
"I rode on Sunday to Cambridge to my bed;* and the next
"morning was up betimes, purposing to have found at Ely
"Mr. Pollard and Mr. Williams.   But they were departed be-
"fore my coming: and so, 'they' being at dinner at Somers-
"ham with the Bishop of Ely, I overtook them 'there.' **   At
"which time, I opened your pleasure unto them in everything.
"Your Lordship, I think, shall shortly perceive the Prior of
"Ely to be of a froward sort, by evident tokens; *** as, at
"our coming home, shall be at large related unto you.

"At the writing hereof we have done nothing at Ramsey;
"saving that one night I communed with the Abbot; whom I
"found comformable to everything, as shall be at this time
"put in act. †   And then, as your Lordship's will is, as soon
"as we have done at Ramsey, we go to Peterborough.   And
"from thence to my House; and so home. ††   The which, I
"trust, shall be at the farthest on this day come seven days.

"That the Blessed Trinity preserve your Lordship's
"health!

"Your Lordship's most bounden Nephew,
"RICHARD CROMWELL.

"From Ramsey, on Tuesday in the morning."†††

.   The other Letter is still more express as to the consanguinity; it says, among other things, "And longer than I may
"have heart so, as my most bounden duty is, to serve the
"King's Grace with body, goods, and all that ever I am

---

* From London, we suppose.

** The words within *single commas,* 'they' and 'there,' are added for
bringing out the sense; a plan we shall follow in all the Original Letters of ·
this Collection.

*** He proved tameable, Sir Richard, — and made *your* Great-grandson
rich, for one consequence of that!

† Brought to legal black-on-white.

†† To London.

††† *Mss. Cotton.* Cleopatra E. IV. p. 204 b.   The envelope and address
are not here; but this docket of address, given in a sixteenth-century hand,
and otherwise indicated by the text, is not doubtful.   The signature alone,
and line preceding that, are in Richard's hand.   In the Letter printed by
Noble the address *remains,* in the hand of Richard's clerk.

"able to make; and your Lordship, as Nature and also your "manifold kindness bindeth, — I beseech God I no longer "live." "As *Nature bindeth*." Richard Cromwell then thanks him, with a bow to the very ground, for "my poore wyef," who has had some kind remembrance from his Lordship; thinks all "his travail but a pastime;" and remains, "at "Stamford the Saturday at eleven of the clock, your humble "Nephew most bounden," as in the other case. A vehement, swift-riding man! Nephew, it has been suggested, did not mean in Henry the Eighth's time so strictly as it now does, brother's or sister's son; it meant *nepos* rather, or kinsman of a younger generation: but on all hypotheses of its meaning, the consanguinity of Oliver Protector of England and Thomas Mauler of Monasteries is not henceforth to be doubted.

Another indubitable thing is, That this Richard, your Nephew most bounden, has signed himself in various Law-deeds and Notarial papers still extant, "Richard Cromwell *alias* Williams;" also that his sons and grandsons continued to sign Cromwell *alias* Williams; and even that our Oliver himself in his youth has been known to sign so. And then a third indubitable thing on this matter is, That Leland, an exact man, sent out by Authority in those years to take cognisance, and make report, of certain points connected with the Church Establishments in England, and whose well-known *Itinerary* is the fruit of that survey, has written in that Work these words; under the head, "Commotes* in Glamorganshire:"

"Kibworth lieth," extendeth, "from the mouth of Remny "up to an Hill in the same Commote, called Kevenon, a six "miles from the mouth of Remny. This Hill goeth as a wall "overthwart betwixt the Rivers of Thave and Remny. A two "miles from this Hill by the south, and a two miles from "Cardiff, be vestigia of a Pile or Manor Place decayed, at "Egglis Newith in the Parish of Llandaff. ** On the south

* Commote is the Welsh word *Cwmwd*, now obsolete as an official division, equivalent to *cantred, hundred*. Kibworth Commote is now Kibbor Hundred.

** "Egglis Newith" is *Eglwys Newydd*, New Church, as the Welsh

"side of this Hill was born Richard Williams alias Cromwell,
"in the Parish of Llanilsen." *

That Richard Cromwell, then, was of kindred to Thomas
Cromwell; that he, and his family after him, signed "alias
Williams;" and that Leland, an accurate man, said and
printed, in the official scene where Richard himself was living
and conspicuous, He was born in Glamorganshire: these three
facts are indubitable; — but to these three we must limit ourselves. For, as to the origin of this same "alias Williams,"
whether it came from the general "Williamses of Berkshire,"**
or from "Morgan Williams a Glamorganshire gentleman
married to the sister of Thomas Cromwell," or from whom or
what it came, we have to profess ourselves little able, and
indeed not much concerned to decide. Williamses are many:
there is Richard Cromwell, in that old Letter, hoping to
breakfast with a Williams at Ely, — but finds both him and
Pollard gone! Facts, even trifling facts, when indisputable
may have significance; but Welsh Pedigrees, "with seventy
shields of arms," "Glothian Lord of Powys" (prior or posterior
to the Deluge), though "written on a parchment eight feet by
"two feet four, bearing date 1602, and belonging to the Miss
"Cromwells of Hampstead'," *** are highly unsatisfactory to
the ingenuous mind! We have to remark two things: First,
that the Welsh Pedigree, with its seventy shields and ample
extent of sheepskin, bears date London, 1602; was not put
together, therefore, till about a hundred years after the birth
of Richard, and at a great distance from the scene of that
event: circumstances which affect the unheraldic mind with
some misgivings. Secondly, that "learned Dugdale," upon
whom mainly, apart from these uncertain Welsh sheepskins,

peasants still name it, though officially it is now called White Church.
River " Thave " means Taff. The description of the wall-like Hill between
the two streams, Taff and Remny, is recognisably correct: Kevenon, spelt
Cevn-on, "Ash-tree ridge," is still the name of the Hill.
    * Noble, i. 238, collated with Leland (Oxford, 1769), iv. fol. 56,
pp. 37, 8. Leland gathered his records "in six years," between 1533 and
1540; he died, endeavouring to assort them, in 1552. They were long
afterwards published by Hearne.
    ** Biographia Britannica (London, 1789), iv. 474.
    *** Noble, i. 1.

the story of this Welsh descent of the Cromwells seems to rest,
has unfortunately stated the matter in *two* different ways, —
as being, and then also as not being, — in two places of his
learned Lumber-Book.* Which circumstance affects the
unheraldic mind with still fataller misgivings, — and in fact
raises irrepressibly the question and admonition, "What
"boots it? Leave the vain region of blazonry, of rusty broken
"shields and genealogical marine stores; let it remain forever
"doubtful! The Fates themselves have appointed it even *so*.
"Let the uncertain Simulacrum of a Glothian, prior or
"posterior to Noah's Deluge, hover between us and the utter
"Void, basing himself on a dust-chaos of ruined heraldries,
"lying genealogies, and saltires checky, the best he can!"

The small Hamlet and Parish Church of Cromwell, or
Crumwell (the Well of Crum, whatever that may be), still
stands on the Eastern edge of Nottinghamshire, not far from
the left bank of the Trent; simple worshippers still doing in it
some kind of divine service every Sunday. From this, without
any ghost to teach us, we can understand that the Cromwell
kindred all got their name, — in very old times indeed. From
torpedo rubbish-records we learn also, without great difficulty,
that the Barons Cromwell were summoned to Parliament from
Edward Second's time and downward; that they had their chief
seat at Tattershall in Lincolnshire; that there were Cromwells
of distinction and of no distinction, scattered in reasonable
abundance over that Fen-country, — Cromwells Sheriffs of their
Counties there in Richard's own time.** The Putney Blacksmith, Father of the *Malleus*, or Hammer that smote Monasteries on the head, — a Figure worthy to take his place beside
Hephaistos, or Smith Mimer, if we ever get a Pantheon in this
Nation, — was probably enough himself a Fen-country man;
one of the junior branches, who came to live by metallurgy in
London here. Richard, also sprung of the Fens, might have
been his kinsman in many ways, have got the name of Williams in many ways, and even been born on the Hill behind

* Dugdale's Baronage, ii. 374, 393.
** Fuller's Worthies, § Cambridgeshire, &c.

Cardiff, independently of Glothian. Enough: Richard Cromwell, on a background of heraldic darkness, rises clearly
visible to us; a man vehemently galloping to and fro, in that
sixteenth century; tourneying successfully before King
Harry,* who loved a man, quickening the death-agonies of
Monasteries; growing great on their spoil; — and fated, he
also, to produce another *Malleus* Cromwell that smote a
thing or two. And so we will leave this matter of the Birth
and Genealogy.

CHAPTER IV.

Events in Oliver's Biography.

Tʜᴇ few ascertained, or clearly imaginable, Events in
Oliver's Biography may as well be arranged, for our present
purpose, in the form of annals.

1603.

Early in January of this year, the old Grandfather, Sir
Henry, "the Golden Knight," at Hinchinbrook, died:**
our Oliver, not quite four years old, saw funeralia and crapes,
saw Father and Uncles with grave faces, and understood not
well what it meant, —understood only, or tried to understand,
that the good old Grandfather was gone away, and would
never pat his head any more. The maternal Grandfather, at
Ely, was yet, and for above a dozen years more, living.

The same year, four months afterwards, King James,
coming from the North to take possession of the English
crown, lodged two nights at Hinchinbrook; with royal retinue,
with immense sumptuosities, addressings, knight-makings,
ceremonial exhibitions; which must have been a grand treat
for little Oliver. His Majesty came from the Belvoir-Castle
region, "hunting all the way," on the afternoon of Wednesday

---

* Stowe's Chronicle (London, 1631), p. 580; Stowe's Survey, Ho-
linshed, &c.

** Poor Noble, unequal sometimes to the copying of a Parish-register,
with his judgment *asleep*, dates this event 1603-4 (at p. 20, vol. i.), and then
placidly (at p. 40) states a fact inconsistent therewith.

27th April 1603; and set off, through Huntingdon and Godmanchester, towards Royston, on Friday forenoon.* The
Cambridge Doctors brought him an Address while here;
Uncle Oliver, besides the ruinously splendid entertainments,
gave him hounds, horses and astonishing gifts at his departure. In return there were Knights created, Sir Oliver first of
the batch, we may suppose; King James had decided that
there should be no reflection for the want of Knights at least.
Among the large batches manufactured next year was Thomas Steward of Ely, henceforth Sir Thomas, Mrs. Robert
Cromwell's Brother, our Oliver's Uncle. Hinchinbrook got
great honour by this and other royal visits; but found it, by
and by, a dear-bought honour. —

Oliver's Biographers, or rather Carrion Heath his first Biographer whom the others have copied, introduce various tales
into these early years of Oliver: of his being run away with by
an ape along the leads of Hinchinbrook, and England being
all but delivered from him, had the Fates so ordered it; of his
seeing prophetic spectres; of his robbing orchards, and fighting tyrannously with boys; of his acting in School Plays; of
his &c. &c. — The whole of which, grounded on "Human
Stupidity" and Carrion Heath alone, begs us to give it Christian burial once for all. Oliver attended the Public School of
Huntingdon, which was then conducted by a worthy Dr.
Beard, of whose writing I possess a Book, ** of whom we shall
hear again: he learned, to appearance moderately well, what
the sons of other gentleman were taught in such places; went
through the universal destinies which conduct all men from

* Stowe's Chronicle, 812, &c.
** *The Theatre of God's Judgements: By Thomas Beard, Doctor of
Divinity, and Preacher of the Word of God in the Town of Huntingdon:
Third Edition, increased by many new Examples* ("Examples" of God's
Justice vindicating itself openly on Violaters of God's Law, — that is the
purport of the Book): Lond. 1631. — A kindly ingenious little Book; still
partly readable, almost lovable; some thin but real vein of perennial
ingenuity and goodness recognisable in it. What one might call a Set of
"Percy-Anecdotes;" but Anecdotes authentic, solemnly select, and *with*
a purpose: "Percy-Anecdotes" for a more earnest Century than ours!
Dedicated to the Mayor and Burgesses of Huntingdon, — for sundry good
reasons; among others, "Because, Mr. Mayor, you were my scholar, and
brought up in my house."

childhood to youth, in a way not particularised in any one point by an authentic record. Readers of lively imagination can follow him on his bird-nesting expeditions, to the top of "Barnabee's big Tree," and elsewhither, if they choose; on his fen-fowling expeditions, social sports and labours manifold; vacation-visits to his Uncles, to Aunt Hampden and Cousin John among others: all these things must have been; but how they specially were is forever hidden from all men. He had kindred of the sort above specified; parents of the sort above specified; rigorous yet affectionate persons, and very religious, as all rational persons then were. He had two sisters elder, and gradually four younger; the only boy among seven. Readers must fancy his growth there, in the North end of Huntingdon, in the beginning of the Seventeenth Century, as they can.

In January 1603—4, * was held at Hampton Court a kind of Theological Convention, of intense interest all over England, and doubtless at Huntingdon too; now very dimly known, if at all known, as the "Hampton-Court Conference."

---

* Here, more fitly perhaps than afterwards, it may be brought to mind, that the English year in those times did not begin till March; that New Year's Day was the 25th of March. So in England, at that time, in all records, writings and books; as indeed in official records it continued so till 1752. In Scotland it was already not so; the year began with January there ever since 1600; — as in all Catholic countries it had done ever since the Papal alteration of the *Style* in 1582; and as in most Protestant countries, excepting England, it soon after that began to do. Scotland in respect of *the day of the month* still followed the Old Style.

"New Year's Day the 25th of March:" this is the whole compass of the fact; with which a reader in those old books has, not without more difficulty than he expects, to familiarise himself. It has occasioned more misdatings and consequent confusions to modern editorial persons than any other as simple circumstance. So learned a man as Whitaker Historian of *Whalley*, editing *Sir George Radcliffe's Correspondence* (London, 1810), with the lofty air which sits well on him on other occasions, has altogether forgotten the above small circumstance: in consequence of which we have Oxford Carriers dying in January, or the first half of March, and to our great amazement going on to forward butter-boxes in the May following; — and similar miracles not a few occurring: and in short the whole Correspondence is jumbled to pieces; a due bit of topsy-turvy being introduced into the Spring of every year; and the learned Editor sits, with his lofty air, presiding over mere Chaos come again! — — In the text here, we of course translate into the modern year, but leaving the day of the month as we find it; and if for greater assurance both forms be written down, as for instance 1603-4, the *last* figure is always the modern one; 1603-4 means 1604 for our calendar.

It was a meeting for the settlement of some dissentient humours in religion. The Millennary Petition, — what we should now call the "Monster Petition," for the like in number of signatures was never seen before, — signed by *near* a thousand Clergymen, of pious straitened consciences: this and various other Petitions to his Majesty, by persons of pious straitened consciences, had been presented; craving relief in some ceremonial points, which, as they found no warrant for them in the Bible, they suspected (with a very natural shudder in that case) to savour of Idol-worship and Mimetic Dramaturgy, instead of God-worship, and to be very dangerous indeed for a man to have concern with! Hampton-Court Conference was accordingly summoned. Four world-famous Doctors, from Oxford and Cambridge, represented the pious straitened class, now beginning to be generally conspicuous under the nickname *Puritans*. The Archbishop, the Bishop of London, also world-famous men, with a considerable reserve of other bishops, deans and dignitaries, appeared for the Church by itself Church. Lord Chancellor, the renowned Egerton, and the highest official persons, many lords and courtiers with a tincture of sacred science, in fact the flower of England, appeared as witnesses; with breathless interest. The King himself presided; having real gifts of speech, and being very learned in Theology, — which it was not then ridiculous but glorious for him to be. More glorious than the monarchy of what we now call Literature would be; glorious as the faculty of a Goethe holding *visibly* of Heaven: supreme skill in Theology then meant that. To know God, *Θεός*, the MAKER, — to know the divine Laws and *inner* Harmonies of this Universe, must always be the highest glory for a man! And not to know them, always the highest disgrace for a man, however common it be! —

Awful devout Puritanism, decent dignified Ceremonialism (both always of high moment in this world, but not of equally high) appeared here facing one another for the first time. The demands of the Puritans seem to modern minds very limited indeed: That there should be a new correct Translation of the

Bible (*granted*), and increased zeal in teaching (*omitted*); That "lay impropriations" (tithes snatched from the old Church by laymen) might be made to yield a "seventh part" of their amount, towards maintaining ministers in dark regions which had none (*refused*); That the Clergy in districts might be allowed to meet together, and strengthen one another's hands as in old times (*refused with indignation*); — on the whole (if such a thing durst be hinted at, for the tone is almost inaudibly low and humble), That pious straitened Preachers, in terror of offending God by Idolatry, and useful to human souls, might not be cast out of their parishes for genuflexions, white surplices and such like, but allowed some Christian liberty in mere external things: these were the claims of the Puritans; — but his Majesty eloquently scouted them to the winds, applauded by all bishops, and dignitaries lay and clerical; said, If the Puritans would not conform, he would "harry them out of the country;" — and so sent Puritanism and the Four Doctors home again, cowed into silence, for the present. This was in January 1604.* News of this, speech enough about it, could not fail in Robert Cromwell's house among others. Oliver is in his fifth year, — always a year older than the Century.

In November 1605, there likewise came to Robert Cromwell's house, no question of it, news of the thrice unutterable Gunpowder Plot. Whereby King, Parliament, and God's Gospel in England, were to have been, in one infernal moment, blown aloft; and the Devil's Gospel, and accursed incredibilities, idolatries, and poisonous confusions of the Romish Babylon, substituted in their room! The eternal Truth of the Living God to become an empty formula, a shamming grimace of the Three-hatted Chimera! These things did fill Huntingdon and Robert Cromwell's house with talk enough, in the winter of Oliver's sixth year. And again, in the summer of his eleventh year, in May 1610, there doubtless failed not news and talk, How the Great Henry was stabbed in Paris streets; assassinated by the Jesuits; —

* Neal's History of the Puritans (London, 1754), i. 411.

black sons of the scarlet woman, murderous to soul and to body.

Other things, in other years, the diligent Historical Student will supply according to faculty. The History of Europe, at that epoch, meant essentially the struggle of Protestantism against Catholicism, — a broader form of that same struggle, of devout Puritanism against dignified Ceremonialism, which forms the History of England then. Henry the Fourth of France, so long as he lived, was still to be regarded as the head of Protestantism; Spain, bound up with the Austrian Empire, as that of Catholicism. Henry's "Grand Scheme" naturally strove to carry Protestant England along with it; James, till Henry's death, held on, in a loose way, by Henry; and his Political History, so far as he has any, may be considered to lie there. After Henry's death, he fell off to "Spanish Infantas," to Spanish interests; and, as it were, ceased to have any History, nay began to have a *negative* one.

Among the events which Historical Students will supply for Robert Cromwell's house, and the spiritual pabulum of young Oliver, the Death of Prince Henry in 1612,* and the prospective accession of Prince Charles, fitter for a ceremonial Archbishop than a governing King, as some thought, — will not be forgotten. Then how the Elector Palatine was married; and troubles began to brew in Germany; and little Dr. Laud was made Archdeacon of Huntingdon: — such news the Historical Student can supply. And on the whole, all students and persons can know always that Oliver's mind was kept *full* of news, and never wanted for pabulum! But from the day of his Birth, which is jotted down, as above, in the Parish-register of St. John's Huntingdon, there is no other authentic jotting or direct record concerning Oliver himself to be met with anywhere, till in the Admission-Book of Sidney-Sussex College, Cambridge, we come to this,**

---

* 6th Nov. (Camden's Annals).
** Noble, 1. 254; — corrected by the College Book itself.

1616.

"*A Festo Annunciationis ad Festum Sancti Michaelis Arch-angeli*, 1616:" such (meaning merely, *From New-year's-day, or 25th March, to 29th September*) is the general Heading of the List of Scholars, or *Admissi*, for that Term; — and first in order there, stands, "*Oliverius Cromwell Huntingdoniensis ad-*"*missus ad commeatum Sociorum, Aprilis vicesimo tertio; Tutore* "*Magistro Ricardo Howlet:*" Oliver Cromwell from Huntingdon admitted Fellow Commoner, 23d April 1616; Tutor Mr. Richard Howlet. — Between which and the next Entry some zealous individual of later date has crowded-in these lines: "*Hic fuit* "*grandis ille Impostor, Carnifex perditissimus, qui pientissimo* "*Rege Carolo Primo nefariâ cæde sublato, ipsum usurpavit Thro-*"*num, et Tria Regna per quinque ferme annorum spatium, sub* "*Protectoris nomine, indomitâ tyrannide vexavit.*" Had the zealous individual specifically dated this entry, it had been a slight improvement, — on a thing not much improvable. We can guess, After 1660, and not long after.

Curious enough, of all days, on this same day Shakspeare, as his stone monument still testifies, at Stratford-on-Avon, died:

Obiit Anno Domini 1616.
Ætatis 53. Die 23 Apr. *

While Oliver Cromwell was entering himself of Sidney-Sussex College, William Shakspeare was taking his farewell of this world. Oliver's Father had, most likely, come with him; it is but some fifteen miles from Huntingdon; you can go and come in a day. Oliver's Father saw Oliver write in the Album at Cambridge: at Stratford, Shakspeare's Ann Hatha-way was weeping over his bed. The first world-great thing that remains of English History, the Literature of Shakspeare, was ending; the second world-great thing that remains of English History, the armed Appeal of Puritanism to the Invisible God of Heaven against many very visible Devils, on Earth and Else-

---

* Collier's Life of Shakspeare (London, 1845), p. 253.

where, was, so to speak, beginning. They have their exits and their entrances. And one People, in its time, plays many parts.

Chevalier Florian, in his *Life of Cervantes*, has remarked that Shakspeare's death-day, 23d April 1616, was likewise that of Cervantes at Madrid. "Twenty-third of April" is, sure enough, the authentic Spanish date: but Chevalier Florian has ommitted to notice that the English twenty-third is of *Old Style*. The brave Miguel died ten days before Shakspeare; and already lay buried, smoothed right nobly into his long rest. The Historical Student can meditate on these things. —

In the foregoing winter, here in England, there was much trying of Ker Earl of Somerset and my Lady once of Essex, and the poisoners of Overbury; and before Christmas the inferior murderers and infamous persons were mostly got hanged; and in these very days, while Oliver began his studies, my Lord of Somerset and my Lady were tried, and not hanged. And Chief Justice Coke, Coke upon Lyttleton, had got into difficulties by the business. And England generally was overspread with a very fetid atmosphere of Court-news, murders, and divorce-cases, in those months; which still a little affects even the History of England. Poor Somerset Ker, King's favourite, "son of the Laird of Ferniehirst," he and his extremely unedifying affairs, — except as they might transiently affect the nostrils of some Cromwell of importance, — do not much belong to the History of England! Carrion ought at length to be *buried*. Alas, if "wise memory" is ever to prevail, there is need of much "wise oblivion" first. —

Oliver's Tutor in Cambridge, of whom legible History and I know nothing, was "Magister Richard Howlet:" whom readers must fancy a grave ancient Puritan and Scholar, in dark antiquarian clothes and dark antiquarian ideas, according to their faculty. The indubitable fact is, that he Richard Howlet did, in Sidney-Sussex College, with his best ability, endeavour to infiltrate something that he called instruction into the soul of Oliver Cromwell and of other youths submitted to him: but how, of what quality, with what method, with what result, will remain extremely obscure to every one. In spite of mountains of books, so are books written, all grows very obscure. About this same date, George Radcliffe, Wentworth Strafford's George, at Oxford, finds his green-baize table-cover, which his mother had sent him, too small; has it cut into "stockings," and goes about with the same.* So unfashionable were young Gentlemen Commoners. Queen Elizabeth was the first person in this country who ever wore knit stockings.

1617.

In March of this year, 1617, there was another royal visit at Hinchinbrook.** But this time, I conceive, the royal enter-tainment would be much more moderate; Sir Oliver's purse growing lank. Over in Huntingdon, Robert Cromwell was lying sick, somewhat indifferent to royal progresses.

King James, this time, was returning northward to visit poor old Scotland again, to get his Pretended-Bishops set into activity, if he could. It is well known that he could not, to any satisfactory extent, neither now nor afterwards: his Pre-tended-Bishops, whom by cunning means he did get instituted, had the name of Bishops, but next to none of the authority, of the respect, or alas, even of the cash, suitable to the reality of that office. They were by the Scotch People derisively called *Tulchan* Bishops. — Did the reader ever see, or fancy in his mind, a Tulchan? A Tulchan is, or rather was, for the thing is long since obsolete, a Calf-skin stuffed into the rude simili-tude of a Calf, — similar enough to deceive the imperfect per-ceptive organs of a Cow. At milking-time the Tulchan, with head duly bent, was set as if to suck; the fond cow looking round fancied that her calf was busy, and that all was right,

---

* 'University College, Oxford, 4th Dec. 1610.

'Loving Mother, — * * Send also, I pray you, by Briggs' (this is Briggs the Carrier, who dies in January, and continues forwarding butter in May), 'a green table-cloth of a yard and half a quarter, and two linen 'table-cloths. * * If the green table-cloth be too little, I will make a pair 'of warm stockings of it. * * — Thus remembering my humble duty, I take 'my leave. — Your loving Son,

"GEORGE RADCLIFFE.'
Radcliffe's Letters, by Whitaker (London, 1810), p. 64-5.

** Camden's Annal's; Nichols's Progresses.

and so gave her milk freely, which the cunning maid was
straining in white abundance into her pail all the while!   The
Scotch milkmaids in those days cried, "Where is the Tulchan;
is the Tulchan ready?"   So of the Bishops.   Scotch Lairds
were eager enough to "milk" the Church Lands and Tithes,
to get the rents out of them freely, which was not always easy.
They were glad to construct a *Form* of Bishops to please the
King and Church, and make the milk come without disturbance.   The reader now knows what a Tulchan Bishop
was.   A piece of mechanism constructed not without difficulty,
in Parliament and King's Council, among the Scots; and torn
asunder afterwards with dreadful clamour, and scattered to
the four winds, so soon as the Cow became awake to it! —

Villiers Buckingham, the new favourite, of whom we say
little, was of the royal party here.   Dr. Laud, too, King's
Chaplain, Archdeacon of Huntingdon, attended the King on
this occasion; had once more the pleasure of seeing Huntingdon, the cradle of his promotions, and the birth-place of Oliver.
In Scotland, Dr. Laud, much to his regret, found "no religion
at all," no surplices, no altars in the east or anywhere; no
bowing, no responding; not the smallest regularity of fugle-
manship or devotional drill-exercise; in short "no religion at
all that I could see," — which grieved me much.*

What to us is greatly more momentous: while these royal
things went on in Scotland, in the end of this same June at
Huntingdon, Robert Cromwell died.   His Will is dated
6th June.**   His burial-day is marked in the Church of All-
Saints, 24th June 1617.   For Oliver, the chief mourner, one
of the most pregnant epochs.   The same year, died his old
Grandfather Steward, at Ely.   Mrs. Robert Cromwell saw
herself at once fatherless and a second time widowed, in this
year of bereavement.   Left with six daughters and an only
son; of whom three were come to years.

Oliver was now, therefore, a young heir; his age eighteen,
last April.   How many of his Sisters, or whether any of them,

* Wharton's Laud (London, 1695), pp. 97, 109, 138.   .
** Noble, I. 84.

were yet settled, we do not learn from Noble's confused searching of records or otherwise. Of this Huntingdon household,
and its new head, we learn next to nothing by direct evidence ;
but can decisively enough, by inference, discern several
things. "Oliver returned no more to Cambridge." It was
now fit that he should take his Father's place here at Huntingdon, that he should, by the swiftest method, qualify himself in
some degree for that.

The universal very credible tradition is, that he, "soon
after," proceeded to London, to gain some knowledge of Law.
"Soon after" will mean certain months, we know not how
many, after July 1617. Noble says, he was entered "of Lincoln's Inn." The Books of Lincoln's Inn, of Gray's Inn, of
all the Inns of Court have been searched; and there is no
Oliver Cromwell found in them. The Books of Gray's Inn
contain these Cromwell Names, which are perhaps worth
transcribing:

Thomas Cromwell, 1524; Francis Cromwell, 1561;
Gilbert Cromwell, 1609; Henry Cromwell, 1620;
Henry Cromwell, 22d February 1653.

The first of which seems to me probably or possibly to mean
Thomas Cromwell *Malleus Monachorum*, at that time returned
from his Italian adventures, and in the service of Cardinal
Wolsey; — taking the opportunity of hearing the "readers,"
old Benchers who then actually read, and of learning Law.
The Henry Cromwell of February 1653-4 is expressly entered
as "Second sonne to his Highness Oliver, Lord Protector:"
an interesting little fact, since it is an indisputable one. For
the rest, Henry Cromwell was already a Colonel in the Army
in 1651:* in 1654, during the spring months he was in Ireland;
in the month of June he was at Chippenham in Cambridgeshire with his father-in-law, being already married;** and
next year he went again on political business to Ireland, where

* Old Newspaper, in Cromwelliana, p. 91.
** "10th May 1653, — Mr. Henry Cromwell to Elizabeth Russel" (Registers of Kensington Church, in Faulkoner's *History of Kensington*, p. 360).

he before long became Lord Deputy:* if for a while, in the end of 1654, he did attend in Gray's Inn, it can only have been, like his predecessor the *Malleus*, to gain some inkling of Law for general purposes; and not with any view towards Advocateship, which did not lie in his course at all, and was never very lovely either to his Father or himself. Oliver Cromwell's, as we said, is not a name found in any of the Books in that period.

Whence is to be inferred that Oliver was never of any Inn; that he never meant to be a professional Lawyer; that he had entered himself merely in the chambers of some learned gentleman, with an eye to obtain some tincture of Law, for doing County Magistracy, and the other duties of a gentleman citizen, in a reputable manner. The stories of his wild living while in Town, of his gambling and so forth, rest likewise exclusively on Carrion Heath; and solicit oblivion and Christian burial from all men. We cannot but believe he did go to Town to gain some knowledge of Law. But when he went, how long he stayed, cannot be known except approximately by years; under whom he studied, with what fruit, how he conducted himself as a young man and law-student, cannot be known at all. Of evidence that he ever lived a wild life about Town or elsewhere, there exists no particle. To assert the affirmative was then a great reproach to him; fit for Carrion Heath and others: it would be now, in our present strange condition of the Moral Law, one knows not what. With a Moral Law gone all to such a state of moonshine; with the hard Stone-tables, the god-given Precepts and eternal Penalties, dissolved all in cant and mealy-mouthed official flourishings, — it might perhaps, with certain parties, be a credit! The admirers and the censurers of Cromwell have alike no word to record on the subject.

* Here are the successive dates: 4th March 1653-4, he arrives at Dublin (Thurloe's *State Papers*, ii. 149); is at Chippenham, 18th June 1654 (*ib*. ii. 381); arrives at Chester on his way to Ireland again, 22d June 1655 (*ib*. iii. 581); — produces his commission as Lord Deputy, 24th or 25th November 1657 (Noble, i. 202).

1618.

Thursday, 29th October 1618. This morning, if Oliver, as is probable, were now in Town studying Law, he might be eye-witness of a great and very strange scene: the Last Scene in the Life of Sir Walter Raleigh.* Raleigh was beheaded in Old Palace-yard; he appeared on the scaffold there "about eight o'clock" that morning; "an immense crowd," all London, and in a sense all England, looking on. A cold hoar-frosty morning. Earl of Arundel, now known to us by his Greek Marbles; Earl of Doncaster ("Sardanapalus" Hay, ultimately Earl of Carlisle): these with other earls and dignitaries sat looking through windows near by; to whom Raleigh in his last brief manful speech appealed, with response from them. He had failed of finding Eldorados in the Indies lately; he had failed, and also succeeded, in many things in his time: he returned home with his brain and his heart "broken," as he said; — and the Spaniards, who found King James willing, now wished that he should die. A very tragic scene. Such a man, with his head grown gray; with his strong heart "breaking," — still strength enough in it to break with dignity. Somewhat proudly he laid his old gray head on the block; as if saying, in better than words, 'There then!' The Sheriff offered to let him warm himself again, within doors again at a fire.   'Nay, let us be swift,' said Raleigh; 'in few minutes my "ague will return upon me, and if I be not dead before that, "they will say I tremble for fear." — If Oliver, among the "immense crowd," saw this scene, as is conceivable enough, he would not want for reflections on it.

What is more apparent to us, Oliver in these days is a visitor in Sir James Bourchier's Town residence. Sir James Bourchier, Knight, a civic gentleman; not connected at all with the old Bourchiers Earls of Essex, says my heraldic friend; but seemingly come of City merchants rather, who by some of their quarterings and cognizances appear to have been "Furriers," says he: — Like enough. Not less but more important, it appears this Sir James Bourchier was a man of some

* Camden; Biog. Britan.

opulence, and had daughters; had a daughter Elizabeth, not without charms for the youthful heart. Moreover he had landed property near Felsted in Essex, where his usual residence was. Felsted, where there is still a kind of School or Free-School, which was of more note in those days than now. That Oliver visited in Sir James's in Town or elsewhere, we discover with great certainty by the next written record of him.

1620.

The Registers of St. Giles's Church, Cripplegate, London, are written by a third party as usual, and have no autograph signatures; but in the List of Marriages for "August 1620," stand these words, still to be read *sic:*

"Oliver Cromwell to Elizabeth Bourcher. 22."

Milton's burial-entry is in another Book of the same memorable Church, "12. Nov. 1674;" where Oliver on the 22d of August 1620 was married.

Oliver is twenty-one years and four months old on this his wedding-day. He repaired, speedily or straightway we believe, to Huntingdon, to his Mother's house, which indeed was now his. His Law-studies, such as they were, had already ended, we infer: he had already set up house with his Mother; and was now bringing a Wife home; the due arrangements for that end having been completed. Mother and Wife were to live together; the Sisters had got or were getting married, — Noble's researches and confused jottings do not say specially when: the Son, as new head of the house, an inexperienced head, but a teachable, ever-learning one, was to take his Father's place; and with a wise Mother and a good Wife, harmonising tolerably well we shall hope, was to manage as he best might. Here he continued, unnoticeable but easily imaginable by History, for almost ten years: farming lands; most probably attending quarter-sessions; doing the civic, industrial, and social duties, in the common way; — living as his Father before him had done. His first child was born here, in October 1621; a son, Robert, baptised at St. John's Church

on the 13th of the month, of whom nothing farther is known. *
A second child, also a son, Oliver, followed, whose baptismal
date is 6th February 1623, of whom also we have almost no
farther account, — except one that can be proved to be erroneous. **   The List of his other children shall be given by
and by.

1623.

In October 1623, there was an illumination of tallow lights,
a ringing of bells, and gratulation of human hearts in all
Towns in England, and doubtless in Huntingdon too; on the
safe return of Prince Charles from Spain *without* the Infanta.***
A matter of endless joy to all true Englishmen of that day,
though no Englishman of this day feels any interest in it one
way or the other.   But Spain, even more than Rome, was the
chosen throne of Popery; which in that time meant temporal
and eternal Damnability, Falsity to God's Gospel, love of
prosperous Darkness rather than of suffering Light, — infinite
baseness rushing short-sighted upon infinite peril for this
world and for all worlds.   King James, with his worldly-wise
endeavourings to marry his son into some first-rate family,
never made a falser calculation than in this grand business of
the Spanish Match.   The soul of England abhorred to have
any concern with Spain or things Spanish.   Spain was as a
black Domdaniel, which, had the floors of it been paved with
diamonds, had the Infanta of it come riding in such a Gig of
Respectability as was never driven since Phaëton's Sun-chariot
took the road, no honest English soul could wish to have
concern with.   Hence England illuminated itself. The articulate tendency of this Solomon King had unfortunately parted

* Date of his burial discovered lately, in the old Parish-Register of
Felsted in Essex; recorded in peculiar terms, and specially in the then
Vicar's hand: "*Robertus Cromwell, Filius honorandi viri Mtis'* (Militis)
"*Oliveris Cromwell et Elizabethæ Uxoris ejus, sepultus fuit 31" die Maii 1639.*
"*Et Robertus fuit eximié pius juvenis, Deum timens suprá multos.*" (See
Edinburgh Review, No. 209, January 1856, p. 54.) So that Oliver's first
great loss in his Family was of this Eldest Son, then in his 18th year; not
of a Younger one as was hitherto supposed. (*Note of* 1857).
   ** Noble, i. 134.
   *** H. L. (Hamond l'Estrange): Reign of King Charles (London, 1656),
p. 3. "October 5th," the Prince arrived.

company altogether with the inarticulate but ineradicable tendency of the Country he presided over. The Solomon King struggled one way; and the English Nation with its very life-fibres was compelled to struggle another way. The rent by degrees became wide enough!

For the present, England is all illuminated, a new Parliament is summoned; which welcomes the breaking of the Spanish Match, as one might welcome the breaking of a Dr. Faustus's Bargain, and a deliverance from the power of sorcerers. Uncle Oliver served in this Parliament, as was his wont, for Huntingdonshire. They and the Nation with one voice impelled the poor old King to draw out his fighting tools at last, and beard this Spanish Apollyon, instead of making marriages with it. No Pitt's crusade against French Sansculottism in the end of the Eighteenth Century could be so welcomed by English Preservers of the Game, as this defiance of the Spanish Apollyon was by Englishmen in general in the beginning of the Seventeenth. The Palatinate was to be recovered, after all; Protestantism, the sacred cause of God's Light and Truth against the Devil's Falsity and Darkness, was to be fought for and secured. Supplies were voted; "drums beat in the City" and elsewhere, as they had done three years ago,* to the joy of all men, when the Palatinate was first to be "defended:" but now it was to be "recovered;" now a decisive effort was to be made. The issue, as is well known, corresponded ill with these beginnings. Count Mansfeldt mustered his levies here, and set sail; but neither France nor any other power would so much as let him land. Count Mansfeldt's levies died of pestilence in their ships; "their bodies, thrown ashore on the Dutch coast, were eaten by hogs," till half the armament was dead on shipboard: nothing came of it, nothing could come. With a James Stuart for Generalissimo, there is no good fighting possible. The poor King himself soon after died; ** left the matter to develop itself in other still fataller ways.

* 11th June 1620 (Camden's Annals).
** Sunday, 27th March 1625 (Wilson, in Kennet, ii. 790).

In those years it must be that Dr. Simcott, Physician in Huntingdon, had to do with Oliver's hypochondriac maladies. He told Sir Philip Warwick, unluckily specifying no date, or none that has survived, 'he had often been sent for at midnight;' Mr. Cromwell for many years was very 'splenetic' (spleen-struck), often thought he was just about to die, and also 'had fancies about the Town Cross.'* Brief intimation; of which the reflective reader may make a great deal. Samuel Johnson too had hypochondrias; all great souls are apt to have, — and to be in thick darkness generally, till the eternal ways and the celestial guiding-stars disclose themselves, and the vague Abyss of Life knit itself up into Firmaments for them. Temptations in the wilderness, Choices of Hercules, and the like, in succinct or loose form, are appointed for every man that will assert a soul in himself and be a man. Let Oliver take comfort in his dark sorrows and melancholies. The quantity of sorrow he has, does it not mean withal the quantity of *sympathy* he has, the quantity of faculty and victory he shall yet have? Our sorrow is the inverted image of our nobleness. The depth of our despair measures what capability, and height of claim we have to hope. Black smoke as of Tophet filling all your universe, it can yet by true heart-energy become *flame*, and brilliancy of Heaven. Courage!

It is therefore in these years, undated by History, that we must place Oliver's clear recognition of Calvinistic Christianity; what he, with unspeakable joy, would name his Conversion; his deliverance from the jaws of Eternal Death. Certainly a grand epoch for a man: properly the one epoch; the turning-point which guides upwards, or guides downwards, him and his activity forevermore. Wilt thou join with the Dragons; wilt thou join with the Gods? Of thee too the question is asked; — whether by a man in Geneva gown, by a man in "Four surplices at Allhallowtide," with words very imperfect; or by no man and no words, but only by the Silences, by the Eternities, by the Life everlasting and the Death everlasting. That the "Sense of difference between Right and Wrong" had filled all

* Sir Philip Warwick's Memoirs (London, 1701), p. 249.

Time and all Space for man, and bodied itself forth into a
Heaven and Hell for him: this constitutes the grand feature
of those Puritan, Old-Christian Ages; this is the element which
stamps them as Heroic, and has rendered their works great,
manlike, fruitful to all generations. It is by far the me-
morablest achievement of our Species; without that element,
in some form or other, nothing of Heroic had ever been
among us.

For many centuries, Catholic Christianity, a fit embodiment
of that divine Sense, had been current more or less, making the
generations noble: and here in England, in the Century called
the Seventeenth, we see the last aspect of it hitherto, — not
the last of all, it is to be hoped. Oliver was henceforth a
Christian man; believed in God, not on Sundays only, but on
all days, in all places, and in all cases.

1624.

The grievance of Lay Impropriations, complained of in the
Hampton-Court Conference twenty years ago, having never
been abated, and many parts of the country being still thought
insufficiently supplied with Preachers, a plan was this year
fallen upon to raise by subscription, among persons grieved at
that state of matters, a Fund for *buying-in* such Impropriations
as might offer themselves; for supporting good ministers therewith, in destitute places; and for otherwise encouraging the
ministerial work. The originator of this scheme was "the
famous Dr. Preston,"* a Puritan College Doctor of immense
"fame" in those and in prior years; courted even by the Duke
of Buckingham, and tempted with the gleam of bishoprics; but
mouldering now in great oblivion, not famous to any man. His
scheme, however, was found good. The wealthy London
Merchants, almost all of them Puritans, took it up; and by
degrees the wealthier Puritans over England at large. Considerable ever-increasing funds were subscribed for this
pious object; were vested in "Feoffees," — who afterwards
made some noise in the world, under that name. They

* Heylin's Life of Laud.

gradually purchased some Advowsons or Impropriations, such as came to market; and hired, or assisted in hiring, a great many "Lecturers," persons not generally in full "Priest's-orders" (having scruples about the ceremonies), but in "Deacon's" or some other orders, with permission to preach, to "lecture," as it was called: whom accordingly we find lecturing in various places, under various conditions, in the subsequent years; — often in some market-town, "on market-day;" on "Sunday-afternoon," as supplemental to the regular Priest when he might happen to be idle, or given to black and white surplices; or as "running Lecturers," now here, now there, over a certain district. They were greatly followed by the serious part of the community; and gave proportional offence in other quarters. In some years hence, they had risen to such a height, these Lecturers, that Dr. Laud, now come into authority, took them seriously in hand, and with patient detail hunted them mostly out; nay brought the Feoffees themselves and their whole Enterprise into the Starchamber, and there, with emphasis enough, and heavy damages, amid huge rumour from the public, suppressed them. This was in 1633; a somewhat strong measure. How would the Public take it now, if, — we say not the gate of Heaven, but the gate of the Opposition Hustings were suddenly shut against mankind, — if our Opposition Newspapers, and their morning Prophesyings, were suppressed! — That Cromwell was a contributor to this Feoffee Fund, and a zealous forwarder of it according to his opportunities, we might already guess; and by and by there will occur some vestige of direct evidence to that effect.

Oliver naturally consorted henceforth with the Puritan Clergy in preference to the other kind; zealously attended their ministry, when possible; — consorted with Puritans in general, many of whom were Gentry of his own rank, some of them Nobility of much higher rank. A modest devout man, solemnly intent "to make his calling and his election sure," to whom, in credible dialect, the Voice of the Highest had spoken. Whose earnestness, sagacity and manful worth

gradually made him conspicuous in his circle among such. —
The Puritans were already numerous.   John Hampden,
Oliver's Cousin, was a devout Puritan, John Pym the like;
Lord Brook, Lord Say, Lord Montague, — Puritans in the
better ranks, and in every rank, abounded.   Already either
in conscious act, or in clear tendency, the far greater part of
the serious Thought and Manhood of England had declared
itself Puritan.

1625.

Mark Noble, citing Willis's *Notitia*, reports that Oliver
appeared this year as Member "for Huntingdon" in King
Charles's first Parliament. *   It is a mistake; grounded on
mere blunders and clerical errors. Browne Willis, in his *Notitia
Parliamentaria*, does indeed specify as Member for Huntingdon*shire* an "Oliver Cromwell, Esq.," who might be our
Oliver.   But the usual member in former Parliaments is Sir
Oliver, our Oliver's Uncle.   Browne Willis must have made,
or have copied, some slip of the pen.   Suppose him to have
found in some of his multitudinous parchments, an "Oliver
Cromwell, Knight of the Shire:" and in place of putting in
the "Sir," to have put in "Esq.;" it will solve the whole difficulty. Our Oliver, when he indisputably did afterwards enter
Parliament, came in for Huntingdon *Town;* so that, on this
hypothesis, he must have first been Knight of the Shire, and
then have sunk (an immense fall in those days) to be a Burgh
Member; which cannot without other ground be credited.
What the original Chancery Parchments say of the business,
whether the error is theirs or Browne Willis's, I cannot decide;
on inquiry at the Rolls' Office, it turns out that the Records,
for some fifty years about this period, have vanished " a good
while ago."   Whose error it may be, we know not; but an
error we may safely conclude it is.   Sir Oliver was then still
living at Hinchinbrook, in the vigour of his years, no reason
whatever why he should not serve as formerly; nay, if he
had withdrawn, his young Nephew, of no fortune for a
Knight of the Shire, was not the man to replace him.   The

* Noble, I. 100.

Members for Huntingdon Town in this Parliament, as in the preceding one, are a Mr. Mainwaring and a Mr. St. John. The County Members in the preceding Parliament, and in this too with the correction of the concluding syllable in this, are "Edward Montague, Esquire," and "Oliver Cromwell, *Knight*."

1626.

In the Ashmole Museum at Oxford stands catalogued a "Letter from Oliver Cromwell to Mr. Henry Downhall, at St. "John's College, Cambridge; dated, Huntingdon, 14 Oc-"tober 1626;" * which might perhaps, in some very faint way, have elucidated Dr. Simcott and the hypochondrias for us. On applying to kind friends at Oxford for a copy of this Letter, I learn that there is now no Letter, only a mere selvage of paper, and a leaf wanting between two leaves. It was stolen, none knows when; but stolen it is; — which forces me to continue my Introduction some nine years farther, instead of ending it at this point. Did some zealous Oxford Doctor cut the Letter out, as one weeds a hemlock from a parsley-bed; that so the Ashmole Museum might be cleansed, and yield only pure nutriment to mankind? Or was it some collector of autographs, eager beyond law? Whoever the thief may be, he is probably dead long since; and has answered for this, — and also, we may fancy, for heavier thefts, which were likely to be charged upon him. If any humane individual ever henceforth get his eye upon the Letter, let him be so kind as send a copy of it to the Publishers of this Book, and no questions will be asked. **

1627.

A Deed of Sale, dated 20 June 1627, still testifies that Hinchinbrook this year passed out of the hands of the Cromwells into those of the Montagues.*** The price was 3000 *l.*; curiously divided into two parcels, down to shillings and

* Bodleian Library: *Codices Mss. Ashmoleani*, no. 8398.
** Letter found, worth nothing: Appendix, No. 1. (*Note to Second Edition*).
*** Noble, 1. 43.

pence, — one of the parcels being already a creditor's. The Purchaser is "Sir Sidney Montague, Knight, of Barnwell, "one of his Majesty's Masters of the Requests." Sir Oliver Cromwell, son of the Golden Knight, having now burnt out his splendour, disappeared in this way from Hinchinbrook; retired deeper into the Fens, to a place of his near Ramsey Mere, where he continued still thirty years longer to reside, in an eclipsed manner. It was to this house at Ramsey that Oliver, our Oliver, then Captain Cromwell in the Parliament's service, paid the domiciliary visit much talked of in the old Books. The reduced Knight, his Uncle, was a Royalist or Malignant; and his house had to be searched for arms, for munitions, for furnishings of any sort, which he might be minded to send off to the King, now at York, and evidently intending war. Oliver's dragoons searched with due rigour for the arms; while the Captain respectfully conversed with his Uncle; and even "insisted" through the interview, say the old Books, "on standing uncovered:" which latter circumstance may be taken as an astonishing hypocrisy in him, say the old blockhead Books. The arms, munitions, furnishings were with all rigour of law, not with more rigour and not with less, carried away; and Oliver parted with his Uncle, for that time, not "craving his blessing," I think, as the old blockhead Books say; but hoping he might, one day, either get it or a *better* than it, for what he had now done. Oliver, while in military charge of that country, had probably repeated visits to pay to his Uncle; and they know little of the man or of the circumstances, who suppose there was any likelihood or need of either insolence or hypocrisy in the course of these.

As for the old Knight, he seems to have been a man of easy temper; given to sumptuosity of hospitality; and averse to severer duties. * When his eldest son, who also showed a turn for expense, presented him a schedule of debts, craving aid towards the payment of them, Sir Oliver answered with a bland sigh, "I wish they were paid." Various Cromwells,

* Fuller's Worthies, § Huntingdonshire.

sons of his, nephews of his, besides the great Oliver, took part in the Civil War, some on this side, some on that, whose indistinct designations in the old Books are apt to occasion mistakes with modern readers. Sir Oliver vanishes now from Hinchinbrook, and all the public business records, into the darker places of the Fens. His name disappears from Willis: — in the next Parliament, the Knight of the Shire for Huntingdon becomes, instead of him, "Sir Capell Bedall, Baronet." The purchaser of Hinchinbrook, Sir Sidney Montague, was brother of the first Earl of Manchester, brother of the third Lord Montague of Boughton; and father of "the valiant Colonel Montague," valiant General Montague, Admiral Montague, who, in au altered state of circumstances, became first Earl of Sandwich, and perished, with a valour worthy of a better generalissimo than poor James Duke of York, in the Seafight of Solebay (Southwold Bay, on the coast of Suffolk) in 1672. *

In these same years, for the dates and all other circumstances of the matter hang dubious in the vague, there is record given by Dugdale, a man of very small authority on these Cromwell matters, of a certain suit instituted, in the King's Council, King's Court of Requests, or wherever it might be, by our Oliver and other relations interested, concerning the lunacy of his Uncle, Sir Thomas Steward of Ely. It seems they alleged, This Uncle Steward was incapable of managing his affairs, and ought to be restrained under guardians. Which allegation of theirs, and petition grounded on it, the King's Council saw good to deny: whereupon — Sir Thomas Steward continued to manage his affairs, in an incapable or semicapable manner; and nothing followed upon it whatever. Which proceeding of Oliver's, if there ever was such a proceeding, we are, according to Dugdale, to consider an act of villany, — if we incline to take that trouble. What we know is, That poor Sir Thomas himself did not so consider it; for, by express testament some years afterwards, he declared Oliver his heir in chief, and left him considerable

* Collins's Peerage (London, 1741), ii. 286-9.

property, as if nothing had happened. So that there is this dilemma: If Sir Thomas was imbecile, then Oliver was right; and unless Sir Thomas was imbecile, Oliver was not wrong! Alas, all calumny and carrion, does it not incessantly cry, "Earth, oh, for pity's sake, a little earth!"

1628.

Sir Oliver Cromwell has faded from the Parliamentary scene into the deep Fen-country, but Oliver Cromwell, Esq. appears there as Member for Huntingdon, at Westminster on "Monday the 17th of March" 1627—8. This was the Third Parliament of Charles: by much the most notable of all Parliaments till Charles's Long Parliament met, which proved his last.

Having sharply, with swift impetuosity and indignation, dismissed two Parliaments, because they would not "supply" him without taking "grievances" along with them; and, meanwhile and afterwards, having failed in every operation foreign and domestic, at Cadiz, at Rhé, at Rochelle; and having failed, too, in getting supplies by unparliamentary methods, Charles "consulted with Sir Robert Cotton what was to be done;" who answered, Summon a Parliament again. So this celebrated Parliament was summoned. It met, as we said, in March 1628, and continued with one prorogation till March 1629. The two former Parliaments had sat but a few weeks each, till they were indignantly hurled asunder again; this one continued nearly a year. Wentworth (Strafford) was of this Parliament; Hampden too, Selden, Pym, Holles, and others known to us: all those had been of former Parliaments as well; Oliver Cromwell, Member for Huntingdon, sat there for the first time.

It is very evident, King Charles, baffled in all his enterprises, and reduced really to a kind of crisis, wished much this Parliament should succeed; and took what he must have thought incredible pains for that end. The poor King strives visibly throughout to control himself, to be soft and patient; inwardly writhing and rustling with royal rage. Unfortunate

King, we see him chafing, stamping, a very fiery steed, but
bridled, check-bitted, by innumerable straps and considerations; struggling much to be composed. Alas, it would not
do. This Parliament was more Puritanic, more intent on
rigorous Law and divine Gospel, than any other had ever
been. As indeed all these Parliaments grow strangely in
Puritanism; more and ever more earnest rises from the hearts
of them all, "O Sacred Majesty, lead us not to Antichrist, to
Illegality, to temporal and eternal Perdition!" The Nobility
and Gentry of England were then a very strange body of men.
The English Squire of the Seventeenth Century clearly appears to have believed in God, not as a figure of speech, but
as a very fact, very awful to the heart of the English Squire.
"He wore his Bible-doctrine round him," says one, "as our
"Squire wears his shot-belt; went abroad with it, nothing
"doubting." King Charles was going on his father's course,
only with frightful acceleration: he and his respectable Tra-
ditions and Notions, clothed in old sheepskin and respectable
Church-tippets, were all pulling one way; England and the
Eternal Laws pulling another; — the rent fast widening till no
man could heal it.

This was the celebrated Parliament which framed the Petition of Right, and set London all astir with "bells and bonfires" at the passing thereof; and did other feats not to be
particularised here. Across the murkiest element in which
any great Entity was ever shown to human creatures, it still
rises, after much consideration, to the modern man, in a dim
but undeniable manner, as a most brave and noble Parliament.
The like of which were worth its weight in diamonds even
now; — but has grown very unattainable now, next door to
incredible now. We have to say that this Parliament chastised
sycophant Priests, Mainwaring, Sibthorp, and other Arminian
sycophants, a disgrace to God's Church; that it had an
eye to other still more elevated Church-Sycophants, as the
mainspring of all; but was cautious to give offence by naming
them. That it carefully "abstained from naming the Duke of
Buckingham." That it decided on giving ample subsidies,

but not till there were reasonable discussion of grievances. That in manner it was most gentle, soft-spoken, cautious, reverential; and in substance most resolute and valiant. Truly with valiant patient energy, in a slow stedfast English manner, it carried, across infinite confused opposition and discouragement, its Petition of Right, and what else it had to carry. Four hundred brave men, — brave men and true, after their sort! One laments to find such a Parliament smothered under Dryasdust's shot-rubbish. The memory of it, could any real memory of it rise upon honourable gentlemen and us, might be admonitory, — would be astonishing at least. We must clip one extract from Rushworth's huge Rag-fair of a Book; the mournfullest torpedo rubbish-heap, of jewels buried under sordid wreck and dust and dead ashes, one jewel to the wagon-load; — and let the reader try to make a visual scene of it as he can. Here, we say, is an old Letter, which "old Mr. Chamberlain of the Court of Wards," a gentleman entirely unknown to us, received fresh and new, before breakfast, on a June morning of the year 1628; of which old Letter we, by a good chance,* have obtained a copy for the reader. It is by Mr. Thomas Alured, a good Yorkshire friend, Member for Malton in that county; — written in a hand which, if it were not naturally stout, would tremble with emotion. Worthy Mr. Alured, called also "Al'red" or "Aldred;" uncle or father, we suppose, to a "Colonel Alured," well known afterwards to Oliver and us: he writes; we abridge and present, as follows:

"Friday, 6th June 1628.

"Sir, — Yesterday was a day of desolation among us in "Parliament; and this day, we fear, will be the day of our "dissolution.

"Upon Tuesday Sir John Eliot moved that as we intended "to furnish his Majesty with money, we should also supply "him with counsel. Representing the doleful state of affairs,

---

* Rushworth's Historical Collections (London, 1682), I. 609-10. (Note, vols. II. and III. of this Copy are of 1680, a *prior* edition seemingly; iv. and v. of 1692; vi. and vii. of 1701; viii., Strafford's Trial, of 1700).

"he desired there might be a *Declaration* made to the King, of
"the danger wherein the Kingdom stood by the decay and
"contempt of religion, by the insufficiency of his Ministers,
"by the" &c. &c. "Sir Humphrey May, Chancellor of the
"Duchy, said, 'it was a strange language;' yet the House
"commanded Sir John Eliot to go on. Whereupon the Chan-
"cellor desired, 'If he went on, *he* the Chancellor might go out.'
"They all bade him 'begone:' yet he stayed, and heard Sir
"John out. The House generally inclined to such a *Declara-*
"*tion;* which was accordingly resolved to be set about.

   "But next day, Wednesday, we had a Message from his
"Majesty by the Speaker, That as the Session was positively
"to end in a week, we should husband the time, and despatch
"our old businesses without entertaining new!" — Intending
nevertheless "to pursue our *Declaration*, we had, yesterday,
"Thursday morning, a new Message brought us, which I
"have here enclosed. Which requiring us *Not to cast or lay*
"*any aspersion upon any Minister of his Majesty*, the House was
"much affected thereby." Did they not in former times proceed by fining and committing John of Gaunt, the King's own
son; had they not, in very late times, meddled with and
sentenced the Lord Chancellor Bacon and others? What are
we arriving at! —

   "Sir Robert Philips of Somersetshire spake, and mingled
"his words with weeping. Mr. Pym did the like. Sir Edward
"Cook" (old Coke upon Lyttleton), "overcome with passion,
"seeing the desolation likely to ensue, was forced to sit down
"when he began to speak, by the abundance of tears." O
Mr. Chamberlain of the Court of Wards, was the like ever
witnessed? "Yea, the Speaker in his speech could not refrain
"from weeping and shedding of tears. Besides a great many
"whose grief made them dumb. But others bore up in that
"storm, and encouraged the rest." We resolved ourselves
into a Committee, to have freer scope for speech; and called
Mr. Whitby to the chair.

   The Speaker, always in close communication with his Majesty, craves leave from us, with much humility, to withdraw

"for half an hour;" which, though we knew well whither he was going, was readily granted him. It is ordered, "No other man leave the House upon pain of going to the Tower." And now the speaking commences, "freer and frequenter," being in Committee, and old Sir Edward Coke tries it again.

"Sir Edward Cook told us, 'He now saw God had not ac-"cepted of our humble and moderate carriages and fair pro-"ceedings; and he feared the reason was, We had not dealt "sincerely with the King and Country, and made a *true* re-"presentation of the causes of all those miseries. Which he, "for his part, repented that he had not done sooner. And "therefore, not knowing whether he should ever again speak "in this House, he would now do it freely; and so did here "protest, That the author and cause of all those miseries was "—'THE DUKE OF BUCKINGHAM.' Which was entertained and an-"swered with a cheerful acclamation of the House." (Yea, yea! Well moved, well spoken! Yea, yea!) "As, when one good "hound recovers the scent, the rest come in with full cry; so "they (*we*) pursued it, and every one came home, and laid "the blame where he thought the fault was," — on the Duke of Buckingham, to wit. "And as we were putting it to the "question, Whether he should be *named* in our intended Re-"monstrance as the chief cause of all our miseries at home and "abroad, — the Speaker, having been, not half an hour, but "three hours absent, and with the King, returned; bringing "this Message, That the House should then rise (being about "eleven o'clock), adjourn till the morrow morning, and no "Committees to sit, or other business to go on, in the in-"terim."

And so, ever since, King's Majesty, Speaker, Duke and Councillors, they have been meditating it all night!

"What we shall expect this morning, therefore, God of "Heaven knows! We shall meet betimes this morning; partly "for the business' sake; and partly because, two days ago, "we made an order, That whoever comes in after Prayers "shall pay twelvepence to the poor.

"Sir, excuse my haste: — and let us have your prayers;

"whereof both you and we have need. I rest, — affectionately
"at your service,

"THOMAS ALURED."

This scene Oliver saw, and formed part of; one of the me-
morablest he was ever in. Why did those old honourable
gentlemen 'weep'? How came tough old Coke upon Lyttleton,
one of the toughest men ever made, to melt into tears like a
girl, and sit down unable to speak? The modern honourable
gentleman cannot tell. Let him consider it, and try if he can
tell! And then, putting off his Shot-belt, and striving to put
on some Bible-doctrine, some earnest God's Truth or other,
— try if he can discover why he cannot tell! —

The Remonstrance against Buckingham was perfected:
the hounds having got all upon the scent. Buckingham was
expressly "named," — a daring feat: and so loud were the
hounds, and such a tune in their baying, his Majesty saw
good to confirm, and ratify beyond shadow of cavil, the invaluable Petition of Right, and thereby produce "bonfires,"
and bob-majors upon all bells. Old London was sonorous; in
a blaze with joy-fires. Soon after which, this Parliament, as
London, and England, and it, all still continued somewhat
too sonorous, was hastily, with visible royal anger, prorogued
till October next, — till January as it proved. Oliver, of
course, went home to Huntingdon to his harvest-work; England continued simmering and sounding as it might.

The day of prorogation was the 26th of June. * One day
in the latter end of August, John Felton, a short swart Suffolk
gentleman of military air, in fact a retired lieutenant of grim
serious disposition, went out to walk in the eastern parts of
London. Walking on Tower Hill, full of black reflections on
his own condition, and on the condition of England, and a
Duke of Buckingham holding all England down into the jaws
of ruin and disgrace, — John Felton saw, in evil hour, on
some cutler's stall there, a broad sharp hunting-knife, price
one shilling. John Felton, with a wild flash in the dark heart

<hr>

* Commons Journals, i. 920.

of him, bought the said knife; rode down to Portsmouth with it, where the great Duke then was; struck the said knife, with one fell plunge, into the great Duke's heart. This was on Saturday the 23d of August of this same year. *

Felton was tried; saw that his wild flashing inspiration had been not of God, but of Satan. It is known he repented: when the death-sentence was passed on him, he stretched out his right hand; craved that this too, as some small expiation, might first be stricken off; which was denied him, as against law. He died at Tyburn; his body was swinging in chains at Portsmouth; — and much else had gone awry, when the Parliament reassembled, in January following, and Oliver came up to Town again.

1629.

The Parliament Session proved very brief; but very energetic, very extraordinary. "Tonnage and Poundage," what we now call Customhouse Duties, a constant subject of quarrel between Charles and his Parliaments hitherto, had again been levied *without* Parliamentary consent; in the teeth of old *Tallagio non concedendo*, nay even of the late solemnly confirmed Petition of Right; and naturally gave rise to Parliamentary consideration. Merchants had been imprisoned for refusing to pay it; Members of Parliament themselves had been "*subpœna'd:*" there was a very ravelled coil to deal with in regard to Tonnage and Poundage. Nay the Petition of Right itself had been altered in the Printing; a very ugly business too.

In regard to Religion also, matters looked equally ill. Sycophant Mainwaring, just censured in Parliament, had been promoted to a fatter living. Sycophant Montague, in the like circumstances, to a Bishopric: Laud was in the act of consecrating him at Croydon, when the news of Buckingham's death came thither. There needed to be a Committee of Religion. The House resolved itself into a Grand Committee

* Clarendon (i. 68); Hamond L'Estrange (p. 90); D'Ewes (MS. Autobiography), &c.; all of whom report the minute circumstances of the assassination, not one of them agreeing completely with another.

of Religion; and did not want for matter. Bishop Neile of Winchester, Bishop Laud now of London, were a frightfully ceremonial pair of Bishops; the fountain they of innumerable tendencies to Papistry and the old-clothes of Babylon! It was in this Committee of Religion, on the 11th day of February 1628-9, that Mr. Cromwell, Member for Huntingdon, stood up and made his first Speech, a fragment of which has found its way into History, and is now known to all mankind. He said, "He had heard by relation from one Dr. Beard" (his old Schoolmaster at Huntingdon), "that Dr. Alablaster had "preached flat Popery at Paul's Cross; and that the Bishop of "Winchester" (Dr. Neile) "had commanded him as his Dio- "cesan, He should preach nothing to the contrary. Main- "waring, so justly censured in this House for his sermons, was "by the same Bishop's means preferred to a rich living. If " these are the steps to Church-preferment, what are we to ex- 'pect?" *

Dr. Beard, as the reader knows, is Oliver's old School-master at Huntingdon; a grave, speculative, theological old gentleman, seemingly, — and on a level with the latest news from Town. Of poor Dr. Alablaster there may be found some indistinct, and instantly forgettable particulars in *Wood's Athenæ*. Paul's Cross, of which I have seen old Prints, was a kind of Stone Tent, "with leaden roof," at the north-east corner of Paul's Cathedral, where Sermons were still, and had long been, preached in the open air; crowded devout congregations gathering there; with forms to sit on, if you came early. Queen Elizabeth used to "tune her pulpits," she said, when there was any great thing on hand; as Governing Persons now strive to tune their Morning Newspapers. Paul's Cross, a kind of *Times Newspaper*, but edited partly by Heaven itself, was then a most important entity! Alablaster, to the horror of mankind, was heard preaching "flat Popery" there — "prostituting our columns" in that scandalous manner! And Neile had forbidden him to preach against it: "what are we to expect?"

* Parliamentary History (London, 1763), viii. 269.

The record of this world-famous utterance of Oliver still lies in manuscript in the British Museum, in Mr. Crewe's Note-book, or another's: it was first printed in a wretched old Book called *Ephemeris Parliamentaria*, professing to be compiled by Thomas Fuller; and actually containing a Preface recognisable as his, but nothing else that we can so recognise: for "quaint old Fuller" is a man of talent; and this Book looks as if compiled by some spiritual Nightmare, rather than a rational Man. Probably some greedy Printer's compilation; to whom Thomas, in ill hour, had sold his name. In the Commons Journals, of that same day, we are farther to remark, there stands, in perennial preservation, this notice: "Upon "question, *Ordered*, That Dr. Beard of Huntingdon be written "to by Mr. Speaker, to come up and testify against the "Bishop; the order for Dr. Beard to be delivered to Mr. Crom-"well." The first mention of Mr. Cromwell's name in the Books of any Parliament. —

A new *Remonstrance* behoves to be resolved upon; Bishops Neile and Laud are even to be *named* there. Whereupon, before they could get well "named," perhaps before Dr. Beard had well got up from Huntingdon to testify against them, the King hastily interfered. This Parliament, in a fortnight more, was dissolved; and that under circumstances of the most unparalleled sort. For Speaker Finch, as we have seen, was a Courtier, in constant communication with the King: one day while these high matters were astir, Speaker Finch refused to "put the question" when ordered by the House! He said he had orders to the contrary; persisted in that; — and at last took to weeping. What was the House to do? Adjourn for two days, and consider what to do! On the second day, which was Wednesday, Speaker Finch signified that by his Majesty's command they were again adjourned till Monday next. On Monday next, Speaker Finch, still recusant, would not put the former nor indeed any question, having the King's order to adjourn *again* instantly. He refused; was reprimanded, menaced; once more took to weeping; then started up to go his ways. But young Mr. Holles, Denzil Holles, the Earl of

Clare's second son, he and certain other honourable members
were prepared for that movement: they seized Speaker Finch,
set him down in his chair, and by main force held him there.
A scene of such agitation as was never seen in Parliament
before. "The House was much troubled." "Let him go,"
cried certain Privy Councillors, Majesty's Ministers as we
should now call them, who in those days sat in front of the
Speaker, "Let Mr. Speaker go!" cried they imploringly. —
"No!" answered Holles; "God's wounds, he shall sit there,
till it please the House to rise!" The House, in a decisive
though almost distracted manner, with their Speaker thus
held down for them, locked their doors; redacted Three em-
phatic Resolutions, their Protest against Arminianism,
against Papistry, against illegal Tonnage and Poundage;
and passed same by acclamation; letting no man out, refusing to let even the King's Usher in; then swiftly vanishing
so soon as the resolutions were passed, for they understood
the Soldiery was coming. * For which surprising procedure,
vindicated by Necessity the mother of Invention and supreme
of Lawgivers, certain honourable gentlemen, Denzil Holles,
Sir John Eliot, William Strode, John Selden, and others less
known to us, suffered fine, imprisonment, and much legal tri-
bulation! nay Sir John Eliot, refusing to submit, was kept in
the Tower till he died.

This scene fell out on Monday, 2d of March 1629. Directly
on the back of which, we conclude, Mr. Cromwell quitted
Town for Huntingdon again; — told Dr. Beard also that he
was not wanted now; that he might at leisure go on with his
Theatre of God's Judgments now. ** His Majesty dissolved the
Parliament by Proclamation; saying something about "vipers"
that had been there.

It was the last Parliament in England for above eleven
years. The King had taken his course. The King went on
raising supplies without Parliamentary law, by all conceivable
devices; of which Shipmoney may be considered the most ori-

* Rushworth, I. 667-9.
** Third Edition, "increased with many new examples," in 1631.

ginal, and sale of Monopolies the most universal. The mono-poly of "soap" itself was very grievous to men.* Your soap was dear, and it would not wash, but only blister. The ceremonial Bishops, Bishop or Archbishop Laud now chief of them, — they, on their side, went on diligently hunting out "Lecturers," erecting "altars in the east end of churches;" charging all clergymen to have, in good repair and order, "Four surplices at Allhallowtide." ** Vexations spiritual and fiscal, beyond what we can well fancy now, afflicted the souls of men. The English Nation was patient; it endured in silence, with prayer that God in justice and mercy would look upon it. The King of England with his chief-priests was going one way; the Nation of England by eternal laws was going another: the split became too wide for healing. Oliver and others seemed now to have done with Parliaments; a royal Proclamation forbade them so much as to speak of such a thing.

1630.

In the "new charter" granted to the Corporation of Hun-tingdon, and dated 8th July 1630, Oliver Cromwell, Esquire, Thomas Beard, D. D. his old Schoolmaster, and Robert Barnard, Esquire, of whom also we may hear again, are named Justices of the Peace for that Borough.*** I suppose there was nothing new in this nomination; a mere confirming and con-tinuing of what had already been. But the smallest authentic fact, any undoubted date or circumstance regarding Oliver and his affairs, is to be eagerly laid hold of.

1631.

In or soon after 1631, as we laboriously infer from the im-broglio record of poor Noble, Oliver decided on an enlarged sphere of action as a Farmer; sold his properties in Hunting-don, all or some of them; rented certain grazing-lands at St. Ives, five miles down the River, eastward of his native place, and removed thither. The Deed of Sale is dated 7th May

---

* See many old Pamphlets.
** Laud's Diary, in Wharton's Laud.   *** Noble, i. 102.

1631;* the properties are specified as in the possession of himself or his Mother; the sum they yielded was 1800*l*. With this sum Oliver stocked his Grazing-Farm at St. Ives. The Mother, we infer, continued to reside at Huntingdon, but withdrawn now from active occupation, into the retirement befitting a widow up in years. There is even some gleam of evidence to that effect: her properties are sold; but Oliver's children born to him at St. Ives are still christened at Huntingdon, in the Church he was used to; which may mean also that their good Grandmother was still there.

Properly this was no change in Oliver's old activities; it was an enlargement of the sphere of them. His Mother still at Huntingdon, within few miles of him, he could still superintend and protect her existence there, while managing his new operations at St. Ives. He continued here till the summer or spring of 1636.** A studious imagination may sufficiently construct the figure of his equable life in those years. Diligent grass - farming; mowing, milking, cattle - marketing: add 'hypochondria,' fits of the blackness of darkness, with glances of the brightness of very Heaven; prayer, religious reading and meditation; household epochs, joys and cares: — we have a solid substantial inoffensive Farmer of St. Ives, hoping to walk with integrity and humble devout diligence through this world; and, by his Maker's infinite mercy, to escape destruction, and find eternal salvation, in wider Divine Worlds. This latter, this is the grand clause in his Life, which dwarfs all other clauses. Much wider destinies than he anticipated were appointed him on Earth; but that, in comparison to the alternative of Heaven·or Hell to all Eternity, was a mighty small matter.

The lands he rented are still there, recognisable to the Tourist; gross boggy lands, fringed with willow-trees, at the east end of the small Town of St. Ives, which is still noted as a cattle-market in those parts. The "Cromwell Barn," the pretended "House of Cromwell," the &c. &c. are, as is usual in these cases, when you come to try them by the documents,

* Noble, 1. 103-4.   ** Ibid. 1. 106.

5*

a mere jumble of incredibilities, and oblivious human platitudes, distressing to the mind.

But a Letter, one Letter signed Oliver Cromwell and dated St. Ives, does remain, still legible and indubitable to us. What more is to be said on St. Ives and the adjacent matters will best arrange itself round that Document. One or two entries here, and we arrive at that, and bring these imperfect Introductory Chronicles to a close.

1632.

In January of this year Oliver's seventh child was born to him; a boy, James; who died the day after baptism. There remained six children, of whom one other died young; it is not known at what date. Here subjoined is the List of them, and of those subsequently born; in a Note, elaborated, as before, from the imbroglios of Noble.*

* OLIVER CROMWELL'S CHILDREN.
(Married to Elizabeth Bourchier, 22d August 1620.)

1. *Robert*; baptised 13th October 1621. Named for his Grandfather. No farther account of him; he died before ripe years.

2. Oliver; baptised 6th February 1662-3; went to Felsted School, "Captain in Harrison's Regiment," — no. At Peterborough in 1643 (Noble i. 133-4). He died, or was killed during the War; date and place not yet discoverable. Noble says it was at Appleby; referring to Whitlocke. Whitlocke (p. 318 of 1st edition, 322 of 2d), on ransacking the old Pamphlets, turns out to be indisputably in error. The Protector on his death-bed alludes to this Oliver's death: "It went to my heart like a dagger, indeed it did."

3. Bridget; baptised 4th August 1624. Married to Ireton, 15th June 1646 (Noble, i. 134, is twice in error); widow, 20th November 1651. Married to Fleetwood (exact date, after long search, remains undiscovered; Noble, ii. 355, says "before" June 1652, — at random seemingly). Died at Stoke Newington, near London, September 1681.

4. Richard; born 4th October 1626. At Felsted School. "In Lincoln's Inn, 27th May 1647:" an error? Married, in 1649, Richard Mayor's daughter, of Hursley, Hants. First in Parliament, 1654. Protector, 1658. Dies, poor idle Triviality, at Cheshunt, 12th July 1712.

5. Henry; baptised at All-Saints (the rest are at St. John's), Huntingdon, 20th January 1627-8. Felsted School. In the army at sixteen. Captain, under Harrison I think, in 1647. Colonel in 1649, and in Ireland with his Father. Lord Deputy there in 1657. In 1660, retired to Spinney Abbey, "near Soham," nearer Wicken, in Cambridgeshire. Foolish story of Charles II. and the "stable-fork" there (Noble, i. 212). Died 23d March 1673-4; buried in Wicken Church. A brave man and true: had *he* been named Protector, there had, most likely, been quite another History of England to write, at present!

6. Elizabeth; baptised 2d July 1629. Mrs. Claypole, 1645-6. Died at 3 in the morning, Hampton-court, 6th August 1658, — four weeks before her

This same year, William Prynne first began to make a noise in England. A learned young gentleman "from Swainswick near Bath," graduate of Oxford, now "an Outer Barrister of Lincoln's Inn;" well read in English Law, and full of zeal for Gospel Doctrine and Morality. He, struck by certain flagrant scandals of the time, especially by that of Play-acting and Masking, saw good, this year, to set forth his *Histriomastix*, or Player's Scourge; a Book still extant, but never more to be read by mortal. For which Mr. William Prynne himself, before long, paid rather dear. The Book was licensed by old Archbishop Abbot, a man of Puritan tendencies, but now verging towards his end. Peter Heylin, "lying Peter" as men sometimes call him, was already with hawk's eye and the intensest interest reading this now unreadable Book, and, by Laud's direction, taking excerpts from the same. —

It carries our thought to extensive world-transactions over sea, to reflect that in the end of this same year, "6th November 1632," the great Gustavus died on the Field of Lützen; fighting against Wallenstein; victorious for the last time. While Oliver Cromwell walked peacefully intent on cattle-husbandry, that winter-day, on the grassy banks of the Ouse at St. Ives, Gustavus Adolphus, shot through the back, was sinking from his horse in the battle-storm far off, with these

Father. A graceful, brave, and amiable woman. The lamentation about Dr. Hewit and "bloodshed" (in Clarendon and others) is fudge.

At St. Ives and Ely :

7. *James;* baptised 8th January 1631-2; died next day.

8. Mary; baptised (at Huntingdon still) 9th February 1636-7. Lady Fauconberg, 18th November 1657. Dean Swift knew her: "handsome and like her Father." Died 14th March 1712 (1712-3? is not decided in Noble). Richard died within a few months of her.

9. Frances; baptised (at Ely now) 6th December 1638. "Charles II. was for marrying her:" not improbable. Married Mr. Rich, Earl of Warwick's grandson, 11th November 1657: he died in three months, 16th February 1657-8. No child by Rich. Married Sir John Russel, — the Checquers Russels. Died 27th January 1720-1.

In all, 5 sons and 4 daughters; of whom 3 sons and all the daughters came to maturity.

The Protector's Widow died at Norborough, her son-in-law Claypole's place (now ruined, patched into a farmhouse; near Market Deeping; it is itself in Northamptonshire), 8th October 1672.

words: "*Ich habe genug, Bruder; rette Dich.*   Brother, I have got enough; save thyself." *

On the 19th of the same month, November 1632, died likewise Frederick Elector Palatine, titular King of Bohemia, husband of King Charles's sister, and father of certain Princes, Rupert and others, who came to be well known in our History. Elizabeth, the Widow, was left with a large family of them in Holland, very bare of money, of resource, or immediate hope; but conducted herself, as she had all along done, in a way that gained much respect.   "*Alles für Ruhm und Ihr*, All for Glory and Her," were the words Duke Bernhard of Weimar carried on his Flag, through many battles in that Thirty-Years War. She was of Puritan tendency; understood to care little about the Four surplices at Allhallowtide, and much for the root of the matter.

Attorney-General Noy, in these months, was busy tearing up the unfortunate old manufacturers of soap; tormenting mankind very much about soap.** He tore them up irresistibly, reduced them to total ruin; good soap became unattainable.

1633.

In May 1633, the second year of Oliver's residence in this new Farm, the King's Majesty, with train enough, passed through Huntingdonshire, on his way to Scotland to be crowned. The loud rustle of him disturbing, for a day, the summer husbandries and operations of mankind. His ostensible business was to be crowned; but his intrinsic errand was, what his Father's formerly had been, to get his Pretended-Bishops set on foot there; his *Tulchans* converted into real Calves; — in which, as we shall see, he succeeded still worse than his Father had done. Dr. Laud, Bishop Laud, now near upon Archbishophood, attended his Majesty thither as formerly; still found "no religion" there, but trusted now to introduce one. The Chapel at Holyrood-house was fitted up with every equipment textile and metallic; and little Bishop Laud in per-

* Schiller: Geschichte des 30jährigen Krieges.
** Rushworth, ii. 135, 252, &c.

son "performed the service," in a way to illuminate the be-
nighted natives, as was hoped, — show them how an Artist
could do it. He had also some dreadful travelling through
certain of the savage districts of that country.

Crossing Huntingdonshire, on this occasion, in his way
Northward, his Majesty had visited the Establishment of Nicholas Ferrar at Little Gidding, on the western border of
that county.* A surprising Establishment, now in full flower;
wherein above fourscore persons, including domestics, with
Ferrar and his Brother and aged Mother at the head of them,
had devoted themselves to a kind of Protestant Monachism,
and were getting much talked of in those times. They followed celibacy, and merely religious duties; employed themselves
in "binding of Prayer-books," embroidering of hassocks,
in almsgiving also, and what charitable work was possible in
that desert region; above all, they kept up, night and day, a
continual repetition of the English Liturgy; being divided
into relays and watches, one watch relieving another as on
shipboard; and never allowing at any hour the sacred fire to
go out. This also, as a feature of the times, the modern
reader is to meditate. In Isaac Walton's *Lives* there is some
drowsy notice of these people, not unknown to the modern
reader. A far livelier notice; record of an actual visit to the
place, by an Anonymous Person, seemingly a religious
Lawyer, perhaps returning from Circuit in that direction, at
all events a most sharp distinct man, through whose clear eyes
we also can still look; — is preserved by Hearne in very unexpected neighbourhood.** The Anonymous Person, after
some survey and communing, suggested to Nicholas Ferrar,
"Perhaps he had but *assumed* all this ritual mummery, in
"order to get a devout life led peaceably in these bad times?"
Nicholas, a dark man, who had acquired something of the
Jesuit in his Foreign travels, looked at him ambiguously, and
said, "I perceive you are a person who know the world!"

* Rushworth, ii. 178.
** Thomæ Caii Vindiciæ Antiquitatis Academiæ Oxoniensis (Oxf. 1730),
ii. 702-794. There are two *Lives* of Ferrar; considerable writings about
him; but, except this, nothing that much deserves to be read.

They did not ask the Anonymous Person to stay dinner, which he considered would have been agreeable. —

Note these other things, with which we are more immediately concerned. In this same year the Feoffees, with their Purchase of Advowsons, with their Lecturers and Running Lecturers, were fairly rooted out, and flung prostrate into total ruin; Laud having set Attorney-General Noy upon them, and brought them into the Starchamber. "God forgive *them*," writes Bishop Laud, "and grant me patience!" — on hearing that they spake harshly of him; not gratefully, but ungratefully, for all this trouble he took! In the same year, by procurement of the same zealous Bishop hounding-on the same invincible Attorney-General, William Prynne our unreadable friend, Peter Heylin having read him, was brought to the Starchamber; to the Pillory, and had his ears cropt off, for the first time; — who also, strange as it may look, manifested no gratitude, but the contrary, for all that trouble!*

1634.

In the end of this the third year of Oliver's abode at St. Ives, came out the celebrated Writ of Shipmoney. It was the last feat of Attorney-General Noy: a morose, amorphous, cynical Law-Pedant, and invincible living heap of learned rubbish; once a Patriot in Parliament, till they made him Attorney-General, and enlightened his eyes: who had fished up from the dust-abysses this and other old shadows of "precedents," promising to be of great use in the present distressed state of the Finance Department. Parliament being in abeyance, how to raise money was now the grand problem. Noy himself was dead before the Writ came out; a very mixed renown following him. The Vintners, says Wood, illuminated at his death, made bonfires, and "drank lusty carouses:" to them, as to every man, he had been a sore affliction. His heart, on dissection, adds old Anthony, was found "all shrivelled up like a leather penny-purse;" which gave rise to

* Rushworth; Wharton's Laud.

comments among the Puritans.*   His brain, said the pasqui-
nades of the day, was found reduced to a mass of dust, his
heart was a bundle of old sheep-skin writs, and his belly consisted of a barrel of soap.** Some indistinct memory of him
still survives, as of a grisly Law Pluto, and dark Law Monster,
kind of Infernal King, Chief Enchanter in the Domdaniel of
Attorneys; one of those frightful men, who, as his contempo-
raries passionately said and repeated, dare to "decree injustice *by a law*."

The Shipmoney Writ has come out, then; and Cousin
Hampden has decided not to pay it! — As the date of Oliver's
St. Ives Letter is 1635-6, and we are now come in sight of that,
we will here close our Chronology.

CHAPTER V.

Of Oliver's Letters and Speeches.

LETTERS and authentic Utterances of Oliver lie scattered,
in print and manuscript, in a hundred repositories, in all varie-
ties of condition and environment. Most of them, all the important of them, have already long since been printed and
again printed; but we cannot in general say, ever read: too
often it is apparent that the very editor of these poor utterances
had, if reading mean understanding, never *read* them. They
stand in their old spelling; mispunctuated, misprinted, un-
elucidated, unintelligible, — defaced with the dark incrusta-
tions too well known to students of that Period. The Speeches
above all, as hitherto set forth in *The Somers Tracts*, in *The
Milton State-Papers*, in *Burton's Diary*, and other such Books,
excel human belief: certainly no such agglomerate of opaque
confusions, printed and reprinted; of darkness on the back of
darkness, thick and threefold; is known to me elsewhere in the
history of things spoken or printed by human creatures. Of
these Speeches, all except one, which was published by autho-

* Wood's Athenæ (Bliss's edition, London, 1815), ii. 583.
** Rushworth.

rity at the time, I have to believe myself, not very exultingly, to be the first actual reader for nearly two Centuries past.

Nevertheless these Documents do exist, authentic though defaced; and invite every one who would know that Period, to study them till they become intelligible again. The words of Oliver Cromwell, — the meaning *they* had, must be worth recovering, in that point of view. To collect these Letters and authentic Utterances, as one's reading yielded them, was a comparatively grateful labour; to correct them, elucidate and make them legible again, was a good historical study. Surely "a wise memory" would wish to preserve among men the written and spoken words of such a man; — and as for the "wise oblivion," that is already, by Time and Accident, done to our hand. Enough is already lost and destroyed; we need not, in this particular case, omit farther.

Accordingly, whatever words authentically proceeding from Oliver himself I could anywhere find yet surviving, I have here gathered; and will now, with such minimum of annotation as may suit that object, offer them to the reader. That is the purport of this Book. I have ventured to believe that, to certain patient earnest readers, these old dim Letters of a noble English Man might, as they had done to myself, become dimly legible again; might dimly present, better than all other evidence, the noble figure of the Man himself again. Certainly there is Historical instruction in these Letters: — Historical, and perhaps other and better. At least, it is with Heroes and god-inspired men that I, for my part, would far rather converse, in what dialect soever they speak! Great, ever fruitful; profitable for reproof, for encouragement, for building up in manful purposes and works, are the words of those that in their day were men. I will advise serious persons, interested in England past or present, to try if they can read a little in these Letters of Oliver Cromwell, a man once deeply interested in the same object. Heavy as it is, and dim and obsolete, there may be worse reading, for such persons in our time.

For the rest, if each Letter look dim, and have little light, after all study; — yet let the Historical reader reflect, such light as it has cannot be disputed at all. These words, expository of that day and hour, Oliver Cromwell did see fittest to be written down. The Letter hangs there in the dark abysses of the Past: if like a star almost extinct, yet like a real star; fixed; about which there is no cavilling possible. That autograph Letter, it was once all luminous as a burning beacon, every word of it a live coal, in its time; it was once a piece of the general fire and light of Human Life, that Letter! Neither is it yet entirely extinct: well read, there is still in it light enough to exhibit its own *self;* nay to diffuse a faint authentic twilight some distance round it. Heaped embers which in the daylight looked black, may still look *red* in the utter darkness. These Letters of Oliver will convince any man that the Past did exist! By degrees the combined small twilights may produce a kind of general feeble twilight, rendering the Past credible, the Ghosts of the Past in some glimpses of them visible! Such is the effect of contemporary letters always; and I can very confidently recommend Oliver's as good of their kind. A man intent to force for himself some path through that gloomy chaos called History of the Seventeenth Century, and to look face to face upon the same, may perhaps try it by this method as hopefully as by another. Here is an irregular row of beacon-fires, once all luminous as suns; and with a certain inextinguishable erubescence still, in the abysses of the dead deep Night. Let us look here. In shadowy outlines, in dimmer and dimmer crowding forms, the very figure of the old dead Time itself may perhaps be faintly discernible here! —

I called these Letters good, — but withal only good of their kind. No eloquence, elegance, not always even clearness of expression, is to be looked for in them. They are written with far other than literary aims; written, most of them, in the very flame and conflagration of a revolutionary struggle, and with an eye to the despatch of indispensable pressing business alone; but it will be found, I conceive, that

for such end they are well written. Superfluity, as if by a
natural law of the case, the writer has had to discard; whatsoever quality *can* be dispensed with is indifferent to him.
With unwieldy movement, yet with a great solid step he
presses through, towards his object; has marked out very decisively what the real steps towards it are; discriminating well
the essential from the extraneous; — forming to himself, in
short, a true, not an untrue picture of the business that is to
be done.   There is in these Letters, as I have said above, a
silence still more significant of Oliver to us than any speech
they have.   Dimly we discover features of an Intelligence,
and Soul of a Man, greater than any speech. The Intelligence
that can, with full satisfaction to itself, come out in eloquent
speaking, in musical singing, is, after all, a small Intelligence.
He that works and *does* some Poem, not he that merely *says*
one, is worthy of the name of Poet. Cromwell, emblem of
the dumb English, is interesting to me by the very inadequacy
of his speech. Heroic insight, valour and belief without
words, — how noble is it in comparison to the adroitest flow
of words without heroic insight! —
   I have corrected the spelling of these Letters; I have
punctuated, and divided them into paragraphs, in the modern
manner. The Originals, so far as I have seen such, have in
general no paragraphs: if the Letter is short, it is usually
found written on the first leaf of the sheet; often with the conclusion, or some postscript, subjoined crosswise on the margin,
— indicating that there was no blotting-paper in those days;
that the hasty writer was loath to turn the leaf. Oliver's
spelling and pointing are of the sort common to educated persons in his time; and readers that so wish, may have specimens
of him in abundance, and of all due dimness, in many printed
Books: but to us, intent here to have the Letters read and
understood, it seemed very proper at once and altogether to
get rid of that encumbrance. Would the rest were all as easily
got rid of!   Here and there, to bring out the struggling sense,
I have added or rectified a word, — but taken care to point

out the same; what words in the Text of the Letters are mine, the reader will find marked off by single commas: it was of course my supreme duty to avoid altering, in any respect, not only the sense, but the smallest feature in the physiognomy, of the Original. And so, "a minimum of annotation" having been added, what minimum would serve the purpose, — here are the *Letters and Speeches of Oliver Cromwell*; of which the reader, with my best wishes, but not with any very high immediate hope of mine in that particular, is to make what he can.

Surely it is far enough from probable that these Letters of Cromwell, written originally for quite other objects, and selected not by the Genius of History, but by blind Accident which has saved them hitherto and destroyed the rest, — can illuminate for a modern man this Period of our Annals, which for all moderns, we may say, has become a gulf of bottomless darkness! Not so easily will the modern man domesticate himself in a scene of things every way so foreign to him. Nor could any measurable exposition of mine, on this present occasion, do much to illuminate the dead dark world of the Seventeenth Century, into which the reader is about to enter. He will gradually get to understand, as I have said, that the Seventeenth Century did exist; that it was not a waste rubbish-continent of Rushworth-Nalson State-papers, of Philosophical Scepticisms, Dilettantisms, Dryasdust Torpedoisms; — but an actual flesh-and-blood Fact; with colour in its cheeks, with awful august heroic thoughts in its heart, and at last with steel sword in its hand! Theoretically this is a most small postulate, conceded at once by everybody; but practically it is a very large one, seldom or never conceded; the due practical conceding of it amounts to much, indeed to the sure promise of all. — I will venture to give the reader two little pieces of advice, which, if his experience resemble mine, may prove furthersome to him in this inquiry: they include the essence of all that I have discovered respecting it.

The first is, By no means to credit the wide-spread report

that these Seventeenth-Century Puritans were superstitious crackbrained persons; given up to enthusiasm, the most part of them; the minor ruling part being cunning men, who knew how to assume the dialect of the others, and thereby, as skilful Machiavels, to dupe them. This is a wide-spread report; but an untrue one. I advise my reader to try precisely the opposite hypothesis. To consider that his Fathers, who had thought about this World very seriously indeed, and with very considerable thinking faculty indeed, were not quite so far behindhand in their conclusions respecting it. That actually their "enthusiasms," if well seen into, were not foolish but wise. That Machiavelism, Cant, Official Jargon, whereby a man speaks openly what he does *not* mean, were, surprising as it may seem, much rarer then than they have ever since been. Really and truly it may in a manner be said, Cant, Parliamentary and other Jargon, were still to invent in this world. O Heavens, one could weep at the contrast! Cant was not fashionable at all; that stupendous invention of "Speech for the purpose of concealing Thought" was not yet made. A man wagging the tongue of him, as if it were the clapper of a bell to be rung for economic purposes, and not so much as attempting to convey any inner thought, if thought he have, of the matter talked of, — would at that date have awakened all the horror in men's minds, which at all dates, and at this date too, is due to him. The accursed thing! No man as yet dared to do it; all men believing that God would judge them. In the History of the Civil War far and wide, I have not fallen in with one such phenomenon. Even Archbishop Laud and Peter Heylin meant what they say; through their words you do look direct into the scraggy conviction they have formed: — or if "lying Peter" do lie, he at least *knows* that he is lying! Lord Clarendon, a man of sufficient unveracity of heart, to whom indeed whatsoever has direct veracity of heart is more or less horrible, speaks always in official language; a clothed, nay sometimes even *quilted* dialect, yet always with some considerable body in the heart

of it, never with none! The use of the human tongue was
then other than it now is. I counsel the reader to leave all
that of Cant, Dupery, Machiavelism, and so forth, decisively lying at the threshold. He will be wise to believe that
these Puritans do mean what they say, and to try unimpeded
if he can discover what that is. Gradually a very stupendous
phenomenon may rise on his astonished eye. A practical
world based on Belief in God; — such as many centuries had
seen before, but as never any century since has been pri-
vileged to see. It was the last glimpse of it in our world, this
of English Puritanism: very great, very glorious; tragical
enough to all thinking hearts that look on it from these days
of ours.

My second advice is, Not to imagine that it was Con-
stitution, "Liberty of the people to tax themselves," Privilege of Parliament, Triennial or annual Parliaments, or any
modification of these sublime Privileges now waxing somewhat
faint in our admirations, that mainly animated our Cromwells, Pyms, and Hampdens to the heroic efforts we still ad-
mire in retrospect. Not these very measurable "Privileges,"
but a far other and deeper, which could not be measured; of
which these, and all grand social improvements whatsoever,
are the corollary. Our ancient Puritan Reformers were, as
all Reformers that will ever much benefit this Earth are
always, inspired by a Heavenly Purpose. To see God's own
Law, then universally acknowledged for complete as it stood
in the holy Written Book, made good in this world; to see
this, or the true unwearied aim and struggle towards this: it
was a thing worth living for and dying for! Eternal Justice;
that God's Will *be* done on Earth as it is in Heaven: corollaries
enough will flow from that, if that be there; if that be not
there, no corollary good for much will flow. It was the
general spirit of England in the Seventeenth Century. In
other somewhat sadly disfigured form, we have seen the same
immortal hope take practical shape in the French Revolution,
and once more astonish the world. That England should all

become a Church, if you like to name it so: a Church presided over not by sham-priests in "Four surplices at Allhallowtide," but by true god-consecrated ones, whose hearts the Most High had touched and hallowed with his fire: — this was the prayer of many, it was the godlike hope and effort of some.

Our modern methods of Reform differ somewhat, — as indeed the issue testifies. I will advise my reader to forget the modern methods of Reform; not to remember that he has ever heard of a modern individual called by the name of Reformer, if he would understand what the old meaning of the word was. The Cromwells, Pyms, Hampdens, who were understood on the Royalist side to be firebrands of the Devil, have had still worse measure from the Dryasdust Philosophies, and sceptical Histories, of later times. They really did resemble firebrands of the Devil, if you looked at them through spectacles of a certain colour. For fire is always fire. But by no spectacles, only by mere blinders and *wooden-eyed* spectacles, can the flame-girt Heaven's-messenger pass for a poor mouldy Pedant and Constitution-monger, such as this would make him out to be!

On the whole, say not, good reader, as is often done, "It was then all one as now." Good reader, it was considerably different then from now. Men indolently say, "The Ages are all alike; ever "the same sorry elements over again, "in new vesture; the issue of it always a melancholy farce- "tragedy, in one Age as in another!" Wherein lies very obviously a truth; but also in secret a very sad error withal. Sure enough, the highest Life touches always, by large sections of it, on the vulgar and universal: he that expects to see a Hero, or a Heroic Age, step forth into practice in yellow Drury-lane stage-boots, and speak in blank verse for itself, will look long in vain. Sure enough, in the Heroic Century as in the Unheroic, knaves and cowards, and cunning greedy persons were not wanting, — were, if you will, extremely abundant. But the question always remains, Did they lie chained, subordinate in this world's business; coerced by steel-whips, or in whatever other effectual way, and sent whimpering into their due subterranean abodes, to beat hemp and repent; a true never-ending attempt going on to hand-cuff, to silence and suppress them? Or did they walk openly abroad, the envy of a general valet-population, and bear sway; professing, without universal anathema, almost with general assent, that they were the Orthodox Party, that they, even they, were such men as you had right to look for? —

Reader, the Ages differ greatly, even infinitely, from one another. Considerable tracts of Ages there have been, by far the majority indeed, wherein the men, unfortunate mortals, were a set of mimetic creatures rather than men; without heart-insight as to this Universe, and its Heights and its Abysses; without conviction or belief of their own regarding it, at all; — who walked merely by hearsays, traditionary cants, black and white surplices, and inane confusions; — whose whole Existence accordingly was a grimace; nothing *original* in it, nothing genuine or sincere but this only, Their greediness of appetite and their faculty of digestion. Such unhappy Ages, too numerous here below, the Genius of Mankind indignantly seizes, as disgraceful to the Family, and with Rhadamanthine ruthlessness — annihilates; tumbles large masses of them swiftly into Eternal Night. These are the Unheroic Ages; which cannot serve, on the general field of Existence, except as *dust*, as inorganic manure. The memory of such Ages fades away forever out of the minds of all men. Why should any memory of *them* continue? The fashion of them has passed away; and as for genuine substance, they never had any. To no heart of a man any more can these Ages become lovely. What melodious loving heart will search into *their* records, will sing of them, or celebrate them? Even torpid Dryasdust is forced to give over at last, all creatures declining to hear him on that subject; whereupon ensues composure and silence, and Oblivion has her own.

Good reader, if you be wise, search not for the secret of Heroic Ages, which have done great things in this Earth,

among their falsities, their greedy quackeries and *un*heroisms!
It never lies and never will lie there.   Knaves and quacks, —
alas, we know they abounded: but the Age was Heroic even
because it had declared war to the death with these, and
would have neither truce nor treaty with these; and went
forth, flame-crowned, as with bared sword, and called the
Most High to witness that it would not endure these! — — But
now for the Letters of Cromwell themselves.

PART I.

TO THE BEGINNING OF THE CIVIL WAR.
1636—1642.

—

LETTER I.

St. Ives, a small Town of perhaps fifteen hundred souls, stands on the left or Northeastern bank of the River Ouse, in flat grassy country, and is still noted as a Cattle-market in those parts. Its chief historical fame is likely to rest on the following one remaining Letter of Cromwell's, written there on the 11th of January 1635-6.

The little Town, of somewhat dingy aspect, and very quiescent except on market-days, runs from Northwest to Southeast, parallel to the shore of the Ouse, a short furlong in length: it probably, in Cromwell's time, consisted mainly of a *row* of houses fronting the River; the now opposite row, which has its back to the River, and still is shorter than the other, still defective at the upper end, was probably built since. In that case, the locality we hear of as the "Green" of St. Ives would then be the space which is now covered mainly with cattle-pens for market-business, and forms the middle of the *street*. A narrow steep old Bridge, probably the same which Cromwell travelled, leads you over, westward, towards Godmanchester, where you again cross the Ouse, and get into Huntingdon. Eastward out of St. Ives, your route is towards Earith, Ely and the heart of the Fens.

At the upper or Northwestern extremity of the place stands the Church; Cromwell's old fields being at the opposite ex-

6*

tremity. The Church from its Churchyard looks down into the very River, which is fenced from it by a brick wall. The Ouse flows here, you cannot without study tell in which direction, fringed with gross reedy herbage and bushes; and is of the blackness of Acheron, streaked with foul metallic glitterings and plays of colour. For a short space downwards here, the banks of it are fully visible; the western row of houses being somewhat the shorter, as already hinted: instead of houses here, you have a rough wooden balustrade, and the black Acheron of an Ouse River used as a washing-place or watering-place for cattle. The old Church, suitable for such a population, stands yet as it did in Cromwell's time, except perhaps the steeple and pews; the flagstones in the interior are worn deep with the pacing of many generations. The steeple is visible from several miles distance; a sharp high spire, piercing far up from amid the willow-trees. The country hereabouts has all a clammy look, clayey and boggy; the produce of it, whether bushes and trees, or grass and crops, gives you the notion of something lazy, dropsical, gross. — This is St. Ives, a most ancient Cattle-market by the shores of the sable Ouse, on the edge of the Fen-country; where, among other things that happened, Oliver Cromwell passed five years of his existence as a Farmer and Grazier.   Who the primitive *Ives* himself was, remains problematic; Camden says he was "Ivo a Persian;" — surely far out of his road here! From him however, Phantasm as he is (being indeed Nothing, — except an ancient "stone-coffin," with bones, and tatters of "bright cloth" in it, accidentally ploughed up in this spot, and acted on by opaque human wonder, miraculous "dreams," and the "Abbot of Ramsey"),* Church and Village indisputably took rise and name; about the Year 1000 or later; — and have stood ever since; being founded on Cattle-dealing and the firm Earth withal. Ives or Yves, the worthy Frenchman, Bishop of Chartres in the time of our Henry Beauclerk; neither he nor the other French Yves, Patron Saint of Attorneys, have any-

* His Legend (*De Beato Yvone, Episcopo Persâ*), with due details, in *Bollandus, Acta Sanctorum*, Junii, tom. ii. (Venetiis, 1742), pp. 288-92.

thing to do with this locality; but miraculous "Ivo the Persian Bishop" and that anonymous stone-coffin alone. —

Oliver, as we observed, has left hardly any memorial of himself at St. Ives. The ground he farmed is still partly capable of being specified, certain records or leases being still in existence. It lies at the lower or Southeast end of the Town; a stagnant flat tract of land, extending between the houses or rather kitchen-gardens of St. Ives in that quarter, and the banks of the River, which, very tortuous always, has made a new bend here. If well drained, this land looks as if it would produce abundant grass, but naturally it must be little other than a bog. Tall bushy ranges of willow-trees and the like, at present, divide it into fields; the River, not visible till you are close on it, bounding them all to the South. At the top of the fields next to the Town is an ancient massive Barn, still used as such; the people call it "Cromwell's Barn:" — and nobody can prove that it was not his! It was evidently some ancient man's or series of ancient men's.

Quitting St. Ives Fen-ward or Eastward, the last house of all, which stands on your right hand among gardens, seemingly the best house in the place, and called Slepe Hall, is confidently pointed out as "Oliver's House." It is indisputably Slepe-Hall House, and Oliver's Farm was rented from the estate of Slepe Hall. It is at present used for a Boarding-school: the worthy inhabitants believe it to be Oliver's; and even point out his "Chapel" or secret Puritan Sermon-room in the lower story of the house: no Sermon-room, as you may well discern, but to appearance some sort of scullery or wash-house or bake-house. 'It was here he used to preach,' say they. Courtesy forbids you to answer, 'Never!' But in fact there is no likelihood that this was Oliver's House at all: in its present state it does not seem to be a century old; * and originally, as is like, it must have served as residence to the Proprietors of Slepe-Hall estate, not to the Farmer of a part thereof. Tradition makes a sad blur of Oliver's memory in his native country! We know, and shall know, only this, for

* Noble, i. 102, 106.

certain here, That Oliver farmed part or whole of these Slepe-Hall Lands, over which the human feet can still walk with assurance; past which the River Ouse still slumberously rolls, towards Earith Bulwark and the Fen-country. Here of a certainty Oliver did walk and look about him habitually, during those five years from 1631 to 1636; a man studious of many temporal and many eternal things. His cattle grazed here, his ploughs tilled here, the heavenly skies and infernal abysses overarched and underarched him here.

In fact there is, as it were, nothing whatever that still decisively to every eye attests his existence at St. Ives, except the following old Letter, accidentally preserved among the Harley Manuscripts in the British Museum. Noble, writing in 1787, says the old branding-irons, "O. C.," for marking sheep, were still used by some Farmer there; but these also, many years ago, are gone. In the Parish-records of St. Ives, Oliver appears twice among some other ten or twelve respectable rate-payers; appointing, in 1633 and 1634, for "St. Ives cum Slepa" fit annual overseers for the "Highway and Green:" — one of the Oliver Signatures is now cut out. Fifty years ago, a vague old Parish-clerk had heard from very vague old persons, that Mr. Cromwell had been seen attending divine service in the Church with "a piece of red flannel round his neck, being subject to inflammation."* Certain letters "written in a very kind style from Oliver Lord Protector to persons in St. Ives," do not now exist; probably never did. Swords "bearing the initials of O. C.," swords sent down in the beginning of 1642, when War was now imminent, and weapons were yet scarce, — do any such still exist? Noble says they were numerous in 1787; but nobody is bound to believe him. Walker** testifies that the Vicar of St. Ives, Rev. Henry Downhall, was ejected with his curate in 1642; an act which Cromwell could have hindered, had he been willing to testify that they were fit clergymen. Alas, had he been able! He attended them in red

---

* See Noble: his confused gleanings and speculations concerning St Ives are to be found, i. 105-6, and again, i. 259-61.
   ** Sufferings of the Clergy. See also Appendix, No. 1.

flannel, but had not exceedingly rejoiced in them, it would seem. — There is, in short, nothing that renders Cromwell's existence completely visible to us, even through the smallest chink, but this Letter alone, which, copied from the Museum Manuscripts, worthy Mr. Harris* has printed for all people. We slightly rectify the spelling, and reprint.

To my very loving friend Mr. Storie, at the Sign of the Dog in the Royal Exchange, London: Deliver these.

MR. STORIE,　　　　　　　　　St. Ives, 11th January 1635.

Amongst the catalogue of those good works which your fellow-citizens and our countrymen have done, this will not be reckoned for the least, That they have provided for the feeding of souls. Building of hospitals provides for men's bodies; to build material temples is judged a work of piety; but they that procure spiritual food, they that build up spiritual temples, they are the men truly charitable, truly pious. Such a work as this was your erecting the Lecture in our Country; in the which you placed Dr. Wells, a man of goodness and industry, and ability to do good every way; not short of any I know in England: and I am persuaded that, sithence his coming, the Lord hath by him wrought much good among us.

It only remains now that He who first moved you to this, put you forward in the continuance thereof: it was the Lord; and therefore to Him lift we up our hearts that He would perfect it. And surely, Mr. Storie, it were a piteous thing to see a Lecture fall, in the

---

* Life of Cromwell: a blind farrago, published in 1761, "after the manner of Mr. Bayle," — a very bad "manner," more especially when a Harris presides over it! Yet poor Harris's Book, his three Books (ou Cromwell, Charles and James I.) have worth: cartloads of Excerpts, carefully transcribed, — and edited, in the way known to us, "by shoving up the shafts." The increasing interest of the subject brought even these to a second edition in 1814.

hands of so many able and godly men, as I am persuaded the founders of this are; in these times, wherein
we see they are suppressed, with too much haste and
violence, by the enemies of God his Truth.   Far be it
that so much guilt should stick to your hands, who live
in a City so renowned for the clear shining light of the
Gospel.   You know, Mr. Storie, to withdraw the pay
is to let fall the Lecture: for who goeth to warfare at
his own cost?   I beseech you therefore in the bowels
of Jesus Christ, put it forward, and let the good man
have his pay.   The souls of God's children will bless
you for it: and so shall I; and ever rest,

Your loving Friend in the Lord,

OLIVER CROMWELL.

Commend my hearty love to Mr. Busse, Mr. Beadly,
and my other good friends.   I would have written to
Mr. Busse; but I was loath to trouble him with a long
letter, and I feared I should not receive an answer from
him: from you I expect one so soon as conveniently
you may.   *Vale.* §

Such is Oliver's first extant Letter.   The Royal Exchange
has been twice burned since this piece of writing was left at the
Sign of the Dog there.   The Dog Tavern, Dog Landlord, fre-
quenters of the Dog, and all their business and concernment
there, and the hardest stone masonry they had, have vanished
irrecoverable.   Like a dream of the Night; like that transient
Sign or Effigies of the Talbot *Dog*, plastered on wood with oil

§ Harris (London, 1814) p. 12.   This Letter, for which Harris, in 1761,
thanks "the Trustees of the British Museum," is not now discoverable in
that Establishment; "a search of three hours through all the Catalogues,
assisted by one of the Clerks," reports itself to me as fruitless. — — Does
exist safe, nevertheless (Sloane mss. no. 2035, f. 125, a venerable brown
Autograph); and, in the "new Catalogue," will be better indicated.
"Busse" is by no means "Bunse," as some have conjectured. (*Note to
Third Edition*).

pigments, which invited men to liquor and house-room in those days! The personages of Oliver's Letter may well be unknown to us.

Of Mr. Story, strangely enough, we have found one other notice: he is amongst the Trustees, pious and wealthy citizens of London for most part, to whom the sale of Bishops' Lands is, by act of Parliament, committed, with many instructions and conditions, on the 9th of October 1646.* "James Story" is one of these; their chief is Alderman Fowke. From Oliver's expression, "our Country," it may be inferred or guessed that Story was of Huntingdonshire: a man who had gone up to London, and prospered in trade, and addicted himself to Puritanism; — much of him, it is like, will never be known! Of Busse and Beadly (unless Busse be a misprint for Bunse, Alderman Bunce, another of the above "Trustees"), there remains no vestige.

Concerning the "Lecture," however, the reader will recal what was said above, of Lecturers, and of Laud's enmity to them; of the Feoffees who supported Lecturers, and of Laud's final suppression and ruin of those Feoffees in 1633. Mr. Story's name is not mentioned in the List of the specific Feoffees; but it need not be doubted he was a contributor to their fund, and probably a leading man among the subscribers. By the light of this Letter we may dimly gather that they still continued to subscribe, and to forward Lectureships where possible, though now in a less ostentatious manner.

It appears there was a Lecture at Huntingdon: but his Grace of Lambeth, patiently assiduous in hunting down such objects, had managed to get that suppressed in 1633,** or at least to get the King's consent for suppressing it. This in 1633. So that "Mr. Wells" could not, in 1636, as my imbecile friend supposes,*** be "the Lecturer in Huntingdon," wherever else he might lecture. Besides Mr. Wells is not in danger of suppression by Laud, but by want of cash! Where Mr. Wells lectured, no mortal knows, or will ever know. Why not at St.

---

* Scobell's Acts and Ordinances (London, 1658), p. 99.
** Wharton's Laud (Loudon, 1695), p. 527.   *** Noble, 1. 259.

Ives on the market-days? Or he might be a "Running Lecturer," not tied to one locality: that is as likely a guess as any.

Whether the call of this Wells Lectureship and Oliver's Letter got due return from Mr. Story we cannot now say; but judge that the Lectureship, — as Laud's star was rapidly on the ascendant, and Mr. Story and the Feoffees had already lost 1,800*l.* by the work, and had a fine in the Starchamber still hanging over their heads, — did in fact come to the ground, and trouble no Archbishop or Market Cattle-dealer with God's Gospel any more. Mr. Wells, like the others, vanishes from History, or nearly so. In the chaos of the King's Pamphlets one seems to discern dimly that he sailed for New England, and that he returned in better times. Dimly once, in 1641 or 1642, you catch a momentary glimpse of a "Mr. Wells" in such predicament, and hope it was this Wells, — preaching for a friend, "in the afternoon," in a Church in London.*

Reverend Mark Noble says, the above Letter is very curious, and a convincing proof how far gone Oliver was, at that time, in religious enthusiasm.** Yes, my reverend imbecile friend, he is clearly one of those singular Christian enthusiasts, who believe that they have a soul to be saved, even as you do, my reverend imbecile friend, that you have a stomach to be satisfied, — and who likewise, astonishing to say, actually take some trouble about that. Far gone indeed, my reverend imbecile friend!

This then is what we know of Oliver at St. Ives. He wrote the above Letter there. He had sold his Properties in Huntingdon for 1800*l.*; with the whole or with part of which sum he stocked certain Grazing-Lands on the Estate of Slepe Hall and farmed the same for a space of some five years. How he lived at St. Ives: how he saluted men on the streets, read Bibles; sold cattle; and walked, with heavy footfall and many thoughts, through the Market Green or old narrow lanes in St. Ives, by the shore of the black Ouse River, — shall be left to the reader's imagination. There is in this man talent for farming;

* Old Pamphlet: Title mislaid and forgotten. ** Noble, i. 259.

there are thoughts enough, thoughts bounded by the Ouse River, thoughts that go beyond Eternity, — and a great black sea of things that he has never yet been able to *think*.

I count the children he had at this time; and find them six: Four boys and two girls; the eldest a boy of fourteen, the youngest a girl of six; Robert, Oliver, Bridget, Richard, Henry, Elizabeth. Robert and Oliver, I take it, are gone to Felsted School, near Bourchier their Grandfather's in Essex. Sir Thomas Bourchier the worshipful Knight, once of London, lives at Felsted; Sir William Masham, another of the same, lives at Otes, hard by, as we shall see.

Cromwell at the time of writing this Letter was, as he himself might partly think probable, about to quit St. Ives. His mother's brother Sir Thomas Steward, Knight, lay sick at Ely in those very days. Sir Thomas makes his will in this same month of January, leaving Oliver his principal heir; and on the 30th it was all over, and he lay in his last home: "Buried in the Cathedral of Ely, 30 January 1635-6."

Worth noting, and curious to think of, since it is indisputable: On the very day while Oliver Cromwell was writing this Letter at St. Ives, two obscure individuals, "Peter Aldridge and Thomas Lane, Assessors of Shipmoney," over in Buckinghamshire, had assembled a Parish Meeting in the Church of Great Kimble, to assess and rate the Shipmoney of the said Parish: there, in the cold weather, at the foot of the Chiltern Hills, "11 January 1635," the Parish did attend, "John Hampden, Esquire," at the head of them, and by a Return still extant, * refused to pay the same or any portion thereof, — witness the above "Assessors," witness also two "Parish Constables" whom we remit from such unexpected celebrity. John Hampden's share for this Parish is thirty-one shillings and sixpence; for another Parish it is twenty shillings; on which latter sum, not on the former, John Hampden was tried.

* Facsimile Engraving of it, in Lord Nugent's Memorials of Hampden (London, 1832), i. 231.

LETTER II.

OLIVER removed to Ely very soon after writing the fore-going Letter.   There is a "receipt for 10*l.*" signed by him, dated "Ely, 10. June 1636;" * and other evidence that he was then resident there.   He succeeded to his Uncle's Farming of the Tithes; the Leases of these, and new Leases of some other small lands or fields granted him, are still in existence. He continued here till the time of the Long Parliament; and his Family still after that, till some unascertained date, seem-ingly about 1647, ** when it became apparent that the Long Parliament was not like to rise for a great while yet, and it was judged expedient that the whole household should remove to London.   His Mother appears to have joined him in Ely; she quitted Huntingdon, returned to her native place, an aged grandmother, — was not, however, to end her days there.

As Sir Thomas Steward, Oliver'sUncle, farmed the Tithes of Ely, it is reasonable to believe that he, and Oliver after him, occupied the House set apart for the Tithe-Farmer there; as Mark Noble, out of dim Tradition, confidently testifies.   This is "the house occupied by Mr. Page;" *** under which name, much better than under that of Cromwell, the inhabitants of Ely now know it.   The House, though somewhat in a frail state, is still standing; close to St. Mary's Churchyard; at the corner of the great Tithe-barn of Ely, or great Square of tithe-barns and offices, — which "is the biggest barn in England but one," say the Ely people.   Of this House, for Oliver's sake, some Painter will yet perhaps take a correct likeness: — it is needless to go to Stuntney, out on the Soham road, as Oliver's Painters usually do; Oliver never lived there, but only his Mother's cousins! Two years ago this House in Ely stood empty; closed finally up, deserted by all the Pages, as "the

---

* Noble, I. 107.

** See Appendix, No. 7, last Letter there.   (*Note to Third Edition*).

*** Noble, I. 106.

Commutation of Tithes" had rendered it superfluous: this year (1845), I find it is an Alehouse, with still some chance of standing. It is by no means a sumptuous mansion; but may have conveniently held a man of three or four hundred a year, with his family, in those simple times. Some quaint air of gentility still looks through its ragged dilapidation. It is of two stories, more properly of one and a half; has many windows, irregular chimneys and gables. Likely enough Oliver lived here; likely his Grandfather may have lived here, his Mother have been born here. She was now again resident here. The tomb of her first husband and child, *Johannes Lynne* and poor little *Catharina Lynne*, is in the Cathedral hard by. "Such are the changes which fleeting Time procureth."—

The Second extant Letter of Cromwell's is dated Ely, October 1638. * It will be good to introduce, as briefly as possible, a few Historical Dates, to remind the reader what o'clock on the Great Horologe it is, while this small Letter is a-writing. Last year in London there had been a very strange spectacle; and in three weeks after, another in Edinburgh, of still more significance in English History.

On the 30th of June 1637, in Old Palaceyard, three men, gentlemen of education, of good quality, a Barrister, a Physician and a Parish Clergyman of London were set on three Pillories; stood openly, as the scum of malefactors, for certain hours there; and then had their ears cut off, — bare knives, hot branding-irons, — and their cheeks stamped "S. L.," Seditious Libeller; in the sight of a great crowd, "silent" mainly, and looking "pale." ** The men were our old friend William Prynne, — poor Prynne, who had got into new trouble, and here lost his ears a *second* and final time, having had them "sewed on again" before: William Prynne, Barrister; Dr. John Bastwick; and the Rev. Henry Burton, Minister of Fridaystreet Church. Their sin was against Laud and his surplices at Allhallowtide, not against any other man

---

* In Appendix, No. 2, another Note of his. (*Third Edition*).
** State Trials (Cobbett's, London, 1809), iii. 746.

or thing. Prynne, speaking to the people, defied all Lambeth, with Rome at the back of it, to argue with him, William Prynne alone, that these practices were according to the Law of England; "and if I fail to prove it," said Prynne, "let them hang my body at the door of that Prison there," the Gate-house Prison. "Whereat the people gave a great shout," — somewhat of an ominous one, I think. Bastwick's wife, on the scaffold, received his ears in her lap, and kissed him. * Prynne's ears the executioner "rather sawed than cut." "Cut me, tear me," cried Prynne; "I fear thee not; I fear the fire of Hell, not thee!" The June sun had shone hot on their faces. Burton, who had discoursed eloquent religion all the while, said, when they carried him, near fainting, into a house in King-street, "It is too hot to last."

Too hot indeed.   For at Edinburgh, on Sunday the 23d of July following, Archbishop Laud having now, with great effort and much manipulation, got his Scotch Liturgy and Scotch Pretended-Bishops ready,** brought them fairly out to action, — and Jenny Geddes hurled her stool at their head. "Let us read the Collect of the Day," said the Pretended-Bishop from amid his tippets; — "De'il *colic* the wame of thee!" answered Jenny, hurling her stool at his head. "Thou foul thief, wilt thou say *mass* at my lug?"*** I thought we had

* Towers's British Biography.
** Rushworth, ii. 321, 349; iii. Appendix, 153-5; &c.
*** — — "No sooner was the Book opened by the Dean of Edinburgh, "but a number of the meaner sort, with clapping of their hands and "outcries, made a great uproar; and one of them, called *Jane* or *Janot* "*Gaddis* (yet living at the writing of this relation), flung a little folding-"stool, whereon she sat, at the Dean's head, saying, 'Out thou false thief! "dost thou say the mass at my lug?' Which was followed with so great a "noise," &c.   These words are in the Continuation of *Baker's Chronicle,* by Phillips (Milton's Nephew); fifth edition of *Baker* (London, 1670), p. 478. They are *not* in the fourth edition of *Baker,* 1665, which is the first that contains the Continuation; they follow as here in all the others.   Thought to be the first grave mention of Jenny Geddes in Printed History; a heroine still familiar to Tradition everywhere in Scotland.

In a foolish Pamphlet, printed in 1661, entitled *Edinburgh's Joy,* &c , — Joy for the Blessed Restoration and *Annus Mirabilis,* — there is mention made of "the immortal Jenet Geddis," whom the writer represents as re-joicing exceedingly in that miraculous event; she seems to be a well-known person, keeping "a cabbage-stall at the Tron Kirk," at that date. Burns, in his Highland Tour, named his mare *Jenny Geddes.* Helen of

got done with the mass some time ago; — and here it is again!
"A Pape, a Pape!" cried others: "Stane him!" * — In
fact the service could not go on at all. This in St. Giles's
Kirk, Edinburgh, on Sunday 23d July 1637. Scotland had
endured much in the bishop way for above thirty years by-
gone, and endeavoured to say nothing, bitterly feeling a great
deal. But now, on small signal, the hour was come. All
Edinburgh, all Scotland, and behind that all England and
Ireland, rose into unappeasable commotion on the flight of
this stool of Jenny's; and his Grace of Canterbury, and King
Charles himself, and many others had lost their heads before
there could be peace again. The Scotch People had sworn
their Covenant, not without "tears;" and were in these very
days of October 1638, while Oliver is writing at Ely, busy with
their whole might electing their General Assembly, to meet at
Glasgow next month. I think the *Tulchan* Apparatus is likely
to be somewhat sharply dealt with, the Cow having become
awake to it! Great events are in the wind; out of Scotland
vague news, of unappeasable commotion risen there.

In the end of that same year, too, there had risen all over
England huge rumour concerning the Shipmoney Trial at
London. On the 6th of November 1637, this important Process of Mr. Hampden's began. Learned Mr. St. John, a dark
tough man, of the toughness of leather, spake with irre-
fragable law-eloquence, law-logic, for three days running,
on Mr. Hampden's side; and learned Mr. Holborn for three
other days; — preserved yet by Rushworth in acres of typography, unreadable now to all mortals. Four other learned
gentlemen, tough as leather, spoke on the opposite side;
and learned judges animadverted; — at endless length, amid
the expectancy of men. With brief pauses, the Trial lasted
for three weeks and three days. Mr. Hampden became the

Troy, for practical importance in Human History, is but a small Heroine
to Jenny: — but she has been luckier in the recording! — For these
bibliographical notices I am indebted to the friendliness of Mr. David Laing
of the Signet Library, Edinburgh.
 * Rushworth, Kennet, Balfour.

most famous man in England,* — by accident partly.   The
sentence was not delivered till April 1638; and then it went
against Mr. Hampden: judgment in Exchequer ran to this
effect, "*Consideratum est per eosdem Barones quod prædictus
"Johannes Hampden de iisdem viginti solidis oneretur*," He must
pay the Twenty shillings, "*et inde satisfaciat.*" **   No hope
in Law-Courts, then; Petition of Right and *Tallagio non concedendo* have become an old song.   If there be not hope in
Jenny Geddes's stool and "De'il colic the wame of thee," we
are in a bad way! —

During which great public Transactions, there had been
in Cromwell's own Fen-country a work of immense local celebrity going on: the actual Drainage of the Fens, so long
talked about; the construction, namely, of the great *Bedford
Level*, to carry the Ouse River direct into the sea; holding it
forcibly aloft in strong embankments, for twenty straight
miles or so; not leaving it to meander and stagnate, and in
the wet season drown the country, as heretofore.   This grand
work began, Dryasdust in his bewildered manner knows not
when; but it "went on rapidly," and had ended in 1637.***
Or rather had *appeared*, and strongly *endeavoured*, to end in
1637; but was not yet by any means settled and ended; the
whole Fen-region clamouring that it could not, and should not,
end so.   In which wide clamour, against injustice done in
high places, Oliver Cromwell, as is well known, though
otherwise a most private quiet man, saw good to interfere; to
give the universal inarticulate clamour a voice, and gain a remedy for it.   He approved himself, as Sir Philip Warwick
will testify,† "a man that would set well at the mark," that
took sure aim, and had a stroke of some weight in him.   We
cannot here afford room to disentangle that affair from the
dark rubbish-abysses, old and new, in which it lies deep
buried: suffice it to assure the reader that Oliver did by no
means "oppose" the Draining of the Fens, but was and had

* Clarendon.   ** Rushworth, iii. Appendix, 159-216; ib. ii. 480.
*** Dugdale's Hist. of Embankments; Cole's, Wells's, &c. &c. History
of the Fens.
    † Warwick's Memoirs (London, 1701), p. 250.

been, as his Father before him, highly favourable to it; that
he opposed the King in Council wishing to do a public injustice in regard to the Draining of the Fens; and by a "great
meeting at Huntingdon," and other good measures, contrived
to put a stop to the same. At a time when, as Old Palaceyard
might testify, that operation of going in the teeth of the royal
will was somewhat more perilous than it would be now! This
was in 1638, according to the good testimony of Warwick.*
Cromwell acquired by it a great popularity in the Fen-country,
acquired the name or nickname "Lord of the Fens;" and what
was much more valuable, had done the duty of a good citizen,
whatever he might acquire by it. The disastrous public Events
which soon followed put a stop to all farther operations in the
Fens, for a good many years.

These clamours of local grievance near at hand, these
rumours of universal grievance from the distance,—they were
part of the Day's noises, they were sounding in Cromwell's
mind, along with many others now silent, while the following
Letter went off towards "Sir William Masham's House called
Otes in Essex," in the year 1638. — Of Otes and the Mashams
in Essex, there must likewise, in spite of our strait limits, be
a word said. The Mashams were distant Cousins of Oliver's;
this Sir William Masham, or Massam as he is often written,
proved a conspicuous busy man in the Politics of his time; on
the Puritan side; — rose into Oliver's Council of State at last.
The Mashams became Lords Masham in the next generation,
and so continued for a while; one Lady Masham was a
daughter of Philosopher Cudworth, and is still remembered as
the friend of John Locke, whom she tended in his old days;
who lies buried, as his monument still shows, at the Church of
High Laver, in the neighbourhood of which Otes Mansion
stood. High Laver, Essex, not far from Harlow Station on
the Northeastern Railway. The Mashams are all extinct, and
their Mansion is swept away as if it had not been. "Some
"forty years ago," says my kind informant, "a wealthy

* Warwick's Memoirs: poor Noble blunders, as he is apt to do.

"Maltster of Bishop's Stortford became the proprietor by pur-
"chase; and pulled the Manorhouse down; leaving the out-
"houses as cottages to some poor people." The name Otes,
the tomb of Locke, and this undestroyed and now inde-
structible fraction of Ragpaper alone preserve the memory of
Mashamdom in this world. We modernise the spelling; let
the reader, for it may be worth his while, endeavour to
modernise the sentiment and subject matter.

There is only this farther to be premised, That St. John,
the celebrated Shipmoney Barrister, has married for his
second wife a Cousin of Oliver Cromwell's, a Daughter of
Uncle Henry's, whom we knew at Upwood long ago;* which
Cousin, and perhaps her learned husband reposing from his
arduous law-duties along with her, is now on a Summer or
Autumn visit at Otes, and has lately seen Oliver there.

*To my beloved Cousin Mrs. St. John, at Sir William Masham his
House called Otes, in Essex: Present these.*

DEAR COUSIN,   Ely, 13th October 1638.
I thankfully acknowledge your love in your kind
remembrance of me upon this opportunity. Alas, you
do too highly prize my lines, and my company. I may be
ashamed to own your expressions, considering how unprofitable I am, and the mean improvement of my talent.

Yet to honour my God by declaring what He hath
done for my soul, in this I am confident, and I will
be so. Truly, then, this I find: That He giveth springs
in a dry barren wilderness where no water is. I live,
you know where, — in Meshec, which they say signifies *Prolonging*; in Kedar, which signifies *Blackness*:
yet the Lord forsaketh me not. Though He do prolong,
yet He will I trust bring me to His tabernacle, to His
resting-place. My soul is with the Congregation of the
Firstborn, my body rests in hope; and if here I may

* Antea, p. 20.

honour my God either by doing or by suffering, I shall be most glad.

Truly no poor creature hath more cause to put himself forth in the cause of his God than I. I have had plentiful wages beforehand; and I am sure I shall never earn the least mite. The Lord accept me in His Son, and give me to walk in the light, — and give us to walk in the light, as He is the light! He it is that enlighteneth our blackness, our darkness. I dare not say, He hideth His face from me. He giveth me to see light in His light. One beam in a dark place hath exceeding much refreshment in it: — blessed be His Name for shining upon so dark a heart as mine! You know what my manner of life hath been. Oh, I lived in and loved darkness, and hated light; I was a chief, the chief of sinners. This is true: I hated godliness, yet God had mercy on me. O the riches of His mercy! Praise Him for me; — pray for me, that He who hath begun a good work would perfect it in the day of Christ.

Salute all my friends in that Family whereof you are yet a member. I am much bound unto them for their love. I bless the Lord for them; and that my Son, by their procurement, is so well. Let him have your prayers, your counsel; let me have them.

Salute your Husband and Sister from me: — He is not a man of his word! He promised to write about Mr. Wrath of Epping; but as yet I receive no letters: — put him in mind to do what with conveniency may be done for the poor Cousin I did solicit him about.

Once more farewell. The Lord be with you: so prayeth
Your truly loving Cousin,
OLIVER CROMWELL. §

§ Thurloe's State Papers (London, 1742), i. 1.

7*

There are two or perhaps three sons of Cromwell's at Felsted School by this time, a likely enough guess is, that he might have been taking Dick over to Felsted on that occasion when he came round by Otes, and gave such comfort by his speech to the pious Mashams, and to the young Cousin, now on a summer visit at Otes.   What glimpses of long-gone summers; of long-gone human beings in fringed trouser-breeches, in starched ruff, in hood and fardingale; — alive, they, within their antiquarian costumes, living men and women; instructive, very interesting to one another! Mrs. St. John came down to breakfast every morning in that summer visit of the year 1638, and Sir William said grave grace, and they spake polite devout things to one another; and they are vanished, they and their things and speeches, — all silent, like the echoes of the old nightingales that sang that season, like the blossoms of the old roses. O Death, O Time! —

For the soul's furniture of these brave people is grown not less unintelligible, antiquarian, than their spanish boots and lappet caps.   Reverend Mark Noble, my reverend imbecile friend, discovers in this Letter evidence that Oliver was once a very dissolute man; that Carrion Heath spake truth in that *Flagellum* Balderdash of his.   O my reverend imbecile friend, hadst thou thyself never any moral life, but only a sensitive and digestive? Thy soul never longed towards the serene heights, all hidden from thee; and thirsted as the hart in dry places wherein no waters be? It was never a sorrow for thee that the eternal pole-star had gone out, veiled itself in dark clouds; — a sorrow only that this or the other noble Patron forgot thee when a living fell vacant? I have known Christians, Moslems, Methodists, — and, alas, also reverend irreverent Apes by the Dead Sea!

O modern reader, dark as this Letter may seem, I will advise thee to make an attempt towards understanding it. There is in it a "tradition of humanity" worth all the rest. Indisputable certificate that man once had a soul; that man once walked with God, — his little Life a sacred island girdled with Eternities and God-hoods.   Was it not a time for heroes?

Heroes were then possible. I say, thou shalt understand that Letter; thou also, looking out into a too brutish world, wilt then exclaim with Oliver Cromwell, — with Hebrew David, as old Mr. Rouse of Truro, and the Presbyterian populations, still sing him in the Northern Kirks:

> Woe's me that I in Meshec am
> A sojourner so long,
> Or that I in the tents do dwell
> To Kedar that belong!

Yes, there is a tone in the soul of this Oliver that holds of the Perennial. With a noble sorrow, with a noble patience, he longs towards the mark of the prize of the high calling. He, I think, has chosen the better part. The world and its wild tumults, — if they will but let him alone! Yet he too will venture, will do and suffer for God's cause, if the call come. What man with better reason? He hath had plentiful wages beforehand; snatched out of darkness into marvellous light: he will never earn the least mite. Annihilation of self; *Selbsttödtung*, as Novalis calls it; casting yourself at the footstool of God's throne, "To live or to die forever; as Thou wilt, not as I will." Brother, hadst thou never, in any form, such moments in thy history? Thou knowest them not, even by credible rumour? Well, thy earthly path was peaceabler, I suppose. But the Highest was never in thee, the Highest will never come out of thee. Thou shalt at best abide by the stuff; as cherished housedog, guard the stuff, —perhaps with enormous gold-collars and provender: but the battle, and the hero death, and victory's fire-chariot carrying men to the Immortals, shall never be thine. I pity thee: brag not, or I shall have to despise thee.

TWO YEARS.

Such is Oliver's one Letter from Ely. To guide us a little through the void gulf towards his next Letter, we will here intercalate the following small fractions of Chronology.

1639.

May — July. The Scots at their Glasgow Assembly * had
rent their *Tulchan* Apparatus in so rough a way, and otherwise so ill comported themselves, his Majesty saw good, in the
beginning of this year, immense negotiation and messaging to
and fro having proved so futile, to chastise them with an
Army. By unheard-of exertions in the Extra-Parliamentary
way, his Majesty got an Army ready; marched with it to Berwick, — is at Newcastle, 8th May 1639.** But, alas, the
Scots, with a much better Army, already lay encamped on
Dunse Law; every nobleman with his tenants there, as a
drilled regiment, round him; old Fieldmarshal Lesley for their
generalissimo; at every Colonel's tent this pennon flying, *For
Christ's Crown and Covenant:* there was no fighting to be
thought of.*** Neither could the Pacification there patched
up be of long continuance. The Scots disbanded their soldiers; but kept the officers, mostly Gustavus-Adolphus men,
still within sight.

1640.

The Scotch Pacification, hastily patched up at Dunse Hill,
did not last; discrepancies arose as to the practical meaning
of this and the other clause in it. Discrepancies which the
farther they were handled, embroiled themselves the more.
His Majesty having burnt Scotch paper Declarations "by the
hands of the common hangman," and almost cut off the poor
Scotch Chancellor Loudon's head, and being again resolute
to chastise the rebel Scots with an Army, decides on sum-
moning a Parliament for that end, there being no money
attainable otherwise. To the great and glad astonishment
of England; which, at one time, thought never to have seen
another Parliament! Oliver Cromwell sat in this Parliament
for Cambridge;† recommended by Hampden, say some; not
needing any recommendation in those Fen-countries, think

---

* Nov. 1638; Baillie's Letters (Edinburgh, 1841), i. 118-176.
** Rushworth, iii. 930.
*** Ib. iii. 926-49; Baillie, i. 184-221; King's Army "dismissed" (*after*
Pacification), 24th June (Rushworth, iii. 946).
† Browne Willis, pp. 229, 30; Rushworth, iii. 1105.

others.   Oliver's Colleague was a Thomas Meautys, Esquire.
This Parliament met, 13th April 1640: it was by no means
prompt enough with supplies against the rebel Scots; the King
dismissed it in a huff, 5th May; after a Session of three weeks:
Historians call it the *Short Parliament.*   His Majesty decides
on raising money and an Army "by other methods;" to which
end, Wentworth, now Earl Strafford and Lord Lieutenant of
Ireland, who had advised that course in the Council, did himself subscribe 20,000*l.*   Archbishop Laud had long ago seen
"a cloud rising" against the Four surplices at Allhallowtide;
and now it is covering the whole sky, in a most dismal and
really thundery-looking manner.

His Majesty by "other methods," commission of array,
benevolence, forced-loan, or how he could, got a kind of Army
on foot,* and set it marching out of the several Counties in
the South towards the Scotch Border: but it was a most hope-
less Army.   The soldiers called the affair a *Bishops' War;*
they mutinied against their officers, shot some of their officers:
in various Towns on their march, if the Clergyman were re-
puted Puritan, they went and gave him three cheers; if of
Surplice tendency, they sometimes threw his furniture out of
window.**   No fighting against poor Scotch Gospellers was
to be hoped for from these men. — Meanwhile the Scots, not
to be behindhand, had raised a good Army of their own; and
decided on going *into* England with it, this time, "to present
their grievances to the King's Majesty."   On the 20th of
August 1640, they cross the Tweed at Coldstream; Montrose
wading in the van of them all.   They wore uniform of hodden
gray, with blue caps; and each man had a moderate haversack
of oatmeal on his back.***

August 28*th.*   The Scots force their way across the Tyne,
at Newburn, some miles above Newcastle; the King's Army
making small fight, most of them no fight; hurrying from
Newcastle, and all town and country quarters, towards York

* Rushworth, iii. 1241.
** Vicars's Parliamentary Chronicle (Lond. 1644), p. 20.
*** Old Pamphlets.

again, where his Majesty and Strafford were. * The *Bishops' War* was at an end. The Scots, striving to be gentle as doves in their behaviour, and publishing boundless brotherly Declarations to all the brethren that loved Christ's Gospel and God's Justice in England, — took possession of Newcastle next day; took possession gradually of all Northumberland and Durham, — and stayed there, in various towns and villages, about a year. The whole body of English Puritans looked upon them as their saviours: some months afterwards, Robert Baillie heard the London ballad-singers, on the streets, singing copiously with strong lungs, "Gramercy, good Master Scot," by way of burden.**

His Majesty and Strafford, in a fine frenzy at this turn of affairs, found no refuge, except to summon a "Council of Peers," to enter upon a "Treaty" with the Scots; and alas, at last, summon a New Parliament. Not to be helped in any way. Twelve chief Peers of the summoned "Council" petitioned for a Parliament; the City of London petitioned for a Parliament, and would not lend money otherwise. A Parliament was appointed for the 3d of November next; — whereupon London cheerfully lent 200,000*l.*; and the treaty with the Scots at Ripon, 1st October 1640,*** by and by transferred to London, went peaceably on at a very leisurely pace. The Scotch Army lay quartered at Newcastle, and over Northumberland and Durham, on an allowance of 850*l.* a-day; an Army indispensable for Puritan objects; no haste in finishing its Treaty. The English Army lay across in Yorkshire; without allowance except from the casualties of the King's Exchequer; in a dissatisfied manner, and occasionally getting into "Army-Plots."

This Parliament, which met on the 3d of November 1640, has become very celebrated in History by the name of the *Long Parliament.* It accomplished and suffered very singular destinies; suffered a Pride's Purge, a Cromwell's Ejectment; suffered Re-instatements, Re-ejectments; and the *Rump* or

---

* Rushworth, iii. 1286, &c.   ** Baillie's Letters.
*** Rushworth, iii. 1282.

Fag-end of it did not finally vanish till 16th March 1659-60.
Oliver Cromwell sat again in this Parliament for Cambridge
Town; Meautys, his old Colleague, is now changed for "John
Lowry, Esquire,"* probably a more Puritanic man. The
Members for Cambridge University are the same in both Par-
liaments.

LETTER III.

*To my loving friend Mr. Willingham, at his House in Swithin's
Lane: These.*

SIR,　　　　　　　　　　　　　　'London, February 1640,'**

I desire you to send me the Reasons of the Scots
to enforce their desire of Uniformity in Religion, expressed in their 8th Article; I mean that which I had
before of you. I would peruse it against we fall upon
that Debate, which will be speedily. Yours,

OLIVER CROMWELL.§

There is a great quantity of intricate investigation requisite to date this small undated Note, and make it entirely
transparent! The Scotch Treaty, begun at Ripon, is going
on, — never ended: the agitation about abolishing Bishops
has just begun, in the House and out of it.

On Friday, 11th December 1640, the Londoners present
their celebrated "Petition," signed by 15,000 hands, craving
to have Bishops and their Ceremonies radically reformed.
Then on Saturday, 23d January 1640-1, comes the still more
celebrated "Petition and Remonstrance from 700 Ministers of
the Church of England,"*** to the like effect. Upon which
Documents, especially upon the latter, ensue strenuous de-

* Willis; Rushworth, iv. 3. See Cooper's *Annals of Cambridge* (London, 1845), iii. 303, 4.

** The words within single commas, here as always in the Text of
Cromwell's Letters, are mine, not his; the date in this instance is con-
jectural or inferential.

§ Harris, p. 517; Sloane mss. no. 2035, f. 126.

*** Commons Journals, ii. 72.

batings,* ensues a "Committee of Twenty-four;" a Bill to abolish Superstition and Idolatry; and, in a week or two, a Bill to take away the Bishops' Votes in Parliament: Bills recommended by the said Committee.   A diligent Committee; which heard much evidence, and theological debating, from Dr. Burgess and others.   Their Bishops Bill, not without hot arguing, passed through the Commons; was rejected by the Lords; — took effect, however, in a much heavier shape, within year and day.   Young Sir Ralph Varney, son of Edmund the Standard-bearer, has preserved very careful Notes of the theological revelations and profound arguments, heard in this Committee from Dr. Burgess and others; intensely interesting at that time to all ingenuous young gentlemen; a mere torpor now to all persons.

In fact, the whole world, as we perceive, in this Spring of 1641, is getting on fire with episcopal, anti-episcopal emotion; and the Scotch Commissioners, with their Desire of Uniformity, are naturally the centre of the latter.   Bishop Hall, Smectymnuus, and one Mr. Milton "near St. Bride's Church," are all getting their Pamphlets ready. — The assiduous contemporary individual who collected the huge stock of loose Printing now known as *King's Pamphlets* in the British Museum, usually writes the date on the title-page of each; but has, with a curious infelicity, omitted it in the case of Milton's Pamphlets, which accordingly remain undateable except approximately.

The exact copy of the Scotch Demands towards a Treaty I have not yet met with, though doubtless it is in print amid the unsorted Rubbish-Mountains of the British Museum. Notices of it are to be seen in Baillie, also in Rushworth.** The first Seven Articles relate to secularities; payment of damages; punishment of incendiaries, and so forth: the Seventh is the "recalling" of the King's Proclamations against the Scots.   The Eighth, "anent a solid peace betwixt the Nations," involves this matter of Uniformity in Religion,

---

* Commons Journals, ii. 81; 8th and 9th of February. See Baillie's Letters, i. 302; and Rushworth, iv. 93 and 174.

** Baillie, i. 297, and *antea* and *postea;* Rushworth, iv. 166.

and therefore is of weightier moment.   Baillie says: "For the
Eighth great Demand some days were spent in preparation."
The Lords would have made no difficulty about dismantling
Berwick and Carlisle, or such like; but finding that the other
points of this Eighth Article were to involve the *permanent*
relations of England, they delayed.   "We expect it this very
day," says Baillie (28th February 1640-1).   Oliver Cromwell
also expects it this very day, or "speedily," — and therefore
writes to Mr. Willingham for a sight of the Documents again.

Whoever wishes to trace the emergence, re-emergence,
slow ambiguous progress, and dim issue of this "Eighth
Article," may consult the opaque but authentic Commons
Journals, and strive to elucidate the same by poor old brown
Pamphlets, in the places cited below.*   It was not finally
voted in the affirmative till the middle of May; and then still
it was far from being ended.   It *ended*, properly, in the Sum-
moning of a "Westminster Assembly of Divines," To ascertain
for us *how* " the two Nations" may best attain to "Uniformity
of Religion."

This "Mr. Willingham my loving friend," of whom I have
found no other vestige anywhere in Nature, is presumably a
London Puritan concerned in the London Petition and other
such matters, to whom the Member for Cambridge, a man of
known zeal, good connexion, and growing weight, is worth
convincing.

Oliver St. John the Shipmoney Lawyer, now Member for
Totness, has lately been made Solicitor-General; on the 2d of
February 1640-1, D'Ewes says of him, "newly created;"** a
date worth attending to.   Strafford's Trial is coming on; to
begin on the 22d of March: Strafford and Laud are safe in the
Tower long since; Finch and Windebank, and other Delinquents in high places, have fled rapidly beyond seas.

* Commons Journals, ii. 84, 85; *Diurnal Occurrences in Parliament*
(Printed for William Cooke, London, 1641, — often erroneous as to the
day), 10th February, 7th March, 15th May.
** Sir Simond D'Ewes's Notes of the Long Parliament (*Harleian Mss.,*
nos. 162-6), fol. 189 a; p. 156 of Transcript *penes me.*

IN THE LONG PARLIAMENT.

That little Note, despatched by a servant to Swithin's Lane in the Spring of 1641, and still saved by capricious destiny while so much else has been destroyed, — is all of Autographic that Oliver Cromwell has left us concerning his proceedings in the first three-and-twenty months of the Long Parliament. Months distinguished, beyond most others in History, by anxieties and endeavours, by hope and fear and swift vicissitude, to all England as well as him: distinguished on his part by much Parliamentary activity withal; of which, unknown hitherto in History, but still capable of being known, let us wait some other opportunity of speaking. Two vague appearances of his in that scene, which are already known to most readers, we will set in their right date and place, making them faintly visible at last; and therewith leave this part of the subject.

In D'Ewes's Manuscript above cited* are these words, relating to *Monday, 9th November* 1640, the sixth day of the Long Parliament: "Mr. Cromwell delivered the Petition of John Lilburn,"—young Lilburn, who had once been Prynne's amanuensis, among other things, and whose "whipping with 200 stripes from Westminster to the Fleet Prison," had already rendered him conspicuous. This is the record of D'Ewes. To which let us now annex the following well-known passage of Sir Philip Warwick; and if the reader fancy the Speeches on the previous Saturday,** and how the "whole of this Monday was spent in hearing grievances," of the like sort, some dim image of a strange old scene may perhaps rise upon him.

"The first time I ever took notice of Mr. Cromwell," says Warwick, "was in the very beginning of the Parliament held "in November 1640; when I," Member for Radnor, "vainly "thought myself a courtly young gentleman, — for we cour-"tiers valued ourselves much upon our good clothes! I came

* D'Ewes, fol. 4.
** Commons Journals, 7th Nov. 1640; Rushworth, iv. 24, &c.

"into the House one morning," Monday morning, "well clad;
"and perceived a gentleman speaking, whom I knew not, —
"very ordinarily apparelled; for it was a plain cloth suit,
"which seemed to have been made by an ill country-tailor;
"his linen was plain, and not very clean; and I remember a
"speck or two of blood upon his little band, which was not
"much larger than his collar. His hat was without a hatband.
"His stature was of a good size; his sword stuck close to his
"side: his countenance swoln and reddish, his voice sharp and
"untuneable, and his eloquence full of fervour.   For the sub-
"ject matter would not bear much of *reason;* it being on behalf
"of a servant of Mr. Prynne's who had dispersed Libels;" —
yes, *Libels,* and had come to Palaceyard for it, as we saw: "I
"sincerely profess, it lessened much my reverence unto that
"Great Council, for this gentleman was very much hearkened
"unto;"* which was strange, seeing he had no gold lace to
his coat, nor frills to his band; and otherwise, to me in my poor
featherhead, seemed a somewhat unhandy gentleman!

The reader may take what of these Warwick traits he can
along with him, and also omit what he cannot take; for though
Warwick's veracity is undoubted, his memory after many
years, in such an element as his had been, may be questioned.
The "band," we may remind our readers, is a linen tippet,
properly the shirt-collar of those days, which, when the hair
was worn long, needed to fold itself with a good expanse of
washable linen over the upperworks of the coat, and defend
these and their velvets from harm.   The "specks of blood," if
not fabulous, we, not without general sympathy, attribute to
bad razors: as for the "hatband," one remarks that men did
not speak with their hats *on;* and therefore will, with Sir
Philip's leave, *omit* that.   The "untuneable voice," or what a
poor young gentleman in these circumstances would consider
as such, is very significant to us.

Here is the other vague appearance; from Clarendon's
Life.**   "He," Mr. Hyde, afterwards Lord Clarendon, "was
"often heard to mention one private Committee, in which he

* Warwick, p. 247.   ** 1. 78 (Oxford, 1761).

"was put accidentally into the chair; upon an Enclosure
"which had been made of great wastes, belonging to the
"Queen's Manors, without the consent of the tenants, the
"benefit whereof had been given by the Queen to a servant of
"near trust, who forthwith sold the lands enclosed to the Earl
"of Manchester, Lord Privy Seal; who together with his Son
"Mandevil were now most concerned to maintain the En-
"closure; against which, as well the inhabitants of other
"manors, who claimed Common in those wastes, as the Queen's
"tenants of the same, made loud complaints, as a great oppres-
"sion, carried upon them with a very high hand, and sup-
"ported by power.

"'The Committee sat in the Queen's Court; and Oliver
"Cromwell being one of them, appeared much concerned to
"countenance the Petitioners, who were numerous together
"with their Witnesses; the Lord Mandevil being likewise
"present as a party, and by the direction of the Committee
"sitting covered. Cromwell, who had never before been heard
"to speak in the House of Commons," — at least not by *me*,
though he had often spoken, and was very well known there,
— "ordered the Witnesses and Petitioners in the method of
"the proceeding; and seconded, and enlarged upon what they
"said, with great passion; and the Witnesses and persons
"concerned, who were a very rude kind of people, interrupted
"the Counsel and Witnesses on the other side, with great
"clamour, when they said anything that did not please them;
"so that Mr. Hyde (whose office it was to oblige men of all sorts
"to keep order) was compelled to use some sharp reproofs, and
"some threats, to reduce them to such a temper that the
"business might be quietly heard. Cromwell, in great fury,
"reproached the Chairman for being partial, and that he dis-
"countenanced the Witnesses by threatening them: the other
"appealed to the Committee; which justified him, and
"declared that he behaved himself as he ought to do; which
"more inflamed him," Cromwell, "who was already too much
"angry. When upon any mention of matter-of-fact, or of the
"proceeding before and at the Enclosure, the Lord Mandevil

"desired to be heard, and with great modesty related what
"had been done, or explained what had been said, Mr. Crom-
"well did answer, and reply upon him with so much indecency
"and rudeness, and in language so contrary and offensive, that
"every man would have thought, that as their natures and
"their manners were as opposite as it is possible, so their
"interest could never have been the same. In the end, his
"whole carriage was so tempestuous, and his behaviour so in-
"solent, that the Chairman found himself obliged to reprehend
"him; and to tell him, That if he" Mr. Cromwell "proceeded
"in the same manner, he" Mr. Hyde "would presently ad-
"journ the Committee, and the next morning complain to the
"House of him. Which he never forgave; and took all oc-
"casions afterwards to pursue him with the utmost malice and
"revenge, to *his* death," — not Mr. Hyde's, happily, but Mr.
Cromwell's, who at length did cease to cherish "malice and
revenge" against Mr. Hyde!

Tracking this matter, by faint indications, through various
obscure courses, I conclude that it related to "the Soke of
Somersham,"* near St. Ives; and that the scene in the Queen's
Court probably occurred in the beginning of July 1641.**
Cromwell knew this Soke of Somersham, near St. Ives, very
well; knew these poor rustics, and what treatment they had
got; and wished, not in the imperturbablest manner it would
seem, to see justice done them. Here too, subtracting the due
subtrahend from Mr. Hyde's Narrative, we have a pleasant
visuality of an old summer afternoon "in the Queen's Court"
two hundred years ago.

Cromwell's next Letters present him to us, not debating, or
about to debate, concerning Parliamentary Propositions and
Scotch "Eighth Articles," but with his sword drawn to enforce
them; the whole Kingdom divided now into two armed con-
flicting masses, the argument to be by pike and bullet henceforth.

* Commons Journals, ii. 172.
** Ibid. 87; 150; 172; 192; 215; 218; 219, — the dates extend from 17th
February to 21st July 1641.

PART II.

TO THE END OF THE FIRST CIVIL WAR.

1642—1646.

PRELIMINARY.

THERE is therefore a great dark void, from February 1641
to January 1643, through which the reader is to help himself
from Letter III. over to Letter IV., as he best may. How has
pacific England, the most solid pacific country in the world,
got all into this armed attitude; and decided itself to argue
henceforth by pike and bullet till it get some solution? Dryas·
dust, if there remained any shame in him, ought to look at
those wagonloads of Printed Volumes, and blush! We, in great
haste, offer the necessitous reader the following hints and considerations.

It was mentioned above that Oliver St. John, the noted Puritan Lawyer, was already, in the end of January 1641, made
Solicitor-General. The reader may mark that as a small
fraction of an event showing itself above ground, completed;
and indicating to him a grand subterranean attempt on the
part of King Charles and the Puritan Leaders, which unfortunately never could become a fact or event. Charles, in
January last or earlier (for there are no dates discoverable but
this of St. John's), perceiving how the current of the Nation
ran, and what a humour men were getting into, had decided
on trying to adopt the Puritan leaders, Pym, Hampden, Holles and others, as what we should now call his "Ministers:"
these Puritan men, under the Earl of Bedford as chief, might
have hoped to become what we should now call a "Majesty's
Ministry," and to execute peaceably, with their King presiding

over them, what reforms had grown inevitable. A most desirable result, if a possible one; for of all men these had the
least notion of revolting, or rebelling against their King!

This negotiation had been entered into, and entertained as
a possibility by both parties: so much is indubitable; so much
and nothing more, except that it ended without result.* It
would in our days be the easiest negotiation; but it was then
an impossible one.   For it meant that the King should content
himself with the Name of King, and see measures the reverse
of what *he* wished and willed, take effect by his sanction.
Which, in sad truth, had become a necessity for Charles I. in
the England of 1641.   His tendency and effort has long been
the reverse of England's; he cannot govern England, whatever
he may govern! And yet to have admitted this necessity, —
alas, was it not to have settled the whole Quarrel, *without* the
eight-and-forty years of fighting, and confused bickering and
oscillation, which proved to be needful first? The negotiation
dropped; leaving for visible result only this appointment of
St. John's.   His Majesty on that side saw no course possible
for him.

Accordingly he tried it in the opposite direction, which also,
on failure by this other, was very natural for him. He entered
into secret tamperings with the Officers of the English Army;
which, lying now in Yorkshire, ill-paid, defeated, and in
neighbourhood of a Scotch Army victoriously furnished with
850*l.* a-day, was very apt for discontent. There arose a "first
Army-Plot" for delivering Strafford from the Tower; then a
second Army-Plot for some equally wild achievement, tending
to deliver Majesty from thraldom, and send this factious Parliament about its business. In which desperate schemes,
though his Majesty strove not to commit himself beyond what
was necessary, it became and still remains indubitable that he
did participate; — as indeed, the former course of listening to
his Parliament having been abandoned, this other of coercing
or awing it by armed force was the only remaining one.

These Army-Plots, detected one after another, and in-

* Whitlocke, Clarendon; see Forster's Statesmen, ii. 150-7.

Carlyle, Cromwell. I.   8

vestigated and commented upon, with boundless interest, in Parliament and out of it, kept the Summer and Autumn of 1641 in continual alarm and agitation; taught all Opposition persons, and a factious Parliament in general, what ground they were standing on; — and in the factious Parliament, especially, could not but awaken the liveliest desire of having the Military Force put in such hands as would be safe for them. "The Lord-Lieutenants of Counties," this factious Parliament conceived an unappeaseable desire of knowing who these were to be: — this is what they mean by "Power of the Militia;" on which point, as his Majesty would not yield a jot, his Parliament and he, — the point becoming daily more important, new offences daily accumulating, and the split ever widening, — ultimately rent themselves asunder, and drew swords to decide it.

Such was the well-known consummation; which in Cromwell's next Letter we find to have arrived. Here are a few Dates which may assist the reader to grope his way thither. From "Mr. Willingham in Swithin's Lane" in February 1641, to the Royal Standard at Nottingham in August 1642, and "Mr. Barnard at Huntingdon" in January 1643, which is our next stage, there is a long vague road; and the lights upon it are mostly a universal dance of will-o'-wisps, and distracted fireflies in a state of excitement, — not *good guidance for the traveller!*

1641.

Monday, 3d May.   Strafford's Trial being ended, but no sentence yet given, Mr. Robert Baillie, Minister of Kilwinning, who was here among the Scotch Commissioners at present, saw in Palaceyard, Westminster, "some thousands of Citizens and Apprentices" (Miscellaneous Persons and City Shopmen, as we should now call them), who rolled about there "all day," bellowing to every Lord as he went in or came out, "with a loud and hideous voice:" "Justice on Strafford! Justice on Traitors!"* — which seemed ominous to the Reverend Mr. Baillie.

* Baillie, i. 351.

In which same hours, amid such echoes from without, the honourable House of Commons within doors, all in great tremor about Army-Plots, Treasons, Death-perils, was busy redacting a "Protestation;" a kind of solemn Vow, or miniature *Scotch Covenant*, the first of a good many such in those earnest agitated times, — to the effect: "We take the Supreme to witness that we will stand by one another to the death in prosecution of our just objects here; in defence of Law, Loyalty and Gospel here." To this effect; but couched in very mild language, and with a "Preamble," in which our Terror of Army-Plots, the moving principle of the affair, is discreetly almost shaded out of sight; it being our object that the House should be "unanimous" in this Protestation. As accordingly the House was; the House, and to a great extent the Nation. Hundreds of honourable Members, Mr. Cromwell one of them, sign the Protestation this day; the others on the following days: their names all registered in due succession in the Books.* Nay, it is ordered that the whole Nation be invited to sign it; that each honourable Member send it down to his constituents, and invite them to sign it. Which, as we say, the constituents, all the reforming part of them, everywhere in England, did; with a feeling of solemnity very strange to the modern mind. Striking terror into all Traitors; quashing down Army-Plots for the present, and the hopes of poor Strafford forever. A Protestation held really sacred; appealed to, henceforth, as a thing from which there was no departing. Cavalcades of Freeholders, coming up from the country to petition the Honourable House, — for instance, the Fourthousand Petitioners from Buckinghamshire, about ten months hence, — rode with this Protestation "stuck in their hats."** A very great and awe-inspiring matter in those days; till it was displaced by greater of the like kind, — Solemn League and Covenant, and others. ***

Monday next, 10*th May*, his Majesty accordingly signed

---

* Commons Journals, ii. 132, 3, &c.; Rushworth, iv. 241, 4.
** 12th January 1641-2; Rushworth, iv. 486.
*** Copy of it, sent to Cambridge: Appendix, No. 3.

sentence on Strafford; who was executed on the Wednesday
following.   No help for it.   A terrible example; the one su-
premely able man the King had.

On the same Monday, 10th May, his Majesty signed likewise another Bill, That this Parliament should not be dissolved
without its own consent.   A Bill signed in order that the City
might lend him money on good Security of Parliament; money
being most pressingly wanted, for our couple of hungry Armies
Scotch and English, and other necessary occasions.   A Bill
which seemed of no great consequence except financial; but
which, to a People reverent of Law, and never, in the wildest
clash of battle-swords, giving up its religious respect for the
constable's baton, proved of infinite consequence.   His Majesty's hands are tied; he cannot dismiss this Parliament, as
he has done the others; — no, not without its own consent.

August 10*th*.   Army-Plotters having fled beyond seas; the
Bill for Triennial Parliaments being passed; the Episcopacy-
Bill being got to sleep; and by the use of royal *varnish* a kind
of composure, or hope of composure, being introduced; above
all things, money being now borrowed to pay the Armies and
disband them, — his Majesty, on the 10th of the month, *
set out for Scotland.   To hold a Parliament, and compose
matters there, as his Majesty gave out.   To see what old or
new elements of malign Royalism could still be awakened to
life there, as the Parliament surmised, who greatly opposed
his going. — Mr. Cromwell got home to Ely again, for six
weeks, this autumn; theer being a recess from 9th September
when the business was got gathered up, till 20th October when
his Majesty was expected back.   An Interim Committee, and
Pym from his "lodging at Chelsea," ** managed what of indispensable might turn up.

November 1*st*.   News came to London, to the reassembled
Parliament, *** that an Irish Rebellion, already grown to be an
Irish Massacre, had broken out.   An Irish Catholic imitation

* Wharton's Laud, p. 62.
** His Report, Commons Journals, ii. 289.
*** Laud, 62; Commons Journals, *in die.*

of the late Scotch Presbyterian achievements in the way of
"religious liberty;" — one of the best models, and one of the
worst imitations ever seen in this world. Erasmus's Ape, observing Erasmus shave himself, never doubted but it too could
shave. One knows what a hand the creature made of itself,
before the edgetool could be wrenched from it again! As this
poor Irish Rebellion unfortunately began in lies and bluster,
and proceeded in lies and bluster, hoping to make itself good
that way, the ringleaders had started by pretending or even
forging some warrant from the King; which brought much un-
deserved suspicion on his Majesty, and greatly complicated his
affairs here for a long while.

November 22*d*. The Irish Rebellion blazing up more and
more into an Irish Massacre, to the terror and horror of all
Antipapist men; and in England, or even in Scotland, except
by the liberal use of *varnish*, nothing yet being satisfactorily
mended, nay all things hanging now, as it seemed, in double
and treble jeopardy, — the Commons had decided on a "Grand
Petition and Remonstrance," to set forth what their griefs
and necessities really were, and really would require to have
done for them. The Debate upon it, very celebrated in those
times, came on this day, Monday 22d November.* The
longest Debate ever yet known in Parliament; and the
stormiest, — nay, had it not been for Mr. Hampden's soft
management, "we had like to have sheathed our swords in
each other's bowels;" says Warwick; which I find otherwise
to be true. The Remonstrance passed by a small majority. It
can be read still in Rushworth,** drawn up in precise business
order; the whole 206 Articles of it, — every line of which
once thrilled electrically into all men's hearts, as torpid as it
has now grown. "The chimes of Margaret's were striking two
in the morning when we came out." — It was on this occasion
that Oliver, "coming down stairs," is reported to have said,
He would have sold all and gone to New England, had the
Remonstrance not passed;***—a vague report, gathered over

---

* Commons Journals, *in die*; D'Ewes mss. f. 179 b.
** iv. 438-51; see also 436, 7.   *** Clarendon.

dining-tables long after, to which the reader need not pay
more deed than it merits. His Majesty returned from Scotland
on the Thursday following; and had from the City a thrice-
glorious Civic Entertainment. *

December 10th. The Episcopal business, attempted last
Spring in vain, has revived in December, kindled into life by
the Remonstrance; and is raging more fiercely than ever;
crowds of Citizens petitioning, Corporation "going in sixty
coaches" to petition;** the Apprentices, or City Shopmen,
and miscellaneous persons, petitioning; — Bishops "much
insulted" in Palaceyard, as they go in or out. Whereupon
hasty Welsh Williams, Archbishop of York, once Bishop of
Lincoln and Lord Keeper, he with Eleven too hasty Bishops,
Smectymnuus Hall being one of them, give in a Protest, on
this 10th of December,*** That they cannot get to their place
in Parliament; that all shall be null and void till they do get
there. A rash step; for which, on the 30th of the same month,
they are, by the Commons, voted guilty of Treason; and
"in a cold evening," with small ceremony, are bundled, the
whole dozen of them, into the Tower. For there is again
rioting, again are cries "loud and hideous;" — Colonel
Lunsford, a truculent one-eyed man, having "drawn his
sword" upon the Apprentices in Westminster Hall, and
truculently slashed some of them; who of course responded in
a loud and hideous manner, by tongue, by fist, and single-
stick: nay, on the morrow, 28th December,† they came
marching many thousands strong, with sword and pistol, out
of the City, "Slash us now! while we wait on the Honourable
House for an answer to our petition!" — and insulted his Majesty's Guard at Whitehall. What a Christmas of that old
London, of that old Year! On the 6th of February following,
Episcopacy will be voted down, with blaze of "bonfires," and
"ringing" of all the bells, — very audible to poor old Dr.
Laud †† over in the Tower yonder.

* Rushworth, iv. 429.   ** Vicars, p. 56.
*** Rushworth, iv. 467.   † Rushworth, iv. 464.
†† Wharton's Laud, p. 62; see also p. 65.

1642.

January 4th. His Majesty seeing these extremities arrive, and such a conflagration begin to blåze, thought now the time had come for snatching the main livecoals away, and so quenching the same. Such coals of strife he counts to the number of Five in the Commons House, and One in the Lords: Pym, Hampden, Haselrig, with Holles and Strode (who held down the Speaker fourteen years ago), these are the Five Commons; Lord Kimbolton, better known to us as Mandevil, Oliver's friend, of the "Soke of Somersham," and Queen's-Court Committee, he is the Lord. His Majesty flatters himself he has gathered evidence concerning these individual firebrands, That they "invited the Scots to invade us" in 1640: he sends, on Monday 3d January,* to demand that they be given up to him as Traitors. Deliberate, slow and, as it were, evasive reply. Whereupon, on the morrow, he rides down to St. Stephen's himself, with an armed very miscellaneous force, of Five-hundred or of Three-hundred truculent braggadocio persons looking in after him from the lobby, — with intent to seize the said Five Members, five principal hot coals; and trample *them* out, for one thing. It was the fatallest step this poor King ever took. The Five Members, timefully warned, were gone into the City; the whole Parliament removed itself into the City, "to be safe from armed violence." From London City, and from all England, rose one loud voice of lamentation, condemnation: Clean against law! Paint an inch thick, there is, was, or can be, no shadow of law in *this.* Will you grant us the Militia now; we seem to need it now! — His Majesty's subsequent stages may be dated with more brevity.

January 10th. The King with his Court quits Whitehall; the Five Members and Parliament purposing to return to-morrow, with the whole City in arms round them.** He left Whitehall; never saw it again till he came to lay down his head there.

* Commons Journals, ii. 367.   ** Vicars, p. 64.

March 9th. The King has sent away his Queen from Dover, "to be in a place of safety," — and also to pawn the Crown Jewels in Holland, and get him arms.   He returns Northward again, avoiding London. Many Messages between the Houses of Parliament and him: "Will your Majesty grant us Power of the Militia; accept this list of Lord-Lieutenants?" On the 9th of March, still advancing Northward without affirmative response, he has got to Newmarket; where another Message overtakes him, earnestly urges itself upon him: Could not your Majesty please to grant us Power of the Militia for a limited time? "No, by God!" answers his Majesty, "not for an hour!" * — On the 19th of March he is at York; where his Hull Magazine, gathered for service against the Scots, is lying near; where a great Earl of Newcastle, and other Northern potentates, will help him; where at least London and its Puritanism, now grown so fierce, is far off.

There we will leave him; attempting Hull Magazine, in vain; exchanging messages with his Parliament; messages, missives, printed and written Papers without limit: — Law-pleadings of both parties before the great tribunal of the English Nation, each party striving to prove itself right, and within the verge of Law: preserved still in acres of typography, once thrillingly alive in every fibre of them; now a mere torpor, readable by few creatures, not remberable by any.   It is too clear his Majesty will have to get himself an army, by Commission of Array, by subscriptions of loyal plate, pawning of crown jewels, or how he can.   The Parliament by all methods is endeavouring to do the like. London subscribed "Horses and Plate," every kind of plate, even to women's thimbles, to an unheard-of amount;** and when it came to actual enlisting, in London alone there were "Four-thousand enlisted in a day."***   Four-thousand, some call it Five-thousand, in a day: the reader may meditate that one fact.   Royal messages, Parliamentary messages; acres of

* Rushworth, iv. 533.
** Vicars, pp. 93, 109; see Commons Journals, 10th June 1642.
*** Wood's Athenæ, iii. 193.

typography thrillingly alive in every fibre of them, — these
go on slowly abating, and military preparations go on steadily
increasing till the 23d of October next. The King's "Commission of Array for Leicestershire" came out on the 12th of
June, commissions for other counties following as convenient;
the Parliament's "Ordinance for the Militia," rising cautiously
pulse after pulse towards clear emergence, had attained com-
pletion the week before.* The question puts itself to every
English soul, Which of these will you obey? — and in all
quarters of English ground, with swords getting out of their
scabbards, and yet the constable's baton still struggling to
rule supreme, there is a most confused solution of it going on.

Of Oliver in these months we find the following things
noted; which the imaginative reader is to spread out into significance for himself the best he can.

February 7th.   "Mr. Cromwell," among others, "offers to
lend Three-hundred Pounds for the service of the Commonwealth, **—towards reducing the Irish Rebellion, and relieving the afflicted Protestants there, or here. Rushworth,
copying a List of such subscribers, of date 9th April 1642, has
Cromwell's name written down for "500*l.*"***—seemingly the
same transaction; Mr. Cromwell having now mended his offer:
or else Mr. Rushworth, who uses the arithmetical cipher in
this place, having misprinted. Hampden's subscription there
is 1,000*l.* In Mr. Cromwell it is clear there is no backwardness,
far from that; his activity in these months notably increases.
In the *D'Ewes* mss.† he appears and reappears; suggesting this
and the other practical step, on behalf of Ireland oftenest; in
all ways zealously urging the work.

July 15th.   "Mr. Cromwell moved that we might make an
"order to allow the Townsmen of Cambridge to raise two
"Companies of Volunteers, and to appoint Captains over
"them."††   On which same day, 15th July, the Commons

---

* Husbands the Printer's *First* Collection (Lond. 1643), pp. 346, 331.
** Commons Journals, ii. 408.   *** Rushworth, iv. 564.
† February—July 1642.   †† D'Ewes mss. f. 658-661.

Clerk writes these words: "Whereas Mr. Cromwell hath sent
"down arms into the County of Cambridge, for the defence
"of that County, it is this day ordered," * — that he shall
have the "100*l.*" expended on that service repaid him by and
by.   Is Mr. Cromwell aware that there lies a colour of high
treason in all this; risk not of one's purse only, but of one's
head? Mr. Cromwell is aware of it, and pauses not. The next
entry is still stranger.

August 15th. "Mr. Cromwell in Cambridgeshire has seized
"the Magazine in the Castle at Cambridge; and hath hindered
"the carrying of the Plate from that University; which, as
"some report, was to the value of 20,000 *l.* or thereabouts."
So does Sir Philip Stapleton, member for Aldborough, member also of our new "Committee for Defence of the Kingdom,"
report this day. For which let Mr. Cromwell have indemnity.**
— Mr. Cromwell has gone down into Cambridgeshire in person, since they began to train there, and assumed the chief
management, — to some effect, it would appear.

The like was going on in all shires of England; wherever
the Parliament had a zealous member, it sent him down to his
shire in these critical months, to take what management he
could or durst.   The most confused months England ever saw.
In every shire, in every parish; in courthouses, alehouses,
churches, markets, wheresoever men were gathered together,
England, with sorrowful confusion in every fibre, is tearing
itself into hostile halves, to carry on the voting by pike and
bullet henceforth.

Brevity is very urgent on us, nevertheless we must give
this other extract. Bramston the Shipmoney Judge, in trouble
with the Parliament and sequestered from his place, is now
likely to get into trouble with the King, who in the last days
of July has ordered him to come to York on business of importance.   Judge Bramston sends his two sons, John and
Frank, fresh young men, to negotiate some excuse. They

* Commons Journals, ii. 674.
** Ibid., ii. 720, 6. See likewise Tanner MSS. lxiii. 116; *Querela Cantabrigiensis* (and wipe away its blubberings and inexactitudes a little), *Life
of Dr. Barwick,* &c., — Cambridge Portfolio (London, 1840), ii. 386-8.

ride to York in three days; stay a day at York with his Majesty; then return, "on the same horses," in three days, — to Skreens in Essex; which was good riding.　John, one of them, has left a most watery incoherent *Autobiography*, now printed, but not edited, — nor worth editing, except by *fire* to ninety-nine hundredths of it; very distracting; in which, however, there is this notable sentence; date about the middle of August, not discoverable to a day.　Having been at York, and riding back on the same horses in three days:

"In our return on Sunday, near Huntingdon, between "that and Cambridge, certain musketeers start out of the "corn, and command us to stand; telling us we must be "searched, and to that end must go before Mr. Cromwell, and "give account from whence we came and whither we were "going.　I asked, Where Mr. Cromwell was?　A soldier told "us, He was four miles off.　I said, It was unreasonable to "carry us out of our way; if Mr. Cromwell had been there, "I should have willingly given him all the satisfaction he "could desire; — and putting my hand into my pocket, I "gave one of them Twelvepence, who said, We might pass. "By this I saw plainly it would not be possible for my Father "to get to the King with his coach;"* — neither did he go at all, but stayed at home till he died.

September 14*th*.　Here is a new phasis of the business.　In a "List of the Army under the command of the Earl of Essex,"** we find that Robert Earl of Essex is "Lord General for King *and* Parliament" (to deliver the poor beloved King from traitors, who have misled him, and clouded his fine understanding, and rendered him as it were a beloved Parent fallen *insane*); that Robert Earl of Essex, we say, is Lord General for King and Parliament; that William the new Earl of Bedford is General of the Horse, and has, or is every hour getting to have, "seventy-five troops of 60 men each;" in

---

* Autobiography of Sir John Bramston, Knt. (Camden Society, 1845). p. 86.
** King's Pamphlets, small 4to, no. 73.

every troop a Captain, a Lieutenant, a Cornet and Quarter-master, whose names are all given.   In *Troop Sixty-seven*, the Captain is "Oliver Cromwell," — honourable member for Cambridge;   many honourable members having now taken arms; Mr. Hampden, for example, having become Colonel Hampden, — busy drilling 'his men in Chalgrove Field at this very time.   But moreover, in *Troop Eight* of Earl Bedford's Horse, we find another "Oliver Cromwell, Cornet;" — and with real thankfulness for this poor flint-spark in the great darkness, recognise him for our honourable member's Son. His eldest Son Oliver,* now a stout young man of twenty. "Thou too, Boy Oliver, thou art fit to swing a sword.   If "there ever was a battle worth fighting, and to be called "God's battle, it is this; thou too wilt come!"   How a staid, most pacific,   solid Farmer of three-and-forty decides on girding himself with warlike iron, and fighting, he and his, against principalities and powers, let readers who have formed any notion of this man conceive for themselves.

On *Sunday*, 23d *October*, was Edgehill Battle, called also Keinton Fight, near Keinton on the south edge of Warwick-shire.   In which Battle Captain Cromwell *was* present, and did his duty, let angry Denzil say what he will.**   The Fight was indecisive; victory claimed by both sides.   Captain Crom-well told Cousin Hampden, They never would get on with a set of poor tapsters and town-apprentice people fighting against men of honour.   To cope with men of honour they must have men of religion.   "Mr. Hampden answered me, It "was a good notion, if it could be executed."   Oliver himself set about executing a bit of it, his share of it, by and by.

"We all thought one battle would decide it," says Richard Baxter;*** — and we were all much mistaken! This winter there arise among certain Counties "Associations" for mutual defence,   against Royalism and plunderous Rupertism;   a

* Antea, p. 54.
** Vicars, p. 198; Denzil Holles's *Memoirs* (in Mazeres's Tracts, vol. i.).
*** Life (London, 1696), Part i. p. 43.

measure cherished by the Parliament, condemned as treason-
able by the King. Of which "Associations," countable to
the number of five or six, we name only one, that of Norfolk,
Suffolk, Essex, Cambridge, Herts; with Lord Grey of Wark
for Commander; where, and under whom, Oliver was now
serving. This "Eastern Association" is alone worth naming.
All the other Associations, no man of emphasis being in the
midst of them, fell in few months to pieces; only this of Cromwell's subsisted, enlarged itself, grew famous; — and indeed
kept its own borders clear of invasion during the whole course
of the War. Oliver, in the beginning of 1643, is serving
there, under the Lord Grey of Wark. Besides his military
duties, Oliver, as natural, was nominated of the Committee
for Cambridgeshire in this Association; he is also of the Committee for Huntingdonshire, which as yet belongs to another
"Association." Member for the Committee of Huntingdonshire; to which also has been nominated a "Robert Barnard,
Esquire,"* — who, however, does not sit, as I have reason
to surmise!

LETTER IV.

The reader recollects Mr. Robert Barnard, how, in 1630,
he got a Commission of the Peace for Huntingdon, along with
"Dr. Beard and Mr. Oliver Cromwell," to be fellow Justices
there. Probably they never sat much together, as Oliver
went to St. Ives soon after, and the two men were of opposite
politics, which in those times meant opposite religions. But
here in twelve years space is a change of many things!

To my assured friend Robert Barnard, Esquire: Present these.

Mr. Barnard,   'Huntingdon,' 23d January 1642.

It's most true, my Lieutenant with some other soldiers of my troop were at your House. I dealt 'so'

_____
* Husbands, i. 892; see for the other particulars, ii. 183, 327, 804, 809;
Commons Journals, &c.

freely 'as' to inquire after you; the reason was, I had heard you reported active against the proceedings of Parliament, and *for* those that disturb the peace of this Country and the Kingdom, — *with* those of this Country who have had meetings not a few, to intents and purposes too-too full of suspect.*

It's true, Sir, I know you have been wary in your carriages: be not too confident thereof. Subtlety may deceive you; integrity never will. With my heart I shall desire that your judgment may alter, and your practice. I come only to hinder men from increasing the rent, — from doing hurt; but not to hurt any man: nor shall I you; I hope you will give me no cause. If you do, I must be pardoned what my relation to the Public calls for.

If your good parts be disposed that way, know me for   Your servant,
                                    OLIVER CROMWELL.

Be assured fair words from me shall neither deceive you of your houses nor of your liberty. §

My Copy, two Copies, of this Letter I owe to kind friends, who have carefully transcribed it from the Original at Lord Gosford's. The present Lady Gosford is "granddaughter of Sir Robert Barnard," to whose lineal ancestor the Letter is addressed. The date of time is given; there never was any date or address of place, — which probably means that it was written in Huntingdon and addressed to Huntingdon, where Robert Barnard, who became Recorder of the place, is known to have resided. Oliver, in the month of January 1642-3,

---

* *Country* is equivalent to *county* or *region; too-too*, in those days, means little more than *too; suspect* is *suspectability*, almost as proper as our modern *suspicion*.

§ Original in the possession of Lord Gosford, at Worlingham in Suffolk.

is present in the Fen-country, and all over the Eastern Association, with his troop or troops, looking after disaffected persons; ready to disperse royalist assemblages, to seize royalist plate, to keep down disturbance, and care in every way that the Parliament Cause suffer no damage.* A Lieutenant and party have gone to take some survey of Robert Barnard, Esquire; Robert Barnard, standing on the right of injured innocence, innocent till he be proved guilty, protests: Oliver responds as here, in a very characteristic way.

It was precisely in these weeks, that Oliver from Captain became Colonel: Colonel of a regiment of horse, raised on his own principles so far as might be, in that "Eastern Association;" and is henceforth known in the Newspapers as Colonel Cromwell. Whether on this 23d of January, he was still Captain, or had ceased to be so, no extant accessible record apprises us. On the 2d March 1642—3, I have found him named as "Col. Cromwell,"** and hitherto not earlier. He is getting "men of religion" to serve in this cause, — or at least would fain get such if he might.

LETTER V.

Cambridge.

In the end of February 1642-3, "Colonel" Cromwell is at Cambridge; "great forces from Essex, Norfolk and Suffolk" having joined him, and more still coming in. *** There has been much alarm and running to and fro, over all those counties. Lord Capel hanging over them with an evident intent to plunder Cambridge, generally to plunder and ravage in this region; as Prince Rupert has cruelly done in Gloucestershire, and is now cruelly doing in Wilts and Hants. Colonel Cromwell, the soul of the whole business, must have had some bestirring of himself; some swift riding and resolving, now here now there. Some "12,000 men," however, or say even "23,000

* Appendix, No. 4.　　　　　** Cromwelliana, p. 2.
*** Cromwelliana, p. 2; Vicars, p. 273.

men" (for rumour runs very high!) from the Associated Counties, are now at last got together about Cambridge, and Lord Capel has seen good to vanish again. *   "He was the first man that rose to complain of Grievances, in this Parliament;" he, while still plain Mr. Capel, member for Herts: but they have made a Lord of him, and the wind sits now in another quarter! —

Lord Capel has vanished; and the 12,000 zealous Volunteers of the Association are dismissed to their counties, with monition to be ready when called for again. Moreover, to avoid like perils in future, it is now resolved to make a Garrison of Cambridge; to add new works to the Castle, and fortify the Town itself. This is now going on in the early spring days of 1643; and Colonel Cromwell and all hands are busy! — Here is a small Document, incidentally preserved to us, which becomes significant if well read.

Fen Drayton is a small Village on the Eastern edge of Cambridgeshire, between St. Ives and Cambridge, — well known to Oliver.   In the small Church of Fen Drayton, after divine service on Sunday the 12th of March 1642-3, the following Warrant, "delivered to the Churchwardings" (by one Mr. Norris, a Constable, who spells very ill), and by them to the Curate, is read to a rustic congregation, — who sit, somewhat agape, I apprehend, and uncertain what to do about it.

COM. CANT. ("CAMBRIDGESHIRE To wit").

To all and every the Inhabitants of Fen Drayton in the Hundred of Papworth.

WHEREAS we have been enforced, by apparent grounds of approaching danger, to begin to fortify the Town of Cambridge, for preventing the Enemy's inroad, and the better to maintain the peace of this County:

Having in part seen your good affections to the

* Vicars; Newspapers, 6th-15th March (in Cromwelliana, p. 2).

Cause, and now standing in need of your further assistance to the perfecting of the said Fortifications, which will cost at least Two-thousand pounds, We are encouraged as well as necessitated to desire a Freewill Offering of a Liberal Contribution from you, for the better enabling of us to attain our desired ends, — viz. the Preservation of our County; — knowing that every honest and well-affected man, considering the vast expenses we have already been at, and our willingness to do according to our ability, will be ready to contribute his best assistance to a work of so high concernment and so good an end.

We do therefore desire that what shall be by you freely given and collected may with all convenient speed be sent to the Commissioners at Cambridge, to be employed to the use aforesaid. And so you shall further engage us to be

Yours ready to serve,
OLIVER CROMWELL.
THOMAS MARTYN. §
('and Six others.')

Cambridge, this 8th of March 1642.

The Thomas Martyn, Sir Thomas, and the Six others whom we suppress, are all of the Cambridge Committees of those times; * zealous Puritan men, not known to us otherwise. Norris did not raise much at Fen Drayton; only 1*l.* 19*s.* 2*d.*, "subscribed by Fifteen persons," according to his Endorsement; — the general public at Fen Drayton, and probably in other such places, hesitates a little to draw its purse as yet! One way or other, however, the work of fortifying Cambridge was got done. ** A regular Force lies henceforth in Cam-

§ Cooper's Annals of Cambridge (Cambridge, 1845), iii. 340.
* Husbands' Second Collection (London, 1646), p. 329; Commons Journals, iii. 153; &c.
** Reported complete, 15th July 1643 (Cooper's Annals, iii. 350).

bridge: Captains Fleetwood, Desborow, Whalley, new soldiers who will become veterans and known to us, are on service here. Of course the Academic stillness is much fluttered by the war-drum, and many a confused brabble springs up between Gown and Garrison; college tippets, and on occasion still more venerable objects, getting torn by the business! The truth is, though Cambridge is not so Malignant as Oxford, the Surplices at Allhallowtide have still much sway there; and various Heads of Houses are by no means what one could wish: of whom accordingly Oliver has had, and still occasionally has, to send, — by instalments as the cases ripen, — a select batch up to Parliament: Reverend Dr. This and then also Reverend Dr. That; who are lodged in the Tower, in Ely House, in Lambeth or elsewhere. in a tragic manner, and pass very troublous years. *

Cambridge continues henceforth the Bulwark and Metropolis of the Association; where the Committees sit, where the centre of all business is. "Colonel Cook," I think, is Captain of the Garrison; but the soul of the Garrison, and of the Association generally, is probably another Colonel. Now here, now swiftly there, wherever danger is to be fronted, or prompt work is to be done: — for example, off to Norwich just now, on important businesses; and, as is too usual, very ill supplied with money.

LETTER V.

Of Captain Nelson I know nothing; seem to see an uncertain shadow of him turn up again, after years of industrious fighting under Irish Inchiquin and others, still a mere Captain, still terribly in arrear even as to pay. ** "It's pity a Gentleman of his affections should be discouraged!" "The Deputy Lieutenants," Suffolk Committee, could be named, if there were room. *** The "business for Norfolk" we guess to be, as

* Querola Cantabrigiensis, &c. &c. In Cooper *ubi suprà.*
** Commons Journals, v. 524, 530. *** Husbands, II. 171, 193.

usual, Delinquents, — symptoms of delinquent Royalists getting to a head.

*To my honoured Friends the Deputy Lieutenants for the County
of Suffolk.*

GENTLEMEN,   Cambridge, 10th March 1642.

I am sorry I should so often trouble you about the
business of money: it's no pleasant subject to be too
frequent upon. But such is Captain Nelson's occasion,
for want thereof, that he hath not wherewith to satisfy for the billet of his soldiers; and so this Business
for Norfolk, so hopeful to set all right there, may fail.
Truly he hath borrowed from me, else he could not
have paid to discharge this Town at his departure.

It's pity a Gentleman of his affections should be
discouraged! Wherefore I earnestly beseech you to
consider him and the Cause. It's honourable that you
do so. — What you can help him to, be pleased to
send into Norfolk; he hath not wherewith to pay a
Troop one day, as he tells me. Let your return be
speedy, — to Norwich.

Gentlemen, command
Your servant,
OLIVER CROMWELL.

'P.S.' I hope to serve you in my return: with your
conjunction, we shall quickly put an end to these
businesses, the Lord assisting.*

By certain official docketings on this same Letter, it appears that Captain Nelson did receive his 100*l*.; touched it
promptly on the morrow, "11th March; — I say received:
JOHN NELSON." How the Norfolk businesses proceeded, and
what end they came to in Suffolk itself, we shall now see.

† Autograph, in the possession of C. Meadows, Esq., Great Bealing.
Woodbridge, Suffolk.

LOWESTOFF.

THE Colonel has already had experience in such Delinquent matters; has, by vigilance, by gentle address, by swift audacity if needful, extinguished more than one incipient conflagration.   Here is one such instance, — coming to its sad maturity, and bearing fruit at Westminster, in these very hours.

On *Monday*, 13*th March* 1642—3, Thomas Conisby, Esquire, High Sheriff of Herts, appears visibly before the House of Commons, to give account of a certain "Pretended Commission of Array," which he had been attempting to execute one Market-day, some time since, at St. Albans in that county. *
Such King's Writ, or Pretended Commission of Array, the said High Sheriff had, with a great *Posse Comitatus* round him, been executing one Market-day at St. Albans (date irrecoverably lost), when Cromwell's Dragoons dashed suddenly in upon him; laid him fast, — not without difficulty: he was first seized by "six troopers," but rescued by his royalist multitude, then "twenty troopers" again seized him; "barricadoed the inn-yard;" ** conveyed him off to London to give what account of the matter he could.   There he is giving account of it, — a very lame and withal an "insolent" one, as seems to the Honourable House, which accordingly sends him to the Tower, where he had to lie for several years.   Commissions of Array are not handy to execute in the Eastern Association at present! Here is another instance; general result of this ride into Norfolk, — "end of these businesses," in fact.

The "Meeting at Laystoff," or Lowestoff in Suffolk, is mentioned in all the old Books; but John·Cory, Merchant Burgess of Norwich, shall first bring us face to face with it. Assiduous Sir Symonds got a copy of Mr. Cory's Letter, ***
one of the thousand Letters which Honourable Members

* Commons Journals, ii. 1000, 1.
** Vicars, p. 246; May's History of the Long Parliament (Guizot's French Translation), ii. 196.
*** D'Ewes mss. f. 1139; Transcript, p. 378.

listened to in those mornings; and here now is a copy of it for the reader, — news all fresh and fresh, after waiting two hundred and two years. Colonel Cromwell is in Norwich: old Norwich becomes visible and audible, the vanished moments buzzing again with old life, — if the reader will read well. Potts, we should premise, and Palgrave, were lately appointed Deputy Lieutenants of Norwich City; * Cory I reckon to be almost a kind of Quasi-Mayor, the real Mayor having lately been seized for Royalism; Knyvett of Ashwellthorpe we shall perhaps transiently meet again. The other royalist gentlemen also are known to antiquaries of that region, and what their "seats" and connexions were: but our reader here can without damage consider merely that they were Sons of Adam, furnished in general with due seats and equipments; and read the best he can:

"*To Sir John Potts, Knight Baronet, of Mannington, Norfolk:*
"*These. Laus Deo.*

"Norwich, 17° Martii 1642. **

"Right honourable and worthy Sir, — I hope you came in "due time to the end of your journey in health and safety; "which I shall rejoice to hear. Sir, I might spare my labour "in now writing; for I suppose you are better informed from "other hands; only to testify my respects:

"Those sent out on Monday morning, the 13th, returned "that night, with old Mr. Castle of Raveningham, and some "arms of his, and of Mr. Loudon's of Alby, and of Captain "Hamond's, with his leading staff-ensign and drum. Mr. "Castle is secured at Sheriff Greenwood's. That night letters "from Yarmouth informed the Colonel,*** That they had, that "day, made stay of Sir John Wentworth, and of one Captain "Allen from Lowestoff, who had come thither to change dol-"lars; both of whom are yet secured; — and further, That the

---

* Commons Journals, 10th December 1642.
** Means 1643 of our Style. There are yet seven days of the Old Year to run.
*** "viz. Cromwell," adds D'Ewes.

"Town of Lowestoff had received-in divers strangers, and was
"fortifying itself.

"The Colonel advised no man might enter in or out the
"gates 'of Norwich,' that night.   And the next morning, be
"tween five and six, with his five troops, with Captain Foun-
"tain's, Captain Rich's, and eighty of our Norwich Volunteers,
"he marched towards Lowestoff; where he was to meet with
"the Yarmouth Volunteers, who brought four or five pieces of
"ordnance.   The Town "of Lowestoff" had blocked them-
"selves up; all except where they had placed their ordnance,
"which were three pieces; before which a chain was drawn to
"keep off the horse.

"The Colonel summoned the Town, and demanded, If
"they would deliver up their strangers, the Town and
"their army? — promising them then favour, if so; if not,
"none.   They yielded to deliver up their strangers, but
"not to the rest.   Whereupon our Norwich dragoons crept
"under the chain before mentioned; and came within pistol-
"shot of their ordnance; proffering to fire upon their
"cannoneer, — who fled: so they gained the two pieces of
"ordnance, and broke the chain; and they and the horse
"entered the Town without more resistance.   Where presently
"eighteen strangers yielded themselves; among whom were,
"of Suffolk men: Sir T. Barker, Sir John Pettus; — of Nor-
"folk: Mr. Knyvett of Ashwellthorpe, 'whom we are to meet
"again;' Mr. Richard Catelyn's Son, — some say his Father
"too was there in the morning; Mr. F. Cory, my unfor-
"tunate cousin, who I wish would have been better per-
"suaded.

"Mr. Brooke, the sometime minister of Yarmouth, and
"some others, escaped, over the river.   There was good
"store of pistols, and other arms: I hear, above fifty cases of
"pistols.   The Colonel stayed there Tuesday and Wednesday
"night.   I think Sir John Palgrave and Mr. Smith went
"yesterday to Berks.   It is rumoured Sir Robert Kemp had
"yielded to Sir John Palgrave; how true it is I know not, for
"I spoke not Sir John yesterday as he came through Town.

"I did your message to Captain Sherwood. Not to trouble
"you further, I crave leave; and am ever
          "Your Worship's at command,
                              "JOHN CORY.

  "*Postscriptum*, 20th March 1642. — Right worthy Sir, The
"above-said, on Friday, was unhappily left behind; for
"which I am sorry; as also that I utterly forgot to send your
"plate. On Friday night the Colonel brought in hither with
"him the prisoners taken at Lowestoff, and Mr. Trott of
"Beccles. On Saturday night, with one troop, they sent
"all the prisoners to Cambridge. Sir John Wentworth is come
"off with the payment of 1000*l.* On Saturday, Dr. Corbett
"of Norwich, and Mr. Henry Cooke * the Parliament-man, and
"our old 'Alderman' Daniell were taken in Suffolk.   Last
"night, several troops went out; some to Lynn-ward, it's
"thought; others to Thetford-ward, it's supposed, — because
"they had a prisoner with them. Sir, I am in great haste,
"and remember nothing else at present.
                              JOHN CORY."

  Cory still adds: "Sir Richard Berney sent to me, last
"night, and showed and gave me the Colonel's Note to testify
"he had paid him the 50 *l.*" — a forced contribution levied by
the Association Committee upon poor Berney, who had shown
himself "backward:" let him be quiet henceforth, and study
to conform.

  This was the last attempt at Royalism in the Association
where Cromwell served. The other "Associations," no man
duly forward to risk himself being present in them, had already fallen, or were fast falling, to ruin; their Counties had
to undergo the chance of War as it came. Huntingdon County
soon joined itself with this Eastern Association. ** Cromwell's

____

  * Corbett is or was "Chancellor of Norwich Diocese;" Henry Cooke
is Son of Coke upon Lyttleton, — has left his place in Parliament, and got
into dangerous courses.
  ** 26th May, — Husbands, ii. 183.

next operations, as we shall perceive, were to deliver Lincolnshire, and give it the power of joining, which in September next took effect. * Lincoln, Norfolk, Suffolk, Essex, Cambridge, Herts, Hunts: these are thenceforth the "Seven Associated Counties," called often the "Association" simply, which make a great figure in the old Books, — and kept the War wholly out of their own borders, having had a man of due forwardness among them.

LETTERS VI. — VIII.

THE main brunt of the War, during this year 1643, is in the extreme Southwest, between Sir Ralph Hopton and the Earl of Stamford; and in the North, chiefly in Yorkshire, between the Earl of Newcastle and Lord Fairfax. The Southwest, Cornwall or Devonshire transactions do not much concern us in this place; but with the Yorkshire we shall by and by have some concern. A considerable flame of War burns conspicuous in those two regions: the rest of England, all in a hot but very dim state, may be rather said to *smoke*, everywhere ready for burning, and incidentally catch fire here and there.

Essex, the Lord General, lies at Windsor, all spring, with the finest Parliamentary Army we have yet had; but unluckily can undertake almost nothing, till he see. For his Majesty in Oxford is also quiescent mostly; engaged in a negotiation with his Parliament; in a Treaty, — of which Colonel Hampden and other knowing men, though my Lord of Essex cannot, already predict the issue. And the Country is all writhing in dim conflict, suffering manifold distress. And from his Majesty's headquarters ever and anon there darts out, now hither now thither, across the dim smoke-element, a swift fierce Prince Rupert, plundering and blazing; and then suddenly darts in again; — too like a streak of sudden *fire*, for he plunders, and even *burns*, a good deal!

---

* Husbands, ii. p. 327.

Which state of things Colonel Hampden and others witness
with much impatience; but cannot get the Lord General to
undertake anything till he see.

An obscure entangled scene of things; all manner of War-
movements and swift-shooting electric influences crossing one
another, with complex action and reaction; — as happens in
a scene of War; much more of Civil War, where a whole
People and its affairs have become *electric*. — Here are Three
poor Letters, reunited at last from their long exile, resus-
citated after long interment: not in a very luminous condition! Vestiges of Oliver in the Eastern Association; which,
however faint, are welcome to us.

LETTER VI.

THE Essex people, at least the Town of Colchester and
Langley their Captain have, in some measure, sent their
contingent to Cambridge; but money is short. Cromwell,
home rapidly again from Norfolk, must take charge of it;
has an order from the Lord General; — nay it seems a Great
Design is in view; and Cromwell too, like Richard Baxter
and the rest of us, imagines one grand effort might perhaps
end these bleeding miseries.

'*To the Mayor*, *&c. of Colchester*, *By Captain Dodsworth:
'   These.'*

GENTLEMEN,   '*Cambridge*,' 23d March 1642.
Upon the coming down of your Townsmen to Cambridge, Captain Langley not knowing how to dispose
of them, desired me to nominate a fit Captain: which
I did, — an honest, religious, valiant Gentleman, Captain Dodsworth, the Bearer hereof.

He hath diligently attended the service, and much
improved his men in their exercise; but hath been unhappy beyond others in not receiving any pay for himself, and what he had for his soldiers is out long ago.

He hath, by his prudence, what with fair and winning carriage, what with money borrowed, kept them together.   He is able to do so no longer: they will presently disband if a course be not taken.

It's pity it should be so!   For I believe they are brought into as good order as most Companies in the Army.   Besides, at this instant, there is great need to use them; I have received a special command from my Lord General, To advance with what force we can, to put an end, if it may be, to this Work, — God so assisting, from whom all help cometh.

I beseech you, therefore, consider this Gentleman, and the soldiers; and if it be possible, make up his Company a Hundred-and-twenty; and send them away with what expedition is possible.   It may, through God's blessing, prove very happy.   One month's pay may prove all your trouble.   I speak to wise men: — God direct you.   I rest,

Yours to serve you,
OLIVER CROMWELL. §

The present Great Design, though it came to nothing, is not without interest for us.   Some three days before the date of this Letter, as certain Entries in the Commons Journals still testify,* there had risen hot alarm in Parliament; my Lord General writing from Windsor "at three in the morning:" Prince Rupert out in one of his forays; in terrible force before the Town of Aylesbury: ought not one to go and fight him? — Without question! eagerly answer Colonel Hampden and others: Fight him, beat him; beat more than him! Why not rise heartily from Windsor with this fine Army; calling the Eastern Association and all friends to aid us; and storm in

§ Morant's History of Colchester (London, 1748), book i. p. 55: "from the Original," he says, but not where that was or is.
* Commons Journals, iii. 10, 12.

upon Oxford itself? It may perhaps quicken the negotiations there! —

This Design came to nothing, and soon sank into total obscurity again. But it seems Colonel Hampden did entertain such a Design, and even take some steps in it. And this Letter of Oliver's, coupled with the Entries in the Commons Journals, is perhaps the most authentic proof we yet have of that fact; an interesting fact which has rested hitherto on the vague testimony of Clarendon,* who seems to think the Design might have succeeded. But it came to nothing; Colonel Hampden could not rouse the Lord General to do more than "write at three in the morning," and send "special commands," for the present.

LETTER VII.

AND now here is a new horde of "Plunderers" threatening the Association with new infall from the North. The old Newspapers call them "Camdeners;" followers of a certain Noel, Viscount Camden, from Rutlandshire; who has seized Stamford, is driving cattle at a great rate, and fast threatening to become important in those quarters. — "Sir John Burgoyne" is the Burgoyne of Potton in Bedfordshire, chief Committee-man in that County: Bedford is not in our Association; but will perhaps lend us help in this common peril.

'To my honoured Friend Sir John Burgoyne, Baronet: These.'

SIR, 'Huntingdon,' 10th April 1643.

These Plunderers draw near. I think it will do well if you can afford us any assistance of Dragooners, to help in this great Exigence. We have here about Six or Seven Troops of Horse; such, I hope, as will fight. It's happy to resist such beginnings betimes.

If you can contribute anything to our aid, let us

* History of the Rebellion (Oxford, 1819), ii. 319; see also May's Long Parliament (Maseres's edition, London, 1812), p. 192.

speedily participate thereof.   In the mean time, and ever, command

Your humble servant,

OLIVER CROMWELL. §

Concerning these Camdeners at Stamford and elsewhere, so soon as Colonel Cromwell has got himself equipt, we shall hear tidings again.   Meanwhile, say the old Newspapers, * "there is a regiment of stout Northfolk blades gone to Wis- "beach, Croyland, and so into Holland" of Lincolnshire, "to preserve those parts," — if they may.   Colonel Cromwell will follow; and give good account of that matter by and by.

Lincolnshire in fact ought to be all subdued to the Parliament; added to the Association.   We could then cooperate with Fairfax across the Humber, and do good service!   So reason the old Committees, as one dimly ascertains. — The Parliament appointed a Lieutenant of Lincolnshire, Lord Willoughby of Parham, a year ago; ** but he is much infested with Camdeners, with enemies in all quarters, and has yet got no secure footing there.   Cromwell's work, and that of the Association, for the next twelvemonth, as we shall perceive, was that of clearing Lincolnshire from enemies, and accomplishing this problem.

LETTER VIII.

MEANWHILE enter Robert Barnard, Esquire, again.   Barnard, getting ever deeper into trouble, has run up to Town; has been persuading my Lord of Manchester and others, That he is not a disaffected man; that a contribution should not be inflicted on him by the County Committee.

---

§ Communicated (from an old Copy) by H. O. Cooper, Esq., Cambridge.

* In Cooper's Annals, iii. 343.

** Commons Journals (ii. 497), 25th March 1642.   New encouragement and sanction given him (Rushworth, v. 106), of date 9th Jan. 1642-3.

To my very loving Friend Robert Barnard, Esquire: Present these.

SIR,   'Huntingdon,' 17th April 1643.

I have received two Letters, one from my Lord of Manchester, the other from yourself; much to the same effect: I hope therefore one answer will serve them both.

Which is in short this: That we *know* you are disaffected to the Parliament; — and truly if the Lords, or any Friends, may take you off from a reasonable Contribution, for my part I should be glad to be commanded to any other employment. Sir, you may, if you will, "come freely into the country about your occasions." For my part, 1 have protected you in your absence; and shall do so to you.

This is all, — but that I am ready to serve you, and rest,

Your loving friend,
OLIVER CROMWELL. §

Let Barnard return, therefore; take a lower level, where the ways are more sheltered in stormy weather; — and so save himself, and "become Recorder after the Restoration." Subtlety may deceive him; integrity never will! —

LETTERS IX.—XI.

CROMWELL, we find, makes haste to deal with these "Camdeners." His next achievement is the raising of their Siege of Croyland (in the end of April, exact date not discoverable); concerning which there are large details in loud-spoken

§ Gentleman's Magazine (London, 1791), lxi. 44: no notice whence, no criticism or commentary there: Letter undoubtedly genuine.

Vicars:* How the reverend godly Mr. Ram and godly Sergeant Horne, both of Spalding, were "set upon the walls to
be shot at," when the Spalding people rose to deliver Croyland; how "Colonel Sir Miles Hobart" and other Colonels
rose also to deliver it, — and at last how "the valiant active
Colonel Cromwell" rose, and did actually deliver it.**

Cromwell has been at Lynn, he has been at Nottingham,
at Peterborough, where the Soldiers were not kind to the
Cathedral and its Surplice furniture:*** he has been here and
then swiftly there; encountering many things.   For Lincolnshire is not easy to deliver; dangers, intricate difficulties
abound in those quarters, and are increasing.   Lincolnshire,
infested with infalls of Camdeners, has its own Malignancies
too; — and, much more, is sadly overrun with the Marquis of
Newcastle's Northern "Popish Army" at present.   An Army
"full of Papists" as is currently reported; officered by renegade Scots, "Sir John Henderson," and the like unclean creatures.   For the Marquis, in spite of the Fairfaxes, has overflowed Yorkshire; flowed across the Humber; has fortified
himself in Newark-on-Trent, and is a sore affliction to the
well-affected thereabouts.   By the Queen's interest he is now,
from Earl, made Marquis, as we see.   For indeed, what is
worst of all, the Queen in late months has landed in these
Northern parts, with Dutch ammunition purchased by English
Crown Jewels; is stirring up all manner of "Northern Papists"
to double animation; tempting Hothams and other waverers
to meditate treachery, for which they will pay dear.   She is
the centre of these new perils.   She marches Southward,
much agitating the skirts of the Eastern Association; joins the
King "on Keinton field" or Edgehill field, where he fought
last autumn. — She was impeached of treason by the Com-

---

* "Thou that with ale, or viler liquors,
"Didst inspire Withers, Prynne and *Vicars*."
Hudibras, canto 1. 645.
** Vicars, p. 322-5; Newspapers (25th April — 2d May), in Cromwelliana,
p. 4.
*** Royalist Newspapers (in Cromwelliana, p. 4); Querela Cantab. &c. &c

mons.   She continued in England till the following summer; *
then quitted it for long years.

Let the following Three Letters, — one of which is farther
distinguished as the first of Cromwell's ever published in the
Newspapers, — testify what progress he is making in the difficult problem of delivering Lincolnshire in this posture of
affairs.

LETTER IX.

THERE was in those weeks, as we learn from the old Newspapers, a combined plan, of which Cromwell was an element,
for capturing Newark; there were several such; but this and
all the rest proved abortive, one element or another of the
combination always failing.   That Cromwell was not the
failing element we could already guess, and may now de-
finitely read.

"Lord Grey," be it remembered, is Lord Grey of Groby,
once Military Chief of the Association, — though now I think
employed mainly elsewhere, nearer home: a Leicestershire
man; as are "Hastings" and "Hartop:" well-known all of
them in the troubles of that County.   Hastings, strong for the
King, holds "Ashby-de-la-Zouch, which is his Father's House,
well fortified;"** and shows and has shown himself a pushing
man.   "His Excellency" is my Lord General Essex.   "Sir
John Gell" is Member and Commander for Derbyshire, has
Derby Town for Garrison.   The Derbyshire forces, the Nottinghamshire forces, the Association forces: if all the "forces"
could but be united!   But they never rightly can.

'*To the Honourable the Committee at Lincoln: These.*'
MY LORDS AND GENTLEMEN,
'Lincolnshire,' 3d May 1643.

I must needs be hardly thought on; because I am
still the messenger of unhappy tidings and delays con-

---

* From February 1642-3 till July 1644 (Clarendon, iii. 195; Rushworth,
v. 684).
** Clarendon, ii. 202.

cerning you, — though I know my heart is to assist you with all expedition!

My Lord Grey hath now again failed me of the rendezvous at Stamford, — notwithstanding that both he and I received Letters from his Excellency, commanding us both to meet, and, together with Sir John Gell and the Nottingham forces, to join with you. My Lord Grey sent Sir Edward Hartop to me, To let me know he could not meet me at Stamford according to our agreement; fearing the exposing of Leicester to the forces of Mr. Hastings and some other Troops drawing that way.

Believe it, it were better, in my poor opinion, Leicester were not, than that there should not be found an immediate taking of the field by our forces to accomplish the common ends. Wherein I shall deal as freely with him, when I meet him, as you can desire. I perceive Ashby-de-la-Zouch sticks much with him. I have offered him now another place of meeting;* to come to which I suppose he will not deny me; and that to be to-morrow. If you shall therefore think fit to send one over unto us to be with us at night, — you do not know how far we may prevail with him: To draw speedily to a head, with Sir John Gell and the other forces, where we may all meet at a general rendezvous, to the end you know of. And then you shall receive full satisfaction concerning my integrity;** — and if no man shall help you, yet will not I be wanting to do my duty, God assisting me.

If we could unite those forces 'of theirs;' and with them speedily make Grantham the general rendezvous,

* Name, not so fit to be *written* for fear of accidents, is very much unknown now!

** Means, "that the blame was not in me."

both of yours and ours, I think it would do well. I shall bend my endeavours that way. Your concurrence by some able instrument to solicit this, might probably exceedingly hasten it; especially having so good a foundation to work upon as my Lord General's commands. Our Norfolk forces, which will not prove so many as you may imagine by six or seven hundred men, will lie conveniently at Spalding; and, I am confident, be ready to meet at Grantham at the general rendezvous.

I have no more to trouble you; but begging of God to take away the impediments that hinder our conjunction, and to prosper our designs, take leave.

Your faithful servant,
OLIVER CROMWELL. §

Some rendezvous at Grantham does take place, some uniting of forces, more or fewer; and strenuous endeavour thereupon. As the next Letter will testify.

LETTER X.

This Letter is the first of Cromwell's ever published in the Newspapers. "That valiant soldier Colonel Cromwell" has written on this occasion to an official Person of name not now discoverable:

"*To* —— ——: *These.*"

SIR, "Grantham, 13th May 1643."
God hath given us, this evening, a glorious victory over our enemies. They were, as we are informed, one-and-twenty colours of horse-troops, and three or four of dragoons.

§ Tanner MSS. (Oxford), lxii. 94: the address lost, the date of place never given; the former clearly restorable from Commons Journals, ii. 75.

It was late in the evening when we drew out; they came and faced us within two miles of the town. So soon as we had the alarm, we drew out our forces, consisting of about twelve troops, — whereof some of them so poor and broken, that you shall seldom see worse: with this handful it pleased God to cast the scale. For after we had stood a little, above musket-shot the one body from the other; and the dragooners had fired on both sides, for the space of half an hour or more; they not advancing towards us, we agreed to charge them. And, advancing the body after many shots on both sides, we came on with our troops a pretty round trot; they standing firm to receive us: and our men charging fiercely upon them, by God's providence they were immediately routed, and ran all away, and we had the execution of them two or three miles.

I believe some of our soldiers did kill two or three men apiece in the pursuit; but what the number of dead is we are not certain. We took forty-five Prisoners, besides divers of their horse and arms, and rescued many Prisoners whom they had lately taken of ours; and we took four or five of their colours. 'I rest'

*   *   *

'OLIVER CROMWELL.' §

On inquiry at Grantham, there is no vestige of tradition as to the scene of this skirmish; which must have been some two miles out on the Newark road. Thomas May, a veracious intelligent man, but vague as to dates, mentions two notable skirmishes of Cromwell's "near to Grantham," in the course of this business; one especially in which "he defeated a strong "party of the Newarkers, where the odds of number on their

---

§ **Perfect Diurnal of the Passages in Parliament, 22d-29th May 1643;** completed from Vicars, p. 332, whose copy, however, is not, except as to sense and facts, to be relied on.

"side was so great that it seemed almost a miraculous vic-
"tory:" that probably is the one now in question. Colonel
Cromwell, we farther find, was very "vigilant of all sallies
"that were made, and took many men and colours at several
"times;"* and did what was in Colonel Cromwell; — but
could not take Newark at present. One element or other of
the combination always fails. Newark, again and again besieged, did not surrender until the end of the War. At present, it is terribly wet weather, for one thing; "thirteen days
of continual rain."

The King, as we observed, is in Oxford: Treaty, of very
slow gestation, came to birth in March last, and was carried
on there by Whitlocke and others till the beginning of April;
but ended in absolute nothing.** The King still continues in
Oxford, — his head-quarters for three years to come. The
Lord General Essex did at one time think of Oxford, but preferred to take Reading first; is lying now scattered about
Thame, and Brickhill in Buckinghamshire, much drenched
with the unseasonable rains, in a very dormant, discontented
condition.*** Colonel Hampden is with him. There is talk of
making Colonel Hampden Lord General. The immediate
hopes of the world, however, are turned on "that valiant soldier and patriot of his country" Sir William Waller, who has
marched to discomfit the Malignants of the West.

On the 4th of this May, Cheapside Cross, Charing Cross,
and other Monuments of Papist Idolatry were torn down by
authority, "troops of soldiers sounding their trumpets, and
all the people shouting;" the Book of Sports was also burnt
upon the ruins of the same.† In which days, too, all the
people are working at the Fortification of London.

* History of Long Parliament, p. 208.
** Whitlocke, 1st edition, pp. 63-5; Husbands, II. 48-119.
** Rushworth, v. 290; May, p. 132.
† Lithgow (in Somers Tracts, iv. 536); Vicars (date incorrect), p. 327.

LETTER XI.

THE "great Service," spoken of in this Letter, we must still understand to be the deliverance of Lincolnshire in general; or if it were another, it did not take effect. No possibility yet of getting over into Yorkshire to cooperate with the Fairfaxes, — though they much need help, and there have been speculations of that and of other kinds.* For the War-tide breaks in very irregular billows upon our shores; at one time we are pretty clear of Newark and its Northern Papists; and anon "the Queen has got into Newark," and we are like to be submerged by them. As a general rule, intricate perilous difficulties abound; and cash is scarce. The Fairfaxes, meanwhile, last week, have gained a Victory at Wakefield;** which is a merciful encouragement.

"To the Mayor, &c. of Colchester: These."

GENTLEMEN,   'Lincolnshire,' 28th May 1643.

I thought it my duty once more to write unto you For more strength to be speedily sent unto us, for this great Service.

I suppose you hear of the great Defeat given by my Lord Fairfax to the Newcastle Forces at Wakefield. It was a great mercy of God to us. And had it not been bestowed upon us at this very present, my Lord Fairfax had not known how to have subsisted. We assure you, should the Force we have miscarry, — expect nothing but a speedy march of the Enemy up unto you.

Why you should not strengthen us to make us subsist, — judge you the danger of the neglect; and how inconvenient this improvidence, or unthrift, may be to

---

* Old Newspapers (30th May—12th June 1643), in Cromwelliana, p. 6.
** 21st May 1643: Letter by Lord Fairfax (in Rushworth, v. 268); Short Memorials, by the younger Fairfax (in Somers Tracts, v. 380.)

you! I shall never write but according to my judgment: I tell you again, It concerns you exceedingly to be persuaded by me. My Lord Newcastle is near Six-thousand foot, and above Sixty troops of horse; my Lord Fairfax is about Three-thousand foot, and Nine troops of horse; and we have about Twenty-four troops of horse and dragooners. The Enemy draws more to the Lord Fairfax: our motion and yours must be exceeding speedy, or else it will do you no good at all.

If you send, let your men come to Boston. I beseech you hasten the supply to us: — forget not money! I press not hard; though I do so need that, I assure you, the foot and dragooners are ready to mutiny. Lay not too much upon the back of a poor gentleman, who desires, without much noise, to lay down his life, and bleed the last drop to serve the Cause and you. I ask not your money for myself: if that were my end and hope, — viz. the pay of my place, — I would not open my mouth at this time. I desire to deny myself; but others will not be satisfied. I beseech you hasten supplies. Forget not your prayers.

Gentlemen, I am
Yours,
OLIVER CROMWELL. §

"Lay not too much upon a poor gentleman," — who is really doing what he can; shooting swiftly, now hither, now thither, wheresoever the tug of difficulty lies; struggling very sore, as beseems the Son of Light and Son of Adam, not to be vanquished by the mud-element!

Intricate struggles; sunk almost all in darkness now: — of which take this other as a token, gathered still luminous from the authentic but mostly inane opacities of the *Commons Jour-*

---

§ Morant's History of Colchester, book i. p. 56.

nals: * "21 June 1643, Mr. Pym reports from the Committee of "the Safety of the Kingdom," our chief authority at present, to this effect, That Captain Hotham, son of the famed Hull Hotham, had, as appeared by Letters from Lord Grey and Colonel Cromwell, now at Nottingham, been behaving very ill; had plundered divers persons without regard to the side they were of; had, on one occasion, "turned two pieces of ordnance *against* Colonel Cromwell;" nay, once, when Lord Grey's quartermaster was in some huff with Lord Grey "about oats," had privily offered to the said quartermaster that they two should draw out their men, and have a fight for it with Lord Grey; — not to speak of frequent correspondences with Newark, with Newcastle, and the Queen now come back from Holland: wherefore he is arrested there in Nottingham, and locked up for trial.

This was on the Wednesday, this report of Pym's: and, alas, while Pym reads it, John Hampden, mortally wounded four days ago in a skirmish at Chalgrove Field, lies dying at Thame; — died on the Saturday following!

LETTERS XII.—XV.

"On Thursday July the 27th," on, or shortly before that day, "news reach London," that Colonel Cromwell has taken Stamford, — retaken it, I think; at all events taken it. Whereupon the Cavaliers from Newark and Belvoir Castle came hovering about him: he drove them into Burleigh House, Burleigh on the Hill in Rutlandshire, and laid siege to the same; "at three in the morning," battered it with all his shot, and stormed it at last. ** Which is "a good help we have had this week."

On the other hand, at Gainsborough we are suffering siege; indisputably the Newarkers threaten to get the upper hand in that quarter of the County.   Here is Cromwell's Letter, —

---

* Commnos Journals, iii. 138.
** Vicars; Newspapers (in Cromwelliana, p. 6).

happily now the original itself; — concerning Lord Willoughby of Parham, and the relief of Gainsborough "with powder
and match."

LETTER XII.

In Rushworth and the old Newspaper copies of this Letter,
along with certain insignificant, perhaps involuntary varia-
tions, there are two noticeable omissions; the whole of the *first*
paragraph, and nearly the whole of the *last*, omitted for cause
by the old official persons; who furthermore have given only
the virtual address "*To the Committee of the Association sitting
at Cambridge,*" not the specific one as here:

*To my noble Friends, Sir Edmund Bacon, Knight and Baronet,
Sir William Spring, Knight and Baronet, Sir Thomas Bar-
nardiston, Knight, and Maurice Barrow, Esquire: Present these.*

GENTLEMEN,   Huntingdon, 31st July 1643.

No man desires more to present you with encouragement than myself, because of the forwardness I find in
you, — to your honour be it spoken, — to promote
this great Cause.   And truly God follows us with encouragements, who is the God of blessings: — and I
beseech you let Him not lose His blessings upon us!
They come in season, and with all the advantages of
heartening: as if God should say, "Up and be doing,
and I will stand by you, and help you!"   There is
nothing to be feared but our own sin and sloth.*

It hath pleased the Lord to give your servant and
soldiers a notable victory now at Gainsborough.   I
marched after the taking of Burleigh House upon Wednesday to Grantham, where I met about 300 horse and
dragooners of Nottingham.   With these, by agreement,
we met the Lincolners at North Scarle, which is about

* This paragraph is omitted in Rushworth and the Newspapers.

ten miles from Gainsborough, upon Thursday in the
evening; where we tarried until two of the clock in the
morning; and then with our whole body advanced towards Gainsborough.

About a mile and a half from the Town, we met a
forlorn-hope of the enemy of near 100 horse. Our dragooners laboured to beat them back; but not alighting
off their horses, the enemy charged them, and beat
some four or five of them off their horses: our horse
charged them, and made them retire unto their main
body. We advanced, and came to the bottom of a
steep hill: we could not well get up but by some tracks;
which our men essaying to do, a body of the enemy
endeavoured to hinder; wherein we prevailed, and got
the top of the hill. This was done by the Lincolners,
who had the vanguard.

When we all recovered the top of the hill, we saw
a great Body of the enemy's horse facing us, at about
a musket-shot or less distance; and a good Reserve of
a full regiment of horse behind it. We endeavoured
to put our men into as good order as we could. The
enemy in the mean time advanced towards us, to take
us at disadvantage; but in such order as we were, we
charged their great body, I having the right wing; we
came up horse to horse; where we disputed it with our
swords and pistols a pretty time; all keeping close order,
so that one could not break the other. At last, they a
little shrinking, our men perceiving it, pressed in upon
them, and immediately routed this whole body; some
flying on one side and others on the other of the
enemy's Reserve; and our men, pursuing them, had
chase and execution about five or six miles.

I perceiving this body which was the Reserve standing still unbroken, kept back my Major, Whalley, from the chase; and with my own troop and the other of my regiment, in all being three troops, we got into a body. In this Reserve stood General Cavendish; who one while faced me, another while faced four of the Lincoln troops, which was all of ours that stood upon the place, the rest being engaged in the chase. At last General Cavendish charged the Lincolners, and routed them. Immediately I fell on his rear with my three troops; which did so astonish him, that he gave over the chase, and would fain have delivered himself from me. But I pressing on forced them down a hill, having good execution of them; and below the hill, drove the General with some of his soldiers into a quagmire; where my Captain-lieutenant slew him with a thrust under his short ribs. The rest of the body was wholly routed, not one man staying upon the place.

We then, after this defeat which was so total, re-lieved the Town with such powder and provision as we brought. Which done, we had notice that there were six troops of horse and 300 foot on the other side of the Town, about a mile off us: we desired some foot of my Lord Willoughby's, about 400; and, with our horse and these foot, marched towards them: when we came towards the place where their horse stood, we beat back with my troops about two or three troops of the enemy's, who retired into a small village at the bottom of the hill. When we recovered the hill, we saw in the bottom, about a quarter of a mile from us, a regiment of foot; after that another; after that the Marquis of Newcastle's own regiment; consisting in all of about 50 foot colours, and a great body of horse;

— which indeed was Newcastle's Army. Which, coming so unexpectedly, put us to new consultations. My Lord Willoughby and I, being in the Town, agreed to call off our foot. I went to bring them off: but before I returned, divers of the foot were engaged; the enemy advancing with his whole body. Our foot retreated in disorder; and with some loss got the Town; where now they are. Our horse also came off with some trouble; being wearied with the long fight, and their horses tired; yet faced the enemy's fresh horse, and by several removes got off without the loss of one man; the enemy following the rear with a great body. The honour of this retreat is due to God, as also all the rest: Major Whalley did in this carry himself with all gallantry becoming a gentleman and a Christian.

Thus you have this true relation, as short as I could. What you are to do upon it, is next to be considered.* If I could speak words to pierce your hearts with the sense of our and your condition, I would! If you will raise 2,000 Foot at present to encounter this Army of Newcastle's, to raise the siege, and to enable us to fight him, — we doubt not, by the grace of God, but that we shall be able to relieve the Town, and beat the Enemy on** the other side of Trent. Whereas if somewhat be not done in this, you will see Newcastle's Army march up into your bowels; being now, as it is, on this side Trent. I know it will be difficult to raise thus many in so short time: but let me assure you, it's necessary, and therefore to *be* done. At least do what you may, with all possible expedition! I would I had the happiness to speak with one of you: — truly I

* The rest of this paragraph, all except the last sentence, is omitted: Postscript, too, omitted.
** Means "to."

cannot come over, but must attend my charge; the Enemy is vigilant. The Lord direct you what to do.
. Gentlemen, I am
Your faithful servant,
OLIVER CROMWELL.

P.S. Give this Gentleman credence; he is worthy to be trusted, he knows the urgency of our affairs better than myself. If he give you intelligence, in point of time, of haste to be made, — believe him: he will advise for your good. §

About two miles south of Gainsborough, on the North-Scarle road, stands the Hamlet and Church of Lea; near which is a "Hill," or expanse of upland, of no great height, but sandy, covered with furze, and full of rabbit-holes, the ascent of which would be difficult for horsemen in the teeth of an enemy. This is understood to be the "Hill" of the Fight referred to here. Good part of it is enclosed, and the ground much altered, since that time; but one of the fields is still called "*Redcoats* Field," and another at some distance nearer Gainsborough "*Graves* Field;" beyond which latter, "on the other or "western face of the Hill, a little over the boundary of Lea "Parish with Gainsborough Parish, on the left hand (as you go "North) between the Road and the River," is a morass or meadow still known by the name of *Cavendish's Bog*, which points out the locality.*

Of the "Hills" and "Villages" rather confusedly alluded to in the second part of the Letter, which probably lay across Trent Bridge on the Newark side of the river, I could obtain no elucidation, — and must leave them to the guess of local antiquaries interested in such things.**

§ Rushworth, v. 278; — given now (*Third Edition*) according to Autograph in the possession of Dawson Turner, Esq., Great Yarmouth. (Papers of Norfolk Archæological Society, Jan. 1848; and Athenæum, London, 11th March 1848.)
* MS. *penes me*.
** Two other Letters on this Gainsborough Action, in Appendix, No. 5.

"General Cavendish," whom some confound with the Earl of Newcastle's brother, was his *Cousin*, "the Earl of Devonshire's second son;" an accomplished young man of three-and-twenty; for whom there was great lamenting; — indeed a general emotion about his death, of which we, in these radical times, very irreverent of human quality itself, and much more justly of the *dresses* of human quality, cannot even with effort form any adequate idea.   This was the first action that made Cromwell to be universally talked of: He dared to kill this honourable person found in arms against him! "Colonel Crom-"well gave assistance to the Lord Willoughby, and performed "very gallant service against the Earl of Newcastle's forces. "'This was the beginning of his great fortunes, and now he "began to appear in the world."*

Waller has an Elegy, not his best, upon "Charles Ca'ndish."** It must have been written some time afterwards: poor Waller, in these weeks, very narrowly escapes death himself, on account of the "Waller Plot;" — makes an abject submission; pays 10,000*l*. fine; and goes upon his travels into foreign parts! —

LETTER XIII.

HERE meanwhile is a small noteworthy thing.   Consider these "Young Men and Maids," and that little joint-stock company of theirs! Amiable young persons, may it prosper with you.   Twelve-score pounds and so many stand of muskets, — well, this little too, in the great Cause, will help.   For a pure preached Gospel, and the ancient liberties of England, who would not try to help? Fine new cloaks and fardingales are good; but a company of musketeers busy on the right side, how much better! — Colonel Cromwell, now home again, has received a Deputation on the matter; and suggests improvements.   "Country" which will take your muskets, means *County*.   Three pounds, we perceive by calculation, will buy a

* Whitlocke (1st edition, London, 1682, — as always, unless the contrary be specified), p. 68.
** Fenton's Waller, p. 209.

war-saddle and pistols.   Who the "Sir" is, guessable as some
Chairman of this "Young Men and Maids" Society; and in
what Town he sits, whether in Huntingdon itself or in another,
—must remain forever uncertain. His Address, by negligence,
has vanished; his affair wholly has vanished; the body of it
gone all to air, and only the *soul* of it now surviving, and like
to survive!

To —— ——.

Sir, 'Huntingdon,' 2d August 1643.

I understand by these Gentlemen the good affections of your Young Men and Maids; for which God is
to be praised.

I approve of the business: only I desire to advise
you that your "foot company" may be turned into a
troop of horse; which indeed will, by God's blessing,
far more advantage the Cause than two or three companies of foot; especially if your men be honest godly
men, which by all means I desire.   I thank God for
stirring up the youth to cast in their mite, which I desire may be employed to the best advantage; therefore
my advice is, thát you would employ your Twelve-score
Pounds to buy pistols and saddles, and I will provide
Four-score horses; for 400*l.* more will not raise a troop
of horse.   As for the muskets that are bought, I think
the Country will take them of you. Pray raise honest
godly men, and I will have them of my regiment. As
for your Officers, I leave it as God shall or hath directed to choose; — and rest,

Your loving friend,
OLIVER CROMWELL. §

§ Fairfax Correspondence (London, 1849), iii. 50: the Original is Autograph; address quite gone; docketed "Colonel Cromwell's Letter to" (in
regard to) "the Bachelors and Maids, 2d August 1643, from Huntingdon."

LETTER XIV.

GAINSBOROUGH was directly taken, after this relief of it; Lord Willoughby could not resist the Newarkers with Newcastle at their head. Gainsborough is lost, Lincoln is lost; unless help come speedily, all is like to be lost. The following Letter, with its enclosure from the Lord Lieutenant Willoughby of Parham, speaks for itself. Read the Enclosure first.

" To my noble Friend Colonel Cromwell at Huntingdon: These.

"Boston, 5th August 1643.

"NOBLE SIR, — Since the business of Gainsborough, the "hearts of our men have been so deaded that we have lost most "of them by running away. So that we were forced to leave "Lincoln upon a sudden: — and if I had not done it then, I "should have been left alone in it. So that now I am at "Boston; where we are very poor in strength; — so that with-"out some speedy supply, I fear we shall not hold this long "neither.

"My Lord General, I perceive, hath writ to you, To draw "all the forces together. I should be glad to see it: for if that "will not be, there can be no good to be expected. If you will "endeavour to stop my Lord of Newcastle, you must presently "draw them to him and fight him! For without we be masters "of the field, we shall be pulled out by the ears, one after "another.

"The Foot, if they will come on, may march very securely "to Boston; which, to me, will be very considerable to your "Association. For if the Enemy get that Town, which is now "very weak for defence for want of men, I believe they will not "be long out of Norfolk and Suffolk.

"I can say no more: but desire you to hasten; — and rest,
"Your servant,
"FRANCIS WILLOUGHBY." *

* Baker MSS. (Trinity-College Library, Cambridge), xxxiv. 429; is in Tanner MSS. too, together with the following.

To my honoured Friends the Commissioners at Cambridge:
These present.

GENTLEMEN, Huntingdon, 6th August 1643.

You see by this Enclosed how sadly your affairs stand. It's no longer Disputing, but Out instantly all you can! Raise all your Bands;* send them to Huntingdon; — get up what Volunteers you can: hasten your Horses.

Send these Letters to Norfolk, Suffolk and Essex, without delay. I beseech you spare not, but be expeditious and industrious! Almost all our Foot have quitted Stamford: there is nothing to interrupt an Enemy, but our Horse, that is considerable. You must act lively; do it without distraction. Neglect no means! — I am

Your faithful servant,
OLIVER CROMWELL. §

In the Commons Journals, *August 4th*,** are various Orders, concerning Colonel Cromwell and his affairs, of a comfortable nature: as, "That he shall have the Three-thousand Pounds, already levied in the Associated Counties, for payment of his men;" likewise privilege of "Free Quarter on the march he is now upon;" and lastly, "That the Six Associated Counties do forthwith raise Two-thousand men more" for his behoof and that of the Cause. On which occasion Speaker Lenthall, as we otherwise find, writes to him on the part of the House, in these encouraging terms: "The House hath commanded me to send "you these enclosed Orders; and to let you know that nothing "is more repugnant to the sense of this House, and dangerous "to this Kingdom, than the unwillingness of their forces to "march out of their several Counties." — "For yourself, they

* Trainbands.
§ Cooper's Annals of Cambridge, iii. 355; Tanner mss. lxii. 229.
** Commons Journals, iii. 193.

"do exceedingly approve of your faithful endeavours to God
"and the Kingdom."*

LETTER XV.

THE Committee's answer, "my return from you," will find
Cromwell at Stamford; to which, as to the place of danger, he
is already speeding and spurring.   Here is his next Letter to
these Honoured Friends:

To my honoured Friends the Commissioners at Cambridge:
These present.

GENTLEMEN,   'Peterborough,' 8th August 1643.

Finding our foot much lessened at Stamford, and
having a great train and many carriages, I held it not
safe to continue there, but presently after my return
from you, I ordered the foot to quit that place and
march into Holland, 'to Spalding;' which they did on
Monday last.** I was the rather induced so to do because of the Letter I received from my Lord Willoughby,
a copy whereof I sent you.

I am now at Peterborough, whither I came this
afternoon. I was no sooner come but Lieutenant Colonel
Wood sent me word, from Spalding, that the Enemy
was marching, with twelve flying colours of horse and
foot, within a mile of Swinstead: so that I hope it
was a good providence of God that our foot were at
Spalding.

It much concerns your Association, and the Kingdom, that so strong a place as Holland is be not possessed by them. If you have any foot ready to march,
send them away to us with all speed. I fear lest the
Enemy should press in upon our foot: — he being thus
far advanced towards you, I hold it very fit that you

---

* Tanner MSS. lxii. (i.), 224.   ** Yesterday.

should hasten your horse at Huntingdon, and what you can speedily raise at Cambridge, unto me. I dare not go into Holland with my horse, lest the enemy should advance with his whole body of horse, this 'way, into your Association; but remain ready here, endeavouring * my Lord Grey's and the Northamptonshire horse towards me, — that so, if we be able, we may fight the enemy, or retreat unto you, with our whole strength. I beseech you hasten your levies, what you can; especially those of foot! Quicken all our friends with new letters upon this occasion; — which I believe you will find to be a true alarm. The particulars I hope to be able to inform you speedily of, more punctually; having sent, in all haste, to Colonel Wood for that purpose.

The money I brought with me is so poor a pittance when it comes to be distributed amongst all my troops that, considering their necessity, — it will not half clothe them, they were so far behind, — if we have not more money speedily, they will be exceedingly discouraged. I am sorry you put me to it to write thus often. It makes it seem a needless importunity in me; whereas, in truth, it is a constant neglect of those that should provide for us. Gentlemen, make them able to live and subsist that are willing to spend their blood for you! — I say no more; but rest

Your faithful servant,

OLIVER CROMWELL. §

Sir William Waller, whom some called William the Conqueror, has been beaten all to pieces on Lansdown Heath, about three weeks ago. The Fairfaxes too are beaten from the field; glad to get into Hull, — which Hotham the Traitor was about delivering to her Majesty, when vigilant persons

---

* "but am ready endeavouring," *in orig.*
§ Fairfax Correspondence, iii. 58.

laid him fast. *   And, in the end of May, Earl Stamford was
defeated in the Southwest; and now Bristol has been suddenly
surrendered to Prince Rupert, — for which let Colonel Nathaniel Fiennes (says Mr. Prynne, still very zealous) be tried by
Court-Martial, and if possible, shot.

LETTERS XVI.—XVIII.

In the very hours while Cromwell was storming the sand-
hill near Gainsborough "by some tracks," honourable gentlemen at St. Stephen's were voting him Governor of the Isle of
Ely.   Ely in the heart of the Fens, a place of great military
capabilities, is much troubled with "corrupt ministers," with
"corrupt trainbands," and understood to be in a perilous
state; wherefore they nominate Cromwell to take charge of
it. ** We understand his own Family to be still resident
in Ely.

The Parliament affairs, this Summer, have taken a bad
course; and except it be in the Eastern Association, look
everywhere declining.   They have lost Bristol, their footing
in the Southwest and in the North is mostly gone; Essex's
Army has melted away, without any action of mark all Summer, except the *loss* of Hampden in a skirmish.   In the beginning of August, the King breaks out from Oxford, very
clearly superior in force; goes to settle Bristol; and might
thence, it was supposed, have marched direct to London,
if he had liked.   He decides on taking Gloucester with him
before he quit those parts.   The Parliament, in much extremity, calls upon the Scots for help; who under conditions
will consent.

In these circumstances, it was rather thought a piece of
heroism in our old friend Lord Kimbolton, or Mandevil, now

* Of Hotham: 29th June 1643 (Rushworth, v. 275, 6); — of the Fairfaxes, at Adderton Moor: 30th June (ib. 279); — of Waller: 13th July
(ib. 285; Clarendon, ii. 376-9).   Stratton Fight in Cornwall, defeat of Stamford by Hopton, was 16th May; Bristol is 22d July (Rushworth, v. 271, 284).
** Commons Journals, iii. 186 (of 28th July 1643); ib. 153, 167, 180, &c.
to 657 (9th October 1644).

become Earl of Manchester, to accept the command of the Eastern Association: he is nominated "Sergeant-Major of the Associated Counties," 10th August 1643; is to raise new force, infantry and cavalry; has four Colonels of Horse under him; Colonel Cromwell, who soon became his second in command, is one of them; Colonel Norton, whom we shall meet afterwards, is another.* "The Associated Counties are busy "listing," intimates the old Newspaper; "and so soon as their "harvest is over, which for the present much retardeth them, "the Earl of Manchester will have a very brave and consider- "able Army, to be a terror to the Northern Papists," Newark- ers and Newcastles, "if they advance Southward."** When specially it was that Cromwell listed his celebrated body of *Ironsides* is of course not to be dated, though some do care- lessly date it, as from the very "beginning of the War;" and in Bates*** and others are to be found various romantic details on the subject, which deserve no credit. Doubtless Crom- well, all along, in the many changes his body of men under- went, had his eye upon this object of getting good soldiers and dismissing bad; and managed the matter by common practical vigilance, not by theatrical claptraps as Dr. Bates represents. Some months ago, it was said in the Newspapers, of Colonel Cromwell's soldiers, "not a man swears but he pays his twelvepence;" no plundering, no drinking, disorder, or impiety allowed.† We may fancy, in this new levy, as Manchester's Lieutenant and Governor of Ely, when the whole force was again winnowed and sifted, he might com- plete the process, and see his Thousand Troopers ranked be- fore him, worthy at last of the name of *Ironsides*. They were men that had the fear of God; and gradually lost all other fear. 'Truly they were never beaten at all,' says he. — Meanwhile:

1643.

August 21*st*. The shops of London are all shut for certain

---

* Commons Journals, iii 199, 200; Husbands, ii. 286, 276-8.
** 29th August 1643, Cromwelliana, p. 7.   *** Elenchus Motuum.
† May 1643, Cromwelliana, p. 5.

11*

days.* Gloucester is in hot siege; nothing but the obdurate valour of a few men there prevents the King, with Prince Rupert, called also Prince Robert and Prince *Robber*, from riding roughshod over us.** The City, with much emotion, ranks its Trained Bands under Essex; making up an Army for him, despatches him to relieve Gloucester. He marches on the 26th; steadily along, in spite of rainy weather and Prince Rupert; westward, westward: on the night of the tenth day, September 5th, the Gloucester people see his signal-fire flame up, amid the dark rain, "on the top of Presbury Hill;" — and understand that they shall live and not die. The King "fired his huts," and marched off without delay. He never again had any real chance of prevailing in this War. Essex, having relieved the West, returns steadily home again, the King's forces hanging angrily on his rear; at Newbury in Berkshire, he had to turn round, and give them battle, — *First* Newbury Battle, 20th September 1643, — wherein he came off rather superior.*** Poor Lord Falkland, in his "clean shirt," was killed here. This steady march, to Gloucester and back again, by Essex, was the chief feat he did during the War; a considerable feat, and very characteristic of him, the slow-going, inarticulate, indignant, somewhat elephantine man.

Here however, in the interim, are some glimpses of the Associated Counties; of the "listing" that now goes on there, a thing attended with its own confused troubles.

LETTER XVI.

Letter Sixteenth is not dated at all; but incidentally names its place; and by the tenor of it sufficiently indicates these autumn days, first days of September, as the approxi-

---

* Rushworth, v. 291.
** See Webb's *Bibliotheca Gloucestrensis, a Collection*, &c. (Gloucester, 1825), or Corbet's contemporary *Siege of Gloucester* (Somers Tracts, v. 296), which forms the main substance of Mr. Webb's Book.
*** Clarendon, ii. 460; Whitlocke, p. 70.

mate time. "Our handful," to be known by and by as *Iron-sides*, they are ready and steady; but we see what an affair the listing of the rest is: cash itself like to be dreadfully short; men difficult to raise, worth little when raised; — add seizure of Malignant neighbours' horses, proclamations, re-clamations, and the Lawyers' tongues, and all men's, every-where set wagging! Spring and Barrow are leading Suffolk Committee-men, whom we shall see again in that capacity. Of Captain Margery, elsewhere than in that Suffolk Troop now mustering, I know nothing; but Colonel Cromwell knows him, can recommend him as a man worth something: if Mar-gery, to mount himself in this pressure, could "raise the horses from Malignants," in some measure, — were it not well?

To my noble Friends, Sir William Spring, Knight and Baronet,' and Maurice Barrow, Esquire: Present these.

GENTLEMEN,   'Cambridge, — September 1643.'

I have been now two days at Cambridge, in ex-pectation to hear the fruit of your endeavours in Suffolk towards the public assistance. Believe it, you will hear of a storm in few days! You have no Infantry at all considerable; hasten your Horses; — a few hours may undo you, neglected. — I beseech you be careful what Captains of Horse you choose, what men be mounted: a few honest men are better than numbers. Some time they must have for exercise. If you choose godly honest men to be Captains of Horse, honest men will follow them; and they will be careful to mount such.

The King is exceeding strong in the West. If you be able to foil a force at the first coming of it, you will have reputation; and that is of great advantage in our affairs. God hath given it to our handful; let us endeavour to keep it.   I had rather have a plain russet-coated Captain that knows what he fights for, and loves what he knows, than that which you call "a Gentleman" and is nothing else.   I honour a *Gentleman* that is so indeed! —

I understand Mr. Margery hath honest men will follow him: if so, be pleased to make use of him; it much concerns your good to have conscientious men. I understand that there is an Order for me to have 3,000 *l.* out of the Association; and Essex hath sent their part, or near it.   I assure you we need exceedingly.   I hope to find your favour and respect.   I protest, if it were for myself, I would not move you. That is all, from

Your faithful servant,

OLIVER CROMWELL.

P. S.   If you send such men as Essex hath sent, it will be to little purpose.   Be pleased to take care of their march; and that such may come along with them as will be able to bring them to the main Body; and then I doubt not but we shall keep them, and make good use of them. — I beseech you, give countenance to Mr. Margery! Help him in raising his Troop; let him not want your favour in whatsoever is needful for promoting this work; — and *command* your servant.   If he can raise the horses from Malignants, let him have your warrant: it will be of special service. §

§ Original in the possession of Dawson Turner, Esq., Great Yarmouth; printed in Papers of Norfolk Archæological Society (Norwich, January 1848).

LETTER XVII.

LISTING still; and with more trouble than ever. Matters go not well: " Nobody to *put-on*," nobody to *push;* cash too is and remains defective: — here, however, is another glimpse of the *Ironsides*, first specific glimpse, which is something.

To my honoured Friend Oliver St. John, Esquire, at Lincoln's Inn: These present.

SIR, 'Eastern Association,' 11th Sept. '1643.'

Of all men I should not trouble you with money matters, — did not the heavy necessities my Troops are in, press me beyond measure. I am neglected exceedingly!

I am now ready for* my march towards the Enemy; who hath entrenched himself over against Hull, my Lord Newcastle having besieged the Town. Many of my Lord of Manchester's Troops are come to me: very bad and mutinous, not to be confided in; — *they* paid to a week almost; *mine* noways provided-for to support them, except by the poor Sequestrations of the County of Huntingdon! — My Troops increase. I have a lovely company; you would respect them, did you know them. They are no "Anabaptists;" they are honest sober Christians: — they expect to be used as men!

If I took pleasure to write to the House in bitterness, I have occasion. 'Of' the 3,000 *l.* allotted me, I cannot get the Norfolk part nor the Hertfordshire: it was gone before I had it. — I have minded your service to forgetfulness of my own and Soldiers' necessities. I desire not to seek myself: — 'but' I have little money of my own to help my Soldiers. My estate is little. I tell you, the business of Ireland and England

---

* "upon" crossed out as ambiguous; "ready for" written over it.

hath had of me, in money, between Eleven and Twelve Hundred pounds; — therefore my Private can do little to help the Public.   You have had my money: I hope in God I desire to venture my skin.   So do mine.   Lay weight upon their patience; but break it not! Think of that which may be a real help.   I believe 5,000 *l.* * is due.

If you lay aside the thought of me and my Letter, I expect no help.   Pray for

Your true friend and servant,

OLIVER CROMWELL.

'P. S.'   There is no care taken how to maintain that Force of Horse and Foot raised and a-raising for my Lord of Manchester.   He hath not one able to put-on 'that business.'   The Force will fall if some help not. Weak counsels and weak actings undo all! — [*two words crossed out*]: — all will be lost, if God help not! Remember who tells you. §

In Lynn Regis there arose "distractions" last Spring; distractions ripening into open treason, and the seizure of Lynn by Malignant forces, — Roger L'Estrange, known afterwards as Sir Roger the busy Pamphleteer, being very active in it.   Lynn lies strong amid its marshes; a gangrene in the heart of the Association itself.   My Lord of Manchester is now, with all the regular Foot, and what utmost effort of volunteers the Country can make, besieging Lynn, does get it, at last, in a week hence.   Ten days hence the Battle of Newbury is got; and much joy for Gloucester and it.   But here in the Association, with such a weight of enemies upon us, and such a stagnancy and staggering want of pith within us, things still look extremely questionable! —

* Erased, as not the correct sum.

§ Additional Ayscough MSS. 5015, art. 25: printed, with some errors, in Annual Register, xxxv. 358.

Monday, 25th September.   The House of Commons and the Assembly of Divines take the Covenant, the old Scotch Covenant, slightly modified now into a "Solemn League and Covenant;" in St. Margaret's Church, Westminster.* They lifted up their hands *seriatim*, and then "stept into the chancel to sign." The list yet remains in Rushworth, — incorrect in some places. There sign in all about 220 Honourable Members that day. The whole Parliamentary Party, down to the lowest constable or drummer in their pay, gradually signed. It was the condition of assistance from the Scotch; who are now calling out "all fencible men from sixteen to sixty," for a third expedition into England. A very solemn Covenant, and Vow of all the People; of the awfulness of which, we, in these days of Customhouse oaths and loose regardless talk, cannot form the smallest notion. — Duke Hamilton, seeing his painful Scotch diplomacy end all in this way, flies to the King at Oxford, — is there "put under arrest," sent to Pendennis Castle near the Land's End.**

LETTER XVIII.

In Rushworth's List of Members covenanting in St. Margaret's Church on Monday September 25th, the name of Oliver Cromwell stands visible: but it is an error; as this Letter and other good evidences still remain to show. Indeed some singular oscitancy must have overtaken the watchful Rushworth, on that occasion of the Convenant; or what is likelier, some inextricable shuffle had got among his Paper-masses there, when he came to redact them long after, — the indefatigable painful man! Thus he says furthermore, and again says, the signing took place "on September 22d," which was Friday; whereas the Rhadamanthine Commons Journals still testify that, on Friday September 22d, there was merely order and appointment made to sign on the 25th; and that the

* Commons Journals, iii. 252, 4; Rushworth (incorrect in various particulars, — unusual with Rushworth), v. 475, 480; the Covenant itself, ib. 478.
** Burnet: Memoirs of the Dukes of Hamilton.

siguing itself took place, accordingly, on Monday September 25th, as we have given it.   With other errors, — incident to the exactest Rushworth, when his Paper-masses get shuffled! — Here is another entry of his, confirmable beyond disputing; which is of itself fatal to that of "Oliver Cromwell" among "those who signed the Covenant that day." Oliver Cromwell had quite other work to do than signing of Covenants, many miles away from him just now; and indeed, I guess, did not sign this one for many days and weeks to come; not till he got to his place in Parliament again, with more leisure on his hands than now.

Tuesday, "26*th September.* The Lord Willoughby" of Parham "and Colonel Cromwell came to Hull, to consult with the Lord "Fairfax; but made no stay: and the same day, Sir Thomas "Fairfax crossed Humber with Twenty Troops of Horse, to "join with Cromwell's forces in Lincolnshire."* For the Marquis of Newcastle is begirdling, and ever more closely besieging, the Lord Fairfax in Hull; which has obliged him to ship his brave Son, with all the horse, across the Humber, in this manner: horse are useless here; under the Earl of Manchester, on the other side, they may be of use.

The landing took place at Saltfleet that same afternoon, say the Newspapers: here now is what followed thereupon, — successful though rather dangerous march into the safe parts of Lincolnshire, and continuance of the drillings, fightings, and enlistments there. Committee-men "Spring and Barrow" are known to us; of Margery and "the Malignants' horses "we have also had some inkling once.

To his honoured Friends, Sir William Spring and Mr. Barrow:
These present.

Gentlemen,   'Holland, Lincolnshire,' 28th Sept. 1643.
It hath pleased God to bring off Sir Thomas Fairfax his Horse over the river from Hull, being about One-and-twenty Troops of Horse and Dragoons. The

---

* Rushworth, v. 280.

Lincolnshire Horse laboured to hinder this work, being about Thirty-four Colours of Horse and Dragoons: we marched up to their landing-place, and the Lincolnshire Horse retreated.

After they were come over, we all marched towards Holland; and when we came to our last quarter upon the edge of Holland, the Enemy quartered within four miles of us, and kept the field all night with his whole body: his intendment, as we conceive, was to fight us; — or hoping to interpose betwixt us and our retreat; having received, to his Thirty-four Colours of Horse, Twenty fresh Troops, ten Companies of 'Dragoons;'* and about a Thousand Foot, being General King's own Regiment. With these he attempted our guards and our quarters; and, if God had not been merciful, had ruined us before we had known of it; the Five Troops we set to keep the watch failing much of their duty. But we got to horse; and retreated in good order, with the safety of all our Horse of the Association; not losing four of them that I hear of, and we got five of theirs. And for this we are exceedingly bound to the goodness of God, who brought our troops off with so little loss.

I write unto you to acquaint you with this; the rather that God may be acknowledged; and that you may help forward, in sending such force away unto us as lie unprofitably in your country. And especially that Troop of Captain Margery's, which surely would** not be wanting, now we so much need it!

I hear there hath been much exception taken to Captain Margery and his Officers, for taking of horses. I am sorry you should discountenance those who (not

----

* Word torn.   ** should.

to make benefit to themselves, but to serve their Country) are willing to venture their lives, and to purchase to themselves the displeasure of bad men, that they may do a Public benefit. I undertake not to justify all Captain Margery's actions: but his own conscience knows whether he hath taken the horses of any but Malignants; — and it were somewhat too hard to put it upon the consciences of your fellow Deputy Lieutenants, whether they have not *freed* the horses of known Malignants? A fault not less, considering the sad estate of this Kingdom, than to take a horse from a known Honest man; the offence being against the Public, which is a considerable aggravation! I know not the measure every one takes of Malignants. I think it is not fit Captain ˙Margery should be the judge: but if he, in this taking of˙horses, hath observed the plain character of a Malignant, and cannot be charged for one horse otherwise taken, — it had been better that some of the bitterness wherewith he and his have been followed had been spared! The horses that his Cornet* Boulry took, he will put himself upon that issue for them all.

If˙these men be accounted "troublesome to the Country," I shall be glad you would send them all to me. I'll bid them welcome. And when they have fought for you, and endured some other difficulties of war which your "honester" men will hardly bear, I pray you then let them go for honest men! I protest unto you, many of those men which are of your Country's choosing, under Captain Johnson, are so far from serving you, that, — were it not that I have honest Troops to master them, — although they be

---

* "Coronett" *in orig.*

well paid, yet they are so mutinous that I may justly fear they would cut my throat! — Gentlemen, it may be it provokes some spirits to see such plain men made Captains of Horse. It had been well that men of honour and birth had entered into these employments: — but why do they not appear? Who would have hindered them? But seeing it was necessary the work must go on, better plain men than none; — but best to have men patient of wants, faithful and conscientious in their employment. And such, I hope, these will approve themselves to be. Let them therefore, if I be thought worthy of any favour, leave your Country with your good wishes and a blessing. I am confident they * will be well bestowed. And I believe before it be long, you will be in their debt; and then it will not be hard to quit scores.

What arms you can furnish them withal, I beseech you do it. I have hitherto found your kindness great to me: — I know not what I have done to lose it; I love it so well, and price it so high, that I would do my best to gain more. You have the assured affection of

Your most humble and faithful servant,
OLIVER CROMWELL.

P. S. — I understand there were some exceptions taken at a Horse that was sent to me, which was seized out of the hands of one Mr. Goldsmith of Wilby. If he be not by you judged a Malignant, and that you do not approve of my having of the Horse, I shall as willingly return him again as you shall desire. And therefore, I pray you, signify your pleasure to me here-

* your wishes.

in under your hands. Not that I would, for ten thousand horses, have the Horse to my own private benefit, saving to make use of him for the Public: — for I will most gladly return the value of him to the State. If the Gentleman stand clear in your judgments, — I beg it as a special favour that, if the Gentleman be freely willing to let me have him for my money, let him set his own price: I shall very justly return him the money. Or if he be unwilling to part with him, but keeps him for his own pleasure, be pleased to send me an answer thereof: I shall instantly return him his Horse; and do it with a great deal more satisfaction to myself than keep him. — Therefore I beg it of you to satisfy my desire in this last request; it shall exceedingly oblige me to you. If you do it not, I shall rest very unsatisfied, and the Horse will be a burden to me so long as I shall keep him. §

The Earl of Manchester, recaptor of Lynn Regislately, is still besieging and retaking certain minor strengths and Fen garrisons, — sweeping the intrusive Royalists out of those Southern Towns of Lincolnshire. This once done, his Foot once joined to Cromwell's and Fairfax's Horse, something may be expected in the Midland parts too.

WINCEBY FIGHT.

Lincolnshire, which has now become one of the Associated Seven, * and is still much overrun by Newarkers and Northern Papists, shall at last be delivered.

Hull siege still continues, with obstinate sally and onslaught; on the other hand, Lynn siege, which the Earl of

§ Original in the possession of Dawson Turner, Esq., Great Yarmouth; printed in Papers of Norfolk Archæological Society (Norwich, January 1848).

* 20th September 1643, Husbands, ii. 327.

Manchester was busy in, has prosperously ended; and the Earl himself, with his foot regiments, is now also here; united, in loose quarters, with Cromwell and Fairfax, in the Boston region, and able probably to undertake somewhat. Cromwell and Fairfax with the horse, we perceive, have still the brunt of the work to do. Here, after much marching and skirmishing, is an account of Winceby Fight, their chief exploit in those parts, which cleared the country of the Newarkers, General Kings, and renegade Sir John Hendersons; — as recorded by loud-spoken Vicars. In spite of brevity we must copy the Narrative. Cromwell himself was nearer death in this action than ever in any other; the victory too made its due figure, and "appeared in the world."

Winceby, a small upland Hamlet, in the Wolds, not among the Fens, of Lincolnshire, is some five miles west of Horncastle. The confused memory of this Fight is still fresh there; the Lane along which the chase went bears ever since the name of "*Slash* Lane," and poor Tradition maunders about it as she can. Hear Vicars, a poor human soul zealously prophesying as if through the organs of an ass, — in a not mendacious, yet loud-spoken, exaggerative, more or less asinine manner:*

* * * "All that night," Tuesday, 10th October 1643, "we were drawing our horse to the appointed rendezvous; and "the next morning, being Wednesday, my Lord" Manchester "gave order that the whole force, both horse and foot, should "be drawn up to Bolingbroke Hill, where he would expect the "enemy, being the only convenient ground to fight with him. "But Colonel Cromwell was no way satisfied that we should "fight; our horse being extremely wearied with hard duty two "or three days together.

"The enemy also drew, that" Wednesday "morning, their "whole body of horse and dragooners into the field, being 74

---

* Third form of *Vicars:* God's Ark overtopping the World's Waves, or the Third Part of the Parliamentary Chronicle: by John Vicars (London, printed by M. Simons and J. Meccock, 1646), p. 45. There are three editions or successive forms of this Book of Vicars's (see Bliss's Wood, *in voce*): it is always, unless the contrary be expressed, the *second* (of 1644) that we refer to here.

"colours of horse, and 21 colours of dragoons, in all 95 colours.
"We had not many more than half so many colours of horse
"and dragooners; but I believe we had as many men,—besides
"our foot, which indeed could not be drawn up until it was
"very late.   The enemy's word was 'Cavendish;'"—he that
was killed in the Bog; "and ours was 'Religion.'   I believe
"that as we had no notice of the enemy's coming towards us,
"so they had as little of our preparation to fight with them.
"It was about twelve of the clock ere our horse and dragoon-
"ers were drawn up.   After that we marched about a mile
"nearer the enemy; and then we began to descry him, by little
"and little, coming towards us.   Until this time we did not
"know we should fight; but so soon as our men had knowledge
"of the enemy's coming, they were very full of joy and resolu-
"tion, thinking it a great mercy that they should now fight
"with him. Our men went on in several bodies, singing Psalms.
"Quartermaster-General Vermuyden with five troops had the
"forlorn-hope, and Colonel Cromwell the van, assisted with
"other of my Lord's troops, and seconded by Sir T. Fairfax.
"Both armies met about Ixbie, if I mistake not the Town's
"name,"—you do mistake, Mr. Vicars; it is Winceby, a mere
hamlet and not a town.

"Both they and we had drawn up our dragooners; who
"gave the first charge; and then the horse fell in.   Colonel
"Cromwell fell with brave resolution upon the enemy,
"immediately after their dragooners had given him the first
"volley; yet they were so nimble, as that, within half pistol-
"shot, they gave him another: his horse was killed under him
"at the first charge, and fell down upon him; and as he rose
"up, he was knocked down again by the Gentleman who
"charged him, who 'twas conceived was Sir Ingram Hopton:
"but afterwards he" the Colonel "recovered a poor horse in
"a soldier's hands, and bravely mounted himself again. Truly
"this first charge was so home-given, and performed with so
"much admirable courage and resolution by our troops, that
"the enemy stood not another; but were driven back upon their
"own body, which was to have seconded them; and at last

"put these into a plain disorder; and thus, in less than half an "hour's fight, they were all quite routed, and"—driven along Slash Lane at a terrible rate, unnecessary to specify.　Sir Ingram Hopton, who had been so near killing Cromwell, was himself killed.　"Above a hundred of their men were found drowned in ditches," in quagmires that would not bear riding; the "dragooners now left on foot" were taken prisoners; the chase lasted to Horncastle or beyond it,—and Henderson the renegade Scot was never heard of in those parts more.　My Lord of Manchester's foot did not get up till the battle was over.

This very day of Winceby Fight, there has gone on at Hull a universal sally, tough sullen wrestle in the trenches all day; with important loss to the Marquis of Newcastle; loss of ground, loss of lives, loss still more of invaluable guns, brass drakes, sackers, what not:—and on the morrow morning the Townsfolk, looking out, discern with emotion that there is now no Marquis, that the Marquis has marched away under cloud of night, and given up the siege.　Which surely are good encouragements we have had; two in one day.

This will suffice for Winceby Fight, or Horncastle Fight, of 11th October 1643;* and leave the reader to imagine that Lincolnshire too was now cleared of the "Papist Army," as we violently nickname it,—all but a few Towns on the Western border, which will be successfully besieged when the Spring comes.

LETTERS XIX., XX.

In the month of January 1643-4, Oliver, as Governor of Ely, is present for some time in that City; lodges, we suppose, with his own family there; doing military and other work of government:—makes a transient appearance in the Cathedral one day; memorable to the Reverend Mr. Hitch and us.

---

* Account of it from the other side, in Rushworth, v. 262; Hull Siege, &c. ib. 280.

The case was this.   Parliament, which, ever since the first meeting of it, had shown a marked disaffection to Surplices at Allhallowtide and "monuments of Superstition and Idolatry," and passed Order after Order to put them down, — has in August last come to a decisive Act on the subject, and specifically explained that go they must and shall. *   Act of Parliament which, like the previous Orders of Parliament, could only have gradual partial execution, according to the humour of the locality; and gave rise to scenes.   By the Parliament's directions, the Priest, Churchwardens, and proper officers were to do it, with all decency: failing the proper officers, *im*proper officers, military men passing through the place, these and such like, backed by a Puritan populace, and a Puritan soldiery, had to do it; — not always in the softest manner.   As many a *Querela*, Peter Heylin's (lying Peter's) *History*, and *Persecutio Undecima*, still testifies with angry tears.   You cannot pull the shirt off a man, the skin off a man, in a way that will please him! — Our Assembly of Divines, sitting earnestly deliberative ever since June last,** will direct us what Form of Worship we are to adopt, — some form, it is to be hoped, not grown dramaturgic to us, but still awfully symbolic for us.   Meanwhile let all Churches, especially all Cathedrals, be stript of whatever the general soul so much as suspects to be stage-property and prayer by machinery, — a thing we very justly hold in terror and horror, and dare not live beside! —

Ely Cathedral, it appears, had still been overlooked, — Ely, much troubled with scandalous ministers, as well as with disaffected trainbands, — and Mr. Hitch, under the very eyes of Oliver, persists in his Choir-service there.   Here accordingly is an official Note copies of which still sleep in some repositories.

---

* 28th August 1643 (Scobell, i. 53; Commons Journals, iii. 220): 2d November 1642 (Commons Journals, and Husbands, ii. 119): 31st August 1641; 23d January 1641 (Commons Journals, *in diebus*).

** Bill for convocation of them, read a third time, 6th January 1642-3 (Commons Journals, ii. 916); Act itself with the Names, 13th June 1643 (Scobell, i. 42-4).

LETTER XIX.

'To the Reverend Mr. Hitch, at Ely: These.'

MR. HITCH,   'Ely,' 10th January 1643.

Lest the Soldiers should in any tumultuary or disorderly way attempt the reformation of the Cathedral Church, I require you to forbear altogether your Choir-service, so unedifying and offensive: — and this as you shall answer it, if any disorder should arise thereupon.

I advise you to catechise, and read and expound the Scripture to the people; not doubting but the Parliament, with the advice of the Assembly of Divines, will direct you farther. I desire your Sermons 'too,' where usually they have been, — but more frequent.

Your loving friend,

OLIVER CROMWELL. §

Mr. Hitch paid no attention; persisted in his Choir-service: — whereupon enter the Governor of Ely with soldiers, "with a rabble at his heels," say the old *Querelas*. With a rabble at his heels, with his hat on, he walks up to the Choir; says audibly: "I am a man under Authority; and am commanded to dismiss this Assembly," — then draws back a little, that the Assembly may dismiss with decency. Mr. Hitch has paused for a moment; but seeing Oliver draw back, he starts again: "As it was in the beginning" — ! — "Leave off your fooling, and come down, Sir!" * said Oliver, in a voice still audible to this Editor; which Mr. Hitch did now instantaneously give ear to. And so, "with his whole congregation," files out, and vanishes from the field of History.

§ Gentleman's Magazine (London, 1778), lviii. 125: copied "from an old Copy, by a Country Rector," who has had some difficulty in reading the name of Hitch, and knows nothing farther about him or it.
 * Walker's Sufferings of the Clergy (London, 1714), Part ii. p. 23.

Friday, 19th January. The Scots enter England by Berwick, 21,000 strong: on Wednesday they left Dunbar "up to the knees in snow;" such a heart of forwardness was in them.[*] Old Lesley, now Earl of Leven, was their General, as before; a Committee of Parliamenteers went with him. They soon drove-in Newcastle's "Papist Army" within narrower quarters; in May, got Manchester with Cromwell and Fairfax brought across the Humber to join them, and besieged Newcastle himself in York. Which, before long, will bring us to Marston Moor, and *Letter Twenty-first.*

In this same month of January, 22d day of it, directly after Hitch's business, Colonel Cromwell, now more properly Lieutenant-General Cromwell, Lieutenant to the Earl of Manchester in the Association, transiently appeared in his place in Parliament; complaining much of my Lord Willoughby, as of a backward General, with strangely dissolute people about him, a great sorrow to Lincolnshire;[**] — and craving that my Lord Manchester might be appointed there instead: which, as we see, was done; with good result.

LETTER XX.

About the end of next month, February 1644, the Lieutenant-General, we find, has been in Gloucester, successfully convoying Ammunition thither; and has taken various strong-houses by the road, — among others, Hilsden-House in Buckinghamshire, with important gentlemen, and many prisoners; which latter, "Walloons, French, and other outlandish men," appear in Cambridge streets in a very thirsty condition; and are, in spite of danger, refreshed according to ability, by the loyal Scholars, and especially by "Mrs. Cumber's maid," with a temporary glass of beer.[***] In this expedition there had gone with Cromwell a certain Major-General Crawford, whom he has left behind in the Hilsden neighbourhood; to whom there

---

[*] Rushworth, v. 603-6.
[**] D'Ewes mss. vol. iv. f. 280 b.
[***] Querela (in Cooper's Annals, iii. 370); Cromwelliana, p. 8 (5th Mar. 1643).

is a Letter, here first producible to modern readers, and connected therewith a tale otherwise known.

Letter Twentieth, which exists as a Copy, on old dim paper, in the Kimbolton Archives, addressed on the back of the sheet, with all reverence, *To the Earl of Manchester*, and forms a very opaque puzzle in that condition, — turns out, after due study, to have been a Copy *by* that Crawford, of a Letter addressed to himself: Copy hastily written off, along with other hasty confused sheets still extant beside it, for the Earl of Manchester's use, on a certain Parliamentary occasion, which will by and by concern us too for a moment.

A "Lieutenant-Colonel," Packer I dimly apprehend is the name of him, has on this Hilsden-and-Gloucester expedition given offence to Major-General Crawford; who again, in a somewhat prompt way, has had Packer laid under arrest, under suspension at Cambridge; in which state Packer still painfully continues. And may, seemingly, continue: for here has my Lord of Manchester just come down with a Parliamentary Commission "to reform the University," a thing of immense noise and moment, and "is employed in regard of many occasions;" is, in fact, precisely in these hours,* issuing his Summonses to the Heads of Houses; and cannot spare an instant for Packer and his pleadings. Crawford is still in Buckinghamshire; nevertheless the shortest way for Packer will be to go to Crawford, and take this admonitory Letter from his superior in command:

'*To Major-General Crawford: These.*'

SIR,　　　　　　　　　　　　Cambridge, 10th March '1643.'

The complaints you preferred to my Lord against your Lieutenant-Colonel, both by Mr. Lee and your own Letters, have occasioned his stay here: — my Lord being 'so' employed, in regard of many occasions which are upon him, that he hath not been at leisure to hear him make his defence: which, in pure justice,

* 11th March (Cooper, iii. 371; details in Neal, ii. 79-89).

ought to be granted him or any man before a judgment
be passed upon him.

During his abode here and absence from you, he
hath acquainted me what a grief it is to him to be absent from his charge, especially now the regiment is
called forth to action: and therefore, asking of me my
opinion, I advised him speedily to repair unto *you*.
Surely you are not well advised thus to turn off one so
faithful to the Cause, and so able to serve you as this
man is. Give me leave to tell you, I cannot be of
your judgment; 'cannot understand,' if a man notorious
for wickedness, for oaths, for drinking, hath as great
a share in your affection as one who fears an oath,
who fears to sin, — that this doth commend your election of men to serve as fit instruments in this work!—

Ay, but the man "is an Anabaptist." Are you sure
of that? Admit he be, shall that render him incapable
to serve the Public? "He is indiscreet." It may be so,
in some things: we have all human infirmities.   I tell
you, if you had none but such "indiscreet men" about
you, and would be pleased to use them kindly, you
would find as good a fence to you as any you have yet
chosen.

Sir, the State, in choosing men to serve it, takes
no notice of their opinions; if they be willing faithfully
to serve it, — that satisfies. I advised you formerly to
bear with men of different minds from yourself: if you
had done it when I advised you to it, I think you
would not have had so many stumblingblocks in your
way.   It may be you judge otherwise; but I tell you
my mind. — I desire you would receive this man into
your favour and good opinion. I believe, if he follow
my counsel, he will deserve no other but respect from

you. Take heed of being sharp, or too easily sharpened by others, against those to whom you can object little but that they square not with you in every opinion concerning matters of religion. If there be any other offence to be charged upon him, — that must in a judicial way receive determination. I know you will not think it fit my Lord should discharge an Officer of the Field but in a regulate way. I question whether you or I have any precedent for that.

I have not further to trouble you: — but rest,

Your humble servant,

OLIVER CROMWELL. §

Adjoined to this Letter, as it now lies, — in its old repository at Kimbolton, copied and addressed in the enigmatic way above-mentioned, — there is, written in a Clerk's hand, but corrected in the hand which copied the Letter, a confused loud-spoken recriminatory Narrative, of some length, about the Second Battle of Newbury; touching also, in a loud confused way, on the case of Packer and others: — evidently the raw-material of the Earl's *Speech in defence of himself*,* in the time of the *Self-denying Ordinance;* of which the reader will hear by and by. Assiduous Crawford had provided the Earl with these helps to prove Cromwell an insubordinate person, and what was equally terrible, a favourer of Anabaptists. Of the *Letter*, Crawford, against whom also there lay accusations, retains the Original; but furnishes this Copy; — of which, unexpectedly, we too have now obtained a reading.

This sharp Letter may be fancied to procure the Lieutenant-Colonel's reinstatement; who, we have some intimation, does march with his regiment again, in hopes to take the Western Towns of Lincolnshire. Indeed Lieutenant-Colonel Packer, if this were verily Packer as he seems to be, became

§ Communicated, with much politeness, by the Duke of Manchester, from Family Papers at Kimbolton.

* Rushworth, v. 733-6.

a distinguished Colonel afterwards, and gave Oliver himself some trouble with his Anabaptistries.*   In the Letter itself, still more in the confused Papers adjoined to it, of Major-General Crawford's writing, — there is evidence enough of smouldering fire-elements in my Lord's Eastern-Association Army! The Lieutenant-General Cromwell, one perceives, is justly suspected of a lenity for Sectaries, Independents, Anabaptists themselves, provided they be "men that fear God," as he phrases it. Lieutenant-Colonel Lilburn (Freeborn John), Lieutenant-Colonel Fleetwood risen from Captaincy now: these and others, in the Crawford Documents, come painfully to view in this Lincolnshire campaign and afterwards; with discontents, with "Petitions," and one knows not what; all tending to Sectarian courses, all countenanced by the Lieutenant-General.** Most distasteful to Scotch Crawford, to my Lord of Manchester, not to say criminal and unforgiveable to the respectable Presbyterian mind.

Reverend Mr. Baillie is now up in Town again with the Scotch Commissioners, — for there is again a Scotch Commission here, now that their Army has joined us: Reverend Mr. Baillie, taking good note of things, has this pertinent passage some six months hence: "The Earl of Manchester, a sweet "meek man, did formerly permit Lieutenant-General Crom- "well to guide all the Army at his pleasure: the man Cromwell "is a very wise and active head" — yes, Mr. Robert! — "uni- "versally well beloved as religious and stout; but a known "Independent or favourer of Sects," — the issues of which might have been frightful! "But now our countryman Craw- "ford has got a great hand with Manchester, stands high "with all that are against Sects;" which is a blessed change indeed,*** — and may. partly explain this Letter and some other things to us!

Of Major-General Crawford, who was once a loud-sounding well-known man, but whose chance for being remembered

* Ludlow (London, 1721), ii. 599.
** ms. by Crawford at Kimbolton.
*** Baillie, ii. 229 (16th September 1644).

much longer will mainly ground itself on a Letter he copied
with very different views, let us say here what little needs to
be said.   He is Scotch; of the Crawfords of Jordan-Hill, in
Renfrewshire; has seen service in the German Wars, and is
deeply conscious of it; — paints himself to us as a headlong
audacious fighter, of loose loud tongue, much of a pedant
and braggart, somewhat given to sycophancy too.   Whose
history may sum itself up, practically, in this one fact, That
he helped Cromwell and the Earl of Manchester to quarrel;
and his character in this other, That he knew Lieutenant-
General Cromwell to be a coward.   This he, Crawford, knew;
had seen it; was wont to assert it, and could prove it.   Nay
once, in subsequent angry months, talking to the Honourable
Denzil Holles in Westminster Hall, he asserted it within ear-
shot of Cromwell himself; "who was passing into the House,
and I am very sure did hear it, as intended;"—who, however,
heard it as if it had been no affair of his at all; and quietly
walked on, as if *his* affairs lay elsewhere than there!*   From
which I too, the knowing Denzil, drew my inferences, — ig-
nominious to the human character! — Poor Crawford, after
figuring much among the Scotch Committee-men and Presbyterian Grandees for a time, joined or rejoined the Scotch
Army under Lesley; and fell at the Siege of Hereford in 1645,
fighting gallantly I doubt not, and was quiet thenceforth.**

In these same weeks there is going on a very famous Treaty
once more, "Treaty of Uxbridge:" with immense apparatus
of King's Commissioners and Parliament and Scotch Commissioners;*** of which however, as it came to nothing, there
need nothing here be said.   Mr. Christopher Love, a young
eloquent divine, of hot Welsh blood, of Presbyterian tendency,
preaching by appointment in the place, said, He saw no prospect of an agreement, he for one; "Heaven might as well

---

* Holles's Memoirs: in Maseres's Select Tracts (London, 1815), i. 199.
** Wood's Athenæ (*Life*, p. 8); Baillie, ii. 295 and *sæpius* (correct ib. ii.
p. 218 *n.*, and Godwin, i. 380); Holles; Scotch Peerages, &c. &c.
*** 29th Jan. — 5th March, Rushworth, v. 844-946; Whitlocke, p. 122, 3.

think of agreeing with Hell;"* words which were remembered against Mr. Christopher. The King will have nothing to do with Presbyterianism, will not stir a step without his Surplices at Allhallowtide; there remains only War; a supreme managing "Committee of Both Kingdoms;" combined forces, and war. On the other hand, his Majesty, to counterbalance the Scots, had agreed to a "Cessation in Ireland," sent for his " Irish Army" to assist him here, — and indeed already got them as good as ruined, or reduced to a mere marauding apparatus.** A new "Papist" or partly "Papist Army," which gave great scandal in this country. By much the remarkablest man in it was Colonel George Monk; already captured at Nantwich, and lodged in the Tower.

But now the Western Towns of Lincolnshire are all taken; Manchester with Cromwell and Fairfax are across the Humber, joined with the Scots besieging York, where Major-General Crawford again distinguishes himself;*** — and we are now at Marston Moor.

LETTER XXI.

Marston Moor.

In the last days of June 1644, Prince Rupert, with an army of some 20,000 fierce men, came pouring over the hills from Lancashire, where he had left harsh traces of himself, to relieve the Marquis of Newcastle, who was now with a force of 6,000 besieged in York, by the united forces of the Scots under Leven, the Yorkshiremen under Lord Fairfax, and the Associated Counties under Manchester and Cromwell. On hearing of his approach, the Parliament Generals raised the Siege; drew out on the Moor of Long Marston, some four miles off, to oppose his coming. He avoided them by crossing the

* Wood, iii. 281; Commons Journals, &c.
** Rushworth, v. 547 (Cessation, 15th September 1643); v. 299-303 (Siege of Nantwich, and ruin of the Irish Army, 21st November).
*** Fires a mine without orders; storms in, hoping to take the city himself; and is disastrously repulsed (Rushworth, v. 631; Baillie, ii. 200).

river Ouse; relieved York, Monday, 1st July; and might have returned successful; but insisted on Newcastle's joining him, and going out to fight the Roundheads. The Battle of Marston Moor, fought on the morrow evening, Tuesday, 2d July 1644, from 7 to 10 o'clock, was the result, — entirely disastrous for him.

Of this Battle, the bloodiest of the whole War, I must leave the reader to gather details in the sources indicated below;* or to imagine it in general as the most enormous hurlyburly, of fire and smoke, and steel-flashings and death-tumult, ever seen in those regions: the end of which, about ten at night, was "Four-thousand one-hundred- and-fifty bodies" to be buried, and total ruin to the King's affairs in those Northern parts.

The Armies were not completely drawn up till after five in the evening; there was a ditch between them; they stood facing one another, motionless except the exchange of a few cannon-shots, for an hour-and-half. Newcastle thought there would be no fighting till the morrow, and had retired to his carriage for the night. There is some shadow of surmise that the stray cannon-shot which, as the following Letter indicates, proved fatal to Oliver's Nephew, did also, rousing Oliver's humour to the charging point, bring on the general Battle. "The Prince of Plunderers," invincible hitherto, here first tasted the steel of Oliver's Ironsides, and did not in the least like it. "The Scots delivered their fire with such constancy "and swiftness, it was as if the whole air had become an element of fire," — in the ancient summer gloaming there.

'To my loving Brother, Colonel Valentine Walton: These.'

DEAR SIR,   'Leaguer before York,' 5th July 1644.

It's our duty to sympathise in all mercies; and to praise the Lord together in chastisements or trials, that so we may sorrow together.

* King's Pamphlets, small 4to, no. 164 (various accounts by eye-witnesses); no. 168, one by Simeon Ash, the Earl of Manchester's Chaplain; no. 167, &c.: Rushworth, v. 632: Carte's Ormond Papers (London, 1739), i. 56: Fairfax's Memorials (Somers Tracts, v. 389). Modern accounts are numerous, but of no value.

Truly England and the Church of God hath had a great favour from the Lord, in this great Victory given unto us, such as the like never was since this War began. It had all the evidences of an absolute Victory obtained by the Lord's blessing upon the Godly Party principally. We never charged but we routed the enemy. The Left Wing, which I commanded, being our own horse, saving a few Scots in our rear, beat all the Prince's horse. God made them as stubble to our swords. We charged their regiments of foot with our horse, and routed all we charged. The particulars I cannot relate now; but I believe, of Twenty-thousand the Prince hath not Four-thousand left. Give glory, all the glory, to God. —

Sir, God hath taken away your eldest Son by a cannon-shot. It brake his leg. We were necessitated to have it cut off, whereof he died.

Sir, you know my own trials this way:* but the Lord supported me with this, That the Lord took him into the happiness we all pant for and live for. There is your precious child full of glory, never to know sin or sorrow any more. He was a gallant young man, exceedingly gracious. God give you His comfort. Before his death he was so full of comfort that to Frank Russel and myself he could not express it, "It was so great above his pain." This he said to us. Indeed it was admirable. A little after, he said, One thing lay upon his spirit. I asked him, What that was? He told

---

* I conclude, the poor Boy Oliver has already fallen in these Wars, — none of us knows where, though his Father well knew! —— *Note to Third Edition:* In the *Squire Papers* (Fraser's Magazine, December 1847) is this passage; "Meeting Cromwell again after some absence, just on the edge "of Marston Battle, Squire says, '1 thought he looked sad and wearied, for "he had had a sad loss; young Oliver got killed to death not long before, "I heard: it was near Knaresborough, and 30 more got killed.'" —— *Note of* 1857: see antea, p. 37 n.

me it was, That God had not suffered him to be any
more the executioner of His enemies. At his fall, his
horse being killed with the bullet, and as I am informed three horses more, I am told he bid them,
Open to the right and left, that he might see the
rogues run. Truly he was exceedingly beloved in the
Army, of all that knew him. But few knew him; for
he was a precious young man, fit for God. You have
cause to bless the Lord. He is a glorious Saint in
Heaven; wherein you ought exceedingly to rejoice. Let
this drink up your sorrow; seeing these are not feigned
words to comfort you, but the thing is so real and undoubted a truth. You may do all things by the strength
of Christ. Seek that, and you shall easily bear your
trial. Let this public mercy to the Church of God
make you to forget your private sorrow. The Lord be
your strength: so prays

Your truly faithful and loving brother,
OLIVER CROMWELL.

My love to your Daughter, and my Cousin Percc-
val, Sister Desborow and all friends with you. §

Colonel Valentine Walton, already a conspicuous man,
and more so afterwards, is of Great-Staughton, Huntingdonshire, a neighbour of the Earl of Manchester's; Member for
his County, and a Colonel since the beginning of the War.
There had long been an intimacy between the Cromwell Family and his. His Wife, the Mother of this slain youth, is
Margaret Cromwell, Oliver's younger Sister, next to him in
the family series. "Frank Russel" is of Chippenham, Cambridgeshire, eldest Son of the Baronet there; already a Colo-

<hr>

§ Seward's Anecdotes (London, 1798), i. 362: reproduced in Ellis's
Original Letters (First Series), iii. 299. "Original once in the possession
of Mr. Langton of Welbeck Street," says Ellis; — "in the Bodleian
Library," says Seward.

nel; soon afterwards Governor of Ely in Oliver's stead.*   It was the daughter of this Frank that Henry Cromwell, some ten years hence, wedded.

Colonel Walton, if he have at present some military charge of the Association, seems to attend mainly on Parliament; and this Letter, I think, finds him in Town. The poor wounded youth would have to lie on the field at Marston while the Battle was fought; the whole Army had to bivouac there, next to no food, hardly even water to be had.   That of "Seeing the rogues run," occurs more than once at subsequent dates in these Wars:** who first said it, or whether anybody ever said it, must remain uncertain.

York was now captured in a few days: Prince Rupert had fled across into Lancashire, and so "south to Shropshire, to recruit again;" Marquis Newcastle with "about eighty gentle-men," disgusted at the turn of affairs, had withdrawn beyond seas.   The Scots moved northward to attend the Siege of Newcastle, — ended it by storm in October next.   On the 24th of which same month, 24th October 1644, the Parliament promulgated its Rhadamanthine Ordinance, To "hang any Irish Papist taken in arms in this country;"*** a very severe Ordinance, but not uncalled for by the nature of the "maraud-ing apparatus" in question there.

LETTERS XXII., XXIII.

The next Two Letters represent the Army and Lieutenant-General got home to the Association again; and can be read with little commentary. "The Committee for the Isle of Ely," we are to remark, consists of Honourable Members connected with that region, and has its sittings in London.   Of "Major Ireton" we shall hear farther.. "Husband" also is slightly met with elsewhere; and "Captain Castle" grew, I think, to be Colonel Castle, and perished at the Storm of Tredah, some years afterwards.

* See Noble, ii. 407, 8, — with vigilance against his blunders.
** Ludlow.   *** Rushworth, v. 783.

LETTER XXII.

*For my noble Friends the Committee for the Isle of Ely:
Present these.*

Gentlemen,   Lincoln, 1st September 1644.

I understand that you have lately released some
persons committed by Major Ireton and Captain
Husband, and one committed by Captain Castle, —
all 'committed' upon clear and necessary grounds as
they are represented unto me; 'grounds' rendering them
as very enemies as any we have, and as much requiring to have them continued secured.

I have given order to Captain Husband to see them
recommitted to the hands of my Marshal, Richard
White. And I much desire you, for the future, Not
to entrench upon me so much as to release them, — or
any committed in the like case by myself, or my Deputy and Commanders in the Garrison, — until myself
or some Superior Authority * be satisfied in the cause,
and do give order in allowance of their enlargement.
For I profess I will be no Governor, nor engage any
other under me to undertake such a charge, upon such
weak terms! —

I am so sensible of the need we have to improve
the present opportunity of our being masters of the
field and having no Enemy near the Isle, and to spare
whatever charge we can towards the making of those
Fortifications, which may render it more defensible
hereafter if we shall have *more* need, — I shall desire
you, for that end, to ease the Isle and Treasury from
the superfluous charge of 'having' Two several Com-

* Not inferior!

mittees for the several parts of the Isle; and that one Committee, settled at March, may serve for the whole Isle.

Wherefore I wish that one of your number may, in your courses, intend* and appear at that Committee, to manage and uphold it the better for all parts of the Isle.

Resting upon your care herein, I remain
Your friend to serve you,
OLIVER CROMWELL. §

LETTER XXIII.

SLEAFORD is in Lincolnshire, a march farther South. Lieut.-General Cromwell with the Eastern-Association Horse, if the "Foot" were once settled, — might not he dash down to help the Lieutenant-General Essex and his "Army in the West?" Of whom, and of whose sad predicament amid the hills of Cornwall there, we shall see the issue anon. Brother Walton, a Parliament man, has written, we perceive, to Cromwell, suggesting such a thing; urging haste if possible. In Cromwell is no delay: but the Eastern-Association Army, horse or foot, is heavy to move, — beset, too, with the old internal discrepancies, Crawfordisms, scandals at Sectaries, and what not.

For Colonel Valentine Walton: These, in London.

SIR,   Sleaford, 6th or 5th September "1644."

We do with grief of heart resent the sad condition of our Army in the West, and of affairs there. That business has our hearts with it; and truly had we wings,

* "Intend" means "take pains;" March is a *Town* in the Ely region.
§ Old Copy, now (January 1846) on sale at Mr. Graves's, Pall-Mall: printed in the *Athenæum* of 13th December 1845. Old copy, such as the Clerks of Honourable Members were wont to take of Letters read in the House, or officially elsewhere; — worth copying for certain parties, in a time without Newspapers like ours.

we would fly thither! So soon as ever my Lord and the
Foot set me loose, there shall be in me no want to
hasten what I can to that service.

For indeed all other considerations are to be laid
aside, and to give place to *it*, as being of far more importance. I hope the Kingdom shall see that, in the
midst of our necessities, we shall serve them without
disputes. We hope to forget our wants, which are exceeding great, and ill cared for; and desire to refer the
many slanders heaped upon us by false tongues to God,
— who will, in due time, make it appear to the world
that we study the glory of God, and the honour and
liberty of the Parliament. For which we unanimously
fight; without seeking our own interests.

Indeed we never find our men so cheerful as when
there is work to do. I trust you will always hear so
of them. The Lord is our strength, and in Him is all
our hope. Pray for us. Present my love to my friends:
I beg their prayers. The Lord still bless you.

We have some amongst us much* slow in action:
— if we could all intend our own ends less, and our
ease too, our business in this Army would go on wheels
for expedition! 'But' because some of us are enemies
to rapine, and other wickednesses, we are said to be
"factious," to "seek to maintain our opinions in religion
by force," — which we detest and abhor. I profess I
could never satisfy myself of the justness of this War,
but from the Authority of the Parliament to maintain
itself in its rights: and in this Cause I hope to approve myself an honest man and single-hearted.

Pardon me that I am thus troublesome. I write

* "much" is old for *very*.

but seldom: it gives me a little ease to pour my mind,
in the midst of calumnies, into the bosom of a Friend.
Sir, no man more truly loves you than
Your brother and servant,
OLIVER CROMWELL. §

THREE FRAGMENTS OF SPEECHES.

Self-denying Ordinance.

THE following Three small Fragments of Speeches will
have to represent for us some six months of occasional loud
debating, and continual anxious gestation and manipulation,
in the Two Houses, in the Committee of Both Kingdoms, and
in many other houses and places; — the ultimate outcome of
which was the celebrated "Self-denying Ordinance," and
"New Model" of the Parliament's Army; which indeed brings
on an entirely New Epoch in the Parliament's Affairs.

Essex and Waller had, for the third or even fourth time,
chiefly by the exertions of ever-zealous London, been fitted
out with Armies; had marched forth together to subdue the
West; — and ended in quite other results than that.   The
two Generals differed in opinion; did not march long together:
Essex, urged by a subordinate, Lord Roberts, who had estates
in Cornwall and hoped to get some rents out of them,* turned
down thitherwards to the left; Waller bending up to the right;
— with small issue either way.   Waller's last action was an
indecisive, rather unsuccessful Fight, or day of skirmishing,
with the King, at Cropredy Bridge on the border of Oxford
and Northampton Shires,** three days before Marston Moor.
After which both parties separated: the King to follow Essex,
since there was now no hope in the North; Waller to wander
Londonwards, and gradually "lose his Army by desertion,'
as the habit of him was.   As for the King, he followed Essex

§ Seward's Anecdotes, *ut suprà*, i. 362.
* Clarendon.   ** 29th June 1644, Clarendon, ii. 655.

into Cornwall with effect; hemmed him in among the hills there, about Bodmin, Lostwithiel, Foy, with continual skirmishing, with evergrowing scarcity of victual; forced poor Essex to escape to Plymouth by the Fleet,* and *leave* his Army to shift for itself as best might be: the horse under Balfour to cut their way through; the foot under Skippon to lay down their arms, cease to be soldiers, and march away "with staves in their hands" into the wide world. This surrender was effected 1st September 1644, two months after Marston Moor. The Parliament's and Cromwell's worst anticipation, in that quarter, is fulfilled.

The Parliament made no complaint of Essex; with a kind of Roman dignity, they rather thanked him. They proceeded to recruit Waller and him, summoned Manchester with Cromwell his Lieutenant-General to join them; by which three bodies, making again a considerable army, under the command of Manchester and Waller (for Essex lay "sick," or seeming to be sick), the King, returning towards Oxford from his victory, was intercepted at Newbury; and there, on Sunday, 27th October 1644, fell out the *Second* Battle of Newbury.** Wherein his Majesty, after four hours confused fighting, rather had the worse; yet contrived to march off, unmolested, "by moonlight at 10 o'clock," towards Wallingford, and got safe home. Manchester refused to pursue; though urged by Cromwell, and again urged. Nay twelve days after, when the King came back, and openly revictualled Dennington Castle, an important strongplace hard by, — Manchester, in spite of Cromwell's urgency, still refused to interfere.

They in fact came to a quarrel here, these two: — and much else that was represented by them came to a quarrel; Presbytery and Independency, to wit. Manchester was reported to have said, If they lost this Army pursuing the King, they had no other; the King "might hang them all." To Cromwell and the thorough-going party, it had become

* His own distinct, downright and somewhat sulky Narrative, in Rushworth, v. 701.
** Clarendon, ii. 717.

13 *

very clear that high Essexes and Manchesters, of limited notions and large estates and anxieties, who besides their fear of being themselves beaten utterly, and forfeited and "hanged," were afraid of beating the King too well, would never end this Cause in a good way.   Whereupon ensue some six months of very complex manipulation, and public and private consultation, which these Three Fragments of Speeches are here to represent for us.

I. *In the House of Commons, on Monday 25th November 1644, Lieutenant-General Cromwell did, as ordered on the Saturday before, exhibit a charge against the Earl of Manchester, to this effect:*

That the said Earl hath always been indisposed and backward to engagements, and the ending of the War by the sword; and 'always' *for* such a Peace as a 'thorough' victory would be a disadvantage to; — and hath declared this by principles express to that purpose, and 'by' a continued series of carriage and actions answerable.

That since the taking of York,* as if the Parliament had now advantage fully enough, he hath declined whatsoever tended to farther advantage upon the Enemy; 'hath' neglected and studiously shifted-off opportunities to that purpose, as if he thought the King too low, and the Parliament too high, — especially at Dennington Castle.

That he hath drawn the Army into, and detained them in, such a posture as to give the Enemy fresh advantages; and this, before his conjunction with the other Armies,** by his own absolute will, against or without his Council of War, against many commands of the Committee of Both Kingdoms, and with con-

---

* Directly after Marston Moor.
** Waller's and Essex's at Newbury.

tempt and vilifying of those commands; — and, *since*
the conjunction, sometimes against the Councils of War,
and sometimes by persuading and deluding the Council
to neglect one opportunity with pretence of another,
and this again of a third, and at last by persuading
'them' that it was not fit to fight at all. §

To these heavy charges, Manchester, — furnished with
his confused Crawford Documents, and not forgetting Letter
Twentieth which we lately read, — makes heavy answer, at
great length, about a week after: of which we shall remember
only this piece of counter-charge, How his Lordship had once,
in those very Newbury days, ordered Cromwell to proceed to
some rendezvous with the horse, and Cromwell, very unsuitably for a Lieutenant-General, had answered, The horses
were already worn off their feet; "if your Lordship want to
have the *skins* of the horses, this is the way to get them!" —
Through which small slit, one looks into large seas of general
discrepancy in those old months!   Lieutenant-General
Cromwell is also reported to have said, in a moment of irrita-
tion surely, "There would never be a good time in England
till we had done with Lords."*   But the most appalling report
that now circulates in the world is this, of his saying once,
"If he met the King in battle, he would fire his pistol at the
King as at another;" — pistol, at our poor semi-divine mis-
guided Father fallen insane: a thing hardly conceivable to the
Presbyterian human mind!**

II. *In the House of Commons, on Wednesday 9th December, all
sitting in Grand Committee, "there was a general silence for a
good space of time," one looking upon the other to see who
would break the ice, in regard to this delicate point of getting
our Essexes and Manchesters softly ousted from the Army; a
very delicate point indeed; — when Lieutenant-General Cromwell stood up, and spake shortly to this effect:*

It is now a time to speak, or forever hold the

§ Rushworth, v. 732; Com. Jour. iii. 703, 5.   * Rushworth, v. 734.
** Old Pamphlets *saepius*, onwards to 1649.

tongue.   The important occasion now, is no less than To save a Nation, out of a bleeding, nay almost dying condition: which the long continuance of this War hath already brought it into; so that without a more speedy, vigorous and effectual prosecution of the War, — casting off all lingering proceedings like 'those of' soldiers-of-fortune beyond sea, to spin out a war, — we shall make the kingdom weary of us, and hate the name of a Parliament.

For what do the enemy say? Nay, what do many say that were friends at the beginning of the Parliament? Even this, That the Members of both Houses have got great places and commands, and the sword into their hands; and, what by interest in Parliament, what by power in the Army, will perpetually continue themselves in grandeur, and not permit the War speedily to end, lest their own power should determine with it. This 'that' I speak here to our own faces, is but what others do utter abroad behind our backs. I am far from reflecting on any. I know the worth of those Commanders, Members of both Houses, who are yet in power: but if I may speak my conscience without reflection upon any, I do conceive if the Army be not put into another method, and the War more vigorously prosecuted, the People can bear the War no longer, and will enforce you to a dishonourable Peace.

But this I would recommend to your prudence, Not to insist upon any complaint or oversight of any Commander-in-chief upon any occasion whatsoever; for as I must acknowledge myself guilty of oversights, so I know they can rarely be avoided in military affairs. Therefore waving a strict inquiry into the causes of these things, let us apply ourselves to the remedy; which is most necessary. And I hope we have such true English hearts, and zealous affections towards the general weal of our Mother Country, as no Members of either House will scruple to *deny* themselves, and their own private interests, for the public good; nor account it to be a dishonour done to them, whatever the Parliament shall resolve upon in this weighty matter. §

III. *On the same day, seemingly at a subsequent part of the debate, Lieutenant-General Cromwell said likewise, as follows:*

Mr. Speaker, — I am not of the mind that the calling of the Members to sit in Parliament will break, or scatter our Armies. I can speak this for my own soldiers, that they look not upon me, but upon you; and for you they will fight, and live and die in your Cause; and if others be of that mind that they are of, you need not fear them. They do not idolise me, but look upon the Cause they fight for. You may lay upon them what commands you please, they will obey your commands in that Cause they fight for. §§

To be brief, Mr. Zouch Tate, Member for Northampton, moved this day a Self-denying Ordinance; which, in a few days more, was passed in the Commons. It was not so easily got through the Lords; but there too it had ultimately to pass. One of the most important clauses was this, introduced not without difficulty, That religious men might now serve *without* taking the Covenant as a *first* preliminary, — perhaps they might take it by and by. This was a great ease to tender consciences; and indicates a deep split, which will grow wider and wider, in our religious affairs. The Scots Commissioners have sent for Whitlocke and Maynard to the Lord General's,

§ Rushworth, vi. 4.   §§ Cromwelliana, p. 12.

to ask in judicious Scotch dialect, Whether there be not ground to prosecute Cromwell as an 'incendiary?' "You ken varry weel!" — The two learned gentlemen shook their heads.*

This Self-denying Ordinance had to pass; it and the New Model wholly; by the steps indicated below.** Essex was gratified by a splendid Pension, — very little of it ever actually paid; for indeed he died some two years after: Manchester was put on the Committee of Both Kingdoms: the Parliament had its New-Model Army, and soon saw an entirely new epoch in its affairs.

LETTER XXIV.

Before the old Officers laid down their commissions, Waller with Cromwell and Massey were sent on an expedition into the West against Goring and Company; concerning which there is some echo in the old Books and Commons Journals, but no definite vestige of it, except the following Letter, read in the House of Commons, 9th April 1645; which D'Ewes happily had given his Clerk to copy.   The Expedition itself, which proved successful, is now coming towards an end. Fairfax the new General is at Windsor all April; full of business, regimenting, discharging, enlisting, new-modelling.

LETTER XXIV.

For the Right Honourable Sir Thomas Fairfax, General of the Army: Haste, Haste: These: At Windsor.

Sir,   'Salisbury,' 9th April (ten o'clock at night) 1645.
Upon Sunday last we marched towards Bruton in

* Whitlocke, iii. p. 111 (December 1644).
** Rushworth, vi. 7, 8: Self-denying Ordinance *passed* in the Commons 19th December, and is sent to the Lords; Conference about it, 7th January; *rejected* by the Lords 15th January, — because 'we do not know what *shape* the Army will now suddenly take.' Whereupon, 21st January, "Fairfax is nominated General;" and on the 19th February, the New Model is completed and passed: '*This* is the shape the Army is to take.' A second Self-denying Ordinance, now introduced, got itself finally passed 3d April 1645.

Somersetshire, which was General Goring's head-quarter: but he would not stand us; but marched away, upon our appearance, to Wells and Glastonbury. Whither we held it unsafe to follow him; lest we should engage our Body of Horse too far into that enclosed country, not having foot enough to stand by them; and partly because we doubted the advance of Prince Rupert with his force to join with Goring; having some notice from Colonel Massey of the Prince his coming this way.

General Goring hath 'Sir Richard' Greenvil in a near posture to join with him. He hath all their Garrisons in Devon, Dorset and Somersetshire, to make an addition to him. Whereupon, Sir William Waller having a very poor Infantry of about 1,600 men, — lest they, being so inconsiderable, should engage* our Horse, — we came from Shaftesbury to Salisbury to secure our Foot; to prevent our being necessitated to a too unequal engagement, and to be nearer a communication with our friends.

Since our coming hither, we hear Prince Rupert is come to Marshfield, a market-town not far from Trowbridge. If the enemy advance altogether, how far we may be endangered, — that I humbly offer to you; entreating you of take care of us, and to send us with all speed such an assistance, to Salisbury, as may enable us to keep the field and repel the enemy, if God assist us: at least to secure and countenance us so, as that we be not put to the shame and hazard of a retreat; which will lose the Parliament many friends in these parts, who will think themselves abandoned on our departure from them. Sir, I beseech you send what

* entangle or incumber.

Horse and Foot you can spare towards Salisbury, by way of Kingscleere, with what convenient expedition may be. Truly we look to be attempted upon every day.

These things being humbly represented to your knowledge and care, I subscribe myself,

Your most humble servant,

OLIVER CROMWELL. *

In Carte's Ormond Papers (i. 79) is a Letter of the same date on the same subject, somewhat illustrative of this. See also Commons Journals *in die.*

LETTERS XXV.—XXVII.

PRINCE RUPERT had withdrawn without fighting; was now at Worcester with a considerable force, meditating new infall. For which end, we hear, he has sent 2,000 men across the country to his Majesty at Oxford, to convoy "his Majesty's person and the Artillery" over to Worcester to him, — both of which objects are like to be useful there. The Committee of Both Kingdoms order the said Convoy to be attacked.

"The charge of this service they recommended particularly "to General Cromwell, who looking on himself now as dis- "charged of military employment by the New Ordinance, "which was to take effect within few days, and to have no "longer opportunity to serve his country in that way, — was, "the night before, come to Windsor, from his service in the "West, to kiss the General's hand and take leave of him: "when, in the morning ere he was come forth of his chamber, "those commands, than which he thought of nothing less in "all the world, came to him from the Committee of Both King- "doms." *

§ D'Ewes mss. vol. v. p. 189; p. 445 of Transcript.
* Sprigge's Anglia Rediviva (London, 1647), p. 10. Sprigge was one of Fairfax's Chaplains; his Book, a rather ornate work, gives florid but authentic and sufficient account of this New-Model Army in all its features and operations, by which "England" had "come alive again." A little

"'The night before" must mean, to all appearance, the 22d of April. How Cromwell instantly took horse; plunged into Oxfordshire, and on the 24th, at Islip Bridge, attacked and routed this said Convoy; and the same day, "merely by dragoons" and fierce countenance, took Bletchington House, for which poor Colonel Windebank was shot, so angry were they: all this is known from Clarendon, or more authentically from Rushworth;* and here now is Cromwell's own account of it:

LETTER XXV.

'COMMITTEE of Both Kingdoms,' first set up in February gone a year, when the Scotch Army came to help, has been the Executive in the War-department ever since; a great but now a rapidly declining authority. Sits at Derby House: Four Scotch: Twenty-one English, of whom Six a quorum. Johnston of Warriston is the notablest Scotchman; among the leading English are Philip Lord Wharton and the Younger Vane.**

'Watlington' is in the Southeast nook of Oxfordshire; a day's march from Windsor. 'Major-General Browne' commands at Abingdon; a City Wood-merchant once; a zealous soldier, of Presbyterian principles at present. The rendezvous at Watlington took place on Wednesday night; the 25th of April is Friday.

To the Right Honourable the Committee of Both Kingdoms, at Derby House: These.

MY LORDS AND GENTLEMEN,

Bletchington, 25th April 1645.

According to your Lordships' appointment, I have

sparing in dates; but correct where they are given. None of the old Books is better worth reprinting. — For some glimmer of notice concerning Joshua Sprigge himself, see Wood *in voce*, — and disbelieve altogether that "Nat. Fiennes" had anything to do with this Book.

 * vi. 23, 4.

 ** List, and light as to its appointment, in Commons Journals (7th Feb. 1643-4), iii. 391; Baillie, ii. 141 *et sæpius*. Its Papers and Correspondence, a curious set of records, lie in very tolerable order in the State-Paper Office.

attended your Service in these parts; and have not had so fit an opportunity to give you an account as now.

So soon as I received your commands, I appointed a rendezvous at Watlington. The body being come up, I marched to Wheatley Bridge, having sent before to Major-General Browne for intelligence; and it being market-day at Oxford, from whence I likewise hoped, by some of the market-people, to gain notice where the Enemy was.

Towards night I received certain notice by Major-General Browne, that the Carriages were not stirred, that Prince Maurice was not here; and by some Oxford scholars, that there were Four Carriages and Wagons ready in one place, and in another Five; all, as I conceived, fit for a march. *

I received notice also that the Earl of Northampton's Regiment was quartered at Islip; wherefore in the evening I marched that way, hoping to have surprised them; but, by the mistake and failing of the forlorn-hope, they had an alarm there, and to all their quarters, and so escaped me; by means whereof they had time to draw all together.

I kept my body all night at Islip: and, in the morning, a party of the Earl of Northampton's Regiment, the Lord Wilmot's, and the Queen's, came to make an infall upon me. Sir Thomas Fairfax's Regiment ** was the first that took the field; the rest drew out with all possible speed. That which is the General's Troop charged a whole squadron of the Enemy, and presently broke it. Our other Troops coming seasonably on, the rest of the Enemy were presently put into

* "march," out towards Worcester.

** "which was once mine," he might have added, but modestly does not; only alluding to it from afar, in the next sentence.

confusion; so that we had the chase of them three or four miles; wherein we killed many, and took near Two-hundred prisoners, and about Four-hundred horse.

Many of them escaped towards Oxford and Woodstock, divers were drowned; and others got into a strong House in Bletchington, belonging to Sir Thomas Cogan; wherein Colonel Windebank kept a garrison with near Two-hundred men. Whom I presently summoned; and after a long Treaty, he went out, about twelve at night, with these Terms here enclosed; leaving us between Two and Three-hundred muskets, besides horse-arms, and other ammunition, and about Threescore-and-eleven horses more.

This was the mercy of God; and nothing is more due than a real acknowledgment. And though I have had greater mercies, yet none clearer: because, in the first 'place,' God brought them to our hands when we looked not for them; and delivered them out of our hands, when we laid a reasonable design to surprise them, and which we carefully endeavoured. His mercy appears in this also, That I did much doubt the storming of the House, it being strong and well manned, and I having few dragoons, and this being not my business; — and yet we got it.

I hope you will pardon me if I say, God is not enough owned. We look too much to men and visible helps: this hath much hindered our success. But 'I hope God will direct all to acknowledge Him alone in all 'things.'

Your most humble servant,
OLIVER CROMWELL. §

§ Pamphlet, in Parliamentary History, xiii. 459: read in the House, Monday 28th April (Commons Journals, iv. 124). — Letter to Fairfax on the same subject, Appendix, No. 6.

Poor Windebank was shot by sudden Court-martial, so en-raged were they at Oxford, — for Cromwell had not even foot-soldiers, still less a battering gun. It was his poor young Wife, they said, she and other "ladies on a visit there," that had confused poor Windebank: he set his back to the wall of Merton College, and received his death-volley with a soldier's stoicism.* The Son of Secretary Windebank, who fled beyond seas long since.

LETTER XXVI.

How Cromwell, sending off his new guns and stores to Abingdon, now shot across westward to "Radcot Bridge" or "Bampton-in-the-Bush;" and on the 26th gained a new vic-tory there; and on the whole made a rather brilliant sally of it: — this too is known from Clarendon, or more authentically from Rushworth; but only the concluding unsuccessful part of this, the fruitless Summons to Farringdon, has left any trace in autograph.

To the Governor of the Garrison in Farringdon.

SIR,   29th April 1645.

I summon you to deliver into my hands the House wherein you are, and your Ammunition, with all things else there; together with your persons, to be disposed of as the Parliament shall appoint. Which if you refuse to do, you are to expect the utmost ex-tremity of war. I rest,

Your servant,

OLIVER CROMWELL. §

———

THIS Governor, "Roger Burgess," is not to be terrified with fierce countenance and mere dragoons; he refuses. Cromwell withdraws into Farringdon Town, and again sum-mons:

* Heath's Chronicle, p. 122.   § Rushworth, vi. 26.

LETTER XXVII.

To the same; same date.

Sir,

I understand by forty or fifty poor men whom you forced into your House, that you have many there whom you cannot arm, and who are not serviceable to you.

If these men should perish by your means, it were great inhumanity surely. Honour and honesty require this, That though you be prodigal of your own lives, yet not to be so of theirs. If God give you into my hands, I will not spare a man of you, if you put me to a storm.

OLIVER CROMWELL. *

Roger Burgess, still unawed, refuses; Cromwell waits for infantry from Abingdon "till 3 next morning," then storms; loses fourteen men, with a captain taken prisoner; — and draws away, leaving Burgess to crow over him. The Army, which rose from Windsor yesterday, gets to Reading this day, and he must hasten thither.

Yesterday, Wednesday, Monthly-fast day, all Preachers, by Ordinance of Parliament, were praying for "God's merci-"ful assistance to this New Army now on march, and His bless-"ing upon their endeavours." * Consider it; actually "praying!" It was a capability old London and its Preachers and Populations had; to us the incrediblest.

LETTER XXVIII.

By Letter Twenty-eighth it will be seen that Lieutenant-General Cromwell has never yet resumed his Parliamentary duty. In fact, he is in the Associated Counties, raising force;

§ Rushworth, vi. 26.   * Rushworth, vi. 25.

"for protection of the Isle of Ely," and other purposes.   To
Fairfax and his Officers, to the Parliament, to the Committee
of Both Kingdoms, to all persons, it is clear that Cromwell
cannot be dispensed with.   Fairfax and the Officers petition
Parliament* that he may be appointed their Lieutenant-General, Commander-in-Chief of the Horse.   There is a clear
necessity in it.   Parliament, the Commons somewhat more
readily than the Lords, continue, by instalments of "forty
days," of "three mouths," his services in the Army; and at
length grow to regard him as a constant element there.   A few
others got similar leave of absence, similar dispensation from
the Self-denying Ordinance.   Sprigge's words, cited above,
are no doubt veracious; yet there is trace of evidence** that
Cromwell's continuance in the Army had, even by the framers
of the Self-denying Ordinance, been considered a thing possible, a thing desirable.   As it well might!   To Cromwell
himself there was no overpowering felicity in getting out to be
shot at, except where wanted; he very probably, as Sprigge
intimates, did let the matter in silence take its own course.

*To the Right Honourable Sir Thomas Fairfax, General of
the Parliament's Army: These.'*

  Sir,   Huntingdon, 4th June 1645.

I most humbly beseech you to pardon my long
silence.   I am conscious of the fault, considering the
great obligations lying upon me.   But since my coming into these parts, I have been busied to secure that
part of the Isle of Ely where I conceived most danger
to be.

Truly I found it in a very ill posture: and it is
yet but weak; without works, ammunition or men considerable, — and of money least: and then, I hope,
you will easily conceive of the defence: and God has

* Their Letter (Newspapers, 9th-16th June), in Cromwelliana, p. 18.
** Godwin's History of the Commonwealth (London, 1824), i. 405.

preserved us all this while to a miracle. The party under Vermuyden waits the King's Army, and is about Deeping; has a command to join with Sir John Gell, if he commands him. So 'too' the Nottingham Horse. I shall be bold to present you with intelligence as it comes to me.

I am bold to present this as my humble suit: That you would be pleased to make Captain Rawlins, this Bearer, a Captain of Horse. He has been so before; was nominated to the Model; is a most honest man. Colonel Sidney leaving his regiment, if it please you to bestow *his* Troop on him, I am confident he will serve you faithfully. So, by God's assistance, will

Your most humble servant,
OLIVER CROMWELL. §

The "Vermuyden" mentioned here, who became Colonel Vermuyden, is supposed to be a son of the Dutch Engineer who drained the Fens. "Colonel Sidney" is the celebrated Algernon; he was nominated in the "Model," but is "leaving his regiment;" having been appointed Governor of Chichester.* Captain Rawlins does obtain a Company of Horse; under "Colonel Sir Robert Pye."** — Colonel Montague, afterwards Earl of Sandwich, has a Foot-Regiment here. Hugh Peters is "Chaplain to the Train."

BY EXPRESS.

FAIRFAX, with his New-Model Army, has been beleaguering Oxford, for some time past; but in a loose way, and making small progress hitherto. The King, not much apprehensive about Oxford, is in the Midland Counties; has just stormed

§ Rushworth, vi. (London, 1701), p. 37.
* Commons Journals, iv. 136 (9th May 1645).
** Army-List, in Sprigge (p. 330).

Leicester ("last night of May," says Clarendon,* a terrible night, and still more terrible "day-break" and day following it), which perhaps may itself relieve Oxford. His Majesty is since at halt, or in loose oscillating movement, "hunting" on the hills, "driving large herds of cattle before him," — nobody, not even himself, yet knows whitherward. Whitherward? This is naturally a very agitating question for the neighbouring populations; but most of all, intensely agitating for the Eastern Association, — though Cromwell, in that Huntingdon Letter, occupied with Ely and other Garrisons, seems to take it rather quietly. But two days later, we have trace of him at Cambridge, and of huge alarm round him there.   Here is an old Piece of Paper still surviving; still emblematic of old dead days and their extinct agitations, when once we get to decipher it! They are the Cambridge Committee that write; "the Army about Oxford," we have seen, is Fairfax's.

'*To the Deputy-Lieutenants of Suffolk: These.*'

Gentlemen,   Cambridge, 6th June 1645.

The cloud of the Enemy's Army hanging still upon the borders, and drawing towards Harborough, make some supposals that they aim at the Association. In regard whereof, we having information that the Army about Oxford was not yesterday advanced, albeit it was ordered so to do, we thought meet to give you intelligence thereof; — and therewith earnestly to propound to your consideration, That you will have in readiness what Horse and Foot may be had, that so a proportion may be drawn forth for this service, such as may be expedient.

And because we conceive that the exigence may require Horse and Dragoons, we desire That all your Horse and Dragoons may hasten to Newmarket; where

* II. 357.

they will receive orders for farther advance, according as the motion of the Enemy and of our Army shall require. And To allow both the several Troops of Dragoons and Horse one week's pay, to be laid down by the owner; which shall be repaid out of the public money out of the County; the pay of each Trooper being 14 shillings per week, and of a Dragoon 10 *s.* 6 *d.* per week.

Your servants,

H. Mildmay,	W. Spring,
W. Heveningham,	Maurice Barrow,
Ti. Midlton (*sic*),	Nathaniel Bacon,

'P. S.' The Place of Rendez- Francis Russell, vous for the Horse and Dragoons Oliver Cromwell, is to be at Newmarket; and for Hum. Walcot, the Foot Bury. — Since the wri- Isaak Puller. ting hereof, we received certain Ed - - - [*illegible*]. intelligence that the Enemy's Body, with 60 carriages, was upon his march towards the Association, 3 miles on this side Harborough, last night at 4 of the clock. *

The Original, a hasty, blotted Paper, with the Signatures in two unequal columns (as imitated here), and with the Post-script crammed hurriedly into the corner, and written from another ink-bottle as is still apparent, — represents to us an agitated scene in the old Committee-rooms at Cambridge that Friday. In *Rushworth* (see vi. 36-8), of the same date, and signed by the same parties, with some absentees (Oliver among them, probably now gone on other business) and more new arrivals, — is a Letter to Fairfax himself, urging him to speed over, and help them in their peril. They say, "We had formerly written to the Counties to raise their Horse and Dra-

* Original, long stationary at Ipswich, is now (Jan. 1849) the property of John Wodderspoon, Esq., Mercury Office, Norwich.

14*

goons, and have now written" as above for one instance, "to quicken them." — The Suffolk and other Horse, old Ironsides not hindmost, did muster; and in about a week hence, there came other news from "this side Harborough last night"!

LETTER XXIX.

Naseby.

THE old Hamlet of Naseby stands yet, on its old hill-top, very much as it did in Saxon days, on the Northwestern border of Northamptonshire; some seven or eight miles from Market-Harborough in Leicestershire; nearly on a line, and nearly midway, between that Town and Daventry. A peaceable old Hamlet, of some eight-hundred souls; clay cottages for labourers, but neatly thatched and swept; smith's shop, saddler's shop, beer-shop, all in order; forming a kind of square, which leads off Southwards into two long streets: the old Church, with its graves, stands in the centre, the truncated spire finishing itself with a strange old Ball, held up by rods; a "hollow copper Ball, which came from Boulogne in Henry the Eighth's time," — which has, like Hudibras's breeches, "been at the Siege of Bullen." The ground is upland, moorland, though now growing corn; was not enclosed till the last generation, and is still somewhat bare of wood. It stands nearly in the heart of England: gentle Dulness, taking a turn at etymology, sometimes derives it from *Navel;* "Navesby, quasi *Navels*by, from being," &c.: Avon Well, the distinct source of Shakspeare's Avon, is on the Western slope of the high grounds; Nen and Welland, streams leading towards Cromwell's Fen-country, begin to gather themselves from boggy places on the Eastern side. The grounds, as we say, lie high; and are still, in their new subdivisions, known by the name of "Hills," "Rutput Hill," "Mill Hill," "Dust Hill," and the like, precisely as in Rushworth's time: but they are not properly hills at all; they are broad blunt clayey masses, swelling towards and from each other, like indolent waves of a sea, sometimes of miles in extent.

It was on this high moor-ground, in the centre of England, that King Charles, on the 14th of June 1645, fought his last battle; dashed fiercely against the New-Model Army, which he had despised till then; and saw himself shivered utterly to ruin thereby. "Prince Rupert, on the King's right wing, charged *up* the hill, and carried all before him;" but Lieutenant-General Cromwell charged downhill on the other wing, likewise carrying all before him, — and did *not* gallop off the field to plunder, he. Cromwell, ordered thither by the Parliament, had arrived from the Association two days before, "amid shouts from the whole Army:" he had the ordering of the Horse this morning. Prince Rupert, on returning from his plunder, finds the King's Infantry a ruin; prepares to charge again with the rallied Cavalry; but the Cavalry too, when it came to the point, "broke all asunder," — never to reassemble more. The chase went through Harborough; where the King had already been that morning, when in an evil hour he turned back, to revenge some "surprise of an outpost at Naseby the night before," and give the Round-heads battle.

Ample details of this Battle, and of the movements prior and posterior to it, are to be found in Sprigge, or copied with some abridgment into Rushworth; who has also copied a strange old Plan of the Battle; half plan, half picture, which the Sale-Catalogues are very chary of, in the case of Sprigge. By assiduous attention, aided by this Plan, as the old names yet stick to the localities, the Narrative can still be, and has lately been, pretty accurately verified, and the Figure of the old Battle dimly brought back again.* The reader shall imagine it, for the present. — On the crown of Naseby Height stands a modern Battle-monument; but, by an unlucky over-sight, it is above a mile to the east of where the Battle really was. There are likewise two modern Books about Naseby and its Battle; both of them without value.

* Appendix, No. 7.

The Parliamentary Army stood ranged on the Height still partly called "Mill Hill," as in Rushworth's time, a mile and half from Naseby; the King's Army, on a parallel "Hill," its back to Harborough; — with the wide table of upland now named *Broad Moor* between them; where indeed the main brunt of the action still clearly enough shows itself to have been. There are hollow spots, of a rank vegetation, scattered over that Broad Moor; which are understood to have once been burial *mounds*; — some of which, one to my knowledge, have been (with more or less of sacrilege) verified as such. A friend of mine has in his cabinet two ancient grinderteeth, dug lately from that ground, — and waits for an opportunity to rebury them there. Sound effectual grinders, one of them very large; which ate their breakfast on the fourteenth morning of June two hundred years ago, and, except to be clenched once in grim battle, had never work to do more in this world! — "A stack of dead bodies, perhaps about 100, "had been buried in this Trench; piled as in a wall, a man's "length thick: the skeletons lay in courses, the heads of one "course to the heels of the next; one figure, by the strange "position of the bones, gave us the hideous notion of its "having been thrown in *before* death! We did not proceed "far: — perhaps some half-dozen skeletons. The bones were "treated with all piety; watched rigorously, over Sunday, "till they could be covered in again."* Sweet friends, for Jesus' sake forbear! —

At this Battle Mr. John Rushworth, our Historical Rushworth, had, unexpectedly, for some instants, sight of a very famous person. Mr. John is Secretary to Fairfax; and they have placed him today among the Baggage-wagons, near Naseby Hamlet, above a mile from the fighting, where he waits in an anxious manner. It is known how Prince Rupert broke our left wing, while Cromwell was breaking their left. "A Gentleman of Public Employment in the late Service near Naseby" writes next day, "Harborough, 15th June, 2 in

---

* MS. *penes me.*

the morning," a rough graphic Letter in the Newspapers, *
wherein is this sentence:

* * "A party of theirs that broke through the left wing of
"horse, came quite behind the rear to our Train; the Leader
"of them being a person somewhat in habit like the General,
"in a red montero, as the General had. He came as a friend;
"our commander of the guard of the Train went with his hat
"in his hand, and asked him, How the day went? thinking
"it had been the General: the Cavalier, who we since heard
"was Rupert, asked him and the rest, If they would have
"quarter? They cried No; gave fire, and instantly beat
"them off. It was a happy deliverance," — without doubt.

There were taken here a good few "ladies of quality in
carriages;"— and above a hundred Irish ladies not of quality,
tattery camp-followers "with long skean-knives about a foot
in length," which they well knew how to use; upon whom I
fear the Ordinance against Papists pressed hard this day. **
The King's Carriage was also taken, with a Cabinet and many
Royal Autographs in it, which when printed made a sad im-
pression against his Majesty, — gave in fact a most melancholy view of the veracity of his Majesty, "On the word of a
King." *** All was lost! —

Here is Cromwell's Letter, written from Harborough, or
"Haverbrowe" as he calls it, that same night; after the hot
Battle and hot chase were over. The original, printed long
since in Rushworth, still lies in the British Museum, — with
"a strong steady signature," which one could look at with
interest. "The Letter consists of two leaves; much worn,
"and now supported by pasting; red seal much defaced; is
"addressed on the second leaf:"

----

* King's Pamphlets, small 4to, no. 212, § 26, p. 2: the punctual con-
temporaneous Collector has named him with his pen: "Mr. Rushworth's
Letter, being the Secretary to his Excellency."
** Whitlocke.
*** The King's Cabinet opened; or Letters taken in the Cabinet at
Naseby Field (London, 1645): — reprinted in Harleian Miscellany (Lon-
don, 1810), v. 514. .

For the Honourable William Lenthall, Speaker of the Commons House of Parliament: These.

Sir,   Harborough, 14th June 1645.

Being commanded by you to this service, I think myself bound to acquaint you with the good hand of God towards you and us.

We marched yesterday after the King, who went before us from Daventry to Harborough; and quartered about six miles from him. This day we marched towards him. He drew out to meet us; both Armies engaged. We, after three hours fight very doubtful, at last routed his Army; killed and took about 5,000, — very many officers, but of what quality we yet know not. We took also about 200 carriages, all he had; and all his guns, being 12 in number, whereof two were demi-cannon, two demi-culverins, and I think the rest sackers. We pursued the Enemy from three miles short of Harborough to nine beyond, even to the sight of Leicester, whither the King fled.

Sir, this is none other but the hand of God; and to Him alone belongs the glory, wherein none are to share with Him. The General served you with all faithfulness and honour: and the best commendation I can give him is, That I daresay he attributes all to God, and would rather perish than assume to himself. Which is an honest and a thriving way: — and yet as much for bravery may be given to him, in this action, as to a man. Honest men served you faithfully in this action. Sir, they are trusty; I beseech you, in the name of God, not to discourage them. I wish this action may beget thankfulness and humility in all that are concerned in it. He that ventures his life for the

liberty of his country, I wish he trust God for the
liberty of his conscience, and you for the liberty he
fights for.   In this he rests, who is
> Your most humble servant,
> OLIVER CROMWELL. §

John Bunyan, I believe, is this night in Leicester, — not
yet writing his *Pilgrim's Progress* on paper, but acting it on
the face of the Earth, with a brown matchlock on his shoulder.
Or rather, *without* the matchlock, just at present; Leicester
and he having been taken the other day.   "Harborough
Church" is getting "filled with prisoners" while Oliver writes,
— and an immense contemporaneous tumult everywhere going
on !

The "honest men who served you faithfully" on this occasion are the considerable portion of the Army who have not
yet succeeded in bringing themselves to take the Covenant.
Whom the Presbyterian Party, rigorous for their own formula, call "Schismatics," "Sectaries," "Anabaptists," and
other hard names; whom Cromwell, here and elsewhere,
earnestly pleads for.   To Cromwell, perhaps as much as to
another, order was lovely, and disorder hateful; but he discerned better than some others what order and disorder really
were.   The forest-trees are not in "order" because they are
all clipt into the same shape of Dutch-dragons, and forced to
die or grow in that way; but because in each of them there
is the same genuine unity of life, from the inmost pith
to the outmost leaf, and they do grow according to that! —
Cromwell naturally became the head of this Schismatic
Party, intent to grow not as Dutch-dragons, but as real
trees; a Party which naturally increased with the increasing
earnestness of events and of men. —

The King stayed but a few hours in Leicester; he had
taken Leicester, as we saw, some days before, and now it
was to be retaken from him some days after: — he stayed but
a few hours here; rode on, that same night, to Ashby-de-la-

§ Harl. mss. no. 7502, art. 5, p. 7; Rushworth, vi. 45.

Zouch, which he reached "at daybreak," — poor wearied King! — then again swiftly Westward, to Wales, to Ragland Castle, to this place and that; in the hope of raising some force, and coming to fight again; which, however, he could never do.* Some ten months more of roaming, and he, "disguised as a groom," will be riding with Parson Hudson towards the Scots at Newark.

The New-Model Army marched into the Southwest; very soon "relieved Colonel Robert Blake" (Admiral Blake), and many others; — marched to ever new exploits and victories, which excite the pious admiration of Joshua Sprigge; and very soon swept all its enemies from the field, and brought this War to a close.**

The following Letters exhibit part of Cromwell's share in that business, and may be read with little commentary.

LETTER XXX.

The Clubmen.

THE victorious Army, driving all before it in the Southwest, where alone the King had still any considerable fighting force, found itself opposed by a very unexpected enemy, famed in the old Pamphlets by the name of *Clubmen*. The design was at bottom Royalist; but the country-people in those regions had been worked upon by the Royalist Gentry and Clergy, on the somewhat plausible ground of taking up arms to defend themselves against the plunder and harassment of *both* Armies. The great mass of them were Neutrals; there even appeared by and by various transient bodies of "Clubmen" on the Parliament side, whom Fairfax entertained occasionally to assist him in pioneering and other such

---

* *Iter Carolinum;* being a succinct Relation of the necessitated Marches, Retreats and Sufferings of his Majesty Charles the First, from 10th January 1641 till the time of his Death, 1648: Collected by a daily Attendant upon his Sacred Majesty during all the said time. London, 1660. — It is reprinted in *Somers Tracts* (v. 263), but, as usual there, without any editing except a nominal one, though it somewhat needed more.

** A Journal of every day's March of the Army under his Excellency Sir Thomas Fairfax (in Sprigge, p. 331).

scrvices. They were called Clubmen, not, as M. Villemain
supposes,* because they united in *Clubs*, but because they
were armed with rough country weapons, mere bludgeons
if no other could be had. Sufficient understanding of them
may be gained from the following Letter of Cromwell, pre-
faced by some Excerpts.

From Rushworth: "Thursday, July 3d, Fairfax marched
"from Blandford to Dorchester, 12 miles; a very hot day.
"Where Colonel Sidenham, Governor of Weymouth, gave
"him information of the condition of those parts; and of the
"great danger from the Club-risers;" a set of men "who would
"not suffer either contribution or victuals to be carried to the
"Parliament's garrisons. And the same night Mr. Hollis
"of Dorsetshire, the chief leader of the Clubmen, with some
"others of their principal men, came to Fairfax: and Mr.
"Hollis owned himself to be one of their leaders; affirming
"that it was fit the people should show their grievances and
"their strength. Fairfax treated them civilly, and promised
"they should have an answer the next morning. For they
"were so strong at that time, that it was held a point of pru-
"dence to be fair in demeanour towards them for a while; for
"if he should engage with General Goring and be put to
"the worst, these Clubmen would knock them on the head
"as they should fly for safety. — That which they desired
"from him was a safe-conduct for certain persons to go to the
"King and Parliament with petitions:"** which Fairfax in a
very mild but resolute manner *refused*.

From Sprigge,*** copied also into Rushworth with some
inaccuracies: "On Monday, August 4th, Lieutenant-General
"Cromwell, having intelligence of some of their places of
"rendezvous for their several divisions, went forth" from
Sherborne "with a party of Horse to meet these Clubmen;

* Our French friends ought to be informed that M. Villemain's Book
on Cromwell is, unluckily, a rather ignorant and shallow one. — Of
M. Guizot, on the other hand, we are to say that his Two Volumes, so far
as they go, are the fruit of real ability and solid studies applied to those
Transactions.
** Rushworth, vi. 52.   *** pp. 78, 9.

"being well satisfied of the danger of their design. As he
"was marching towards Shaftesbury with the party, they
"discovered some colours upon the top of a high Hill, full
"of wood and almost inaccessible. A Lieutenant with a small
"party was sent to them to know their meaning, and to ac-
"quaint them that the Lieutenant-General of the Army was
"there;   whereupon Mr. Newman, one of their leaders,
"thought fit to come down, and told us, The intent was to
"desire to know why the gentlemen were taken at Shaftes-
"bury on Saturday? The Lieutenant-General returned him
"this answer: That he held himself not bound to give him or
"them an account; what was done was by Authority; and
"they that did it were not responsible to them that had none:
"but not to leave them wholly unsatisfied, he told him, Those
"persons so met had been the occasion and stirrers of many
"tumultuous and unlawful meetings; for which they were to be
"tried by law; which trial ought not by them to be questioned
"or interrupted.   Mr. Newman desired to go up to return the
"answer; the Lieutenant-General with a small party went
"with him; and had some conference with the people; to this
"purpose: That whereas they pretended to meet there to
"save their goods, they took a very ill course for that: to
"leave their houses was the way to *lose* their goods; and it
"was offered them, That justice should be done upon any who
"offered them violence; and as for the gentlemen taken at
"Shaftesbury, it was only to answer some things they were
"accused of, which they had done contrary to law and the
"peace of the Kingdom. — Herewith they seeming to be well
"satisfied, promised to return to their houses; and accord-
"ingly did so.

"These being thus quietly sent home, the Lieutenant-
"General advanced further, to a meeting of a greater num-
"ber, of about 4000, who betook themselves to Hambledon
"Hill, near Shrawton.   At the bottom of the Hill ours met a
"man with a musket, and asked, Whither he was going? he
"said, To the Club Army; ours asked, What he meant to
"do? he asked, What they had to do with that? Being re-

"quired to lay down his arms, he said He would first lose his
"life; but was not so good as his word, for though he cocked
"and presented his musket, he was prevented, disarmed,
"and wounded, but not" — Here, however, is Cromwell's
own Narrative:

*To the Right Honourable Sir Thomas Fairfax, Commander-in-
Chief of the Parliament's Forces, 'at Sherborne: These.'*

SIR,   'Shaftesbury,' 4th August 1645.

I marched this morning towards Shaftesbury. In
my way I found a party of Clubmen gathered together,
about two miles on this side of the Town, towards you;
and one Mr. Newman in the head of them, — who was
one of those who did attend you at Dorchester, with
Mr. Hollis. I sent to them to know the cause of their
meeting: Mr. Newman came to me; and told me, That
the Clubmen in Dorset and Wilts, to the number of
ten-thousand, were to meet about their men who were
taken away at Shaftesbury, and that their intendment
was to secure themselves from plundering. To the first
I told them, That although no account was due to
them, yet I knew the men were taken by your authority,
to be tried judicially for raising a Third Party in the
Kingdom; and if they should be found guilty, they
must suffer according to the nature of their offence; if
innocent, I assured them you would acquit them. Upon
this they said, If they have deserved punishment, they
would not have any thing to do with them; and so
were quieted as to that point. For the other 'point,'
I assured them, That it was your great care, not to
suffer them in the least to be plundered, and that they
should defend themselves from violence, and bring to
your Army such as did them any wrong, where they
should be punished with all severity: upon this, very

quietly and peaceably they marched away to their houses, being very well satisfied and contented.

We marched on to Shaftesbury, where we heard a great body of them was drawn together about Hambledon Hill; — where indeed near two-thousand were gathered. I sent 'up' a forlorn-hope of about fifty Horse; who coming very civilly to them, they fired upon them; and ours desiring some of them to come to me, were refused with disdain. They were drawn into one of the old Camps,* upon a very high Hill: I sent one Mr. Lee** to them, To certify the peaceableness of my intentions, and To desire them to peaceableness, and to submit to the Parliament. They refused, and fired at us. I sent him a second time, To let them know, that if they would lay down their arms, no wrong should be done them. They still (through the animation of their leaders, and especially two vile Ministers) refused; I commanded your Captain-Lieutenant to draw up to them, to be in readiness to charge; and if upon his falling on, they would lay down arms, to accept them and spare them. When we came near, they refused his offer, and let fly at him; killed about two of his men, and at least four horses. The passage not being for above three a-breast, kept us out: whereupon Major Desborow wheeled about; got in the rear of them, beat them from the work, and did some small execution upon them; — I believe killed not twelve of them, but cut very many, "and put them all to flight." We have taken about 300; many of which are poor silly creatures, whom if you please to let me send home,

---

* Roman Camps (Gough's Camden, 1. 52).
** "One Mr. Lee who, upon the approach of ours, had come from them." (Sprigge, p. 79).

they promise to be very dutiful for time to come, and "will be hanged before they come out again."

The ringleaders which we have, I intend to bring to you. They had taken divers of the Parliament soldiers prisoners, besides Colonel Fiennes his men; and used them most barbarously; bragging, They hoped to see my Lord Hopton, and that he is to command them. They expected from Wilts great store; and gave out they meant to raise the siege at Sherborne, when 'once' they were all met. We have gotten great store of their arms, and they carried few or none home. We quarter about ten miles off, and purpose to draw our quarters near to you tomorrow.

Your most humble servant,
OLIVER CROMWELL. §

"On Tuesday at night, August 5th, the Lieutenant-General" Cromwell "with his party returned to Sherborne," where the General and the rest were very busy besieging the inexpugnable Sir Lewis Dives.

"This work," which the Lieutenant-General had now been upon, continues Sprigge, "though unhappy, was very necessary."* No messenger could be sent out but he was picked up by these Clubmen; these once dispersed, "a man might ride very quietly from Sherborne to Salisbury." The inexpugnable Sir Lewis Dives (a thrasonical person known to the readers of Evelyn), after due battering, was now soon stormed: whereupon, by Letters found on him, it became apparent how deeply Royalist this scheme of Clubmen had been; "Commissions for raising Regiments of Clubmen;" the design to be extended over England at large, "yea into the Associated Counties:" however, it has now come to nothing; and the Army turns Northward to the Siege of

§ Newspapers (Cromwelliana, p. 20).
* Sprigge, p. 81.

Bristol, where Prince Rupert is doing all he can to entrench himself.

LETTER XXXI.

Storm of Bristol.

"On the Lord's Day, September 21, according to Order "of Parliament, Lieutenant-General Cromwell's Letter on "the taking of Bristol was read in the several Congregations "about London, and thanks returned to Almighty God for "the admirable and wonderful reducing of that city. The "Letter of the renowned Commander is well worth observa-"tion."* For the Siege itself and what preceded and followed it, see, besides this Letter, Rupert's own account,** and the ample details of Sprigge copied with abridgment by Rush-worth: Sayer's *History of Bristol* gives Plans, and all manner of local details, though in a rather vague way.

For the Honourable William Lenthall, Speaker of the Commons House of Parliament: These.

Sir,   Bristol, 14th September 1645.

It has pleased the General to give me in charge to represent unto you a particular account of the taking of Bristol; the which I gladly undertake.

After the finishing of that service at Sherborne, it was disputed at a council of war, Whether we should march into the West or to Bristol? Amongst other arguments, the leaving so considerable an enemy at our backs, to march into the heart of the Kingdom, the un-doing of the country about Bristol, which was 'already' exceedingly harassed by the Prince his being there-abouts but a fortnight; the correspondency he might hold in Wales; the possibility of uniting the Enemy's

* Newspapers, Cromwelliana, p. 24.
** Rushworth, vi. 69, &c.

forces where they pleased, and especially of drawing
to an head the disaffected Clubmen of Somerset, Wilts
and Dorset, when once our backs were toward them:
these considerations, together with 'the hope of' taking
so important a place, so advantageous for the opening
of trade to London, — did sway the balance, and beget
that conclusion.

When we came within four miles of the City, we
had a new debate, Whether we should endeavour to
block it up, or make a regular siege? The latter being overruled, Colonel Welden with his brigade marched
to Pile Hill, on the South side of the City, being within
musket-shot thereof: — where in a few days they
made a good quarter, overlooking the City. Upon our
advance, the enemy fired Bedminster, Clifton, and
some other villages lying near to the City; and would
have fired more, if our unexpected coming had not
hindered. The General caused some Horse and Dragoons under Commissary-General Ireton to advance
over Avon, to keep-in the enemy on the North side of
the Town, till the foot could come up: and after a
day, the General, with Colonel Montague's and Colonel
Rainsborough's Brigades, marched over at Kensham to
Stapleton, where he quartered that night. The next
day, Colonel Montague, having this post assigned with
his brigade, To secure all between the Rivers Froom
and Avon; he came up to Lawford's Gate,* within
musket-shot thereof. Colonel Rainsborough's post was
near to Durham Down, whereof the Dragoons and three
regiments of Horse made good a post upon the Down,
between him and the River Avon, on his right hand.
And from Colonel Rainsborough's quarters to Froom

* One of the Bristol Gates.

River, on his left, a part of Colonel Birch's, and 'the whole of' General Skippon's regiment were to maintain that post.

These posts thus settled, our Horse were forced to be upon exceeding great duty; to stand by the Foot, lest the Foot, being so weak in all their posts, might receive an affront.   And truly herein we were very happy, that we should receive so little loss by sallies; considering the paucity of our men to make good the posts, and strength of the enemy within.   By sallies (which were three or four) I know not that we lost thirty men, in all the time of our siege.   Of officers of quality, only Colonel Okey was taken by mistake (going 'of himself' to the enemy, thinking they had been friends), and Captain Guilliams slain in a charge. We took Sir Bernard Astley; and killed Sir Richard Crane, — one very considerable with the Prince.

We had a council of war concerning the storming of the Town, about eight days before we took it; and in that there appeared great unwillingness to the work, through the unseasonableness of the weather, and other apparent difficulties.   Some inducement to bring us thither had been the report of the good affection of the Townsmen to us; but that did not answer expectation. Upon a second consideration, it was overruled for a storm.   And all things seemed to favour the design; — and truly there hath been seldom the like cheerfulness to any work like to this, after it was once resolved upon.   The day and hour of our storm was appointed to be on Wednesday morning, the Tenth of September, about one of the clock.   We chose to act it so early because we hoped thereby to surprise the Enemy.   With this resolution also, to avoid confusion and falling foul one upon another, That when 'once' we had recovered* the Line, and Forts upon it, we should not advance further till day. The General's signal unto a storm, was to be, The firing of straw, and discharging four pieces of cannon at Pryor's Hill Fort.

The signal was very well perceived of all; — and truly the men went on with great resolution; and very presently recovered the Line, making way for the Horse to enter. Colonel Montague and Colonel Pickering, who stormed at Lawford's Gate, where was a double work, well filled with men and cannon, presently entered; and with great resolution beat the Enemy from their works, and possessed their cannon. Their expedition was such that they forced the Enemy from their advantages, without any considerable loss to themselves. They laid down the bridges for the Horse to enter; — Major Desborow commanding the Horse; who very gallantly seconded the Foot. Then our Foot advanced to the City Walls; where they possessed the Gate against the Castle Street: whereinto were put a Hundred men; who made it good. Sir Hardress Waller with his own and the General's regiment, with no less resolution, entered on the other side of Lawford's Gate, towards Avon River; and put themselves into immediate conjunction with the rest of the brigade.

During this, Colonel Rainsborough and Colonel Hammond attempted Pryor's Hill Fort, and the Line downwards towards Froom; and the Major-General's regiment being to storm towards Froom River, Colonel Hammond possessed the Line immediately, and beating

* *recovered* means "taken," "got possession of:" *the Line* is a new earthen work outside the walls; very deficient in height, according to Rupert's account.

15*

the enemy from it, made way for the Horse to enter. Colonel Rainsborough, who had the hardest task of all at Pryor's Hill Fort, attempted it; and fought near three hours for it. And indeed there was great despair of carrying the place; it being exceeding high, a ladder of thirty rounds scarcely reaching the top thereof; but his resolution was such that, notwithstanding the inaccessibleness and difficulty, he would not give it over. The Enemy had four pieces of cannon upon it, which they plied with round and case shot upon our men: his Lieutenant-Colonel Bowen, and others, were two hours at push of pike, standing upon the palisadoes, but could not enter. 'But now' Colonel Hammond being entered the Line (and 'here' Captain Ireton,* with a forlorn of Colonel Rich's regiment, interposing with his Horse between the Enemy's Horse and Colonel Hammond, received a shot with two pistol-bullets, which broke his arm), — by means of this entrance of Colonel Hammond, they did storm the Fort on that part which was inward; 'and so' Colonel Rainsborough's and Colonel Hammond's men entered the Fort, and immediately put almost all the men in it to the sword.

And as this was the place of most difficulty, so 'it was' of most loss to us on that side, — and of very great honour to the undertaker. The Horse 'too' did second them with great resolution: both these Colonels do acknowledge that *their* interposition between the Enemy's Horse and their Foot was a great means of obtaining of this strong Fort. Without which all the rest of the Line to Froom River would have done us

* This is not the famous Ireton; this is his Brother. "Commissary-General Ireton," as we have seen (p. 294), is also here; ho is not wedded yet.

little good: and indeed neither Horse nor Foot could have stood in all that way, in any marner of security, had not the Fort been taken. — Major Bethel's were the first Horse that entered the Line; who did behave himself gallantly; and was shot in the thigh, had one or two shot more, and had his horse shot under him. Colonel Birch with his men, and the Major-General's regiment, entered with very good resolution where their post was; possessing the Enemy's guns, and turning them upon them.

By this, all the Line from Pryor's Hill Fort to Avon (which was a full mile), with all the forts, ordnance and bulwarks, were possessed by us; — save one, wherein were about Two-hundred and twenty men of the Enemy; which the General summoned, and all the men submitted.

The success on Colonel Welden's side did not answer with this. And although the Colonels, and other the officers and soldiers both Horse and Foot, testified as much resolution as could be expected, — Colonel Welden, Colonel Ingoldsby, Colonel Herbert, and the rest of the Colonels and Officers, both of Horse and Foot, doing what could be well looked for from men of honour, — yet what by reason of the height of the works, which proved higher than report made them, and the shortness of the ladders, they were repulsed, with the loss of about a Hundred men. Colonel Fortescue's Lieutenant-Colonel was killed, and Major Cromwell* dangerously shot; and two of Colonel Ingoldsby's brothers hurt; with some Officers.

* A cousin.

Being possessed of thus much as hath been related, the Town was fired in three places by the Enemy; which we could not put out. Which begat a great trouble in the General, and us all; fearing to see so famous a City burnt to ashes before our faces. Whilst we were viewing so sad a spectacle, and·consulting which way to make further advantage of our success, the Prince sent a trumpet to the General to desire a treaty for the surrender of the Town. To which the General agreed; and deputed Colonel Montague, Colonel Rainsborough, and Colonel Pickering for that service; authorising them with instructions to treat and conclude the Articles, — which 'accordingly' are these enclosed. For performance whereof hostages were mutually given.

On Thursday about two of the clock in the afternoon, the Prince marched out; having a convoy of two regiments of Horse from us; and making election of Oxford for the place he would go to, which he had liberty to do by his Articles.

The cannon which we have taken are about a Hundred-and-forty mounted; about a Hundred barrels of powder already ʹcome to our hands, with a good quantity of shot, ammunition, and arms. We have found already between Two and Three-thousand muskets. The Royal Fort had victual in it for a Hundred-and-fifty men, for Three-hundred-and-twenty days; the Castle victualled for nearly half so long. The Prince had in Foot of the Garrison, as the Mayor of the City informed me, Two-thousand five-hundred, and about a thousand Horse, besides the Trained Bands of the Town, and Auxiliaries a Thousand, some say a Thousand five-hundred. — I hear but of one man that

hath died of the plague in all our Army, although we
have quartered amongst and in the midst of infected
persons and places. We had not killed of ours in the
Storm, nor in all this Siege, Two-hundred men.

Thus I have given you a true, but not a full account of this great business; wherein he that runs may
read, That all this is none other than the work of God.
He must be a very Atheist that doth not acknowledge it.
It may be thought that some praises are due to
those gallant men, of whose valour so much mention is
made: — their humble suit to you and all that have
an interest in this blessing, is, That in the remembrance of God's praises they be forgotten. It's their
joy that they are instruments of God's glory, and their
country's good. It's their honour that God vouchsafes
to use them. Sir, they that have been employed 'in
this service know, that faith and prayer obtained this
City for you: I do not say ours only, but of the people
of God with you and all England over, who have
wrestled with God for a blessing in this very thing.
Our desires are, that God may be glorified by the
same spirit of faith by which we ask all our suffi-
ciency, and have received it. It is meet that He have
all the praise. Presbyterians, Independents, all have
here the same spirit of faith and prayer; the same
presence and answer; they agree here, have no names
of difference: pity it is it should be otherwise anywhere! All that believe, have the real unity, which is
most glorious; because inward, and spiritual, in the
Body, and to the Head.* For being united in forms,
commonly called Uniformity, every Christian will for

* "Head" means *Christ;* "Body" is *True Church of Christ.*

peace-sake study and do, as far as conscience will permit.   And for brethren, in things of the mind we look for no compulsion, but that of light and reason.   In other things, God hath put the sword in the Parliament's hands, — for the terror of evil-doers, and the praise of them that do well.   If any plead exemption from that, — he knows not the Gospel: if any would wring that out of your hands, or steal it from you under what pretence soever, I hope they shall do it without effect.   That God may maintain it in your hands, and direct you in the use thereof, is the prayer of

Your humble servant,
OLIVER CROMWELL. §

These last paragraphs are, as the old Newspapers say, "very remarkable."   If modern readers suppose them to be "cant," it will turn out an entire mistake.   I advise all modern readers not only to believe that Cromwell here means what he says; but even to try how *they*, each for himself in a new dialect, could mean the like or something better! —

Prince Rupert rode out of Bristol amid seas of angry human faces, glooming unutterable things upon him; growling audibly, in spite of his escort, "Why not hang *him!*" For indeed the poor Prince had been necessitated to much plunder; commanding "the elixir of the Blackguardism of the Three Kingdoms," with very insufficient funds for most part! — He begged a thousand muskets from Fairfax on this occasion, to assist his escort in protecting him across the country to Oxford; promising, on his honour, to return them after that service.   Fairfax lent the muskets, the Prince did honourably return them, what he had of them, — honourably apologising that so many had "deserted" on the road, of whom neither man nor musket were recoverable at present.

§ Rushworth, vi. 85; Sprigge, pp. 112-118.

LETTERS XXXII.—XXXV.

From Bristol the Army turned Southward again, to deal with the yet remaining force of Royalism in that quarter. Sir Ralph Hopton, with Goring and others under him, made stubborn resistance; but were constantly worsted, at Langport, at Torrington, wheresoever they rallied and made a new attempt. The Parliament Army went steadily and rapidly on; storming Bridgewater, storming all manner of Towns and Castles; clearing the ground before them: till Sir Ralph was driven into Cornwall; and, without resource or escape, saw himself obliged next spring * to surrender, and go beyond seas. A brave and honourable man; respected on both sides; and of all the King's Generals the most deserving respect. He lived in retirement abroad; taking no part in Charles Second's businesses; and died in honourable poverty before the Restoration.

The following Three Letters ** are what remain to us concerning Cromwell's share in that course of victories. He was present in various general or partial Fights from Langport to Bovey Tracey; became especially renowned by his Sieges, and took many Strong Places besides those mentioned here.

LETTER XXXII.

'*To the Right Honourable Sir Thomas Fairfax, General of the Parliament's Army: These.*'

Sir,   '*Winchester, 6th October 1645.*'

I came to Winchester on the Lord's day, the 28th of September; with Colonel Pickering, — commanding his own, Colonel Montague's, and Sir Hardress Waller's regiments. After some dispute with the Governor, we entered the Town. I summoned the Castle; was denied; whereupon we fell to prepare batteries, — which we

* Truro, 14th March 1645-6 (Rushworth, vi. 110).
** Appendix, No. 8, contains Two more: Battle of Langport, and Summons to Winchester (*Note of* 1857).

could not perfect (some of our guns being out of order)
until Friday following.   Our battery was six guns;
which being finished, — after firing one round, I sent
in a second summons for a treaty; which they refused.
Whereupon we went on with our work, and made a
breach in the wall near the Black Tower; which, after
about 200 shot, we thought stormable; and purposed
on Monday morning to attempt it.   On Sunday night,
about ten of the clock, the Governor beat a parley,
desiring to treat.   I agreed unto it; and sent Colonel
Hammond and Major Harrison in to him, who agreed
upon these enclosed Articles.

Sir, this is the addition of another mercy.   You
see God is not weary in doing you good: I confess,
Sir, His favour to you is as visible, when he comes by
His power upon the hearts of your enemies, making
them quit places of strength to you, as when He gives
courage to your soldiers to attempt hard things.   His
goodness in this is much to be acknowledged: for the
Castle was well manned with Six-hundred-and-eighty
horse and foot, there being near Two-hundred gentlemen, officers, and their servants; well victualled, with
fifteen hundred-weight of. cheese, very great store of
wheat and beer; near twenty barrels of powder, seven
pieces of cannon; the works were exceeding good and
strong.   It's very likely it would have cost much blood
to have gained it by storm.   We have not lost twelve
men: this is repeated to you, that God may have all
the praise, for it's all His due.

Sir, I rest,

Your most humble servant,

OLIVER CROMWELL. §

§ Sprigge, p. 128; Newspapers (in Cromwelliana, p. 25); Rushworth,
vi. 91.

"Lieutenant-General Cromwell's Secretary," who brings this Lettter, gets 50*l.* for his good news. * By Sprigge's account, ** he appears to have been "Mr. Hugh Peters," this Secretary. Peters there makes a verbal Narrative of the affair, to Mr. Speaker and the Commons, which, were not room so scanty, we should be glad to insert.

It was at this surrender of Winchester that certain of the captive enemies having complained of being plundered contrary to Articles, Cromwell had the accused parties, six of his own soldiers, tried: being all found guilty, one of them by lot was hanged, and the other five were marched off to Oxford, to be there disposed of as the Governor saw fit. The Oxford Governor politely returned the five prisoners, "with an acknowledgment of the Lieutenant-General's nobleness. ***

LETTER XXXIII.

Basing House, Pawlet Marquis of Winchester's Mansion, stood, as the ruined heaps still testify, at a small distance from Basingstoke in Hampshire. It had long infested the Parliament in those quarters; and been especially a great eyesorrow to the "Trade of London with the Western Parts." With Dennington Castle at Newbury, and this Basing House at Basingstoke, there was no travelling the western roads, except with escort, or on sufferance. The two places had often been attempted; but always in vain. Basing House especially had stood siege after siege, for four years; ruining poor Colonel This and then poor Colonel That; the jubilant Royalists had given it the name of *Basting* House: there was, on the Parliament side, a kind of passion to have Basing House taken. The Lieutenant-General, gathering all the artillery he can lay hold of; firing incessantly, 200 or 500 shot at some given point till he see a hole made; and then storming like a fireflood:— he perhaps may manage it.

* Commons Journals, 7th October 1645.   ** p. 129.
*** Sprigge, p. 133.

To the Honourable William Lenthall, Speaker of the Commons House of Parliament: These.

SIR,   Basingstoke, 14th October 1645.

I thank God, I can give you a good account of Basing. After our batteries placed, we settled the several posts for the storm: Colonel Dalbier was to be on the north side of the House next the Grange; Colonel Pickering on his left hand, and Sir Hardress Waller's and Colonel Montague's regiments next him. We stormed, this morning, after six of the clock: the signal for falling on was the firing four of our cannon; which being done, our men fell on with great resolution and cheerfulness. We took the two Houses without any considerable loss to ourselves. Colonel Pickering stormed the New House, passed through, and got the gate of the Old House; whereupon they summoned a parley, which our men would not hear.

In the mean time Colonel Montague's and Sir Hardress Waller's regiments assaulted the strongest work, where the Enemy kept his Court of Guard; — which, with great resolution, they recovered; beating the Enemy from a whole culverin, and from that work: which having done, they drew their ladders after them, and got over another work, and the house-wall, before they could enter. In this Sir Hardress Waller, performing his duty with honour and diligence, was shot in the arm, but not dangerously.

We have had little loss: many of the Enemy our men put to the sword, and some officers of quality; most of the rest we have prisoners, amongst whom the Marquis 'of Winchester himself,' and Sir Robert Peak, with divers other officers, whom I have ordered to be sent up to you. We have taken about ten pieces of ordnance, with much ammunition, and our soldiers a good encouragement.

I humbly offer to you, to have this place utterly slighted, for these following reasons: It will ask about Eight-hundred men to manage it; it is no frontier; the country is poor about it; the place exceedingly ruined by our batteries and mortar-pieces, and by a fire which fell upon the place since our taking it. If you please to take the Garrison at Farnham, some out of Chichester, and a good part of the foot which were here under Dalbier, and to make a strong Quarter at Newbury with three or four troops of horse, — I dare be confident it would not only be a curb to Dennington, but a security and a frontier to all these parts; inasmuch as Newbury lies upon the River, and will prevent any incursion from Dennington, Wallingford or Farringdon into these parts; and by lying there, will make the trade most secure between Bristol and London for all carriages. And I believe the gentlemen of Sussex and Hampshire will with more cheerfulness contribute to maintain a garrison on the frontier than in their bowels, which will have less safety in it.

Sir, I hope not to delay, but to march towards the West tomorrow; and to be as diligent as I may in my expedition thither. I must speak my judgment to you, That if you intend to have your work carried on, recruits of Foot must be had, and a course taken to pay your Army; else, believe me, Sir, it may not be able to answer the work you have for it to do.

I entrusted Colonel Hammond to wait upon you, who was taken by a mistake whilst we lay before this Garrison, whom God safely delivered to us, to our great joy; but to his loss of almost all he had, which the Enemy took from him. The Lord grant that these mercies may be acknowledged with all thankfulness: God exceedingly abounds in His goodness to us, and will not be weary until righteousness and peace meet; and until He hath brought forth a glorious work for the happiness of·this poor Kingdom. Wherein desires to serve God and you, with a faithful heart,

Your most humble servant,

OLIVER CROMWELL. *

Colonel Hammond, whom we shall by and by see again, brought this good news to London, and had his reward, of 200*l.*; * Mr. Peters also, being requested "to make a relation to the House of Commons, spake as follows." The reader will like to hear Mr. Peters for once, a man concerning whom he has heard so many falsehoods, and to see an old grim scene through his eyes. Mr. Peters related:

"That he came into Basing House some time after the "storm," on Tuesday 14th of October 1645; — "and took a "view first of the works; which were many, the circumvalla- "tion being above a mile in compass. The Old House had "stood (as it is reported) two or three hundred years, a nest of "Idolatry; the New House surpassing that, in beauty and "stateliness; and either of them fit to make an emperor's "court.

"The rooms before the storm (it seems), in both Houses, "were all completely furnished; provisions for some years "rather than months; 400 quarters of wheat; bacon divers "rooms-full, containing hundreds of flitches; cheese propor- "tionable; with oatmeal, beef, pork; beer divers cellars-full, "and that very good," — Mr. Peters having taken a draught of the same.

"A bed in one room, furnished, which cost 1,300*l.* Popish

§ Spriggc, pp. 137-9; Newspapers (Cromwelliana, p. 27); and Harl. MSS. 787.

* Commons Journals (15th Oct. 1645), iv. 309.

"books many, with copes, and such utensils. In truth, the
"House stood in its full pride; and the Enemy was persuaded
"that it would be the last piece of ground that would be taken
"by the Parliament, because they had so often foiled our
"forces which had formerly appeared before it. In the several
"rooms and about the House, there were slain seventy-four,
"and only one woman, the daughter of Dr. Griffith, who by
"her railing," poor lady "provoked our soldiers (then in heat)
"into a further passion. There lay dead upon the ground,
"Major Cuffle; — a man of great account amongst them, and
"a notorious Papist slain by the hands of Major Harrison,
"that godly and gallant gentleman," — all men know him;
"and Robinson the Player, who, a little before the storm, was
"known to be mocking and scorning the Parliament and our
"Army. Eight or nine gentlewomen of rank, running forth
"together, were entertained by the common soldiers some-
"what coarsely; — yet not uncivilly, considering the action in
"hand.

"The plunder of the soldiers continued till Tuesday night:
"one soldier had a Hundred-and-twenty Pieces in gold for his
"share; others plate, others jewels; — among the rest, one got
"three bags of silver, which (he being not able to keep his
"own counsel) grew to be common pillage amongst the rest,
"and the fellow had but one half-crown left for himself at last.
"— The soldiers sold the wheat to country-people; which
"they held up at good rates awhile; but afterwards the
"market fell, and there were some abatements for haste.
"After that, they sold the household stuff; whereof there was
"good store, and the country loaded away many carts; and
"they continued a great while, fetching out all manner of
"household stuff, till they had fetched out all the stools,
"chairs, and other lumber, all which they sold to the country-
"people by piecemeal.

"In all these great buildings, there was not one iron bar
"left in all the windows (save only what were on fire), before
"night. And the last work of all was the lead; and by Thurs-
"day morning, they had hardly left one gutter about the

"House. And what the soldiers left, the fire took hold on;
"which made more than ordinary haste; leaving nothing but
"bare walls and chimneys in less than twenty hours; — being
"occasioned by the neglect of the Enemy in quenching a fire-
"ball of ours at first." — What a scene!

"We know not how to give a just account of the number of
"persons that were within. For we have not quite Three-hun-
"dred prisoners; and it may be, have found a Hundred slain,
"— whose bodies, some being covered with rubbish, came not
"at once to our view.   Only, riding to the House on Tuesday
"night, we heard divers crying in vaults for quarter; but our
"men could neither come to them, nor they to us. Amongst
"those that we saw slain, one of their officers lying on the
"ground, seeming so exceeding tall, was measured; and from
"his great toe to his crown was 9 feet in length' (*sic*).

"The Marquis being pressed, by Mr. Peters arguing with
"him,' which was not very chivalrous in Mr. Peters, 'broke out
"and said, "'That if the King had no more ground in England
"but Basing House, he would adventure as he did, and so
"maintain it to the uttermost;' — meaning with these Papists;
"comforting himself in this disaster, 'That Basing House was
"called *Loyalty*.' But he was soon silenced in the question
"concerning the King and Parliament; and could only hope
"'That the King might have a day again.' — And thus the
"Lord was pleased in a few hours to show us what mortal seed
"all earthly glory grows upon; and how just and righteous the
"ways of God are, who takes sinners in their own snares, and
"lifteth up the hands of His despised people.

"This is now the Twentieth garrison that hath been taken
"in, this Summer, by this Army; — and, I believe most of them
"the answers of the prayers, and trophies of the faith, of some
"of God's servants. The Commander of this Brigade," Lieutenant-General Cromwell, "had spent much time with God in
"prayer the night before the storm; — and seldom fights with-
"out some Text of Scripture to support him. This time he
"rested upon that blessed word of God, written in the Hundred-
"and-fifteenth Psalm, eighth verse, *They that make them are like*

"*unto them; so is every one that trusteth in them.*   Which, with
"some verses going before, was now accomplished."*

"Mr. Peters presented the Marquis's own Colours, which
"he brought from Basing; the Motto of which was, *Donec pax*
"*redeat terris;* the very same as King Charles gave upon his
"Coronation-money, when he came to the Crown."** — So Mr.
Peters; and then withdrew, — getting by and by 200*l.* a-year
settled on him. ***

This Letter was read in all Pulpits next Sunday, with
thanks rendered to Heaven, by order of Parliament.   Basing
House is to be carted away; "whoever will come for brick or
stone shall freely have the same for his pains."†

Among the names of the Prisoners taken here one reads
that of *Inigo Jones,* — unfortunate old Inigo. Vertue, on what
evidence I know not, asserts farther that Wenceslaus Hollar,
with his graving tools, and unrivalled graving talent, was
taken here. ††   The Marquis of Winchester had been addicted to the Arts, — to the Upholsteries perhaps still more.
A magnificent kind of man; whose "best bed," now laid bare
to general inspection, excited the wonder of the world.

LETTER XXXIV.

FAIRFAX, with the Army, is in Devonshire; the following
Letter will find him at Tiverton; Cromwell marching that way,
having now ended Basing. It is ordered in the Commons House
that Cromwell be thanked; moreover that he now attack Den-

---

* "Not unto us, O Lord, not unto us, but unto thy Name give glory;
"for thy mercy and for thy truth's sake. Wherefore should the Heathen
"say, Where is now their God? Our God is in the Heavens: he hath
"done whatsoever he hath pleased! — Their Idols are silver and gold; the
"work of men's hands. They have mouths, but they speak not; eyes have
"they, but they see not: they have ears, but they hear not; noses have
"they, but they smell not; they have hands, but they handle not; feet have
"they, but they walk not: neither speak they through their throat! They
"that make them are like unto them; so is every one that trusteth in
"them." — These words, awful as the words of very God, were in Oliver
Cromwell's heart that night.

** Sprigge, pp. 139-41.   *** Whitlocke.
  † Commons Journals, iv. 309.   †† Life of Hollar.

nington Castle, of which we heard already at Newbury. These messages, as I gather, reached him at Basing, late "last night," — Wednesday 15th, the day they were written in London. * Thursday morning early, he marched; has come ("came," he calls it) as far as Wallop; purposes still to make a forced march "to Langford House to-night" (probably with horse only, and leave the foot to follow); — answers meanwhile his messages *here* (see next Letter), and furthermore writes this:

To the Right Honourable Sir Thomas Fairfax, *General of the Parliament's Army:*** *Haste: These.*

SIR,   Wallop, 16th October 1645.

In today's march I came to Wallop, twenty miles from Basing, towards you. Last night I received this enclosed from the Speaker of the House of Commons; which I thought fit to send you; and to which I returned an Answer, a copy whereof I have also sent enclosed to you.

I perceive that it's their desire to have the place*** taken-in. But truly I could not do other than let them know what the condition of affairs in the West is, and submit the business to them and you. I shall be at Langford House tonight, if God please. I hope the work will not be long. If it should, I will rather leave a small part of the Foot (if Horse will not be sufficient to take it in), than be detained from obeying such commands as I shall receive. I humbly beseech you to be confident that no man hath a more faithful heart to serve you than myself, nor shall be more strict to obey your commands than

Your most humble servant,

OLIVER CROMWELL.

* Commons Journals (iv. 309), 15th Oct. 1645.
** Marching from Collumpton to Tiverton, while Cromwell writes (Sprigge, p. 334).   *** Dennington Castle.

Sir, I beseech you to let me know your resolution in this business with all the possible speed that may be; because whatsoever I be designed to, I wish I may speedily endeavour it, time being so precious for action in this season.§

Langford House, whither Oliver is now bound, hoping to arrive to-night, is near Salisbury.   He did arrive accordingly; drew out part of his brigade, and summoned the place; — here is his own most brief account of the business.

LETTER XXXV.

To the Honourable William Lenthall, Esquire, Speaker to the Honourable House of Commons: These.

SIR,   Salisbury, 17th October (12 at night) 1645.

I gave you an account, the last night, of my marching to Langford House.   Whither I came this day, and immediately sent them in a Summons.   The Governor desired I should send two Officers to treat with him; and I accordingly appointed Lieutenant-Colonel Hewson and Major Kelsey thereunto.   The Treaty produced the Agreement, which I have here enclosed to you.

The General, I hear, is advanced as far West as Collumpton, and hath sent some Horse and Foot to Tiverton.   It is earnestly desired, that more Foot might march up to him; — it being convenient that we stay 'here' a day for our Foot that are behind and coming up.

I wait your answer to my Letter last night from

§ Sloane MSS. 1519, fol. 61: — only the Signature is in Oliver's hand.

16*

Wallop: I shall desire that your pleasure may be
speeded to me; — and rest,
                    Sir,
          Your humble servant,
                    OLIVER CROMWELL. §

Basing is black ashes, then; and Langford is ours, the Garrison "to march forth to-morrow at twelve of the clock, being
the 18th instant."*   And now the question is, Shall we attack
Dennington or not? —
    Colonel Dalbier, a man of Dutch birth, well known to
readers of the old Books, is with Cromwell at present; his Second in command.   It was from Dalbier that Cromwell first of
all learned the mechanical part of soldiering; he had Dalbier
to help him in drilling his Ironsides; so says Heath, credible
on such a point.   Dennington Castle was not besieged at present; it surrendered next Spring to Dalbier.**   Cromwell returned to Fairfax; served through Winter with him in the
West, till all ended there.

    About a month before the date of this Letter, the King had
appeared again with some remnant of force, got together in
Wales; with intent to relieve Chester, which was his key to
Ireland: but this force too he saw shattered to pieces on Row-
ton Heath, near that City.*** He had also had an eye towards
the great Montrose in Scotland, who in these weeks was blazing
at his highest there: but him too David Lesley with dragoons,
emerging from the mist of the Autumn morning, on Philips-
haugh near Selkirk, had, in one fell hour, trampled utterly out.
The King had to retire to Wales again; to Oxford and
obscurity again.
    On the 14th of next March, as we said, Sir Ralph Hopton

    § King's Pamphlets, small 4to, no. 229, art. 19 (no. 42 of *The Weekly
Account*).
      * Sprigge, p. 145.
     ** 1st April 1646 (Rushworth, vi. 252).
    *** 24th September 1645 (Rushworth, vi. 117; Lord Digby's account of
it, Ormond Papers, ii. 90.\

surrendered himself in Cornwall.*   On the 22d of the same month, Sir Jacob Astley, another distinguished Royalist General, the last of them all, — coming towards Oxford with some small force he had gathered, — was beaten and captured at Stow among the Wolds of Gloucestershire:** surrendering himself, the brave veteran said, or is reported to have said, "You have now done your work, and may go to play, —unless you will fall out among yourselves."

On Monday night, towards twelve of the clock, 27th April 1646, the King in disguise rode out of Oxford, somewhat uncertain whitherward, — at length towards Newark and the Scots Army.*** On the Wednesday before, Oliver Cromwell had returned to his place in Parliament.† Many detached Castles and Towns still held out, Ragland Castle even till the next August; scattered fires of an expiring conflagration, that need to be extinguished with effort and in detail. Of all which victorious sieges, with their elaborate treaties and moving accidents, the theme of every tongue during that old Summer, let the following one brief glimpse, notable on private grounds, suffice us at present.

Oxford, the Royalist metropolis, a place full of Royalist dignitaries, and of almost inexpugnable strength, had it not been so disheartened from without, — was besieged by Fairfax himself in the first days of May. There was but little fighting, there was much negotiating, tedious consulting of Parliament and King; the treaty did not end in surrender till Saturday 20th June. And now, dated on the Monday before, at Holton, a country Parish in those parts, there is this still legible in the old Church Register, — intimately interesting to some friends of ours! "HENRY IRETON, Commissary-General to Sir Thomas "Fairfax, and BRIDGET, Daughter to Oliver Cromwell, Lieute-"nant-General of the Horse to the said Sir Thomas Fairfax, — "were married, by Mr. Dell, in the Lady Whorwood her

* Hopton's own account of it, Ormond Papers, ii. 109-26.
** Rushworth, vi. 139-41.
*** Ibid., vi. 267; Iter Carolinum.
† Cromwelliana, p. 31.

"House in Holton, 15th June 1646. — ALBAN EALES,
"Rector." *

Ireton, we are to remark, was one of Fairfax's Commissioners on the Treaty for surrendering Oxford, and busy under the walls there at present: Holton is some five miles east of the City; Holton House we guess by various indications to have been Fairfax's own quarter. Dell, already and afterwards well known, was the General's Chaplain at this date. Of "the Lady Whorwood" I have traces, rather in the Royalist direction; her strong moated House, very useful to Fairfax in those weeks, still stands conspicuous in that region, though now under new figure and ownership; draw-bridge become *fixed*, deep ditch now dry, moated island changed into a flower-garden; — "rebuilt in 1807." Fairfax's Lines, we observe, extended "from Headington Hill to Marston," several miles in advance of Holton House, then "from Marston across the Cherwell, and over "from that to the Isis on the North side of the City;" southward and elsewhere, the besieged, "by a dam at St. Clement's Bridge, had laid the country all under water:" ** — in such scene, with the treaty just ending and general Peace like to follow, did Ireton welcome his Bride, — a brave young damsel of twenty-one; escorted, doubtless by her Father among others, to the Lord General's house; and there, by the Rev. Mr. Dell, solemnly handed over to new destinies!

This wedding was on Monday 15th June; on Saturday came the final signing of the treaty: and directly thereupon, on Monday *next*, Prince Rupert and Prince Maurice took the road, with their attendants, and their passes to the sea-coast; a sight for the curious. On Tuesday "there went about 300 persons, mostly of quality;" and on Wednesday all the Royalist force, "3,000" (or say 2,000) "to the Eastward, 500 to the North;" with "drums beating, colours flying," for the last time; all

---

* Parish Register of Holton (copied, Oct. 1846). Poor Noble (i. 134) seems to have copied this same Register, and to have misread his own Note: giving instead of Holton, *Nalton*, an imaginary place; and instead of June, *January*, an impossible date. See *antea*, p. 54; *postea*, Letter XLI. p. 211.
** Rushworth, vi. 279-285.

with passes, with agitated thoughts and outlooks: and in sacred Oxford, as poor Wood intimates,* the abomination of desolation supervened!—Oxford surrendering with the King's sanction quickened other surrenders; Ragland Castle itself, and the obstinate old Marquis, gave in before the end of August: and the First Civil War, to the last ember of it, was extinct.

The Parliament, in these circumstances, was now getting itself "recruited,"—its vacancies filled up again. The Royalist Members who had deserted three years ago, had been, without much difficulty, successively "disabled," as their crime came to light: but to issue new writs for new elections, while the quarrel with the King still lasted, was a matter of more delicacy; this too, however, had at length been resolved upon, the Parliament Cause now looking so decidedly prosperous, in the Autumn of 1645. Gradually, in the following months, the new Members were elected, above Two-hundred-and-thirty of them in all. These new Members, "Recruiters," as Anthony Wood and the Royalist world reproachfully call them, were by the very fact of their standing candidates in such circumstances, decided Puritans all, — Independents many of them. Colonel, afterwards Admiral Blake (for Taunton), Ludlow, Ireton (for Appleby), Algernon Sidney, Hutchinson known by his Wife's *Memoirs*, were among these new Members. Fairfax, on his Father's death some two years hence, likewise came in.**

* Fasti, li. 58, sec. edit.
** The Writ is issued 16th March 1647-8 (Commons Journals).

PART III.

BETWEEN THE TWO CIVIL WARS.
1646 — 1648.

———

LETTERS XXXVI.— XLII.

The conquering of the King had been a difficult operation; but to make a Treaty with him now when he was conquered, proved an impossible one. The Scots, to whom he had fled, entreated him, at last, "with tears" and "on their knees," to take the Covenant, and sanction the Presbyterian worship, if he could not adopt it: on that condition they would fight to the last man for him; on no other condition durst or would a man of them fight for him. The English Presbyterians, as yet the dominant party, earnestly entreated to the same effect. In vain, both of them. The King had other schemes: the King, writing privately to Digby before quitting Oxford, when he had some mind to venture privately on London, as he ultimately did on the Scotch Camp, to raise Treaties and Caballings there, had said, "— endeavouring to get to Lon-"don; being not without hope that I shall be able so to draw "either the Presbyterians or the Independents to side with me "for extirpating one another, that I shall be really King "again."* Such a man is not easy to make a Treaty with, — on the word of a King! In fact, his Majesty, though a belligerent party who had not now one soldier on foot, considered

* Oxford, 26th March 1646; Carte's Life of Ormond, iii. (London, 1735), p. 452.

himself still a tower of strength; as indeed he was; all men
having a to us inconceivable reverence for him, till bitter
Necessity and he together drove them away from it..   Equi-
vocations, spasmodic obstinacies, and blindness to the real
state of facts, must have an end. —

The following Seven Letters, of little or no significance
for illustrating public affairs, are to carry us over a period of
most intricate negotiation; negotiation with the Scots, managed manfully on both sides, otherwise it had ended in
quarrel; negotiations with the King; infinite public and private negotiations; — which issue at last in the Scots marching
home with 200,000 *l.* as "a fair instalment of their arrears," in
their pocket; and the King marching, under escort of Parliamentary Commissioners, to Holmby House in Northamptonshire, to continue in strict though very stately seclusion, "on
50 *l.* a-day," * and await the destinies there.

LETTER XXXVI.

KNYVETT, of Ashwellthorpe in Norfolk, is one of the unfortunate Royalist Gentlemen whom Cromwell laid sudden hold
of at Lowestoff, some years ago, and lodged in the Castle of
Cambridge, — suddenly snuffing out their Royalist light in
that quarter. Knyvett, we conclude, paid his "contribution,"
or due fine, for the business; got safe home again; and has
lived quieter ever since. Of whom we promised the reader
some transitory glimpse once more.**

Here accordingly is a remarkable Letter to him, now first
adjusted to its right place in this Series. The Letter used to
be in the possession of the Lords Berners, whose ancestor this
Knyvett was, one of whose seats this Ashwellthorpe in Norfolk still is. With them, however, there remains nothing but
a Copy now, and that without date, and otherwise not quite
correct. Happily it had already gone forth in print with
date and address in full; — has been found among the
lumber and innocent marine-stores of *Sylvanus Urban*, communicated, in an incidental way, by "a Gentleman at Shrews-

* Whitlocke, p. 244.   ** Antea, p. 109.

bury," who, in 1787, had got possession of it, — honestly, we hope; and to the comfort of readers here.

For my noble Friend Thomas Knyvett, Esquire, at his House at Ashwellthorpe: These.

SIR.   London, 27th July 1646.

I cannot pretend any interest in you for anything I have done, nor ask any favour for any service I may do you. But because I am conscious to myself of a readiness to serve any gentleman in all possible civilities, I am bold to be beforehand with you to ask your favour on behalf of your honest poor neighbours of Hapton, who, as I am informed, are in some trouble, and are likely to be put to more, by one Robert Browne your Tenant, who, not well pleased with the way of these men, seeks their disquiet all he may.

Truly nothing moves me to desire this, more than the pity I bear them in respect of their honesties, and the trouble I hear they are likely to suffer for their consciences. And however the world interprets it, I am not ashamed to solicit for such as are anywhere under pressure of this kind; doing even as I would be done by. Sir, this is a quarrelsome age; and the anger seems to me to be the worse, where the ground is difference of opinion; — which to cure, to hurt men in their names, persons or estates, will not be found an apt remedy. Sir, it will not repent you to protect those poor men of Hapton from injury and oppression: which that you would is the effect of this Letter. Sir, you will not want the grateful acknowledgment, nor utmost endeavours of requital from

Your most humble servant,

OLIVER CROMWELL. §

§ Gentleman's Magazine (1787), liv. 337.

Hapton is a Parish and Hamlet some seven or eight miles south of Norwich, in the Hundred of Depwade; it is within a mile or two of this Ashwellthorpe; which was Knyvett's residence at that time. What "Robert Browne your Tenant" had in hand or view against these poor Parishioners of Hapton, must, as the adjoining circumstances are all obliterated, remain somewhat indistinct to us. We gather in general that the Parishioners of Hapton were a little given to Sectarian, Independent notions; which Browne, a respectable Christian of the Pesbyterian strain, could not away with. The oppressed poor Tenants have contrived to make their case credible to Lieutenant-General Cromwell, now in his place in Parliament again; — have written to him; perhaps clubbed some poor sixpences, and sent up a rustic Deputation to him: and he, "however the respectable Presbyterian world may interpret it, is not ashamed to solicit for them:" with effect, either now or soon.

LETTER XXXVII.

For his Excellency the Right Honourable Sir Thomas Fairfax,
General of the Parliament's Forces: * *These.*

Sir,   'London,' 31st July 1646.

I was desired to write a Letter to you by Adjutant Fleming. The end of it is, To desire your Letter in his recommendation. He will acquaint you with the sum thereof, more particularly what the business is. I most humbly submit to your better judgment, when you hear it from him.

Craving pardon for my boldness in putting you to this trouble,

I rest,

Your most humble servant,

OLIVER CROMWELL. §

* At Ragland, or about leaving Bath for the purpose of concluding Ragland Siege (Rushworth, vi. 293).
§ Sloane mss. 1519, fol. 70.

Adjutant Fleming is in Sprigge's Army-List. I suppose him to be the Fleming who, as Colonel Fleming, in Spring 1648, had rough service in South Wales two years afterwards; and was finally defeated, — attempting to "seize a Pass" near Pembroke Castle, then in revolt under Poyer; was driven into a Church, and there slain, — some say, slew himself.*

Of Fleming's present "business" with Fairfax, whether it were to solicit promotion here, or continued employment in Ireland, nothing can be known. The War, which proved to be but the "First War," is now, as we said, to all real intents, ended: Ragland Castle, the last that held out for Charles, has been under siege for some weeks; and Fairfax, who had been "at the Bath for his health," was now come or coming into those parts for the peremptory reduction of it.** There have begun now to be discussions and speculations about sending men to Ireland;*** about sending Massey (famed Governor of Gloucester) to Ireland with men, and then also about disbanding Massey's men.

Exactly a week before, 24th July 1646, the united Scots and Parliamentary Commissioners have presented their "Propositions" to his Majesty at Newcastle: Yes or No, is all the answer they can take.   They are most zealous that he should say Yes.   Chancellor Loudon implores and prophesies in a very remarkable manner: "All England will rise against you; they," these Sectarian Parties, "will process and depose you, and set up another Government," unless you close with the Propositions.   His Majesty, on the 1st of August (writing at Newcastle, in the same hours whilst Cromwell writes this in London), answers in a haughty way, No.†

* Rushworth, vii. 1097, 38 : — a little "before" 27th March 1648.
** Ibid., vi. 293; — Fairfax's first Letter from Ragland is of 7th August;
14th August he dates from Usk; and Ragland is surrendered on the 17th.
*** Cromwelliana, April 1646, p. 31.
† Rushworth, vi. 819-21.

LETTER XXXVIII.

August 10*th*. The Parliamentary Commissioners have returned, and three of the leading Scots with them, — to see what is now to be done. The "Chancellor" who comes with Argyle is Loudon, the Scotch Chancellor, a busy man in those years. Fairfax is at Bath; and "the Solicitor," St. John the Shipmoney Lawyer, is there with him.

For his Excellency Sir Thomas Fairfax, the General: These.

Sir,   London, 10th August 1646.

Hearing you were returned from Ragland to the Bath, I take the boldness to make this address to you.

Our Commissioners sent to the King came this night to London.* I have spoken with two of them, and can only learn these generals, That there appears a good inclination in the Scots to the rendition of our Towns, and to their march out of the Kingdom. When they bring in their Papers, we shall know more. Argyle, and the Chancellor, and Dunfermline are come up. Duke of Hamilton is gone from the King into Scotland. I hear that Montrose's men are *not* disbanded. The King gave a very general answer. Things are not well in Scotland; — would they were in England! We are full of faction and worse.

I hear for certain that Ormond has concluded a Peace with the Rebels. Sir, I beseech you command the Solicitor to come away to us. His help would be welcome. — Sir, I hope you have not cast me off. Truly I may say, none more affectionately honours nor loves you. You and yours are in my daily prayers.

* Commons Journals, 11th Aug. 1646.

You have done enough to command the uttermost of,

Your faithful and most obedient servant,
OLIVER CROMWELL.§

'P.S.' I beseech you, my humble service may be
presented to your Lady.

'P.S. 2d.'* The money for disbanding Massey's
men is gotten, and you will speedily have directions
about them from the Commons House.

"Our Commissioners" to Charles at Newcastle, who have
returned "this night," were: Earls Pembroke and Suffolk,
from the Peers; from the Commons, Sir Walter Earle (Weymouth), Sir John Hippesley (Cockermouth), Robert Goodwin
(East Grinstead, Sussex), Luke Robinson (Scarborough).**

"Duke of Hamilton:" the Parliamentary Army found him
in Pendennis Castle, — no, in St. Michael's Mount Castle, —
when they took these places in Cornwall lately. The Parliament has let him loose again; — he has begun a course of new
diplomacies, which will end still more tragically for him.

Ormond is, on application from the Parliament, ostensibly
ordered by his Majesty not to make peace with the outlaw
Irish rebels; detestable to all men; — but he of course follows
his own judgment of the necessities of the case, being now
nearly over with it himself, and the King under restraint unable to give any real "orders." The truth was, Ormond's
Peace, odious to all English Protestants, had been signed and
finished in March last; with this condition among others, That
an Army of 10,000 Irish were to come over and help his Majesty; which truth is now beginning to ooze out. A new Ormond Peace: — not materially different I think from the late
very sad Glamorgan one; which had been made in secret,

§ Sloane mss. 1519. fol. 63.
* This second Postscript has been squeezed-in *above* the other, and is
evidently written *after* it.
** Rushworth, vi. 309, where the proposals are also given.

through the Earl of Glamorgau, in Autumn last; and then, when by ill chance it came to light, had needed to be solemnly denied in Winter following, and the Earl of Glamorgan to be thrown into prison to save appearances! On the word of an unfortunate King!* — It would be a comfort to understand farther, what the fact soon proves, that this new Peace also will not hold; the Irish Priests and Pope's Nuncios disapproving of it.   Even while Oliver writes, an Excommunication or some such Document is coming out, signed "Frater O'Farrel," "Abbas O'Teague," and the like names: poor Ormond going to Kilkenny, to join forces with the Irish rebels, is treacherously set upon, and narrowly escapes death by them. **

Concerning "the business of Massey's men," there are some notices in Ludlow.*** The Commons had ordered Fairfax to disband them, and sent the money, as we see here; whereupon the Lords ordered him, Not.   Fairfax obeyed the Commons; apologised to the Lords, — who had to submit, as their habit was.   Massey's Brigade was of no particular religion; Massey's Miscellany, — "some of them will require passes to Æthiopia," says ancient wit.   But Massey himself was strong for Presbyterianism, for strict Drill-sergeantcy and Anti-heresy of every kind: the Lords thought his Miscellany and he might have been useful.

LETTER XXXIX.

His Excellency, in the following Letter, is Fairfax; John Rushworth, worthy John, we already know! Fairfax has returned to the Bath, still for his health; Ragland being taken, and the War ended.

For John Rushworth, Esquire, Secretary to his Excellency, at the Bath: These.

MR. RUSHWORTH,   The House 'of Commons,' 26 Aug. '1646.'
I must needs entreat a favour on the behalf of

* Rushworth, vi. 242, 239-247; Birch's Inquiry concerning Glamorgan; Carte's Ormond; &c. Correct details in Godwin, ii. 102-124.
** Rushworth, vi. 416; Carte's Life of Ormond.
*** Memoirs of Edmund Ludlow (London, 1722), ii. 181.

Major Lilburn; who has a long time wanted employment, and by reason good his necessities may grow upon him.

You should do very well to move the General to take him into favourable thoughts. I know, a reasonable employment will content him. As for his honesty and courage, I need not speak much of 'that,' seeing he is so well known both to the General and yourself.

I desire you answer my expectation herein so far as you may. You shall very much oblige,

Sir,
Your real friend and servant,
OLIVER CROMWELL. §

This is not "Freeborn John," the Sectarian Lieutenant-Colonel once in my Lord of Manchester's Army; the Lilburn whom Cromwell spoke for, when Sir Philip Warwick took note of him; the John Lilburn "who could not live without a "quarrel; who if he were left alone in the world would have to "divide himself in two, and set the John to fight with Lilburn, "and the Lilburn with John!" Freeborn John is already a Lieutenant-Colonel by title; was not in the New Model at all; is already deep in quarrels, — lying in limbo since August last, for abuse of his old master Prynne.* He has quarrelled, or is quarrelling, with Cromwell too; calls the Assembly of Divines an Assembly of *Dry-vines;* — will have little else but quarrelling henceforth. — This is the Brother of Freeborn John; one of his two Brothers. Not Robert, who already is or soon becomes a Colonel in the New Model, and does not "want employment." This is Henry Lilburn: appointed, probably in consequence of this application, Governor of Tynemouth Castle: revolting to the Royalists, his own Soldiers slew him there, in 1648. These Lilburns were from Durham County.

§ Sloane mss. 1519, fol. 71   — Signature alone is Oliver's.
* Wood, iii. 353.

LETTER XL.

"Delinquents," conquered Royalists, are now getting themselves fined, according to rigorous proportions, by a Parliament Committee, which sits, and will sit long, at Goldsmiths' Hall, making that locality very memorable to Royalist gentlemen.*

The Staffordshire Committee have sent a Deputation up to Town. They bring a Petition; very anxious to have 2,000*l.* out of their Staffordshire Delinquents from Goldsmiths' Hall, or even 4,000*l.*, — to pay off their forces, and send them to Ireland; which lie heavy on the County at present.

For his Excellency Sir Thomas Fairfax, 'General of the Parliament's Army:' These.

SIR,   'London,' 6th October 1646.

I would be loath to trouble you with anything; but indeed the Staffordshire Gentlemen came to me this day, and with more than ordinary importunity did press me to give their desires furtherance to you. Their Letter will show what they entreat of you. Truly, Sir, it may not be amiss to give them what ease may well be afforded, and the sooner the better, especially at this time.**

I have no more at present, but to let you know the business of your Army is like to come on tomorrow. You shall have account of that business so soon as I am able to give it. I humbly take leave, and rest,

Your Excellency's most humble servant,
OLIVER CROMWELL.§

* The proceedings of it, all now in very superior order, still lie in the State-Paper Office.

** "and the sooner," &c.: these words are inserted above the line, by way of *caret* and afterthought.

§ Sloane MSS. 1519, fol. 72: — Oliver's own hand. — Note, his signature seems generally to be *Oliver* Cromwell, not *O.* Cromwell; to which practice we conform throughout, though there are exceptions to it.

The Commons cannot grant the prayer of this Petition;* Staffordshire will have to rest as it is for some time.   "The business of your Army" did come on "tomorrow;" and assessments for a new six-months were duly voted for it, and other proper arrangements made.**

LETTER XLI.

COLONEL IRETON, now Commissary-General Ireton, was wedded, as we saw, to Bridget Cromwell on the 15th of June last.   A man "able with his pen and his sword;" a distinguished man.   Once B.A. of Trinity College, Oxford, and Student of the Middle Temple; then a gentleman trooper in my Lord General Essex's Lifeguard; now Colonel of Horse, soon Member of Parliament; rapidly rising.   A Nottinghamshire man; has known the Lieutenant-General ever since the Eastern-Association times.   Cornbury House, not now conspicuous on the maps, is discoverable in Oxfordshire, disguised as *Blandford Lodge*, — not too far from the Devizes, at which latter Town Fairfax and Ireton have just been, disbanding Massey's Brigade.   The following Letter will require no commentary.

For my beloved Daughter Bridget Ireton, at Cornbury, General's Quarters: These.

DEAR DAUGHTER,   London, 25th October 1646.

I write not to thy Husband; partly to avoid trouble, for one line of mine begets many of his, which I doubt makes him sit up too late; partly because I am myself indisposed*** at this time, having some other considerations.

Your Friends at Ely are well: your Sister Claypole is, I trust in mercy, exercised with some perplexed thoughts.   She sees her own vanity and carnal mind;

* 7th December 1646, Commons Journals, v. 3.
** 7th October 1646, Commons Journals, iv. 687.
*** not in the mood at this time, having other matters in view.

bewailing it: she seeks after (as I hope also) what will
satisfy.   And thus to be a seeker is to be of the best
sect next to a finder; and such an one shall every
faithful humble seeker be at the end.   Happy seeker,
happy finder!   Who ever tasted that the Lord is gracious, without some sense of self, vanity, and badness?
Who ever tasted that graciousness of His, and could go
less* in desire, — less than pressing after full enjoy-
ment?   Dear Heart, press on; let not Husband, let not
anything cool thy affections after Christ.   I hope he**
will be an occasion to inflame them.   That which is
best worthy of love in thy Husband is that of the
image of Christ he bears.   Look on that, and love it
best, and all the rest for that.   I pray for thee and
him; do so for me.

My service and dear affections to the General and
Generaless.   I hear she is very kind to thee; it adds
to all other obligations.

I am
Thy dear Father,
OLIVER CROMWELL. §

Bridget Ireton is now Twenty-two.   Her Sister Claypole
(Elizabeth Cromwell) is five years younger.   They were both
wedded last Spring.   "Your Friends at Ely" will indicate

---

* *less*, is an adjective; to *go*, in such case, signifies to *become*, as
"go mad," &c.
** thy Husband.
§ "A Copy of Oliver Cromwell's Letter to his Daughter Ireton, exactly
taken from the Original." Harleian mss. no. 6988, fol. 224 (not mentioned
in Harleian Catalogue). — In another Copy sent me, which exactly cor-
responds, is this Note: "Memo: The above Lettr of Oliver Cromwell
"Jno Caswell Mercht of London had from his Mother Linington, who
"had it from old Mrs. Warner, who liv'd with Oliver Cromwell's Daugh-
"ter. — — And was Copied from the Original Letter, which is in the
"hands of John Warner Esqr of Swanzey, by Chas Norris, 25th Mart
"1749."

17*

that the Cromwell Family was still resident in that City;* though, I think, they not long afterwards removed to London.   Their first residence here was King-street, Westminster;**   Oliver for the present lodges in Drury Lane: fashionable quarters both, in those times.

General Fairfax had been in Town only three days before, attending poor Essex's Funeral: a mournful pageant, consisting of "both the Houses, Fairfax and all the Civil and "Military Officers then in Town, the Forces of the City, a "very great number of coaches and multitudes of people;" with Mr. Vines to preach; — regardless of expense, 5,000*l.* being allowed for it. ***

LETTER XLII.

The intricate Scotch negotiations have at last ended. The paying of the Scots their first instalment, and getting them to march away in peace, and leave the King to our disposal, is the great affair that has occupied Parliament ever since his Majesty refused the Propositions. Not till Monday the 21st December could it be got "perfected" or "almost perfected." After a busy day spent in the Commons House on that affair,† Oliver writes the following Letter to Fairfax. The "Major-General" is Skippon. Fairfax, "since he left Town," is most likely about Nottingham, the head-quarters of his Army, which had been drawing rather Northward, ever since the King appeared among the Scots. Fairfax came to Town 12th November, with great splendour of reception; left it again "18th December."

On the morrow after that, 19th December 1646, the Londoners presented their Petition, not without tumult; complaining of heavy expenses and other great grievances from the Army; and craving that the same might be, so soon as possible, disbanded, and a good Peace with his Majesty made.†† The first note of a very loud controversy which arose

* See also Appendix, No. 7, last Letter there (*Note to Third Edition*).
** Cromwelliana, p. 60.   *** Rushworth, vi. 239; Whitlocke, p. 230.
† Commons Journals, v. 22, 3.
†† King's Pamphlets, small 4to, no. 290 (cited by Godwin, ii. 269).

between the City and the Army, between the Presbyterians
and the Independents, on that matter. Indeed the humour of
the City seems to be getting high; impatient for "a just peace"
now that the King is reduced. On Saturday 6th December,
it was ordered that the Lord Mayor be apprised of tumultuous
assemblages which there are, "to the disturbance of the
peace;" and be desired to quench them, — if he can.

*For his Excellency Sir Thomas Fairfax, General of the
Parliament's Armies: These.*

SIR,   'London,' 21st December 1646.

Having this opportunity by the Major-General to
present a few lines unto you, I take the boldness to let
you know how our affairs go on since you left Town.

We have had a very long Petition from the City;
how it strikes at the Army, and what other aims it
has, you will see by the contents of it; as also what is
the prevailing temper at this present, and what is to
be expected from men. But this is our comfort, God
is in Heaven, and He doth what pleaseth Him; His
and only His counsel shall stand, whatsoever the designs of men, and the fury of the people be.

We have now, I believe, almost* perfected all our
business for Scotland. I believe Commissioners will
speedily be sent down to see agreements performed; it's
intended that Major-General Skippon have authority
and instructions from your Excellency to command the
Northern Forces, as occasion shall be, and that he have
a Commission of Martial Law. Truly I hope that the
having the Major-General to command** this Party will
appear to be a good thing, every day more and more.

* "almost" is inserted with a *caret*.
** At this point, the bottom of the page being reached, Oliver takes to
the broad margin, and writes the remainder there lengthwise, continuing
till there is barely room for his signature, on the outmost verge of the

Here has been a design to steal away the Duke of York from my Lord of Northumberland: one of his own servants, whom he preferred to wait on the Duke, is guilty of it; the Duke himself confessed so.   I believe you will suddenly hear more of it.

I have no more to trouble you 'with;' but praying for you, rest,

Your Excellency's most humble servant,

OLIVER CROMWELL. §

Skippon, as is well known, carried up the cash, 200,000*l.*, to Newcastle successfully, in a proper number of wagons; got it all counted there, "bags of 100*l.*, chests of 1000*l.*," (5th-16th January 1646-7); after which the Scots marched peaceably away.

The little Duke of York, entertained in a pet-captive fashion at St. James's, did not get away at this time; but managed it, by and by, with help of a certain diligent intriguer and turncoat called Colonel Bamfield; * of whom we may hear farther.

On Thursday, 11th February 1646-7, on the road between Mansfield and Nottingham, — road between Newcastle and Holmby House, — "Sir Thomas Fairfax went and met 'the "King; who stopped his horse: Sir Thomas alighted, and "kissed the King's hand; and afterwards mounted, and dis-"coursed with the King as they passed towards Notting-ham."** The King had left Newcastle on the 3d of the month; got to Holmby, or Holdenby, on the 13th; — and "there," says the poor *Iter Carolinum*, "during pleasure."

sheet; which, as we remarked already, is a common practice with him in writing Letters: — he is always loath to turn the page; — having *no blotting-paper* at that epoch; having only sand to dry his ink with, and a natural indisposition to pause till he finish!

§ Sloane MSS. 1519, fol. 78, p. 147.

* Clarendon, iii. 188.

** Whitlocke, p. 242; *Iter Carolinum* (in Somers Tracts, vi. 274): Whitlocke's date, as usual, is inexact.

LETTERS XLIII., XLIV.

BEFORE reading these two following Letters, read this Extract from a work still in Manuscript, and not very sure of ever getting printed:

"The Presbyterian 'Platform' of Church Government, "as recommended by the Assembly of Divines or 'Dry-"'Vines,' has at length, after unspeakable debatings, passings "and repassings through both Houses, and soul's-travail nõt "a little, about 'ruling-elders,' 'power of the keys,' and such "like,—been got *finally* passed, though not without some mel-"ancholy shades of Erastianism, or 'the Voluntary Principle,' "as the new phrase runs.   The Presbyterian Platform is "passed by Law; and London and other places, busy 'elect-"'ing their ruling-elders,' are just about ready to set it actually "on foot. And now it is hoped there will be some 'uniformity' "as to that high matter.

"Uniformity of free-growing healthy forest-trees is good; "uniformity of clipt Dutch-dragons is not so good! The ques-"tion, Which of the two? is by no means settled,—though the "Assembly of Divines, and majorities of both Houses, would "fain think it so.   The general English mind, which, loving "good order in all things, loves regularity even at a high "price, could be content with this Presbyterian scheme, which "we call the Dutch-dragon one; but a deeper portion of the "English mind inclines decisively to growing in the forest-"tree way, — and indeed will shoot out into very singular ex-"crescences, Quakerisms and what not, in the coming years. "Nay already we have Anabaptists, Brownists, Sectaries and "Schismatics springing up very rife: already there is a Paul "Best, brought before the House of Commons for Soci-"nianism; nay we hear of another distracted individual who "seemed to maintain, in confidential argument, that 'God was "mere Reason.'*   There is like to be need of garden-shears, "at this rate! The devout House of Commons, viewing these

* Whitlocke.

"things with a horror inconceivable in our loose days, knows
"not well what to do. London City cries, 'Apply the shears!'
"— the Army answers, 'Apply them *gently;* cut off nothing
"that is sound!' The question of garden-shears, and how far
"you are to apply them, is really difficult; — the settling of *it*
"will lead to very unexpected results. London City knows
"with pain, that there are 'many persons in the Army
"who have never yet taken the Covenant;' the Army be-
"gins to consider it unlikely that certain of them will ever
"take it!" —

These things premised, we have only to remark farther,
that the House of Commons, meanwhile, struck with devout
horror, has, with the world generally, spent Wednesday the
10th of March 1646-7, as a Day of Fasting and Humiliation for
Blasphemies and Heresies.* Cromwell's Letter, somewhat
remarkable for the grieved mind it indicates, was written next
day. Fairfax with the Army is at Saffron Walden in Essex;
there is an Order this day** that he is to quarter where he sees
best. There are many Officers about Town; soliciting pay-
ments, attending private businesses: their tendency to Schism,
to Anabaptistry and Heresy, or at least to undue tolerance for
all that, is well known. This Fast-day, it would seem, is regarded as a kind of covert rebuke to them. Fastday was Wednesday; this is Thursday evening;

LETTER XLIII.

*For his Excellency Sir Thomas Fairfax, General of the
Parliament's Army, 'at Saffron Walden:' These.*

SIR,   'London, 11th March 1646.'

Your Letters about your head-quarters, directed to
the Houses,*** came seasonably, and were to very good
purpose. There want not, in all places, men who have
so much malice against the Army as besots them: the

---

* Whitlocke, p. 243.   ** Commons Journals, v. 110.
*** Commons Journals, v. 110, 11th March 1646 (Letter is dated Saffron
Walden, 9th March).

late Petition, which suggested a dangerous design upon the Parliament in 'your' coming to those quarters* doth sufficiently evidence the same: but they got nothing by it, for the Houses did assoil the Army from all suspicion, and have left you to quarter where you please.**

Never were the spirits of men more embittered than now. Surely the Devil hath but a short time. Sir, it's good the heart be fixed against all this. The naked simplicity of Christ, with that wisdom He is pleased to give, and patience, will overcome all this. That God would keep your heart as He has done hitherto, is the prayer of

Your Excellency's most humble servant,
OLIVER CROMWELL.

'P.S.'*** I desire my most humble service may be presented to my Lady. — Adjutant Allen desires Colonel Baxter, sometime Governor of Reading, may be remembered. I humbly desire Colonel Overton may not be out of your remembrance. He is a deserving man, and presents his humble services to you. — — Upon the Fast-day, divers soldiers were raised (as I heard), both horse and foot, near 200 in Covent Garden, To prevent us soldiers from cutting the Presbyterians' throats! These are fine tricks to mock God with.§

This flagrant insult to "us soldiers," in Covent Garden and doubtless elsewhere, as if the zealous Presbyterian Preacher

---

* Saffron Walden, in the Eastern Association: "*Not* to quarter in the Eastern Association," had the Lords, through Manchester their Speaker, lately written (Commons Journals, *infra*); but without effect.

** Commons Journals, v. 110, 11th March 1646.

*** Written across on the margin, according to custom.

§ Sloane MSS. 1519, fol. 62.

were not safe from violence in bewailing Schism, — is very significant. The Lieutenant-General himself might have seen as well as "heard" it, — for he lived hard by, in Drury Lane I think; but was of course at his own Church, bewailing Schism too, though not in so strait-laced a manner. —

Oliver's Sister Anna, Mrs. Sewster, of Wistow, Huntingdonshire, had died in these months, 1st November 1646.* Among her little girls is one, Robina, for whom there is a distinguished Scotch Husband in store; far off as yet, an "Ensign in the French Army" as yet, William Lockhart by name; of whom we may hear more.

This Letter lies contiguous to Letter XXXIV. in the Sloane Volume: Letter XXXIV. is sealed conspicuously with red wax; this Letter, as is fit, with black.   The Cromwell crest, "lion with ring on his fore-gamb," — the same big seal, is on both.

LETTER XLIV.

Commons Journals, 17th March 1646: "*Ordered*, That the "Committee of the Army do write unto the General, and ac- "quaint him that this House takes notice of his care in order- "ing that none of the Forces under his Command should "quarter nearer than Five-and-twenty Miles of this City: "That notwithstanding his care and directions therein, the "House is informed that some of his Forces are quartered "much nearer than that; and To desire him to take course "that his former Orders, touching the quartering of his Forces "no nearer than Twenty-five Miles, may be observed."

To his Excellency Sir Thomas Fairfax, General of the Parliament's Army: These.

SIR,   'London,' 19th March 1646.

This enclosed Order I received; but, I suppose, Letters from the Committee of the Army to the effect of this are come to your hands before this time.   I

* See *antea*, p. 20; and Noble, 1. 89.

think it were very good that the distance of Twenty-
five Miles be very strictly observed; and they are to
blame that have exceeded the distance, contrary to your
former appointment. This Letter I seceived this evening from Sir William Massam,* a Member of the House
of Commons; which I thought fit to send you; his
House being much within that distance of Twenty-five
Miles of London. I have sent the Officers down, as
many as I could well light of.

Not having more at present, I rest,
Your Excellency's most humble servant,
OLIVER CROMWELL. §

The troubles of the Parliament and Army are just beginning. The order for quartering beyond twenty-five miles
from London, and many other "orders" were sadly violated
in the course of this season. "Sir W. Massam's House,"
"Otes in Essex," is a place known to us since the beginning of
these *Letters*.

The Officers ought really to go down to their quarters in
the Eastern Counties; Oliver has sent them off, as many of
them as he "could well light of."

The Presbyterian System is now fast getting into action:
on the 20th of May 1647, the Synod of London, with due Pro-
locutor or Moderator, met in St. Paul's.** In Lancashire too
the System is fairly on foot; but I think in other English
Counties it was somewhat lazy to move, and never came
rightly into action, owing to impediments. — Poor old Laud is
condemned of treason, and beheaded, years ago; the Scots,
after Marston Fight, pressing heavy on him; Prynne too
being very ungrateful. That "performance" of the Service
to the Hyperborean populations in so exquisite a way, has
cost the Artist dear! He died very gently; his last scene much
the best, for himself and for us. The two Hothams also, and
other traitors, have died.

* Masham.   § Sloane MSS. 1519, fol. 74.
** Rushworth, vi. 489; Whitlocke (p. 249) dates wrong.

ARMY MANIFESTO.

Our next entirely authentic Letter is at six months distance: a hiatus not unfrequent in this Series; but here most
especially to be regretted; such a crisis in the affairs of Oliver
and of England transacting itself in the interim. The Quarrel
between City and Army, which we here see begun; the split
of the Parliament into two clearly hostile Parties of Presbyterians and Independents, represented by City and Army; the
deadly wrestle of these two Parties, with victory to the latter,
and the former flung on its back, and its "Eleven Members"
sent beyond Seas: all this transacts itself in the interim, without autograph note or indisputably authentic utterance of
Oliver's to elucidate it for us.   We part with him labouring to
get the Officers sent down to Saffron Walden; sorrowful on
the Spring Fast-day in Covent Garden: we find him again at
Putney in Autumn; the insulted Party now dominant, and he
the most important man in it.   One Paper which I find among
the many published on that occasion, and judge pretty confidently, by internal evidence, to be of his writing, is here introduced; and there is no other that I know of.

How this Quarrel between City and Army, no agreement
with the King being for the present possible, went on waxing;
developing itself more and more visibly into a Quarrel between
Presbyterianism and Independency; attracting to the respec-
tive sides of it the two great Parties in Parliament and in England generally: all this the reader must endeavour to imagine
for himself, — very dimly, as matters yet stand.   In books, in
Narratives old or new, he will find little satisfaction in regard
to it.   The old Narratives, written all by baffled enemies of
Cromwell,* are full of mere blind rage, distraction and darkness; the new Narratives, believing only in "Machiavelism,"
&c., disfigure the matter still more. Common History, old
and new, represents Cromwell as having underhand, — in a

---

* Holles's Memoirs; Waller's Vindication of his Character; Clement
Walker's History of Independency, &c. &c.

most skilful and indeed prophetic manner, — fomented or ori-
ginated all this commotion of the elements; steered his way
through it by "hypocrisy," by "master-strokes of duplicity,"
and such like.   As is the habit hitherto of History.

   "The fact is," says a Manuscript already cited from, "poor
"History, contemporaneous and subsequent, has treated this
"matter in a very sad way.   Mistakes, misdates; exaggera-
"tions, unveracities, distractions; all manner of misseeings
"and misnotings in regard to it, abound.   How many grave
"historical statements still circulate in the world, accredited
"by Bishop Burnet and the like, which on examination you
"will find melt away into after-dinner rumours, — gathered
"from ancient red-nosed Presbyterian gentlemen, Harbottle
"Grimston and Company, sitting over claret under a Blessed
"Restoration, and talking to the loosely recipient Bishop in a
"very loose way!   Statements generally with some grain of
"harmless truth, misinterpreted by those red-nosed honour-
"able persons; frothed up into huge bulk by the loquacious
"Bishop above mentioned, and so set floating on Time's
"Stream.   Not very lovely to us, they, nor the red-noses they
"proceeded from!   I do not cite them here; I have examined
"most of them; found not one of them fairly believable; —
"wondered to see how already in one generation, earnest Puri-
"tanism being hung on the gallows or thrown out in St. Mar-
"garet's Churchyard, the whole History of it had grown *myth-
"ical*, and men were ready to swallow all manner of nonsense
"concerning it.   Ask for dates, ask for proofs: Who saw it,
"heard it; when was it, where?   A misdate, of itself, will do
"much.   So accurate a man as Mr. Godwin, generally very
"accurate in such matters, makes 'a master-stroke of dupli-
"'city' merely by mistake of dating:* the thing when Oliver
"did say it, was a credible truth, and no master-stroke or
"stroke of any kind!

   "'Master-strokes of duplicity;'   'false protestations;'
"'fomenting of the Army discontents:' alas, alas!   It was
"not Cromwell that raised these discontents; not he, but the

<hr>

* Godwin, ii. 300, — citing Walker, p. 31 (should be p. 33).

"elemental Powers! Neither was it, I think, 'by master-
"strokes of duplicity' that Cromwell steered himself victo-
"riously across such a devouring chaos; no, but by *conti-
"nuances* of noble manful *simplicity*, I rather think, — by
"meaning one thing before God, and meaning the same be-
"fore men, not as a weak but as a strong man does. By con-
"scientious resolution; by sagacity, and silent wariness and
"promptitude; by religious valour and veracity, — which,
"however it may fare with *foxes*, are really, after all, the
"grand source of clearness for a *man* in this world!" — — We
here close our Manuscript.

Modern readers ought to believe that there was a real im-
pulse of heavenly Faith at work in this Controversy; that on
both sides, more especially on the Army's side, here lay the
central element of all; modifying all other elements and pas-
sions; — that this Controversy was, in several respects, very
different from the common wrestling of Greek with Greek for
what are called "Political objects!" — Modern readers,
mindful of the French Revolution, will perhaps compare these
Presbyterians and Independents to the Gironde and the
Mountain. And there is an analogy; yet with differences.
With a great difference in the situations; with the difference,
too, between Englishmen and Frenchmen, which is always
considerable; and then with the difference between believers
in Jesus Christ and believers in Jean Jacques, which is still
more considerable!

A few dates, and chief summits of events, are all that can
be indicated here, to make our "Manifesto" legible.

From the beginnings of this year 1647 and earlier, there
had often been question as to what should be done with the
Army. The expense of such an Army, between twenty and
thirty thousand men, was great; the need of it, Royalism
being now subdued, seemed small; besides it was known that
there were many in it who "had never taken the Covenant,"
and were never likely to take it. This latter point, at a time

when Heresy seemed rising like a hydra, * and the Spiritualism of England was developing itself in really strange ways,
became very important too, — became gradually most of all
important, and the soul of the whole Controversy.

Early in March, after much debating, it had been got
settled that there should be Twelve-thousand men employed
in Ireland,** which was now in sad need of soldiers. The
rest were, in some good way, to be disbanded. The "way,"
however, and whether it might really be a good way, gave
rise to considerations. — Without entering into a sea of
troubles, we may state here in general that the things this
Army demanded were strictly their just right: Arrears of pay,
"three-and-forty weeks" of hard-earned pay; indemnity for
acts done in War; and clear discharge according to contract,
not service in Ireland except under known Commanders and
conditions, — "our old Commanders," for example. It is also
apparent that the Presbyterian party in Parliament, the
leaders of whom were, several of them, Colonels of the *Old*
Model, did not love this victorious Army; that indeed they
disliked and grew to hate it, useful as it had been to them.
Denzil Holles, Sir William Waller, Harley, Stapleton,
these men, all strong for Presbyterianism, were old unsuccessful Colonels or Generals under Essex; and for very ob-
vious reasons looked askance on this Army, and wished to be,
so soon as possible, rid of it. The first rumour of a demur or
desire on the part of the Army, rumour of some Petition to
Fairfax by his Officers as to the "way" of their disbanding,
was by these Old-Military Parliament men very angrily re-
pressed; nay, in a moment of fervour, they proceeded to decree that whoever had, or might have, a hand in promoting
such Petition in the Army was an "Enemy to the State, and
a Disturber of the Public Peace," — and sent forth the same in
a "Declaration of the 30th of March," which became very
celebrated afterwards. This unlucky "Declaration," Waller

* See Edwards's *Gangraena* (London, 1646) for many furious details
of it.
** 6th March, Commons Journals, v. 107.

says, was due to Holles, who smuggled it one evening through
a thin House.   "Enemies to the State, Disturbers of the
Peace:" it was a severe and too proud rebuke; felt to be un-
just, and looked upon as "a blot of ignomiy;" not to be forgotten, nor easily forgiven, by the parties it was addressed
to.   So stood matters at the end of March.

At the end of April they stand somewhat thus.   Two Parliament Deputations, Sir William Waller at the head of them,
have been at Saffron Walden, producing no: agreement: *
five dignitaries of the Army, "Lieutenant-General Hammond, Colonel Hammond, Lieutenant-Colonel Pride," and
two others, have been summoned to the bar;** some sub-
alterns given into custody; Ireton himself "ordered to be
examined;" — and no "satisfaction to the just desires of the
Army;" on the contrary, the "blot of ignominy" fixed deeper
on it than before.   We can conceive a universal sorrow and
anger, and all manner of dim schemes and consultations going
on at Saffron Walden and the other Army-quarters, in those
days.   Here is a scene from Whitlocke, worth looking at,
which takes place in the Honourable House itself; date 30th
April 1647: ***

"Debate upon the Petition and Vindication of the Army.
"Major-General Skippon, in the House, produced a Letter
"presented to him the day before by some Troopers, in behalf
of Eight Regiments of the Army of Horse.   Wherein they
"expressed some reasons, Why they could not engage in the
"service of Ireland under the present Conduct," under the
proposed Commandership, by Skippon and Massey; "and
"complained, Of the many scandals and false suggestions
"which were of late raised against the Army and their pro-
"ceedings; That they were taken as enemies; That they saw
"designs upon them, and upon many of the Godly Party in
"the Kingdom; That they could not engage for Ireland till

* Waller, pp. 42-85.
** Commons Journals, v. 129 (29th March 1647).
*** Whitlocke, p. 249; Commons Journals *in die;* and a fuller account
in Rushworth, vi. 474.   The "Letter," immediately referred to, is in Cary's
Memorials (Selections from the Tanner MSS.; London, 1842), i. 201.

"they were satisfied in their expectations, and their just
"desires granted. — Three Troopers, Edward Sexby, Wil-
"liam Allen, Thomas Sheppard, who brought this Letter,
"were examined in the House, touching the drawing and sub-
"scribing of it; and, Whether their Officers were engaged in
"it or not? They affirmed, That it was drawn up at a Rendez-
"vous of several of those Eight Regiments; and afterwards
"at several meetings by Agents or Agitators, for each Regi-
"ment; and that few of their Officers knew or took notice
"of it.

"Those Troopers being demanded, Whether they had not
"been Cavaliers? — it was attested by Skippon, that they
"had constantly served the Parliament, and some of them
"from the beginning of the War. Being asked concerning
"the meaning of some expressions in the Petition," especially
concerning "certain men aiming at a *Sovereignty*," — "they
"answered, That the Letter being a joint act of those Regi-
"ments, they could not give a punctual answer, being only
"Agents; but if they might have the queries in writing, they
"would send or carry them to those Regiments, and return
"their own and their answers. — They were ordered to attend
"the House upon summons."

Three sturdy fellows, fit for management of business; let
the reader note them. They are "Agents" to the Army: a
class of functionaries called likewise "Adjutators" and mis-
spelt "Agitators;" elected by the common men of the Army,
to keep the ranks in unison with the Officers in the present
crisis of their affairs. This is their first distinct appearance
in the eye of History; in which, during these months, they
play a great part. Evidently the settlement with the Army
will be a harder task than was supposed.

During these same months some languid negotiation with
the King is going on; Scots Commissioners come up to help
in treating with him; but as he will not hear of Covenant or
Presbytery, there can no result follow. It was an ugly aggravation of the blot of ignominy which the Army smarts under,
— the report raised against it, That some of the Leaders had

said, "If the King would come to *them*, they would put the crown on his head again." — Cromwell, from his place in Parliament, earnestly watches these occurrences; waits what the great "birth of Providence" in them may be; — "carries himself with much wariness;" is more and more looked up to by the Independent Party, for his interest with the Soldiers. One day, noticing the "high carriages" of Holles and Company, he whispers Edmund Ludlow who sat by him, "These men will never leave till the Army pull them out by the ears!" * Holles and Company, who at present rule in Parliament, pass a New Militia Ordinance for London; put the Armed Force of London into hands more strictly Presbyterian. ** There have been two London Petitions against the Army, and two London Petitions covertly in favour of it; the Managers of the latter, we observe, have been put in prison.

May 8th. A new and more promising Deputation, Cromwell at the head of it. "Cromwell, Ireton, Fleetwood, Skippon," proceed again to Saffron Walden; investigate the claims and grievances of the Army;*** engage, as they had authority to do, that real justice shall be done them; and in a fortnight return with what seems an agreement and settlement; for which Lieutenant-General Cromwell receives the thanks of the House.† The House votes what *it* conceives to be justice, "eight weeks of pay" in ready money, bonds for the rest, — and so forth. Congratulations hereupon; a Committee of Lords and Commons are ordered to go down to Saffron Walden, to *see* the Army disbanded.

May 28th. On arriving at Saffron Walden, they find that their notions of what is justice, and the Army's notions, differ widely. 'Eight weeks of pay,' say the Army; 'we want nearer eight times eight!' Disturbances in several of the quarters: — at Oxford the men seize the disbanding-money as *part* of

* Ludlow, i. 189; see Whitlocke, p. 252.
** 4th May 1647, Commons Journals, v. 160: — "Thirty-one Persons," their names given.
*** Letters from them, in Appendix, No. 9.
† May 21st, Commons Journals, v. 181.

payment, and will not disband till they get the whole.   A
meeting of Adjutators, by authority of Fairfax, convenes at
Bury St. Edmund's, — a regular Parliament of soldiers, "each
common man paying fourpence to meet the expense:" it is
agreed that the Army's quarters shall be "contracted",
brought closer together; that on Friday next, 4th of June,
there shall be a Rendezvous, or General Assembly of all the
Soldiers, there to decide on what they will do. *

    June 4th and 5th.   The Newmarket Rendezvous, "on
Kentford Heath," a little east of Newmarket, is held; a kind
of Covenant is entered into, and other important things are
done: — but elsewhere in the interim a thing still more important had been done.   On Wednesday June 2d, Cornet
Joyce, — once a London tailor they say, evidently a very
handy active man, — he, and Five-hundred common troopers,
a volunteer Party, not expressly commanded by anybody, but
doing what they know the whole Army wishes to be done, sally
out of Oxford, where things are still somewhat disturbed;
proceed to Holmby House; and, after two days of talking,
bring "the King's Person" off with them.   To the horror and
despair of the Parliament Commissioners in attendance there;
but clearly to the satisfaction of his Majesty, — who hopes, in
this new shuffle-and-deal, some good card will turn up for him;
hopes, with some ground, "the Presbyterians and Independents *may* now be got to extirpate one another."   His Majesty
rides willingly; the Parliament Commissioners accompany,
wringing their hands: — to Hinchinbrook, that same Friday
night; where Colonel Montague receives them with all hospitality, entertains them for two days.   Colonel Whalley with
a strong party, deputed by Fairfax, had met his Majesty;
offered to deliver him from Joyce, back to Holmby and the
Parliament; but his Majesty positively declined. — Captain
Titus, *quasi* Tighthose, very well known afterwards, arrives at
St. Stephen's with the news; has 50*l.* voted him "to buy a
horse," for his great service; and fills all men with terror and
amazement.   The Honourable Houses agree to "sit on the

      * Rushworth, pp. 496-510.

Lord's day;" have Stephen Marshall to pray for them; never were in such a plight before.   The Controversy, at this point, has risen from Economical into Political: Army Parliament in the Eastern Counties, against Civil Parliament in Westminster; and, "How the Nation shall be settled" between them; whether its growth shall be in the forest-tree fashion, or in the clipt Dutch-dragon fashion? —

Monday, June 7th.   All Officers in the House are ordered forthwith to go down to their regiments.   Cromwell, without order, not without danger of detention, say some, — has already gone: this same day, "General Fairfax, Lieutenant-General Cromwell and the chief men of the Army," have an interview with the King, "at Childerley House between Huntingdon and Cambridge:" his Majesty will not go back to Holmby; much prefers "the air" of these parts, the air of New-market for instance; and will continue with the Army.*   Parliament Commissioners, with new Votes of Parliament, are coming down; the Army must have a new Rendezvous, to meet them. New Rendezvous at Royston, more properly on Triploe Heath near Cambridge, is appointed for Thursday; and in the interim a "Day of Fasting and Humiliation" is held by all the soldiers, — a real Day of Prayer (very inconceivable in these days), For God's enlightenment as to what should now be done.

Here is Whitlocke's account of the celebrated Rendezvous itself, — somewhat abridged from Rushworth, and dim enough; wherein, however, by good eyes a strange old Historical Scene may be discerned.   The new Votes of Parliament do not appear still to meet "the just desires" of the Army; mean while, let all things be done decently and in order.

"The General had ordered a Rendezvous at Royston;" properly on Triploe Heath, as we said; on Thursday 10th June 1647: the Force assembled was about Twenty-one thousand men, the remarkablest Army that ever wore steel in this world. "The General and the Commissioners rode to each Regiment. "They first acquainted the General's Regiment with the Votes

<hr>

* Rushworth, vi. 549.

"of the Parliament; and Skippon," one of the Commissioners, "spake to them to persuade a compliance. An Officer of the "Regiment made answer, That the Regiment did desire that "their answer might be returned *after* perusal of the Votes by "some select Officers and Agitators, whom the Regiment had "chosen; and said, This was the motion of the Regiment.

"He desired the General and Commissioners to give him "leave to ask the whole Regiment if this *was* their answer. "Leave being given, they cried, 'All.' Then he put the "question, If any man were of a contrary opinion he should "say, No;—and not one man gave his 'No.'—The Agitators "in behalf of the soldiers pressed to have the question put at "once, Whether the Regiment did acquiesce and were satisfied "with the Votes?" The Agitators knew well what the answer would have been!—"But in regard the other way was more "orderly, and they might after perusal proceed more deliber- "ately, that question was laid aside.

"The like was done in the other Regiments; and all were "very unanimous; and always after the Commissioners had "done reading the Votes, and speaking to each Regiment, and "had received their answer, all of them cried out, 'Justice, "'Justice!'"—not a very musical sound to the Commissioners.

"A Petition was delivered in the field to the General, in "the name of 'many well-affected people in Essex;' desiring, "That the Army might *not* be disbanded; in regard the Com- "monwealth had many enemies, who watched for such an "occasion to destroy the good people."*

Such, and still dimmer, is the jotting of dull authentic Bul- strode, — drowning in official oil, and somnolent natural pedantry and fat, one of the remarkablest scenes our History ever had: An Armed Parliament, extra-official, yet not without a kind of sacredness, and an Oliver Cromwell at the head of it; demanding with one voice, as deep as ever spake in England, "Justice, Justice!" under the vault of Heaven.

That same afternoon, the Army moved on to St. Albans, nearer to London; and from the Rendezvous itself, a joint

* Whitlocke, p. 255.

Letter was despatched to the Lord Mayor and Aldermen, which the reader is now at last to see.   I judge it, pretty confidently, by evidence of style alone, to be of Cromwell's own writing.   It differs totally in this respect from any other of those multitudinous Army-Papers; which were understood, says Whitlocke, to be drawn up mostly by Ireton, "who had a subtle working brain;" or by Lambert, who also had got some tincture of Law and other learning, and did not want for brain. They are very able Papers, though now very dull ones.   This is in a far different style; in Oliver's worst style; his style when he writes in haste, — and not in haste of the pen merely, for that seems always to have been a most rapid business with him; but in haste before the matter had matured itself for him, and the real kernels of it got parted from the husks.   A style of composition like the structure of a block of oak-root, — as tortuous, unwedgeable, and as strong!   Read attentively, this Letter can be understood, can be believed: the tone of it, the "voice" of it, reminds us of what Sir Philip Warwick heard; the voice of a man risen justly into a kind of *chaunt*, — very dangerous for the City of London at present.

To the Right Honourable the Lord Mayor, Aldermen, and
Common Council of the City of London: These.

Royston, 10th June 1647.

RIGHT HONOURABLE AND WORTHY FRIENDS,

Having, by our Letters and other Addresses presented by our General to the Honourable House of Commons, endeavoured to give satisfaction of the clearness of our just Demands; and 'having' also, in Papers published by us, remonstrated the grounds of our proceedings in prosecution thereof; — all of which being published in print, we are confident 'they' have come to your hands, and received at least a charitable construction from you.

The sum of all these our Desires as Soldiers is no other than this: Satisfaction to our undoubted Claims as Soldiers; and reparation upon those who have, to the utmost, improved all opportunities and advantages, by false suggestions, misrepresentations and otherwise, for the destruction of this Army with a perpetual blot of ignominy upon it. Which 'injury' we should not value, if it singly concerned our own particular 'persons;' being ready to deny ourselves in this, as we have done in other cases, for the Kingdom's good: but under this pretence, we find, no less is involved than the overthrow of the privileges both of Parliament and People; — and that rather than they* shall fail in their designs, or we receive what in the eyes of all good men is 'our' just right, the Kingdom is endeavoured to be engaged in a new War. 'In a new War,' and this singly by those who, when the truth of these things shall be made to appear, will be found to be the authors of those 'said' evils that are feared; — and who have no other way to protect *themselves* from question and punishment but by putting the Kingdom into blood, under the pretence of their honour and of their love to the Parliament. As if that were dearer to them than to us; or as if they had given greater proof of their faithfulness to it than we.

But we perceive that, under these veils and pretences, they seek to interest in their design the City of London: — as if that City ought to make good their miscarriages, and should prefer a few self-seeking men before the welfare of the Public. And indeed we have found these men so active to accomplish their designs, and to have such apt instruments for their turn in that City, that we have cause to suspect they may engage

* The Presbyterian leaders in Parliament, Holles, Stapleton, Harley, Waller, &c.

many therein upon mistakes, — which are easily swallowed, in times of such prejudice against them * that have given (we may speak it without vanity) the most public testimony of their good affections to the Public, and to that City in particular.

'As' for the thing we insist upon as Englishmen, — and surely our being Soldiers hath not stript us of that interest, although our malicious enemies would have it so, — we desire a Settlement of the Peace of the Kingdom and of the Liberties of the Subject, according to the Votes and Declarations of Parliament, which, *before* we took arms, were, by the Parliament, used as arguments and inducements to invite us and divers of our dear friends out; some of whom have lost their lives in this War. Which being now, by God's blessing, finished, — we think we have as much right to demand, and desire to see, a happy Settlement, as we have to our money and 'to' the other common interest of Soldiers which we have insisted upon. We find also the ingenuous and honest People, in almost all parts of the Kingdom where we come, full of the sense of ruin and misery if the Army should be disbanded *before* the Peace of the Kingdom, and those other things before mentioned, have a full and perfect Settlement.

We have said before, and profess it now, We desire no alteration of the Civil Government. As little do we desire to interrupt, or in the least to intermeddle with, the settling of the Presbyterial Government. Nor did we seek to open a way for licentious liberty, under pretence of obtaining ease for tender consciences. We profess, as ever in these things, When once the State

* Oblique for "us."

has made a Settlement, we have nothing to say but to submit or suffer. Only we could wish that every good citizen, and every man who walks peaceably in a blameless conversation, and is beneficial to the Commonwealth, might have liberty and encouragement; this being according to the true policy of all States, and even to justice itself.

These in brief are our Desires, and the things for which we stand; beyond which we shall not go. And for the obtaining of these things, we are drawing near your City;* — professing sincerely from our hearts, 'That' we intend not evil towards you; declaring, with all confidence and assurance, That if you appear not against us in these our just desires, to assist that wicked Party which would embroil us and the Kingdom, neither we nor our Soldiers shall give you the least offence. We come not to do any act to prejudice the being of Parliaments, or to the hurt of this 'Parliament' in order to the present Settlement of the Kingdom. We seek the good of all. And we shall wait here, or remove to a farther distance to abide there, if once we be assured that a speedy Settlement of things is in hand, — until it be accomplished. Which done, we shall be most ready, either all of us, or so many of the Army as the Parliament shall think fit, — to disband, or to go for Ireland.

And although you may suppose that a rich City may seem an enticing bait to poor hungry Soldiers to venture far to gain the wealth thereof, — yet, if not provoked by you, we do profess, Rather than any such

* That is the remarkable point!

evil should fall out, the soldiers shall make their way through our blood to effect it.   And we can say this for most of them, for your better assurance, That they so little value their pay, in comparison of higher concernments to a Public Good, that rather than they will be unrighted in the matter of their honesty and integrity (which hath suffered by the Men they aim at and desire justice upon), or want the settlement of the Kingdom's Peace, and their 'own' and their fellow-subjects' Liberties, — they will lose all.   Which may be a strong assurance to you that it's not your wealth they seek, but the things tending in common to your and their welfare.   That they may attain 'these,' you shall do like Fellow-Subjects and Brethren if you solicit the Parliament for them, on their behalf.

If after all this, you, or a considerable part of you, be seduced to take up arms in opposition to, or hindrance of, these our just undertakings, — we hope we have, by this brotherly premonition, to the sincerity of which we call God to witness, freed ourselves from all that ruin which may befall that great and populous City; having thereby washed our hands thereof.

We rest,

Your affectionate Friends to serve you,

THOMAS FAIRFAX.	HENRY IRETON.
OLIVER CROMWELL.	ROBERT LILBURN.
ROBERT HAMMOND.	JOHN DESBOROW.
THOMAS HAMMOND.	THOMAS RAINSBOROW.
HARDRESS WALLER.	JOHN LAMBERT.
NATHANIEL RICH.	THOMAS HARRISON. §
THOMAS PRIDE.	

§ Rushworth, vi. 554.

This Letter was read next day in the Commons House, *
— not without emotion. Most respectful answer went from
the Guildhall, "in three coaches with the due number of out-
riders."

On June 16th, the Army, still at St. Albans, accuses of treason Eleven Members of the Commons House by name, as chief
authors of all these troubles; whom the Honourable House is
respectfully required to put upon their Trial, and prevent from
voting in the interim. These are the famed Eleven Members;
Holles, Waller, Stapleton, Massey are known to us; the whole
List, for benefit of historical readers, we subjoin in a Note. **
They demurred; withdrew; again returned; in fine, had to
"ask leave to retire for six months," on account of their
health, we suppose. They retired swiftly in the end; to
France; to deep concealment, — to the Tower otherwise.

The history of these six weeks, till they did retire and the
Army had its way, we must request the reader to imagine for
himself. Long able Papers, drawn by men of subtle brain
and strong sincere heart: the Army retiring always to a safe
distance when their Demands are agreed to; straightway advancing if otherwise, — which rapidly produces an agreement.
A most remarkable Negotiation; conducted with a method, a
gravity and decorous regularity beyond example in such cases.
The "shops" of London were more than once "shut;" tremor
occupying all hearts: — but no harm was done. The Parliament regularly paid the Army; the Army lay coiled round
London and the Parliament, now advancing, now receding;
saying in the most respectful emblematic way, "Settlement
with us and the Godly People, or—!" — The King, still with

* Commons Journals, v. 208.
** Denzil Holles (Member for Dorchester), Sir Philip Stapleton (Bo-
rough-bridge), Sir William Waller (Andover), Sir William Lewis (Peters-
field), Sir John Clotworthy (Malden), Recorder Glynn (Westminster), Mr.
Anthony Nichols (Bodmin); these Seven are old Members, from the beginning of the Parliament; — the other Four are "recruiters," elected since
1645: Major-General Massey (Wootton Basset), Colonel Walter Long
(Ludgershall), Colonel Edward Harley (Herefordshire), Sir John Maynard
(Lostwithiel).

the Army, and treated like a King, endeavoured to play his game, "in meetings at Woburn" and elsewhere; but the two Parties could not be brought to extirpate one another for his benefit.

Towards the end of July, matters seem as good as settled: the Holles "Declaration," that "blot of ignominy," being now expunged from the Journals; * the Eleven being out; and now at last, the New Militia Ordinance for London (Presbyterian Ordinance brought in by Holles on the 4th of May) being revoked, and matters in that quarter set on their old footing again.   The two Parties in Parliament seem pretty equal in numbers; the Presbyterian Party, shorn of its Eleven, is cowed down to the due pitch; and there is now prospect of fair treatment for all the Godly Interest, and such a Settlement with his Majesty as may be the best for that.   Towards the end of July, however, London City, torn by factions, but Presbyterian by the great majority, rallies again in a very extraordinary way.   Take these glimpses from contemporaneous Whitlocke; and rouse them from their fat somnolency a little.

July 26*th*.   Many young men and Apprentices of London came to the House in a most rude and tumultuous manner; and presented some particular Desires.   Desires, That the Eleven may come back; that the Presbyterian Militia Ordinance be *not* revoked, — that the Revocation of it be revoked.   Desire, in short, That there be no peace made with Sectaries, but that the London Militia may have a fair chance to fight them! — Drowsy Whitlocke continues; almost as if he were in Paris in the eighteenth century: "The Apprentices, and many other "rude boys and mean fellows among them, came into the "House of Commons; and kept the Door open and their hats "on; and called out as they stood, 'Vote, Vote!' and in this "arrogant posture, stood till the votes passed in that way, To "repeal the Ordinance for change of the Militia, to" &c.   "In "the evening about seven o'clock, some of the Common Coun-

* Asterisks still in the place of it, Commons Journals, 29th March 1647.

"cil came down to the House:" but finding the Parliament and Speaker already *had* been forced, they, astute Common-Council men, ordered their Apprentices to go home again, the work they had set them upon being now finished. * This disastrous scene fell out on Monday 26th July 1647: the Houses, on the morrow morning, without farther sitting, adjourned till Friday next.

On Friday next, — — behold, the Two Speakers, "with the Mace," and many Members of both Houses, have withdrawn; and the Army, lately at Bedford, is on quick march towards London! Alarming pause. "About noon," however, the Remainders of the Two Houses, reinforced by the Eleven who reappear for the last time, proceed to elect new Speakers, "get the City Mace;" order, above all, that there be a vigorous enlistment of forces under General Massey, General Poyntz, and others. "St. James's Fields" were most busy all Saturday, all Monday; shops all shut; drums beating in all quarters; a most vigorous enlistment going on. Presbyterianism will die with harness on its back. Alas, news come that the Army is at Colnebrook, advancing towards Hounslow; news come that they have rendezvoused at Hounslow, and received the Speakers and fugitive Lords and Commons with shouts. Tuesday, 3d August 1647, was such a day as London and the Guildhall never saw before or since! Southwark declares that it will not fight; sends to Fairfax for Peace and a "sweet composure;" comes to the Guildhall in great crowds petitioning for Peace; — at which sight, General Poyntz, pressing through for orders about his enlistments, loses his last drop of human patience; "draws his sword" on the whining multitudes, "slashes several persons, whereof some died." The game is nearly up. Look into the old Guildhall on that old Tuesday night; the palpitation, tremulous expectation; wooden Gog and Magog themselves almost sweating cold with terror:

"General Massey sent out scouts to Brentford: but Ten "men of the Army beat Thirty of his; and took a flag from a

* Whitlocke, p. 263.

"Party of the City.   The City Militia and Common Council
"sat late; and a great number of people attended at Guild-
"hall.   When a scout came in and brought news, That the
"Army made a halt; or other good intelligence, — they cry,
"'One and all!'   But if the scouts reported that the Army
"was advancing nearer them, then they would cry as loud,
"'Treat, treat, treat!'   So they spent most part of the night.
"At last they resolved to send the General an humble Letter,
"beseeching him that there might be a way of composure." *

On Friday morning, was "a meeting at the Earl of Holland's House in Kensington" (the Holland House that yet
stands), and prostrate submission by the Civic Authorities and
Parliamentary Remainders; after which the Army marched
"three deep by Hyde Park" into the heart of the City, "with
boughs of laurel in their hats;" — and it was all ended.   Fair
treatment for all the Honest Party: and the Spiritualism of
England shall not be forced to grow in the Presbyterian
fashion, however it may grow.   Here is another entry from
somnolent Bulstrode.   The Army soon changes its head-quarters to Putney; ** one of its outer posts is Hampton Court,
where his Majesty, obstinate still, but somewhat despondent
now of getting the two Parties to extirpate one another, is
lodged.

Saturday, "*September* 18*th*.   After a Sermon in Putney
"Church, the General, many great Officers, Field-Officers, in-
"ferior Officers and Adjutators, met in the Church; debated
"the Proposals of the Army" towards a Settlement of this
bleeding Nation; "altered some things in them; — and were
"very full of the Sermon, which had been preached by Mr.
"Peters." ***

* Whitlocke, p. 265.   ** 28th August, Rushworth, vii. 791.
*** Whitlocke, p. 272.

LETTERS XLV. — LVIII.

THESE Fourteen Letters, touching slightly on public affairs with one or two glimpses into private, must carry us, without commentary, in a very dim way, across to the next stage in Oliver's History and England's: the Flight of the King from Hampton Court and the Army, soon followed by the actual breaking-out of the Second Civil War.

LETTER XLV.

WILLIAMS, Archbishop of York, "hasty hot Welsh Williams," — whom we once saw, seven years ago, as Bishop of Lincoln, getting jostled in Palaceyard, protesting thereupon, and straightway getting lodged in the Tower, * — is to concern us again for one moment. A man once very radiant to men, as obscure as he has now grown: a most high-riding far-shining Solar Luminary in that epoch; obscure to no man in England for thirty years last past! A man of restless mercurial vivacity, of endless superficial dexterity and ingenuity, of next to no real wisdom; — very fit to have swift promotions and sudden eclipses in a Stuart Court; not worthy of much memory otherwise. Of his rapid rises, culminations, miraculous faculties and destinies, to us all useless, indifferent and extinct, let there be silence here, — reference to Bishop Hacket and the Futile Ingenuities. **

Archbishop Williams, — for he got delivered from the Tower at that time, and recovered favour, and was "enthroned Archbishop at York" while his Majesty was raising his War-standard there, — found, after a while, that there was little good to be got of his Archbishophood; that his best weapon would be, not the crosier, but the linstock and cannon-rammer, at present: he went to his Welsh estate of Aberconway, and "procuring a Commission from his Majesty," fortified Conway Castle "at his own expense," and invited the neigh-

* Antea, p. 118.
** Hacket's Life of Archbishop Williams (a considerable Folio, Lond. 1712); Philips's Life of Williams (an Octavo Abridgment of that); &c.

bouring gentry to lodge their plate and valuables there, as in a place of security. Good;—for the space of a year or two. But now, some time ago in the death-throes of the late War, while North Wales was bestirring itself as in last-agony for his Majesty's behoof,—there came a certain Colonel Sir John Owen, of whom we shall hear again: he, this Owen, came before Castle Conway with large tumultuary force, demanded the same in his Majesty's name, to be governed by him Sir John Owen, as essential for his Majesty's occasions at that time. High-sniffing, indignant refusal on the part of Williams: impetuous capture and forcible possession on the part of Owen. Hot Williams, blown all to flame hereby, applied to Col. Mitton, the Parliamentary Colonel of those parts; said to him, "Expel me this intolerable Owen; Owen out, I will hold this Castle for the Parliament and you,—his Majesty seems nearly done with fighting now." A thing difficult to explain completely to the Royalist mind: Bishop Hacket has his own ados with it; and in stupid Saunderson * and others, it is one loud howl, "Son of the morning, how art thou fallen!" —

Explained or not, "my Lord of York" does hold Conway Castle on those terms, at this date; is taking a certain charge of North Wales in his busy way; and has even been corresponding with Cromwell, on the subject. They had known one another in old years: Buckden, the Bishop of Lincoln's House, is in the neighbourhood of Huntingdon; where Cromwell, it is understood, used occasionally to wait upon him; pleading for oppressed Lecturers and the like,—the Bishop having, from political or other biases, a kind of lenity for Puritans.

Cromwell is very brief with him here; courteous as to an old neighbour rather in eclipse; but evidently wishing to have no unnecessary business with the Governor of Conway. We see he could on occasion jocosely claim "kindred" with him, as himself a "Williams:" and that perhaps is the chief interest of this small Document, which the reader will now abundantly understand.

* History of Charles I.

For the Right Honourable my Lord of York: These.

MY LORD,   'Putney,' 1st September 1647.

Your Advices will be seriously considered by us. We shall endeavour, to our uttermost, so to settle the affairs of North Wales as, to the best of our understandings, does most conduce to the public good thereof and of the whole. And that without private respect, or to the satisfaction of any humour, — which has been too much practised on the occasion of our Troubles.

The Drover you mention will be secured, as far as we are able, in his affairs, if he come to ask it. Your Kinsman shall be very welcome: I shall study to serve him for Kindred's sake; among whom let not be forgotten,

My Lord,
Your cousin and servant,
OLIVER CROMWELL. §

My Lord of York still lived some year or two in Conway Castle; saw his enemy Sir John Owen in trouble enough; but died before long, — chiefly of broken heart for the fate of his Majesty, thinks Bishop Hacket.   A long farewell to him.

LETTER XLVI.

THE Marquis of Ormond, a man of distinguished integrity, patience, activity and talent, had done his utmost for the King in Ireland, so long as there remained any shadow of hope there.   His last service, as we saw, was to venture secretly on a Peace with the Irish Catholics, — Papists, men of the Massacre of 1641, men of many other massacres, falsities, mad blusterings and confusions, — whom all parties considered as sanguinary Rebels, and regarded with abhorrence.   Which

§ Gentleman's Magazine (1789), lix. 877.

Peace, we saw farther, Abbas O'Teague and others threatening to produce excommunication on it, the "Council of Kilkenny" broke away from, — not in the handsomest manner. Ormond, in this Spring of 1647, finding himself reduced to "seven barrels of gunpowder" and other extremities, without prospect of help or trustworthy bargain on the Irish side, — agreed to surrender Dublin, and what else he had left, rather to the Parliament than to the Rebels; his Majesty, from England, secretly and publicly advising that course. The Treaty was completed: "Colonel Michael Jones," lately Governor of Chester, arrived with some Parliamentary Regiments, with certain Parliamentary Commissioners, on the 7th of June:* the surrender was duly effected, and Ormond withdrew to England.

A great English force had been anticipated; but the late quarrel with the Army had rendered that impossible. Jones, with such inadequate force as he had, made head against the Rebels; gained "a great victory" over them on the 8th of August, at a place called Dungan Hill, not far from Trim:** "the most signal victory we had yet gained;" for which there was thankfulness enough. — Four days before that Sermon by Hugh Peters, followed by the military conclave in Putney Church, Cromwell had addressed this small Letter of Congratulation to Jones, whom, by the tone of it, he does not seem to have as yet personally known:

For the Honourable Colonel Jones, Governor of Dublin, and . Commander-in-Chief of all the Forces in Leinster: These.

SIR,   'Putney,' 14th September 1647.

The mutual interest and agreement we have in the same Cause*** give me occasion, as to congratulate, so 'likewise' abundantly to rejoice in God's gracious Dispensation unto you and by you. We have, both in England and Ireland, found the immediate presence

* Carte's Ormond, 1. 603.
** Rushworth, vii. 779; Carte, ii. 5.
*** Word uncertain to the Copyist; sense not doubtful.

and assistance of God, in guiding and succeeding our endeavours hitherto; and therefore ought, as I doubt not both you and we desire, to ascribe the glories of all to Him, and to improve all we receive from Him unto Him alone.

Though, it may be, for the present a cloud may lie over our actions to those who are not acquainted with the grounds of them; yet we doubt not but God will clear our integrity, and innocency from any other ends we aim at but His glory and the Public Good. And as you are an instrument herein, so we shall, as becometh us, upon all occasions, give you your due honour. For my own particular, — wherein I may have your commands to serve you, you shall find none more ready than he that sincerely desires to approve himself,

Your affectionate friend and humble servant,
OLIVER CROMWELL. §

Michael Jones is the name of this Colonel; there are several Colonel Joneses; difficult to distinguish. One of them, Colonel *John* Jones, Member for Merionethshire, and known too in Ireland, became afterwards the Brother-in-law of Cromwell; and ended tragically as a Regicide in 1661. Colonel Michael gained other signal successes in Ireland; welcomed Oliver into it in 1649; and died there soon after of a fever.

One of the remarkablest circumstances of this new Irish Campaign is, that Colonel Monk, George Monk, is again in it. He was taken prisoner, fresh from Ireland, at Nantwich, three years ago. After lying three years in the Tower, seeing his Majesty's affairs now desperate, he has consented to take the Covenant, embark with the Parliament; and is now doing good service in Ulster.

§ Ms. Volume of Letters in Trinity-College Library, Dublin (marked: F. 3. 18), fol. 62. Autograph; docketed by Jones himself, of whom the Volume contains other memorials.

19*

LETTER XLVII.

For his Excellency Sir Thomas Fairfax: These.

SIR,   Putney, 13th October 1647.

The case concerning Captain Middleton hears * ill; inasmuch as it is delayed, upon pretences, from coming to a trial. It is not, I humbly conceive, fit that it should stay any longer. The Soldiers complain thereof, and their witnesses have been examined. Captain Middleton, and some others for him, have made stay thereof hitherto.

I beseech your Excellency to give order it may be tried on Friday, or Saturday at farthest, if you please; and that so much may be signified to the Advocate.

Sir, I pray excuse my not-attendance upon you. I feared 'to' miss the House a day, where it's very necessary for me to be. I hope your Excellency will be at the Head-quarter tomorrow, where, if God be pleased, I shall wait upon you.

I rest,
Your Excellency's most humble servant,
OLIVER CROMWELL. §

Captain Middleton and his case have vanished completely out of the records; whether it was tried on Saturday, and how decided, will never now be known. Doubtless Fairfax "signified" somewhat to the Advocate about it, but let us not ask what. "The Advocate" is called "John Mills, Esquire, Judge-Advocate;"** whose military Law-labours have mostly become silent now. The former Advocate was Dr. Dorislaus; of whom also a word. Dr. Dorislaus, by birth Dutch; appointed Judge-Advocate at the beginning of Essex's campaignings;

* sounds.   § Sloane MSS. 1519, fol. 80.   ** Spriggo, p. 326.

known afterwards on the King's Trial; and finally, for that latter service, assassinated at the Hague, one evening, by certain highflying Royalist cut-throats, Scotch several of them. The Portraits represent him as a man of heavy, deep-wrinkled, elephantine countenance, pressed down with the labours of life and law; the good ugly man here found his quietus.

The business in the House, "where it's necessary for me to be" without miss of a sitting, is really important, or at least critical, in these October days: Settlement of Army arrears, duties and arrangements; Tonnage and Poundage; business of the London Violence upon the Parliament (pardoned for the most part); business of Lieutenant-Colonel John Lilburn, now growing very noisy; — above all things, final Settlement with the King, if that by any method could be possible. The Army-Parliament too still sits; "Council of War" with its Adjutators meeting frequently at Putney.* In the House, and out of the House, Lieutenant-General Cromwell is busy enough.

This very day, "Wednesday 13th October 1647," we find him deep in debate "On the *farther* establishment of the Presbyterial Government" (for the law is still loose, the Platform except in London never fairly on foot); and Teller on no fewer than three divisions. *First*, Shall the Presbyterian Government be limited to three years? Cromwell answers *Yea*, in a House of 73; is beaten by a majority of 3. *Second*, Shall there be a limit of time to it? Cromwell again answers *Yea;* beats, this time, by a majority of 14, in a House now of 74 (some individual having dropt in). *Third*, Shall the limit be seven years? Cromwell answers *Yea;* and in a House still of 74 is beaten by 8. It is finally got settled that the limit of time shall be "to the end of the next Session of Parliament "after the end of this Present Session,"—a very vague Period, "this present session" having itself already proved rather long! Note, too, this is not yet a Law; it is only a Proposal to be made to the King, if his Majesty will concur, which seems doubtful. Debating enough! — Saturday last there was

* Rushworth, vii. 849, &c.

a call of the House, and great quantities of absent Members;
"*ægrotantes*," fallen ill, a good many of them, — sickness
being somewhat prevalent in those days of waiting upon Providence. *

LETTER XLVIII.

*'For his Excellency Sir Thomas Fairfax, General of the
Parliament's Army: These.'*

Sir,   Putney, 22d October 1647.

Hearing the Garrison of Hull is most distracted in
the present government, and that the most faithful and
honest Officers have no disposition to serve there any
longer under the present Governor; and that it is their
earnest desires, with all the trusty and faithful inhabitants of the Town, to have Colonel Overton sent
to them to be your Excellency's Deputy over them, —
I do humbly offer to your Excellency, Whether it
might not be convenient that Colonel Overton be
speedily sent down; that so that Garrison may be
settled in safe hands. And that your Excellency would
be pleased to send for Colonel Overton, and confer
with him about it. That either the Regiment 'now' in
the Town may be so regulated as your Excellency may
be confident that the Garrison may be secured by them;
or otherwise it may be drawn out, and his own Regiment in the Army be sent down thither with him. —
But I conceive, if the Regiment in Hull can be made
serviceable to your Excellency, and included in the
Establishment, it will be better to continue it there,
than to bury a Regiment of your Army in the Garrison.

Sir, the expedient will be very necessary, in regard of the present distractions here. This I thought

---

* Commons Journals, v. 329; ib. 332.

fit to offer to your Excellency's consideration. I shall humbly take leave to subscribe myself,
        Your Excellency's
            Humble 'and faithful servant,
                OLIVER CROMWELL.'§

After Hotham's defection and execution, the Lord Ferdinando Fairfax, who had valiantly defended the place, was appointed Governor of Hull; which office had subsequently been conferred on the Generalissimo Sir Thomas, his Son; and was continued to him, on the readjustment of all Garrisons in the Spring of this same year.* Sir Thomas therefore was express Governor of Hull at this time. Who the Substitute or Deputy under him was, I do not know. Some Presbyterian man; unfit for the stringent times that had arrived, when no algebraic formula, but only direct vision of the relations of things would suffice a man.

Colonel Overton was actually appointed Governor of Hull: there is a long Letter from the Hull people about Colonel Overton's laying free billet upon them, a Complaint to Fairfax on the subject, next year.** He continued long in that capacity; zealously loyal to Cromwell and his cause,*** till the Protectorship came on. His troubles afterwards, and confused destinies, may again concern us a little.

This Letter is written only three weeks before the King took his flight from Hampton Court. One spark illuminating (very faintly) that huge dark world, big with such results, in the Army's quarters about Putney, and elsewhere!

§ Sloane MSS. 1519, fol. 82: — Signature, and all after "humble," is torn off. The Letter is not an autograph; it has been dictated, apparently in great haste.
* 13th March 1646-7 (Commons Journals, v. 111).
** 4th March 1647-8 (Rushworth, vii. 1020).
*** Sir James Turner's Memoirs. Milton State-Papers (London, 1743), pp. 10, 24, 161, — where the Editor calls him Colonel *Richard* Overton: his name was Robert: "Richard Overton" is a "Leveller," unconnected with him; "*Colonel* Richard Overton" is a non-existence.

LETTER XLIX.

. The immeasurable Negotiations with the King, "Proposals of the Army," "Proposals of the Adjutators of the Army," still occupying tons of printed paper, the subject of intense debatings and considerations in Westminster, in Putney Church, and in every house and hut of England, for many months past, — suddenly contract themselves for us, like a universe of gaseous vapour, into one small point: the issue of them all is failure. The Army Council, the Army Adjutators, and serious England at large, were in earnest about one thing; the King was not in earnest, except about another thing: there could be no bargain with the King.

Cromwell and the Chief Officers have for some time past ceased frequenting his Majesty or Hampton Court; such visits being looked upon askance by a party in the Army: they have left the matter to Parliament; only Colonel Whalley, with due guard, and Parliament Commissioners, keep watch "for the security of his Majesty." In the Army, his Majesty's real purpose becoming now apparent, there has arisen a very terrible "Levelling Party;" a class of men demanding punishment not only of Delinquents, and Deceptive Persons who have involved this Nation in blood, but of the "Chief Delinquent:" minor Delinquents getting punished, how should the Chief Delinquent go free? A class of men dreadfully in earnest; — to whom a King's Cloak is no impenetrable screen; who within the King's Cloak discern that there is a Man, accountable to a God! The Chief Officers, except when officially called, keep distant: hints have fallen that his Majesty is not out of danger. — In the Commons Journals this is what we read:

"*Friday* 12*th November* 1647. A Letter from Lieutenant-"General Cromwell, of 11th November, twelve at night, was "read; signifying the escape of the King; who went away "about 9 o'clock yesterday" evening.*

<hr>

* Commons Journals, v. 356.

Cromwell, we suppose, lodging in head-quarters about Putney, had been roused on Thursday night by express That the King was gone; had hastened off to Hampton Court; and there about "twelve at night" despatched a Letter to Speaker Lenthall.   The Letter, which I have some confused recollection of having, somewhere in the Pamphletary Chaos, seen in full, refuses to disclose itself at present except as a Fragment:

'For the Honourable William Lenthall, Speaker of the House of Commons: These.'

     'SIR,'   'Hampton Court, Twelve at night, 11th November 1647.'

*   *   *   *   Majesty   *   *   withdrawn himself *   *   at nine o'clock.

The manner is variously reported; and we will say little of it at present, but That his Majesty was expected at supper, when the Commissioners and Colonel Whalley missed him; upon which they entered the Room: — they found his Majesty had left his cloak behind him in the Gallery in the Private Way. He passed, by the backstairs and vault, towards the Waterside.

He left some Letters upon the table in his withdrawing room, of his own handwriting; whereof one was to the Commissioners of Parliament attending him, to be communicated to both Houses, 'and is here enclosed.'

*   *   *

'OLIVER CROMWELL.' §

We do not give his Majesty's Letter "here enclosed:" it is that well-known one where he speaks, in very royal style, still every inch a King, Of the restraints and slights upon him, — men's obedience to their King seeming much abated of late.

§ Rushworth, vii. 871.

So soon as *they* return to a just temper, "I shall instantly break through this cloud of retirement, and show myself ready to be *Pater Patriæ*," — as I have hitherto done.

LETTER L.

THE Ports are all ordered to be shut; embargo laid on ships.   Read in the Commons Journals again: "*Saturday* 13*th* "*Nov.* Colonel Whalley was called in; and made a particular "Relation of all the circumstances concerning the King's "going away from Hampton Court. He did likewise deliver-in "a Letter directed unto him from Lieutenant-General Crom- "well, concerning some rumours and reports of some design of "danger to the person and life of the King: The which was "read.   *Ordered*, That Colonel Whalley do put in writing the "said Relation, and set his hand to it; and That he do leave "a Copy of the said Letter from Lieutenant-General Crom- "well." *

Colonel Whalley's Relation exists; and a much fuller Relation and pair of Relations concerning this Flight and what preceded and followed it, as viewed from the Royalist side, by two parties to the business, exist:** none of which shall concern us here.   Lieutenant-General Cromwell's Letter to Whalley also exists; a short insignificant Note: here it is, fished from the Dust-Abysses, which refuse to disclose the other.   Whalley is "Cousin Whalley," as we may remember; Aunt Frances's and the Squire of Kerton's Son, — a Nottinghamshire man.***

'*For my beloved Cousin, Colonel Whalley, at Hampton Court: These.*'

DEAR COS. WHALLEY,   '*Putney, November 1647.*'
There are rumours abroad of some intended at-

* Commons Journals, v. 358.
** Berkley's Memoirs (printed, London, 1699); Ashburnham's Narrative (printed, London, 1830), — which require to be sifted, and contrasted with each other and with third parties, by whoever is still curious on this matter; each of those Narratives being properly a Pleading, intended to clear the Writer of all blame, in the first place.
*** See antea, p. 26, note.

tempt on his Majesty's person.　Therefore I pray have a care of your guards.　If any such thing should be done, it would be accounted a most horrid act. * * *
　　　　Yours,
　　　　　　OLIVER CROMWELL. §

See, among the Old Pamphlets, Letters to the like effect from Royalist Parties: also a Letter of thanks from the King to Whalley; — ending with a desire, "to send the black-gray bitch to the Duke of Richmond," on the part of his Majesty: Letters from &c., Letters to &c., in great quantities. *　For us here this brief notice of one Letter shall suffice:

"*Monday 15th November* 1647.　Letter from Colonel Robert "Hammond, Governor of the Isle of Wight, *Cowes*, 13° *No-* "*vembris*, signifying that the King is come into the Isle of "Wight."** The King, after a night and a day of riding, saw not well whither else to go.　He delivered himself to Robert Hammond;*** came into the Isle of Wight. Robert Hammond is ordered to keep him strictly within Carisbrook Castle and the adjoining grounds, in a vigilant though altogether respectful manner.

This same "Monday" when Hammond's Letter arrives in London is the day of the mutinous Rendezvous "in Corkbush Field, between Hertford and Ware;" † where Cromwell and the General Officers had to front the Levelling Principle, in a most dangerous manner, and trample it out or be trampled out by it on the spot.　Eleven Mutineers are ordered from the ranks; tried by Court-Martial on the Field; three of them condemned to be shot; — throw dice for their life, and one *is* shot, there and then.　The name of him is Arnald; long memorable among the Levellers.　A very dangerous Review service! — Head-quarters now change to Windsor.

---

§ King's Pamphlets, small 4to, no. 337, §. 15, p. 7.
＊ Parl. Hist. xvi. 324-30.　　　** Commons Journals, *in die* (v. 359).
*** Berkley's and Ashburnham's Narratives.
† Rushworth, vii. 875.

LETTER LI.

A SMALL charitable act, for one who proved not very worthy. Friends of a young gentleman in trouble, Mr. Dudley Wyatt by name, have drawn this word from the Lieutenant-General, who on many grounds is powerful at Cambridge.

'To Dr. Thomas Hill, Master of Trinity College, Cambridge.'

SIR,   Windsor, 23d December 1647.

As I am informed, this Gentleman the Bearer hereof, in the year 1641, had leave of his College to travel into Ireland for seven years; and in his absence, he (being then actually employed against the Rebels in that Kingdom) was ejected out of his College by a mistake, the College Registry being not looked into, to inquire the cause of his non-residence.

I cannot therefore but think it a just and reasonable request, That he be readmitted to all the benefits, rights and privileges which he enjoyed before that ejection; and therefore desire you would please to effect it accordingly. Wherein you shall do a favour will be owned by

> Your affectionate friend and servant,
> OLIVER CROMWELL. §

Dudley Wyatt, Scholar of Trinity College, 25th April 1628; B.A., 1631; Fellow, 4th October 1633; vanishes from the Bursar's Books in 1645: no notice of him farther, or of

§ "Muniment Room, Trinity College, Cambridge (Collection entitled "*Papers relating to Trin. Coll.*, vol. 3): a Transcript, Original not now "forthcoming, — docketed in the hand of one Porter, Clerk to Thomas "Parne, about 1724, *L. P. Cromwell's Letter concerning Sir Dudley Wyatt.*" (Communicated by the Rev. J. Edleston, Fellow of Trinity, March 1849.) — Harl. mss., no. 7058. f. 153 b.: printed, from the latter, in Hartshorne's *Book Rarities in the University of Cambridge* (London, 1829), p. 277. The Harl. mss. copy adds: "N. B. Upon this Letter, Sir Dudley Wyatt was re-admitted," — but did not stay, as would appear.

any effect produced by the Lieutenant-General's Letter on
his behalf, is found in the College records. Indeed, directly
after this Letter, the young gentleman, of a roving turn
at any rate, appears to have discovered that there was new
war and mischief in the wind, and better hope at Court than
at College for a youth of spirit. He went to France to the
Queen (as we may gather); went and came; developed himself into a busy spy and intriguer; — attained to Knighthood,
to be the "*Sir* Dudley Wyatt" of Clarendon's History;*
whom, and not us, he shall henceforth concern.

LETTER LII.

Robert Hammond, Governor of the Isle of Wight, who
has for the present become so important to England, is a
young man "of good parts and principles:" a Colonel of Foot;
served formerly as Captain under Massey in Gloucester; —
where, in October 1644, he had the misfortune to kill a
brother Officer, one Major Gray, in sudden duel, "for giving
him the lie;" he was tried, but acquitted, the provocation
being great. He has since risen to be Colonel, and become
well known. Originally of Chertsey, Surrey; his Grandfather, and perhaps his Father, a Physician there. His Uncle,
Thomas Hammond, is now Lieutenant-General of the Ordnance; a man whom, with this Robert, we saw busy in the
Army Troubles last year. The Lieutenant-General, Thomas
Hammond, persists in his democratic course; patron at this
time of the Adjutator speculations; sits afterwards as a
King's-Judge.

In strong contrast with whom is another Uncle, Dr. Henry
Hammond, a pattern-flower of loyalty, one of his Majesty's
favourite Chaplains. It was Uncle Thomas that first got this
young Robert a Commission in the Army: but Uncle Henry
had, in late months, introduced him to his Majesty at Hampton
Court, as an ingenuous youth, repentant, or at least sym-

* ii. 959, iii. 22, &c.

pathetic and not without loyalty. Which circumstance, it is supposed, had turned the King's thoughts in that bewildered Flight of his, towards Colonel Robert and the Isle of Wight.

Colonel Robert, it would seem, had rather disliked the high course things were sometimes threatening to take, in the Putney Council of War; and had been glad to get out of it for a quiet Governorship at a distance. But it now turns out, he has got into still deeper difficulties thereby. His "temptation" when the King announced himself as in the neighbourhood, had been great: Shall he obey the King in this crisis; conduct the King whitherward his Majesty wishes? Or be true to his trust and the Parliament? He "grew suddenly pale;"— he decided as we saw.

The Isle of Wight, holding so important a deposit, is put under the Derby-House Committee, old "Committee of Both Kingdoms," some additions being made thereto, and some exclusions. Oliver is of it, and Philip Lord Wharton, among others. Lord Wharton, a conspicuous Puritan and intimate of Oliver's; of whom we shall afterwards have occasion to say somewhat.

This Committee of Derby House was, of course, in continual communication with Robert Hammond. Certain of their Letters to him had, after various fortune, come into the hands of the Honourable Mr. Yorke (Lord Hardwicke); and were lying in his house, when it and they were, in 1752, accidentally burnt. A Dr. Joseph Litherland had, by good luck, taken copies; Thomas Birch, lest fire should again intervene, printed the Collection, — a very thin Octavo, London, 1764. He has given some introductory account of Robert Hammond; copying, as we do mainly here, from Wood's *Athenæ*; * and has committed — as who does not? — several errors. His Annotations are sedulous but ineffectual. What of the Letters are from Oliver we extract with thanks.

A former Letter, of which Oliver was "the penner," is now lost. "Our brethren" in the following letter are the Scots, now all *excluded* from Derby-House Committee of Both

* III. 500.

Kingdoms. The "Recorder" is Glyn, one of the vanished Eleven, Stapleton being another; for both of whom it has been necessary to appoint substitutes in the said Committee.

For Colonel Robert Hammond, Governor of the Isle of Wight: These, for the Service of the Kingdom. Haste: Post Haste.

DEAR ROBIN,   'London,' 3d January 1647.
          (My Lord Wharton's, near Ten at night.)

Now, blessed be God, I can write and thou receive freely. I never in my life saw more deep sense, and less will to show it unchristianly, than in that which thou didst write to us when we were at Windsor, and thou in the midst of thy temptation, — which indeed, by what we understand of it, was a great one, and occasioned * the greater by the Letter the General sent thee; of which thou wast not mistaken when thou didst challenge me to be the penner.

How good has God been to dispose all to mercy! And although it was trouble for the present, yet glory has come out of it; for which we praise the Lord with thee and for thee. And truly thy carriage has been such as occasions much honour to the name of God and to religion. Go on in the strength of the Lord; and the Lord be still with thee.

But, dear Robin, this business hath been, I trust, a mighty providence to this poor Kingdom and to us all. The House of Commons is very sensible of the King's dealings, and of our brethren's, ** in this late transaction. You should do well, if you have anything that may discover juggling, to search it out, and let us know it. It may be of admirable use at this time; because we shall, I hope, instantly go upon business in relation to them, *** tending to prevent danger.

* rendered.   ** the Scots.   *** the Scots.

The House of Commons has this day voted as follows: 1st, They will make no more Addresses to the King; 2nd, None shall apply to him without leave of the Two Houses, upon pain of being guilty of high treason; 3rd, They will receive nothing from the King, nor shall any other bring anything to them from him, nor receive anything from the King; *lastly*, the Members of both Houses who were of the Committee of Both Kingdoms are established in all that power in themselves, for England and Ireland, which they 'formerly' had to act with England and Scotland; and Sir John Evelyn of Wilts is added in the room of Mr. Recorder, and Nathaniel Fiennes in the room of Sir Philip Stapleton, and my Lord of Kent in the room of the Earl of Essex. *   I think it good you take notice of this, the sooner the better.

Let us know how it is with you in point of strength, and what you need from us.   Some of us think the King well with you, and that it concerns us to keep that Island in great security, because of the French, &c.: and if so, ** where can the King be better? If you have more force 'sent,' you will be sure of full provision for them.

The Lord bless thee.   Pray for
Thy dear friend and servant,
OLIVER CROMWELL. *

In these same days noisy Lilburn has accused Cromwell of meaning or having meant to make his own bargain with the King, and be Earl of Essex and a great man.   Noisy John

* Essex is dead; Stapleton, one of the Eleven who went to France, is dead; Recorder Glyn, another of them, is in the Tower. For the "Votes," see Commons Journals, v. 415 (3d January 1647-8).

** If we do secure and fortify it.

§ Birch's Hammond Letters, p. 23. Given also in Harris, p. 497.

thinks all great men, especially all Lords, ought to be brought
low.   The Commons have him at their bar in this month.*

LETTER LIII.

HERE, by will of the Destinies preserving certain bits of
paper and destroying others, there introduces itself a little
piece of Domesticity; a small family-transaction, curiously
enough peering through by its own peculiar rent, amid these
great world-transactions: Marriage-treaty for Richard Cromwell, the Lieutenant-General's eldest Son.

What Richard has been doing hitherto no Biographer
knows.   In spite of Noble, I incline to think he too had been
in the Army; in October last there are two Sons mentioned expressly as being officers there: "One of his Sons, Captain of
"the General's Life-guard; his other Son, Captain of a troop
"in Colonel Harrison's Regiment," — so greedy is he of the
Public Money to his own family!** Richard is now heir-ap-
parent; our poor Boy Oliver therefore, "Cornet Oliver," we
know not in the least where, must have died.   "It went to my
heart like a dagger; indeed it did!" The phrase of the
Pamphlet itself, we observe, is "his other Son," not "*one* of
his other Sons," as if there were now but two left.   If Richard
was ever in the Army, which these probabilities may dimly
intimate, the Lifeguard, a place for persons of consequence,
was the likeliest for him.   The Captain in Harrison's Regiment
will in that case be Henry. — The Cromwell family, as we
laboriously guess and gather, has about this time removed to
London.   Richard, if ever in the Lifeguard, has now quitted
it: an idle fellow, who could never relish soldiering in such an
Army; he now wishes to retire to Arcadian felicity and wedded
life in the country.

The "Mr. M." of this Letter is Richard Mayor, Esquire, of
Hursley, Hants,*** the young lady's father. Hursley, not far
from Winchester, is still a manorhouse, but no representative

* 19th January, Commons Journals, v. 437.
** 5th October 1647 (Royalist Newspaper, citing a Pamphlet of Lilburn's), Cromwelliana, p. 36.   *** Noble, ii. 436-42.

of Richard Mayor's has now place there or elsewhere. The treaty, after difficulties, did take effect.   Mayor, written also Major and Maijor, a pious prudent man, becomes better known to Oliver, to the world and to us in the sequel. Richard Norton, Member for Hants since 1645, is his neighbour; an old fellow-soldier under Manchester, fellow-colonel in the Eastern Association, seemingly very familiar with Oliver, he is applied to on this delicate occasion.

For my noble Friend Colonel Richard Norton: These.

DEAR NORTON,   'London,' 25th February 1647.

I have sent my Son over to thee, being willing to answer Providence; and although I had an offer of a very great proposition, from a father, of his daughter, yet truly I rather incline to this in my thoughts; because, though the other be very far greater, yet I see difficulties, and not that assurance of godliness, — though indeed of fairness. I confess that which is told me concerning the estate of Mr. M. is more than I can look for, as things now stand.

If God please to bring it about, the consideration of piety in the Parents, and such hopes of the Gentlewoman in that respect, make the business to me a great mercy; concerning which I desire to wait upon God.

I am confident of thy love; and desire things may be carried with privacy. The Lord do His will: that's best; — to which submitting, I rest,

Your humble servant,

OLIVER CROMWELL. §

What other Father it was that made "the offer of a very great proposition" to Oliver, in the shape of his Daughter as

§ Harris, p. 501.   Copy of this, and of the next Two Letters to Norton, by Birch, in Ayscough MSS. 4162. f. 56, &c.

Wife to Oliver's Son, must remain totally uncertain for the present; perhaps some glimpse of it may turn up by and by. There were "difficulties" which Oliver did not entirely see through; there was not that assurance of "godliness" in the house, though there was of "fairness" and natural integrity; in short, Oliver will prefer Mayor, at least will try him, — and wishes it carried with privacy.

The Commons, now dealing with Delinquents, do not forget to reward good Servants, to "conciliate the Grandees" as splenetic Walker calls it. For above two years past ever since the War ended, there has been talk and debate about settling 2,500*l.* a-year on Lieutenant-General Cromwell; but difficulties have arisen. First they tried Basing-House Lands, the Marquis of Winchester's, whom Cromwell had demolished; but the Marquis's affairs were in disorder; it was gradually found the Marquis had for most part only a Life-rent there: — only "Abbotston and Itchin" in that quarter could be realised. Order thereupon to settle "Lands of Papists and Delinquents" to the requisite amount, wheresoever convenient. To settle especially what Lands the Marquis of Worcester had in that "County of Southampton;" which was done, — though still with insufficient result.* Then came the Army Quarrels, and an end of such business. But now in the Commons Journals, 7th March, the very day of Oliver's next Letter, this is what we read:** "An Ordinance for passing unto Oliver Cromwell, "Esquire, Lieutenant-General, certain Lands and Manors in "the Counties of Gloucester, Monmouth and Glamorgan, late "the Earl of Worcester's, was this day read the third time and, "upon the question, passed; and ordered to be sent unto the

* Commons Journals (iv. 416), 23d January 1645-6: the Marquis of *Worcester's* Hampshire Lands. Ib. 426, a week afterwards: "Abberston and Itchell," meaning Abbotston and Itchin, Marquis of *Winchester's* there. See also Letter of Oliver St. John to Cromwell, in *Thurloe*, i. 75. — Commons Journals (v. 36) about a year afterwards, 7th January 1646-7: "remainder of the 2,500*l.*" from Marquis of Winchester's Lands in general; which in a fortnight more is found to be impossible: whereupon "Lands of Deliquents and Papists," as in the Text. None of these Hampshire Lands, except Abbotston and Itchin, are named. Noble says, "Fawley Park" in the same County; which is possible enough.
** v. 482.

"Lords for their concurrence."   Oliver himself, as we shall
find, has been dangerously sick. This is what Clement Walker,
the splenetic Presbyterian, "an elderly gentleman of low sta-
"ture, in a gray suit, with a little stick in his hand," reports
upon the matter of the Grant:

"The 7th of March, an Ordinance to settle 2,500*l.* a-year of
"Land, out of the Marquis of Worcester's Estate," — old Marquis of Worcester at Ragland, father of my Lord Glamorgan,
who in his turn became Marquis of Worcester and wrote the
Century of Inventions, — 2,500*l.* a-year out of this old Marquis's Estate "upon Lieutenant-General Cromwell! I have
"heard some gentlemen that know the Manor of Chepstow and
"the other Lands affirm" that in reality they are worth 5,000*l.*
or even 6,000*l.* a-year; — which is far from the fact, my little
elderly friend! "You see," continues he, "though they have
not made King Charles 'a Glorious King,'" as they sometimes
undertook, "they have settled a Crown-Revenue upon Oliver,
"and have made *him* as glorious a King as ever John of Leyden
"was!"* — — A very splenetic old gentleman in gray; —
verging towards Pride's Purge, and lodgment in the Tower, I
think! He is from the West; known long since in Gloucester
Siege; Member now for Wells; but terminates in the Tower,
with ink, and abundant *gall* in it, to write the History of Independency there.

LETTER LIV.

For his Excellency Sir Thomas Fairfax, General of the Par-
liament's Armies, 'at Windsor:' These.

SIR,   'London,' 7th March 1647.
It hath pleased God to raise me out of a dangerous
sickness; and I do most willingly acknowledge that the
Lord hath, in this visitation, exercised the bowels of a
Father towards me. I received in myself the sentence
of death, that I might learn to trust in Him that

---

* History of Independency (London, 1648), Part 1. 83 and 55.

raiseth from the dead, and have no confidence in the flesh. It's a blessed thing to die daily. For what is there in this world to be accounted of! The best men according to the flesh, and things, are lighter than vanity. I find this only good, To love the Lord and His poor despised people, to do for them, and to be ready to suffer with them: — and he that is found worthy of this hath obtained great favour from the Lord; and he that is established in this shall (being confirmed to Christ and the rest of the Body *) participate in the glory of a Resurrection which will answer all. **

Sir, I must thankfully confess your favour in your last Letter. I see I am not forgotten; and truly, to be kept in your remembrance is very great satisfaction to me; for I can say in the simplicity of my heart, I put a high and true value upon your love, — which when I forget, I shall cease to be a grateful and an honest man.

I most humbly beg my service may be presented to your Lady, to whom I wish all happiness, and establishment in the truth. Sir, my prayers are for you, as becomes

Your Excellency's
Most humble servant,
OLIVER CROMWELL.

'P. S.' Sir, Mr. Rushworth will write to you about the Quartering, and the Letter lately sent; and therefore I forbear. §

* Christ's Body, his Church.
** Turns now to the margin of the sheet, lengthwise.
§ Sloane mss. 1519, fol. 79.

FREE OFFER.

From the Committee of the Lords and Commons sitting at Derby House, Sir John Evelyn reports a certain offer from Lieutenant-General Cromwell; which is read in the words following:

'*To the Honourable the Committee of Lords and Commons for the Affairs of Ireland, sitting at Derby House: The Offer of Lieutenant-General Cromwell for the Service of Ireland.*'

21° Martii 1647.

The two Houses of Parliament having lately bestowed 1,680 *l. per annum* upon me and my heirs, out of the Earl of Worcester's Estate; the necessity of affairs requiring assistance, I do hereby offer One-thousand Pounds annually to be paid out of the rents of the said lands; that is to say, 500 *l.* out of the next Michaelmas rent, and so on, by the half year, for the space of five years, if the War in Ireland shall so long continue, or that I live so long: to be employed for the service of Ireland, as the Parliament shall please to appoint; provided the said yearly rent of 1,680 *l.* become not to be suspended by war or other accident.

And whereas there is an arrear of Pay due unto me whilst I was Lieutenant-General unto the Earl of Manchester, of about 1,500 *l.*, audited and stated; as also a great arrear due for about Two Years being Governor of the Isle of Ely: I do hereby discharge the State from all or any claim to be made by me thereunto.

OLIVER CROMWELL. §

§ Commons Journals, v. 513.

"*Ordered*, That the House doth accept the Free Offer of
"Lieutenant-General Cromwell, testifying his zeal and good
"affection."   My splenetic little gentleman in gray, with the
little stick in his hand, takes no notice of this; which modifies
materially what the Chepstow Connoisseurs and their "five or
six thousand a-year" reported lately!

LETTER LV.

HERE is Norton and the Marriage again.   Here are news
out of Scotland that the Malignant Party, the Duke of Hamilton's Faction, are taking the lead there; and about getting up
an Army to attack us, and deliver the King from Sectaries:* Reverend Stephen Marshall reports the news.   Let
us read:

For my noble Friend Colonel Richard Norton: These.

DEAR DICK,   Farnham, 28th March 1648.
It had been a favour indeed to have met you here
at Farnham. But I hear you are a man of great business; therefore I say no more: — if it be a favour to
the House of Commons to enjoy you, what is it to me!
But, in good earnest, when will you and your Brother
Russel be a little honest, and attend your charge there?
Surely some expect it; especially the good fellows who
chose you! —
I have met with Mr. Mayor; we spent two or three
hours together last night. I perceive the gentleman is
very wise and honest; and indeed much to be valued.
Some things of common fame ** did a little stick: I
gladly heard his doubts, and gave such answer as was
next at hand, — I believe, to some satisfaction. Nevertheless I exceedingly liked the gentleman's plainness

* Rushworth, vii. 1040, &c.
** Against myself: — "favour for Sectaries," and so forth.

and free dealing with me. I know God has been above
all ill reports, and will in His own time vindicate me;
I have no cause to complain. I see nothing but that
this particular business between him and me may go on.
The Lord's will be done.

For news out of the North there is little; only the
Malignant Party is prevailing in the Parliament of
Scotland. They are earnest for a war; the Ministers *
oppose as yet. Mr. Marshall is returned, who says so.
And so do many of our Letters. Their great Com-
mittee of Danger have two Malignants for one right.
It's said they have voted an Army of 40,000 in Par-
liament; so say some of Yesterday's Letters. But
I account my news ill bestowed, because upon an idle
person.

I shall take speedy course in the business concerning my Tenants; for which thanks. My service to your
Lady. I am really,

Your affectionate servant,
OLIVER CROMWELL. §

Had Cromwell come out to Farnham on military business?
Kent is in a ticklish state; it broke out some weeks hence in
open insurrection,** — as did many other places, when once
the "Scotch Army of 40,000" became a certainty.

"The business concerning my Tenants" will indicate that
in Hampshire, within ken of Norton, in Fawley Park, in Itchin,
Abbotston, or elsewhere, "my Tenants" are felling wood,
cutting copses, or otherwise not behaving to perfection: but
they shall be looked to.

For the rest, Norton really ought to attend his duties in
Parliament! In earnest "an idle fellow," as Oliver in sport
calls him. Given to Presbyterian notions; was purged out by

* Clergy.   § Harris, p. 502.
** 24th or 25th May 1648 (Rushworth, vii. 1128).

Pride; came back; dwindled ultimately into Royalism. "Brother Russel" means only brother Member. He is the Frank Russel of the Letter on Marston Moor. Now Sir Francis; and sits for Cambridgeshire. A comrade of Norton's; seemingly now in his neighbourhood, possibly on a visit to him.

The attendance on the House in these months is extremely thin; the divisions range from 200 to as low as 70. Nothing going on but Delinquents' fines, and abstruse negotiations with the Isle of Wight, languid Members prefer the country till some result arrive.

LETTER LVI.

HERE is a new phasis of the Wedding-treaty; which, as seems, "doth now a little stick." Prudent Mr. Mayor insists on his advantages; nor is the Lieutenant-General behindhand. What "lands" all these of Oliver's are, in Cambridgeshire, Norfolk, Hampshire, no Biographer now knows. Portions of the Parliamentary Grants above alluded to; perhaps "Purchases by Debentures," some of them. Soldiers could seldom get their Pay in money; with their "Debentures" they had to purchase Forfeited Lands; — a somewhat uncertain investment of an uncertain currency.

The Mr. Robinson mentioned in this Letter is a pious Preacher at Southampton.* "My two little Wenches" are Mary and Frances: Mary aged now near twelve; Frances ten.**

'*For my noble Friend Colonel Richard Norton: These.*'

DEAR NORTON,   'London,' 3d April 1648.

I could not in my last give you a perfect account of what passed between me and Mr. Mayor; because we were to have a conclusion of our speed that morning after I wrote my Letter to you.*** Which we had;

* Harris, p. 504.   ** See antea, p. 60.   *** Letter LV.

and having had a full view of one another's minds, we parted with this: That both would consider with our relations, and according to satisfactions given there, acquaint one another with our minds.

I cannot tell better how to do, 'in order' to give or receive satisfaction, than by you; who, as I remember, in your last, said That, if things did stick between us, you would use your endeavour towards a close.

The things insisted upon were these, as I take it: Mr. Mayor desired 400*l. per annum* of Inheritance, lying in Cambridgeshire and Norfolk, to be presently settled,* and to be for maintenance; wherein I desired to be advised by my Wife. I offered the Land in Hampshire for present maintenance; which I dare say, with copses and ordinary fells,** will be, *communibus annis*, 500*l. per annum:* and besides 'this,' 500*l. per annum* in Tenants' hands holding but for one life; and about 300*l. per annum*, some for two lives, some for three lives. — But as to this, if the latter offer be not liked of, I shall be willing a farther conference be held in 'regard to' the first.

In point of jointure I shall give satisfaction. And as to the settlement of lands given me by the Parliament, satisfaction to be given in like manner, according as we discoursed. 'And' in what else was demanded of me, I am willing, so far as I remember any demand was, to give satisfaction. Only, I having been informed by Mr. Robinson that Mr. Mayor did, upon a former match, offer to settle the Manor wherein he lived, and to give 2,000*l.* in money, I did insist upon that; and do desire it may not be with difficulty. The money I shall need for my two little Wenches; and

<hr>

* on the Future Pair.   ** fellings.

thereby I shall free my Son from being charged with
them. Mr. Mayor parts with nothing at present but
that money; except the board 'of the young Pair,'
which I should not be unwilling to give them, to enjoy
the comfort of their society; — which it's reason he
smart for, if he will rob me altogether of them.

Truly the land to be settled, — both what the
Parliament gives me, and my own — is very little less
than 3,000*l. per annum*, all things considered, if I be
rightly informed. And a Lawyer of Lincoln's Inn,
having searched all the Marquis of Worcester's writings, which were taken at Ragland and sent for by the
Parliament, and this Gentleman appointed by the Committee to search the said writings, — assures me there
is no scruple concerning the title. And it so fell out
that this Gentleman who searched was my own Lawyer,
a very godly able man, and my dear friend; which I
reckon no small mercy. He is also possessed of the
writings for me.*

I thought fit to give you this account; desiring you
to make such use of it as God shall direct you: and I
doubt not but you will do the part of a friend between
two friends. I account myself one; and I have heard
you say Mr. Mayor was entirely so to you. What the
good pleasure of God is, I shall wait; there alone is
rest. Present my service to your Lady, to Mr. Mayor, &c.
I rest,

Your affectionate servant,
OLIVER CROMWELL.

'P.S.' I desire you to carry this business with all

---

* holds these Ragland Documents on my behalf.

privacy. I beseech you to do so, as you love me. Let me entreat you not to lose a day herein, that I may know Mr. Mayor's mind; for I think I may be at leisure for a week to attend this business, to give and take satisfaction; from which perhaps I may be shut up afterwards by employment.* I know thou art an idle fellow: but prithee neglect me not now; delay may be very inconvenient to me; I much rely upon you. Let me hear from you in two or three days. I confess the principal consideration as to me, is the absolute settlement 'by Mr. Mayor' of the Manor where he lives; which he would not do but conditionally, in case they have a son, and but 3,000l. in case they have no son. But as to this, I hope farther reason may work him to more. §

Of "my two little Wenches," Mary, we may repeat, became Lady Fauconberg; Frances was wedded to the Honourable Mr. Rich; then to Sir John Russell. Elizabeth and Bridget are already Mrs. Claypole and Mrs. Ireton. Elizabeth, the younger, was first married. They were all married very young; Elizabeth, at her wedding, was little turned of sixteen.

LETTER LVII.

For Colonel Robert Hammond.

DEAR ROBIN,   'London,' 6th April 1648.

Your business is done in the House: your 10l. by the week is made 20l.; 1000l. given you; and Order to Mr. Lisle to draw up an Ordinance for 500l. *per annum* to be settled upon you and your heirs. This was done with smoothness; your friends were not wanting to you. I know thy burden; this is an addition to it: the Lord direct and sustain thee.

* Went to Wales in May.   § Harris, p. 502.

Intelligence came to the hands of a very consider-able Person, That the King attempted to get out of his window; and that he had a cord of silk with him whereby to slip down, but his breast was so big the bar would not give him passage. This was done in one of the dark nights about a fortnight ago. A Gentleman with you led him the way, and slipped down. The Guard, that night, had some quantity of wine with them. The same party assures that there is aquafortis gone down from London, to remove that obstacle which hindered; and that the same design is to be put in execution in the next dark nights. He saith that Captain Titus, and some others about the King are not to be trusted. He is a very considerable Person of the Parliament who gave this intelligence, and desired it should be speeded to you.

The Gentleman that came out of the window was Master Firebrace; the Gentlemen doubted are Cresset, Burrowes, and Titus; the time when this attempt of escape was, the 20th of March.

Your servant,
OLIVER CROMWELL. §

Henry Firebrace is known to Birch, and his *Narrative* is known. "He became Clerk of the Kitchen to Charles II." — The old Books are full of King's Plots for escape, by aquafortis and otherwise.* His Majesty could make no agreement with the Parliament, and began now to smell War in the wind. His presence in this or the other locality might have been of clear advantage. But Hammond was too watchful. Titus, with or without his new horse, attends upon his Majesty; James Harrington also (afterwards author of *Oceana*); and "the Honourable Thomas Herbert," who has left a pleasing

§ Birch, p. 41. The Original in cipher.
* Lilly's Life; Wood, § Hammond; &c. &c.

Narrative concerning that affair.   These, though appointed by the Parliament, are all somewhat in favour with the King. Hammond's Uncle the Chaplain, as *too* favourable, was ordered out of the Island about Christmas last.

LETTER LVIII.

"THE Gentleman I mentioned to you," who is now travelling towards Dover with this hopeful Note in his pocket, must remain forever anonymous.   Of Kenrick I have incidentally heard, at Worcester Fight or elsewhere; but of "the Gentleman" nowhere ever.   A Shadow, sunk deep, with all his business, in the Land of Shadows; yet still indisputably visible there: that is the miracle of him!

To Colonel Kenrick, 'Lieutenant of Dover Castle: These.'

SIR,   'London,' 18th April 1648.

This is the Gentleman I mentioned to you.   I am persuaded you may be confident of his fidelity to you in the things you will employ him in.

I conceive he is fit for any Civil employment; having been bred towards the Law, and having besides very good parts.   He hath been a Captain-Lieutenant: and therefore I hope you will put such a value on him, in 'the' Civil way, as one that hath borne such a place shall be thought by you worthy of.   Whereby you will much oblige,

Your affectionate servant,

OLIVER CROMWELL.

'P.S.'   I expect to hear from you about your defects in the Castle, that so you may be timely supplied. §

"Defects in the Castle," and in all Castles, were good to be amended speedily, — in such predicaments as we are now again on the eve of.

§ Gentleman's Magazine (1791), lxi. 520; without comment or indication of any kind.

PRAYER-MEETING.

THE Scotch Army of Forty-thousand, "to deliver the King from Sectaries," is not a fable but a fact. Scotland is distracted by dim disastrous factions, very uncertain what it will do with the King when he *is* delivered; but in the meanwhile Hamilton has got a majority in the Scotch Parliament; and drums are beating in that country: the "Army of Forty-thousand, certainly coming," hangs over England like a flaming comet, England itself being all very combustible too. In few weeks hence, discontented Wales, the Presbyterian Colonels declaring now for Royalism, will be in a blaze; large sections of England, all England very ready to follow, will shortly after be in a blaze.

The small Governing Party in England, during those early months of 1648, are in a position which might fill the bravest mind with misgivings. Elements of destruction everywhere under and around them; their lot either to conquer, or ignominiously to die. A King not to be bargained with; kept in Carisbrook, the centre of all factious hopes, of world-wide intrigues: that is one element. A great Royalist Party, subdued with difficulty, and ready at all moments to rise again: that is another. A great Presbyterian Party, at the head of which is London City, "the Purse-bearer of the Cause," highly dissatisfied at the course things had taken, and looking desperately round for new combinations and a new struggle: reckon that for a third element. Add lastly a head-long Mutineer, Republican or Levelling Party: and consider that there is a working House of Commons which counts about Seventy, divided in pretty equal halves too,—the rest waiting what will come of it. Come of *it*, and of the Scotch Army advancing towards it!—

Cromwell, it appears, deeply sensible of all this, does in these weeks make strenuous repeated attempts towards at least a union among the friends of the Cause themselves, whose aim is one, whose peril is one. But to little effect.

Ludlow, with visible satisfaction, reports how ill the Lieuten-
ant-General sped, when he brought the Army Grandees and
Parliament Grandees "to a Dinner" at his own house, "in
King Street," and urged a cordial agreement: they would not
draw together at all.*   Parliament would not agree with
Army; hardly Parliament with itself: as little, still less, would
Parliament and City agree.   At a Common Council in the
City, prior or posterior to this Dinner, his success, as angry
little Walker intimates, was the same.   "Saturday 8th April
1648," having prepared the ground beforehand, Cromwell with
another leader or two, attended a Common Council; spake, as
we may fancy, of the common dangers, of the gulfs now yawn-
ing on every side: "but the City," chuckles my little gentleman in gray, with a very shrill kind of laughter in the throat
of him, "were now wiser than our First Parents; and rejected
"the Serpent and his subtleties."** In fact, the City wishes
well to Hamilton and his Forty-thousand Scots; the City has,
for some time, needed regiments quartered in it, to keep down
open Royalist-Presbyterian insurrection.   It was precisely
on the morrow after this visit of Cromwell's that there rose,
from small cause, huge Apprentice-riot in the City: discom-
fiture of Trainbands, seizure of arms, seizure of City Gates,
Ludgate, Newgate, loud wide cry of "God and King Charles!"
— riot not to be appeased but by "desperate charge of cavalry," after it had lasted forty hours.*** Such are the aspects
of affairs, near and far.

Before quitting Part Third, I will request the reader to
undertake a small piece of very dull reading; in which however, if he look till it become credible and intelligible to him,
a strange thing, much elucidative of the heart of this matter,
will disclose itself.   At Windsor, one of these days, unknown
now which, there is a Meeting of Army Leaders.   Adjutant-
General Allen, a most authentic earnest man, whom we shall
know better afterwards, reports what they did.   Entirely

* Ludlow, i. 238.
** History of Independency, part i. 85.
*** Rushworth, vii. 1051.

amazing to us. These are the longest heads and the strongest hearts in England; and this is the thing they are doing; this is the way they, for their part, begin despatch of business. The reader, if he is an earnest man, may look at it with very many thoughts, for which there is no word at present.

"In the year Forty-seven, you may remember," says Adjutant Allen, "we in the Army were engaged in actions of a "very high nature; leading us to very untrodden paths, — "both in our Contests with the then Parliament, as also Con- "ferences with the King. In which great works, — wanting "a spirit of faith, and also the fear of the Lord, and also being "unduly surprised with the fear of man, which always brings "a snare, we, to make haste, as we thought, out of such per- "plexities, measuring our way by a wisdom of our own, fell "into Treaties with the King and his Party: which proved "such a snare to us, and led into such labyrinths by the end "of that year, that the very things we thought to avoid, by "the means we used of our own devising, were all, with many "more of a far worse and more perplexing nature, brought "back upon us. To the overwhelming of our spirits, weaken- "ing of our hands and hearts; filling us with divisions, con- "fusions, tumults, and every evil work; and thereby endan- "gering the ruin of that blessed Cause we had, with such suc- "cess, been prospered in till that time.

"For now the King and his Party, seeing us not answer "their ends, began to provide for themselves, by a Treaty "with the then Parliament, set on foot about the beginning "of Forty-eight. The Parliament also was, at the same time, "highly displeased with us for what we had done, both as to "the King and themselves. The good people likewise, even " our most cordial friends in the Nation, beholding our turning " aside from that path of *simplicity* we had formerly walked in, "and been blessed in, and thereby much endeared to their "hearts, — began now to fear, and withdraw their affections "from us, in this *politic* path which we had stepped into, and "walked in to our hurt, the year before. And as a farther

"fruit of the wages of our backsliding hearts, we were also
"filled with a spirit of great jealousy and divisions amongst
"ourselves; having left that Wisdom of the Word, which is
"first pure and then peaceable; so that we were now fit for
"little but to tear and rend one another, and thereby prepare
"ourselves, and the work in our hands, to be ruined by our
"common enemies.   Enemies that were ready to say, as many
"others of like spirit in this day do,* of the like sad occasions
"amongst us, 'Lo this is the day we looked for.'   The King
"and his Party prepare accordingly to ruin all; by sudden In-
"surrections in most parts of the Nation: the Scot, concurring
"with the same designs, comes in with a potent Army under
"Duke Hamilton.   We in the Army, in a low, weak, divided,
"perplexed condition in all respects, as aforesaid: — some of
"us judging it a duty to lay down our arms, to quit our sta-
"tions, and put ourselves into the capacities of private men,
"— since what we had done, and what was yet in our hearts
"to do, tending as we judged to the good of these poor Na-
"tions, was not accepted by them.

"Some also even encouraged themselves and us to such a
"thing, by urging for such a practice the example of our Lord
"Jesus; who, when he had borne an eminent testimony to the
"pleasure of his Father in an active way, sealed it at last by
"his sufferings; which was presented to us as our pattern for
"imitation.   Others of us, however, were different-minded;
"thinking something of another nature might yet be farther
"our duty; — and these therefore were, by joint advice, by a
"good hand of the Lord, led to this result; viz., To go solemnly
"to search out our own iniquities, and humble our souls before
"the Lord in the sense of the same; which, we were persuaded,
"had provoked the Lord against us, to bring such sad per-
"plexities upon us at that day.   Out of which we saw no way
"else to extricate ourselves.

"Accordingly we did agree to meet at Windsor Castle

---

* 1659; Allen's Pamphlet is written as a Monition and Example to
Fleetwood and the others, now in similar peril, but with no Oliver now
among them.

"about the beginning of Forty-eight. And there we spent
"one day together in prayer; inquiring into the causes of that
"sad dispensation," — let all men consider it; "coming to no
"farther result that day; but that it was still our duty to seek.
"And on the morrow we met again in the morning; where
"many spake from the Word, and prayed; and the then
"Lieutenant-General Cromwell," — unintelligible to Poste-
rity, but extremely intelligible to himself, to these men, and
to the Maker of him and of them, — "did press very earnestly
"on all there present, to a thorough consideration of our
"actions as an Army, and of our ways particularly as private
"Christians: to see if any iniquity could be found in them; and
"what it was, that if possible we might find it out, and so re-
"move the cause of such sad rebukes as were upon us (by *rea-
"son* of our iniquities, as we judged) at that time. And the
"way more particularly the Lord led us to herein was this: To
"look back and consider what time it was when with joint
"satisfaction we could last say to the best of our judgments,
"The presence of the Lord *was* amongst us, and rebukes and
"judgments were not as then upon us. Which time the Lord
"led us jointly to find out and agree in; and having done so,
"to proceed, as we then judged it our duty, to search into all
"our public actions as an Army afterwards. Duly weighing
"(as the Lord helped us) each of them, with their grounds,
"rules, and ends, as near as we could. And so we concluded
"this second day, with agreeing to meet again on the morrow.
"Which accordingly we did upon the same occasion, reas-
"suming the consideration of our debates the day before, and
"reviewing our actions again.

"By which means we were, by a gracious hand of the Lord,
"led to find out the very steps (as we were all then jointly con-
"vinced) by which we had departed from the Lord, and pro-
"voked Him to depart from us. Which we found to be those
"cursed carnal Conferences our own conceited wisdom, our
"fears, and want of faith had prompted us, the year before,
"to entertain with the King and his Party. And at this time,
"and on this occasion, did the then Major Goffe (as I remem-

"ber was his title) make use of that good Word, *Proverbs*
"First and Twenty-third, *Turn you at my reproof: behold,*
"*I will pour out my Spirit unto you, I will make known my words*
"*unto you.*   Which, we having found out our sin, he urged as
"our duty from those words.   And the Lord so accompanied
"by His Spirit, that it had a kindly effect, like a word of His,
"upon most of our hearts that were then present: which begot
"in us a great sense, a shame and loathing of ourselves for
"our iniquities, and a justifying of the Lord as righteous in
"His proceedings against us.

   "And in this path the Lord led us, not only to see our sin,
"but also our duty; and this so unanimously set with weight
"upon each heart that none was able hardly to speak a word
"to each other for bitter weeping," — does the modern reader
mark it; this weeping, and who they are that weep!   Weeping "partly in the sense and shame of our iniquities; of our
"unbelief, base fear of men, and carnal consultations (as the
"fruit thereof) with our own wisdoms, and not with the Word
"of the Lord, — which only is a way of wisdom, strength and
"safety, and all besides it are ways of snares.   And yet we
"were also helped, with fear and trembling, to rejoice in the
"Lord; whose faithfulness and loving-kindness, we were made
"to see, yet failed us not; — who remembered us still, even
"in our low estate, because His mercy endures for ever.   Who
"no sooner brought us to His feet, acknowledging Him in
"that way of His (viz. searching for, being ashamed of, and
"willing to turn from, our iniquities), but He did direct our
"steps; and presently we were led and helped to a clear agree-
"ment amongst ourselves, not any dissenting, That it was the
"duty of our day, with the forces we had, to go out and fight
"against those potent enemies, which that year in all places
"appeared against us."   Courage!   "With an humble con-
"fidence, in the name of the Lord only, that we should destroy
"them.   And we were also enabled then, after serious seeking
"His face, to come to a very clear and joint resolution, on
"many grounds at large there debated amongst us, That it
"was our duty, if ever the Lord brought us back again in

"peace, to call Charles Stuart, that man of blood, to an ac-
"count for that blood he had shed, and mischief he had done
"to his utmost, against the Lord's Cause and People in these
"poor Nations." Mark that also!

"And how the Lord led and prospered us in all our under-
"takings that year, in this way; cutting His work short, in
"rightcousness; making it a year of mercy, equal if not trans-
"cendent to any since these Wars began; and making it
"worthy of remembrance by every gracious soul, who was
"wise to observe the Lord and the operations of His hands, —
"I wish may never be forgotten." Let Fleetwood, if he have
the same heart, go and do likewise.*

Abysses, black chaotic whirlwinds: — does the reader look
upon it all as Madness? Madness lies close by; as Madness
does to the Highest Wisdom, in man's life always: but this is
not mad! This dark element, it is the mother of the lightnings and the splendours; it is very sane this! —

* A faithful Memorial of that remarkable Meeting of many Officers of
the Army in England at Windsor Castle, in the year 1648, &c. &c. (in Somers Tracts, vi. 499-501.)

END OF VOL. I.